No Never No More

ISBN: 0-9856-3282-8
ISBN-13: 9780985632823

No Never No More

a novel

Michael J. Malone

Well Lit Books
WellLitBooks.com
2013

Lower East Side, NYC

1999

I grab the stack of index cards and a Sharpie marker from my desk, and count off four from the pile. On one I write TISA. On another I write MA, then HALEY, then GABBY. I've got to address this shit, take Gabby's proverbial Pamplona bull by the horns.

Tisa, Ma, Haley, Gabby. This is rock bottom—it has to be. I'm putting my life back together. My birthday is in exactly four weeks. I'll give myself a week to take care of each one. And then I'll turn 30.

How the hell did I get into this mess?

State of Contusion

Gabby's walking back to our boys after talking to the ref, so I pull my shorts up and sprint back onto the field. I like the fact that Gabby's our captain; he's a hard bastard, and you want a hard bastard for your captain, but mostly because he goes out to meet the ref and the other captain before the match. The other captain's always got his hair parted to the side, looks like his name is Ted or Scottie, lives out in Long Island or Jersey with his wife and small child, and this is the only shit he does for fun. Us, we're all downtown dudes: bartenders and actors and freaks and novelist-wanna-be's. And Gabby, with his buzz cut, sideburns that almost connect at his chin, nose ring and an accent like an FDNY captain, sort of captures all that.

"We're receivin'," he says in a no-nonsense voice. His Rockaway burr always comes out before games. "The ref's watchin' any stompin', so use yuh heads if yuh givin' someone the boots. Release as soon as yuh tackled. No lip, he says, or he's gonna toss yuh. Don't fuck wid 'im. Any problems, talk tuh me."

We nod and put our hands together in the middle. I close my eyes. It sounds corny, but I feel safe when we're huddled in tight. Maybe it's because Ma denied me affection as a kid, who the hell knows. Gabby barks "One, two, three," and we yell "Vipers!" as loud as we can. It's Friends and Family Day, a ploy to get more chicks out to our games, but our sideline crowd features only a couple dozen or so spectators, pretty much the same ones that come out every week. They cheer, and Mental Ben's German shepherd barks madly.

I take my position with the rest of the forwards. Their kicker, a real ugly bastard with a shaved head, squatty legs and a scar above his eye that's noticeable from 20 yards away, is about to hoist it skyward and start the match. Everything around me melts into surreality. I'm scared to death. It's hard to explain. Sure, I could break a leg, finally crack my neck all the way through or even die—yeah, it's happened, though not to me—in the next 90 minutes, but that's not what scares me. If it happens, it happens. It ain't that. I can't explain; not now, anyway. I see the Kiwi, Shady Brady, Flyboy, Spartacus, Gabby, Dr. Demento, Ghetto Ron, Mental Ben and Gentle Ben. We look at each other solemnly, nod expressionless nods, and the ref blows the whistle.

The kicker approaches the ball and I think of Haley. She's away for the weekend, visiting her sister in Vermont, and I'm bummed—thought it would be cool if she was there to watch me play, like I was the high school quarterback and she was the cheerleader or something. Oh well. At least she sounded interested. Tisa never freakin' came out to watch me play. That Haley isn't here is my final thought as the ball floats lazily through the air, end over end, towards, of course, yours truly. A drop of pee drips down my leg as I field the ball. The Bayonne Barbarians' pack, desperate for that crucial first contact, converges on me like underfed tigers on a wounded doe. I take three steps and offer them my forearm. It's on.

And it's off.
Nothing.
Black.
Then brilliant yellow. Everywhere. Is it heaven? I listen for angels but hear only an English accent. It sure is hot. Hot as a mofo and English people. Is it … hell? Jesus, no. I mean it, Jesus—no! Can't I appeal? I tried to be good. I swear.

I slowly open my eyes and look up into the sun, a ring of familiar faces surrounding it like demented Boy Scouts around a campfire. How much time has passed? I wish I could tell the time by the sun, but I'm just a city kid. I'm alive, thank God, but I'm paralyzed. The neck has finally broken clear through. That really puts a damper on my weekend. I envision myself in a wheelchair and diapers, sipping a cheeseburger & fries frappé, never able to play ball with my kid. Fuck.

I try to move my head, my arms and my legs. Slowly, reluctantly, they all oblige, thank the Lord. I'm lying in the early summer sun and my lungs are on fire and the Randalls Island grime is sticking to my sweaty face and the sun is relentless and I should've worn sunblock because I burn like nobody's business. And I can't fucking get up.

"Deckie?" says my teammate. What the hell's his name? Big Rockaway dude, our captain, sideburns. My best bud.

"He took a good knock," says another teammate, a stocky guy with a goatee. "Got him with an elbow."

"Coal-turr, ya pussy," another says. It's… Dr. Demento. A real doctor, thankfully, although one from…Oklahoma, I think? Somewhere flat and boring that you fly over to get someplace.

I try to say 'fuck off,' but nothing comes out except dust.

"What month we in?" he asks.

"Fuck off."

There it is.

"Not the answer I was looking for, Coal-turr. The month, please."

Good question. "May," I try.

"*Baaaaahhhhh*! Missed it by one. OK, double or nothin'. What's the day of the week?"

I look around and take a deep breath.

"Seeing as we've got a rugby game," I say, "it must be Saturday."

"Not bad, not bad," Dr. Demento says. "What's your name?"

I roll my eyes. What's with the kindergarten questions?

"Coal-turr?" Demento repeats.

"Declan Coulter," I say. I'm using the test to take the test, as my old Social Studies teacher at Art & Design used to say. The guy supposedly had a wooden leg or a glass eye, or maybe it was a wooden eye or a glass leg, I don't remember.

"Very good. What's your girlfriend's name?"

I pause, and a wave of anxiety hits me, which gives way to a strangely happy feeling all over. I can see her pretty smile, her hair pulled back in a pony tail. I smile back at her image.

"Coal-turr?"

"I know her fucking name, Demento. Help me up."

Teresa? Lisa?

"Not til I get a name, Coal-turr. It's for your own good."

I can picture her face. Jeez, what's her name?

Demento hums the theme to "Happy Days."

"Joanie?" I guess. It doesn't sound right. Who's named Joanie anymore?

"Incorrectamundo!" shouts Demento. *Rock—around—the clock tonight. Gonna rock rock rock til broad daylight...* Who sang it?"

Demento has lost his mind.

"Bill blah blah and the Comets," he continues.

What's he talking about? Who took the knock on the head?

"Last chance...C'mon, man—we're trying to play a game here."

Was it Buddy Holly?

"Holly," I say as I push myself up on my elbows.

"Sorry, pal," says Demento, pushing me back down. "Your day is done."

I stare up at the sun again.

Where the fuck am I?

Me

I'm Declan and I'm 29, but only for five more months. I live in the Village View, a project on the edge of Alphabet City in New York. Alphabet City sticks out like a pimple on Manhattan's chin; while the rest of the city is dissected vertically by numbered avenues, every avenue east of 1st gets letters: A, B, C and D. Giving Alphabet City's avenues negative numbers would not have done much for the already fragile psyche of the neighborhood.

The Village View's kind of like a poor man's Stuyvesant Town…not that Stuy Town's exactly the home to New York's elite. Nobody calls the Village View a project, because there's a handful of white people here. But it's a project: bunch of big ugly brick buildings that look the same, like a college campus you'd go to only if you'd totally shit the bed on the SATs. Some patches of grass, crappy playground, inbred squirrels and a bunch of people who can't afford to live anywhere else.

It's about 90% Latino, with a smattering of Russians, Ukes, Poles and other bo-hunk types that're good with their hands. But mostly Latinos. Not sure which countries they're from, just like they don't know if some white dude's a Pole, a Uke, a Russian or a Yank-Mick bastard, like me.

My full-time job is associate editor—a title I can't shake—at a shitty wine magazine. There's the good wine mag and the pretty good one and the shitty one that tries to rip off the other two; I work for the latter at a fucked up place called Avatar Publishing. My heart's not really in the job—it's in writing fiction. My new novel, which I'm starting tomorrow and hopefully will finish by my birthday, will be my second, and will play a huge part in keeping my mind off…oh, never mind. The first I wrote at work over the course of five years, and it reads like it. Unless you're freakin' Tisa or a lowly assistant for a literary agency starting with A through F and listed in *Writer's Market*, you haven't read it. And if you did, I'm sorry. To say *Lend Me Ten Bucks and I'll Buy You a Drink* is flawed is to imply there was some sort of plan to it. There was no plan. To call it a *roman a clef* flatters it by giving it a genre. My book didn't have no freakin' genre. It just was crap.

Sadly, I thought it was great when it was done. Amped by my accomplishment, if we can call it that, I sent the manuscript to 31 literary agencies, and got 34 rejections. After rejecting it, did the agency assistants show it to their agency assistant friends at happy hour as some sort of benchmark of bad submissions, and those friends were so struck by its wretchedness that they felt compelled to reject me themselves, so as to prevent my subsequent literary endeavors? I have no idea.

But that's not to say I'm not a published author. Don't let the double negative confuse you—I've had books published. More than one, in fact. I write children's books. I invented a character named "Honey Bunny" who goes around doing nice things for people and bailing them out of difficult situations. He's sort of like a lucky rabbit's foot, only he's the whole rabbit. Got the idea when I was an exchange student in Liverpool—Ma loved that one, calling me a *fookin' Limey Lover* and a *wee Brit Twit*, pronouncing *wee* like *way*—or something else your mother should not be saying. She wanted me to go to school in Ireland, preferably somewhere in *de narth*, but I was hot for a girl at City College who was doing a year exchange in Liverpool, so I followed. (It's probably only fair to mention that my student advisor, who was in charge of pushing this new exchange program, suggested I go to Liverpool to avoid getting booted from City College.) Over there, I saw a kiddie program called "Magic Roundabout." There was a rabbit named Dylan who walked around with a guitar all the time, kind of a Greek chorus to the emotions of the other animals around him. I was all hopped up on some wack shit my roommate Madoo from Brixton brought back from Morocco, and dreamed up Honey Bunny.

So I've done four Honey Bunny books, but you won't find them under my name. Look under "Sarah Appleton." Don't ask—my editor Sally insisted. It's probably for the best; this way, I can keep it from the rugby guys that I write books about a benevolent bunny. They'd never let go of that one. Kids love Honey Bunny, and so do I; at $2,500 a pop, plus royalties, who wouldn't? No, seriously. Honey Bunny is very close to my heart, and has helped me through tough times. I love him dearly.

But, like any Lower East Side writer, I want to do novels about people and conflict and drugs and sex. The second novel's going to be good; I can feel it. You just can't do a good novel while you're sneaking around at work, minimizing the screen every time your boss walks by, though it'd be great if you could. I just sunk every dime I had—about 5,000 of the shiny little things—on a new computer.

So I write in my crummy little apartment on Avenue A, across from a diner that recently installed this huge fan on the roof that blows out the greasy air from the grill, rattling and humming 24-7 right across from my apartment. This just started happening, so it's too early to tell how this will affect my mental health and my writing here in the project where I've spent my entire life, minus the year in Liverpool. I can't say I'm happy about it. Neither's Ma. *Fookin' 'ell,* I hear her screech through my window—it's how she begins most sentences—*it's like living by the fookin' airpart.*

I started seeing this classy blond chick called Haley—I seem to be drawn to the WASP-y types, to Ma's eternal disgust—and like my second novel, she's helping me get my mind off Tisa, who we're not going to talk about anymore. And if we do, we won't flatter her by referring to her by name. We'll just call her the Bunt, sort of a cross between a bitch and the C-word. Actually, the C-word suits her just fine, but I know some people are offended by it. So we'll call her the Bunt. Maybe I'll even come up with a bunt sign or something.

So I thought about doing a novel about that whole turning 30 thing, but who the hell wants to read that? I mean, maybe it means something to you if you're at that age, which narrows my potential readership down considerably, and even if you *are* that age, chances are you've already read your share of turning-30 cliché crap. And mine would likely just depress you even more.

Ya know, I goof on my first novel, but to be honest, I'm pretty proud that I did it. It's crap, and it deserved the unsolicited rejections. But it's a book: has a beginning, middle and end, and it makes a noise when you drop the damn thing. I remember when everyone in the neighborhood who was just out of school—back when kids just out of school could afford the neighborhood—was writing a book. It was the trendy thing to talk about at parties. But no one finished them. My fucking book's done. I always had trouble finishing shit and, fucking A, I had trouble finishing *Lend Me Ten Bucks*. But I did it.

My lifelong finishing-shit problem is pretty well symbolized by this ridiculous tattoo on my shoulder blade. You might say the stupid tattoo-in-progress helped me finish my book. I always wanted a tattoo, and Ma said I could do it if I got something Irish—not that a grown man needs his mommy's permission to get ink, but she was willing to pay half if she liked the tat. Ma wanted some Fenian rhetoric that she saw on a wall along *the Shankill Road*, some 'Kill the Brit Bastards' crap, but we agreed on a Celtic harp. She checked out Ink-a-Dink Cappuccino & Tattoo on St. Mark's beforehand, made sure they're legit and not dipping needles in jars marked 'HIV,' because she's a nurse at NYU and is worried about that stuff. I'm generally not one of those Irish-Americans who drape themselves in the goddamn Paddy flag—Mick mooks that Gabby would call "turbo-Irish"—but I do appreciate my ancestry.

I'm less appreciative of needles. Absolutely fucking despise them, as in, nothing freaks me out more than someone sticking a needle in me. Or in them. Or in lab rats. Anyway, you have to get a buncha needles stuck in you if you're going to get a tat. So I get absolutely bombed on this cheap-ass whiskey called Clan MacGregor. The homeless buy it because it costs about the same as a pack of cigarettes; you always see broken bottles of the shit on the sidewalk next to a smashed storefront window, a bleeding guy, some other blighted sight. I'm crocked on the Clan Mac-Gregor, and I'm kind of OK, what with my eyes closed and Tisa holding my hand…

Shit.

So it's taking a while for the tattoo. The whiskey's starting to wear off and I feel the mother of all anxiety attacks coming on: sweating, gagging, thinking I was going to piss myself, or worse. I jump out of the dentist chair and run out the door with a half-finished tattoo. It's supposed to look like a Celtic harp and it looks like, geez, I don't know, a big, fancy capital D, or something. At least my name starts with D. But what kind of dork gets their initial tattooed on their shoulder blade?

I'm running out onto St. Mark's, the Bunt squealing behind me, and the tat dude, this big burly fucker, is yelling, "Man, you can't run outta here with half a tattoo. Shit's gonna look *wack*." The guy ain't exactly sprinting after me down St. Mark's, because Ma paid him up front. So me and the Bunt go to Tompkins to sit and chill. I had to get out of there. I just knew I couldn't take him sticking any more needles in me. Scared to fucking *death* of needles.

And that's probably for the best.

The security guys here at the Village View are cool. They've got two guards on duty at all times, which is probably overkill, with the neighborhood the way it is now, but I guess a little extra security's not a bad thing. They know me because I've lived here my whole life, and most of them have been here as long as I have. Me and Ma—Ms. Paula Coulter from West Belfast—lived in Apartment 23B up until I was a year or so out of college—mind you, "out of college" does not always mean "graduated college," but that's another story. Mrs. Walker in 34B died—old biddie couldn't get around without a walker, which always sort of cracked me up, slit tennis balls like Pac Man's stuck to the hind legs of the thing—so I was able to get my ass into her place for crazy cheap.

The security guys know I like to sleep outside sometimes. Living in Manhattan, you get used to not seeing the stars; I had no idea how bright they were until Ma took me to the Shamrock House in the Catskills when I was a kid, her dragging my sorry ass onto the dance floor to do the stiffest, clumsiest Siege of Ennis ever seen. Even if you walk around with your head tilted up all the time—bumping into people, like a Times Square tourist with a bad moustache and a Stone Cold Steve Austin t-shirt—the visibility's for shit, and you don't see much more than little tiny dots through the haze. So you just get used to living life without stars. Trouble is, I can't.

So a lot of times, when I'm feeling kind of fucked up, or not, I lay down on one of the benches in the courtyard, check out the stars and drift off to sleep. From afar, the security guys might think I'm just some neighborhood junkie—one that doesn't belong there, anyway—but they see it's me, and everything's chill. Sometimes they wake me up and tell me to go inside, thinking I fell asleep by mistake. Other times, they just let me be, knowing that crazy white boy, that son of the crazy Irish lady, digs sleeping outside. I love the feel of the cool air at night, especially in early fall. There's nothing better than sleeping under the stars. And being a Manhattan resident doesn't necessarily deny you that pleasure. Look at me. Better yet, don't.

Me and Tisa used to come here all the time; bring a six-pack, smoke some butts, just hang out under the big "No Alcoholic Beverages" sign. There's this little playground in the middle of the project, with a purple slide shaped like a whale, and me and Tisa would sit on the whale's back, her leaning back against me, when all the kids were done with kickball and spud and skelly and had gone to bed, and we'd hang for hours. You could lean back against the whale's tail, and you were in a perfect position to check out the stars. And pour beer down your throat. So we'd do both.

But Tisa isn't around anymore. So sometimes I go there with Gabby, or maybe Shady Brady too. When I go with the guys, we don't sit on the whale—that was me and Tisa's spot, and it's got bad memories. We just grab a bench and kick back. I play rugby with Gabby and Shady Brady, and another 30 or so assorted freaks, hellions and drunks. Gabby's a strange fucker, like all my friends. Strange looking, strange acting, strange everything. Want to slug him sometimes, but most times he's cool. We went to high school together at Art & Design, back when he was known as Paul.

A bunch of years ago, we were coming home from a game on the Jersey Shore and the Kiwi's driving. The Kiwi drives like he's being chased by some huge Maori who found out he was banging his missus, and he's flying along the Jersey Turnpike near Newark Airport, and doesn't see the traffic in front of him stopping. So the Kiwi locks them up. Gabby, who's Paul at the time, is sitting in the front, and when the Kiwi jams on the brakes, his head goes slamming into the dash. Presumably there's an air bag there, though we never got to see it. But we know there's one there, because there're raised plastic letters on the dash that say AIR BAG. The Kiwi avoids an accident, but Paul's got the letters GAB RIA engraved into his forehead. He's rubbing it, and it's all red, and it's still freakin' there when we get back to MacLennane's. Gabby isn't much of a talker, speaking reluctantly and in half-sentences, so the nickname stuck.

It's a shitty nickname, but it's better than mine: Deckie. By law, guys have to stick an 'ie' or a 'y' after the first syllable of every guy's name. It's just something we do. So Ma gives me a nice ethnic name, and now it's shortened to Deckie. At best, it sounds like that dork Duckie from *Pretty in Pink*. At worst, it sounds like Dickie, like a fake turtleneck or undersized genitalia.

Shady Brady's got the better nickname. His real name—or "Christian name," as he would say—is Malcolm Brady, with like five names in between (Michael Dundee David Weir Simon, something or other), and he grew up in London. He's got tattoos of Arsenal, the soccer team back home that he loves, all over his fore-

Michael J. Malone

arms, and little scars on both corners of his mouth. Over there, they call that look the "Chelsea Smile"—when the *aggro* is going down, as Shady says, a thug who supports the other team, often Chelsea, gets behind you and slips a wire garrote into your mouth, then pulls on it until the sides of your mouth rip. Shady ain't got it too bad—you hardly even notice it when you've known him for a while. Makes him look like he's happy all the time or, when he's drinking or playing rugby, sort of evil.

Chelsea Smile notwithstanding, there's nothing shady about Brady, except that he deals the odd bag of pot now and then, but it rhymes. Shady has an Irish dad and a Scottish mom, but still somehow learned to put together the most preposterous blue blood English accent you've ever heard. He went to Oxford and now he's a bartender at some Avenue A dive, as well as a flyhalf on our little Village Vipers rugby team. His parents must be proud.

So sometimes me and Gabby or Shady Brady go and hang out on the playground, and never sit on the whale.

But mostly I go alone.

Squirrel Crazy

I was sitting in that little playground, hanging out and thinking of our match that weekend—it's against the Montclair Vikings—when the strangest thing happened. This squirrel was climbing down a tree headfirst, inching along with measured control the way squirrels do. He scrambled to within about five feet of the ground, and he just fell. Couldn't believe my eyes. I mentioned the damn things were inbred. The poor little guy was crafty enough to get his ass down and land on all four feet, so I don't think he was hurt badly, but he sure as hell fucking fell.

So the poor little squirrel was on the ground, looking a bit dazed, and he stared over at me, who was pretty dazed too. We were staring at each other and, for a split second, we were just about the only two of God's creatures on this earth. We stared for a second longer, and he scampered off all gingerly.

That got me thinking. You assume the squirrel's always going to make that descent safely, just like his leap from tree to tree never ends with him splattered on the sidewalk. Ever seen a dead squirrel? Me either. But I saw the poor little guy fall. And that sort of blows everything up. It's like, you go on the roller coaster and it's scary, but no one ever dies, right? No matter how scary it is, no matter how close to peril this lurching steel beast brings you, you'll end up OK, ready for cotton candy and a souvenir t-shirt. But then you read about someone who died on a roller coaster, and your guarantee is down the drain.

So the squirrel's got me thinking. There's meaning in there somewhere.

Fortunately, Gabby comes along before I can dig it out.

"Hey, yo, Deckie. What up?"

"Not much, Gab. Just hangin'."

Gabby plays eight-man on the Village Vipers. I'm a flanker, right next to Gabby in the scrum. Soon as the ball comes out, we chase it—putting hits on their guys if they have it, and supporting our boys if we have it. He's got on these seersucker pants he must've found at the Salvation Army and a shirt that says "Ridgewood Wrestling." Thrift shop as well, I'm sure. I know he never wrestled, and he sure isn't from Ridgewood, wherever that is. Where he's from, there are neither ridges nor woods, though I know the mooks out there love wrestling in the bars once they've had a few dozen Buds.

"Y'awright? You seem...subdued."

"Yeah, I'm fine," I say. "Just hangin'."

"Awright, what's on yer mind?"

"Nothin'," I say in sort of a hangdog way that should invite a follow-up question.

"C'mon, girl trouble?"

"Ah, just fucking Tisa."

"Teaser! You're not still talkin' to that cunt, are ya?"

"Yes and no," I respond. Unlike me, Gabby doesn't shy away from the C-word. "We're havin' that talk next week."

"Oh, the one about her getting married."

"Right, right," I say.

Tisa met someone right after we broke up, and we're not going to mention his name. (It's Earl. Can you fucking believe it? Fucking *Earl*. Earl!) Every few months, she would get sort of hung up on me and call, and it got so that every time I saw the goddamn blinking on my answering machine, I thought it was her. About 99 times out of a hundred, it wasn't, so I forbade her to call me anymore. So now she sends me letters every few months, telling me she can't get me out of her head. For a while there, her return address was L.A., and there was comfort knowing that we had Nevada and Colorado and all those "I" states I've never been to/never will see to between us. But the last one had 39 West 17th Street on it, New York Fucking City. Haven't been by 39 West 17th Street yet, but I've got a feeling I will.

That last letter talked about meeting up, so I called the number she gave me, felt my stomach nearly implode when I heard her voice on the recording and left my number, which she should know, because it used to be *our* number. She called back, and we're supposed to meet.

Tisa said she keeps having what she calls these "Declan flashes." Sounds sexy, doesn't it? I got a flash named after me. She figures she's got to get past this if she's going to get married. I have to admit I like knowing I still have that effect on her—*any* effect on her—especially with her breaking up with me. That's right, she broke up with me. Few guys will admit that. So Tisa says we have to meet up, says she needs "closure." Yup, the C-word used the c-word. I suppose the whole turning 30 thing wouldn't be a big deal if Tisa weren't knocking on my door, so to speak, and likewise, the Tisa thing wouldn't be a big deal—wouldn't be *as* big a deal—if I wasn't turning 30. But Tisa's calling, I'm turning 30 in five months and now my life's all fucked up.

Not that it wasn't before. This just sort of puts everything in focus. Out of focus, is more like it.

Gabby cracks his knuckles and burps loudly. A squirrel with what looks like a cigarette burn on his back inches up to us, trying us for handouts. Gabby stamps his foot and he scoots away.

"So you're all freaked about meetin' her," he says.

"Sort of. I mean, it's not like I expect anything to come out of it."

So what do you do when you're about to meet up with the ex-girlfriend? Naturally, our lives will be compared to each other's, like we're adding up points based on how we each did following our parting of ways. She's engaged to some rich actor guy (Earl!), and I'm sort of dating Haley, though I'm not ready to really get back into it. By the looks of Tisa's engagement ring, she certainly is. Not that I've seen it…but I can picture it. I'm living in the same fucking place, in the zit that is Alphabet City, and I've got $21 in the bank…though at least I've got a new computer that will eventually house my novel. Tisa's way ahead on points.

Since she hit me with the letter, I made a few little changes. First off, I went out and bought some funky new Skechers biker boots that ran me a hundred bucks. Tisa got me a pair of Doc Martens for my birthday when we were going out, and I'd worn them pretty much every day since. She knew I had no dough and couldn't afford good shoes; you think I'm broke now, you shoulda known me then. After three years, the Docs look like hell—yes, you can wear a hole in the inch-and-a-half thick bottom of a Doc Marten—and I'd rather walk in to meet Tisa barefoot, or in those dreadful New England L.L. Bean duck boots the preps wear, than in the old Doc Martens. So it's like, yeah, I'm still living in the same project, yeah, I ain't got a real girlfriend and yeah, I'm still a freakin' associate editor, but at least I'm not wearing the old Docs you bought me with the hole. I just have to scuff the boots up on the street before we meet, make it look like I didn't just run out and get new boots because I was going to meet my ex-girlfriend, the actress who's engaged to *Earl* and who, as we speak, is probably planning some huge wedding in the picturesque English village Somer-something-or-other-shire-something-or-other she grew up in.

I also joined a gym, or at least the extremely cheap, for city residents, community center with the prison-yard weights over on Carmine, and now I do volunteer work. The gym is important because it shows people you're serious about self-improvement, and the volunteer thing just plain sounds good. I was going to do stuff in a homeless shelter, like feed the folks and help carry their coin rolls to the bank when they open accounts, but I scoped out some of the shelters along the Bowery, and it was just too depressing. They kick these guys out of the place as soon as the sun comes up, like around 6 or so, and they just stand outside the shelter, with no dough and no place to go. Depressed the shit out of me.

Instead, I go every Monday to this place on Avenue C called the Lower East Side Harm Reduction Center, known to its customers and workers alike as Needles R Us. They used to give out methadone there, but guys were selling their cups on the street. The workers made the guys drink it at the counter, but they would keep it in their mouths, go outside, spit it into a cup and sell it. So now the place is out of the methadone biz, and just gives out needles. Most of the customers are fairly coherent, and they seem to like me. Hell, I'm giving them clean works for dirty ones, so why shouldn't they? It's only an hour each week, and it sort of serves as a good penance for the fucked up shit I did—do—all weekend. And it's helping me get over my fear of needles.

My life suitably changed and infinitely more interesting, I'm now ready to meet Tisa. I think.

"But deep down…," says Gabby, dragging hard on a cigarette. Lots of the rugby guys smoke butts. We keep talking about getting Marlboro or Camel to sponsor the team, stitch their logo right on our chests. "Part of you still wants to keep that flame burning."

I shrug.

Another squirrel hops by. The Village View squirrels aren't afraid of people, just slink right up next to them. Me and Jimmy Gulotta, my old pal from Village View before he went, quite literally, up the river, named them all when we were kids.

"Here's the deal," he says. "Ya go, ya show her how cool ya are with shit, she gets married. It's done. Ya get on with your life."

"Mmmm," I utter in partial agreement. "It all sounds good, man."

"It *is* good. Tisa's a cunt. I never liked her."

"Mmmm," I repeat.

"How's the new broad?"

"Haley's great."

"Cool, man," says Gabby. "She's a hottie. Shady Brady didja nice."

"I know, man."

"Harley know about all this Tisa nonsense?"

"*Haley*. Nah."

"That's good. Get your fuckin' mind off her until you see her, then just go and get it over with. You're tough, sort of. Harley's way better'n freakin' Teaser."

"*Haley*. You're right."

"Course I'm right," says Gabby. "Let's head over to the Homestead. I feel like beating your ass in pool."

I hate pool. Nearly every scuffle you see in a bar is because of pool. It's not the violence that bugs me; I *like* violence. It's the disorder. As you might gather from the squirrel episode, I prefer order. Put a pool table in a place that serves alcohol, and it's a recipe for chaos. *I've* got next. Those're *my* quarters. *I'm* Jack. See my name? Yeah, well I'm Lou. That's on top of Jack. No, those are *my* quarters. Wait your turn. I'm next. Fuck you. Go time! Now Jack's on top of Lou. Repeat.

Hate the game.

"I'm in," I say, and get to my feet.

The Homestead's got ancient wood paneling that's smoke-stained beige and old Pabst and Schaefer signs on the wall alongside framed newspaper cutouts of polka festivals and accordion-world heroes; it looks like the basement of some Polish family's New World dream house. I've been coming here since I was a kid—it's one of the few neighborhood bars that just never got trendy, where drinking cans of Pabst Blue Ribbon stayed blissfully unironic. It's where I had my first beer in a bar, my first alcohol-induced puke, my first kiss. Come to think of it, they may have all been in the same night. The place is owned by Christine, this Polish lady who's old as dirt, but has a disposition like sugar. Man, she was old even when I first started coming here about a dozen years ago.

"I wanna move to San Fran," says Gabby, chalking up his stick and wiping his hands on his pants. He *always* wants to move somewhere: San Fran, London, Sydney. Start a graphic design business, see if he can get paid to play rugby.

I line up my shot. I'm going for the 6 in the corner pocket. I don't feel good about the shot. There's a lot of green, as the pool nuts say, between the cue and the 6.

"You always say that," I say.

"This time I mean it."

"You always say that too."

I miss the shot. Too much green.

"What're ya gonna find in San Fran?"

"I don't know," he says, sucking on a Winston and resting it on the edge of the table. "Just a change of pace, I s'pose. Even just for a year."

Gabby's like me—another NYC redneck. A local. A townie. He grew up in New York City, only in its furthest point from midtown Manhattan. He's from the tail end of Rockaway, in a little beach neighborhood that's guarded by a gate, with a Checkpoint Charlie there to make sure you're Irish-American before letting you in. Houses an arm's length from each other, everyone up in everyone else's business. That's why Gabby dislikes the Irish, despite being pure-bred. He's had me out there a few times—had a bunch of guys out for Christmas, all the ex-pats with no family nearby, and me. We drink a bunch of beers and have fun, but it feels really claustrophobic. The houses were all summer bungalows back when it was called the Irish Riviera, but now people live in them year-round, a view of each other's laundry hanging on the line. There're two bars, and all the chicks are somebody's sister or cousin or ex, and the locals don't seem to like the visitors all that much. It always feels like there's tension, over a spilled beer, or a pool game, or a cop that doesn't like a firefighter, or a Bronx-Irish dude that doesn't like a Brooklyn-Irish dude. Or the rowdy bunch of boys visiting from Manhattan.

Gabby got out of there before turning into a lifer, which is surprising, because he's got some of that in him. That's why I know he'll never go to San Fran.

Michael J. Malone

"There's way more hi-tech shit going on out there," he says.

"Go for it, man," I say.

"What about you? Stayin' at the wine mag?"

"Prolly," I say.

"Free wine. Can't beat that."

"True, true."

"Perfect for a lush like you. So how 'bout runnin' with the bulls? You wanna do that?"

Like leaving New York, Gabby's brought this up before.

"No."

"C'mon, man," says Gabby. "We'll go to Pamplona for a long weekend. It's comin' up. Ghetto Ron got a flight for $250 online."

"Why the fuck would I want to run with the bulls?"

"Why? You really gotta ask why?" Gabby says, shaking his head.

"Yeah," I say, aiming the 3 at the side pocket.

"The fuckin' party. The Spanish women. The rush of the bulls breathin' down yuh neck. And we get the fuck outta the city for a bit."

"Nah, man," I say, as my shot bumps off the side of the pocket. "Running with the bulls does nothing for me."

Gabby shakes his head.

"Ask Shady," I suggest. "He'll go."

"He's got no dough. I can't believe you wouldn't wanna go. Why the fuck not?"

"Same reason I didn't join a frat," I say, though City College didn't have frats.

"What the fuck's that mean?"

"Thousands of frat boys from Jersey," I say. "That's what running with the bulls means to me."

Gabby shakes his head.

"Yeah, well, maybe ya get to see one of 'em get gored."

"That'd be nice," I say.

I aim the 5-ball for the far corner pocket, but nearly put the cue ball in the side pocket.

"How's your book comin'?"

I have a moment of anxiety, as I think Gabby's talking about Honey Bunny. But then I remember I mentioned starting my new novel to him a few weeks ago, right after I bought the new computer.

"Slow goin'. Can't force these things."

"Haven't started, have ya?"

"I'm in the Gathering Notes stage."

"Haven't started yet, have ya?"

16

"Nah, man. Soon. Tomorrow."

Shane MacGowan's ragged rasp comes from the tinny juke box.

Jimmy played harmonica in the pub where I was born
He played it from the nighttime, til the peaceful, early morn
He soothed the souls of psychos and the men who had the horn
And they all looked very happy in the morning

"When did they put Shane on the box?" I ask. Shane and the Pogues next to Bobby Vinton and Jimmy Roselli and Weird Al Yankovic's dad. It puts me in a good mood, makes me want to do a shot or hit somebody or write that novel. Shane, the last great gutter poet, is like that. My dad probably had Dylan when he was young and impressionable, and I got Shane.

"Dunno, man. Freakin' donkey music."

"Easy," I say. "You're a Paddy too."

"I'm a fuckin' American," he growls.

I-I-I-I'm sad to say, I must be on me way
So buy me beer and whiskey, 'cuz I'm goin' far away

I look over to the bar, where Christine gives me a bashful wave and smile. She's seen me in my favorite Pogues t-shirt, Shane's toothless grin on the front and the Ireland flag on the back, and sure enough, she put the Pogues on the box. I used to wear a London Irish rugby jersey that Tisa bought me back in England, big Guinness logo on the front, and Christine put a Guinness tap right next to the Rheingold and the Miller. You just don't get that at the trendy places.

"You hear about this Y2K thing?" Gabby asks. "Like, everything's gonna freeze up at midnight on New Year's, and then the world turns into freakin' *Road Warrior*?"

"Yeah," I say, missing the 7-ball entirely for a scratch. "All I need—one more thing to stress about. Hopefully it's nothing. Hopefully it's just some media creation. Either way, it's like half a year off."

Gabby places the cue ball strategically behind the 8-ball and sinks it. The cue stops on a dime upon impact. He wins. Thank God.

"Nice game," I say. We slap hands.

"Nice game," he says back.

"Beer?" I say.

"Sure."

It's a few hours later. The sun's down and me and Gabby are drunk. We're heading up Avenue A to Tompkins. It's a warm evening, late spring, a perfect night to sit outside. We enter the park at the southwest entrance, where the junkies who smell like piss sit and play chess and smoke butts all day. They sit there trying to kick, bangin' pawns to get their minds off fixing. I recognize a few from the Harm

Reduction Center. They're a miserable bunch, squirming like they all got poison ivy on their asses. Some do the junkie stagger—walking along, then stopping, nodding, looking like they're going to fall, but never quite falling. Then walking along, stopping, doing it all again. The fiend lean. Arguments break out all the time, though no one's got the energy to actually fight, and about half the chess games end with one of the guys throwing the table up in the air, pieces all a-flying, and storming off. Quitting the quitting, fixing to fix. A sign nearby admonishes park goers to "Keep off the Grass," but it's not the pot they jones for.

"Dog-run?" I suggest.

"Sure," says Gabby. We hop over the dog-run fence and get a bench facing Avenue B. I'm always struck by the change in the neighborhood when I see it from a different vantage point. Things always look different. Ninety percent of the neighborhood's still shitty as it ever was, but there's a new luxury building just off B, chic black-and-white photos of jazz dudes who once partied here blown up huge and framed, hanging in the foyer. I used to work with a guy who lived there. He wore a ponytail and a necktie. We had nothing in common, other than the neighborhood. A fancy Belgian restaurant here, a jazz club there. The stretch of B near us has been renamed "Charlie Parker Place" after one of the neighborhood's most successful junkies, and a huge portrait of another neighborhood doper icon, Lou Reed, hangs in a new photo finishing place. It used to be there was nothing past A; now you can freakin' *bar hop* on Avenue C. And you better dress up, and bring lots of money. Shit's crazy.

We've got a sixer of Rolling Rock and Styrofoam cups. We pour Exhibit A into Exhibit B and toast. A coupla cops walk by—even a full decade after the Tompkins riots, there's still a cop presence in the park. But they don't give a couple local white boys a second glance.

Like city kids during recess, the dogs canter around the run, introducing themselves to each other and howling happily, elated to be sprung from their tiny apartments. I love the dog-run.

"Montclair Vikings this weekend, huh?" I say.

"Yup," says Gabby. "Fuckin' hate those guys. All they do is ram it atcha with those two big centuhs. Same shit every year."

"They beat us every year."

"No shit," says Gabby. "Everyone's afraid to hit those dudes. Fuck 'em. Hit 'em low. They'll go down."

"Fuck 'em," I echo. "Got your cell?"

"Yeah. Calling Haley?"

"Checking my messages," I say.

"Wuss," he says, handing me the phone. "And buy your own damn cell phone—it's 1999."

Hi Declan, it's Tisa. My heart takes off when I hear the voice, then plummets to the pavement when I hear the message.

Her voice sounds different, like she was on Prozac or was practicing a new breathing technique she learned in acting class.

Listen, I'm so sorry, I must postpone our little rendezvous again, though we simply must get together. Please call my cell. Cheers. Ta!

I hand Gabby back his phone.

"She call?" he asks.

"Who?"

"I dunno. You tell me who."

"Tisa."

"Fuckin' Teaser," says Gabby.

I drain my beer and fill up a new one. A chocolate lab puppy approaches me and I push him away. Why do I let this chick fuck me up like this? It had been such a pleasant day. Haley blows Tisa away. Why can't I get this through my fucking thick Irish skull?

Haley &
The Happiest Birthday

Haley's place is on Charles Street. It's the West Village, the prettiest part of the city; leafy streets with proper names—not numbers or letters, like cell blocks—that wind around with no apparent plan, well-scrubbed gay couples walking hand in hand, old ladies riding ancient bicycles or walking fluffy dogs. Don't think I could actually live here, but it sure is pretty to look at. Could probably get lots of writing done here. Maybe I'll set up a little writing space in the West Village when my big book deal comes through.

"Hey, babe," I say.

"Declan," says Haley, peering over her sunglasses like a movie star. "How are you?"

"I'm well, Hale. I'm hale and well."

To be honest, I didn't really expect my blind date with Haley to amount to anything. I mean, it's not like I'm still hung up on fucking Tisa after a year and a half, but she just kind of soured me on relationships. Relationships mean you lose your freedom, which I need a lot of, and they mean that shitty feeling in the pit of your gut now and then too, even in healthy ones. Had that for about six straight months with Tisa; thought it was a freakin' ulcer. Now, I'd take just about any precautionary step possible to avoid that feeling for the rest of my life, even if it means avoiding all relationships entirely.

But Haley sort of snuck up on me. Shady Brady's girl, whose name is Melanie but who we call Lady Brady (how could we not?), got talking to me one night at MacLennane's, saying she worked with this chick who she thought I'd "get on with"—Shady's got his girl talking like a Brit too. They're teachers together at some unthinkably quaint little rich kid school over on Bleecker—check it out, the school's called "Little Red Schoolhouse," no lie—and Lady Brady insisted I meet her. Tell you the truth, I was intrigued by Haley's name. I've dated hundreds of girls in my life—well, either hooked up with or dated that many, or at least a hundred—and I'm into cool names. I've already dated about six Mary's and eight Kristin's (or Kristen's) and all the common names, and vowed to date only chicks with different names, ones that sound good on a wedding invite. *Declan and Haley, Table 14.* Got a nice ring, huh? *Tisa and Earl?* Ha!

So Lady Brady brought Haley out to MacLennane's a week or so later, and I saw Lady walk in with this tall chick—pretty, minimal make-up, kind of natural and done up at the same time, straight blonde hair, clothes that were both classy and totally sexy, the kind of girl that probably gets seats offered to her on the subway all the time. And I felt kind of a jolt, an actual physical reaction, to this girl. So I knew I had to give it a go. I was all nervous and shit, and the music's kind of loud at MacLennane's, which makes it hard to talk, but we got introduced, and started talking, and hit it off pretty well. She's like this classy broad, but totally drinks beer—pints, no less—and talks about cool stuff. And I just thought she was hot as hell. First time I'd felt that way since Tisa dumped my ass.

So we had one at MacLennane's and it was going good, and I decided I'd be wise to shift our convo to another bar, as the boys start getting drunk and making a scene and singing rude songs, and it's fun as fuck when you're not with a chick, but might not be the ideal environment for trying to impress a classy West Village broad. So we snuck out to Chumley's, this funky little speakeasy from the Prohibition days over by 7th Ave. You have to know where it is or you'll never find it, and for the first time in my life, I found it without having to ask directions or peer in the windows. It was a badge of a true New Yorker, like knowing how to pronounce Joralemon Street or where the hell Bialystoker Place is. (Hint: It's not on Broadway.) Haley was suitably impressed, and we continued our pleasant, easy convo inside.

I still kind of feel that jolt when I see Haley weeks later, and I get it when I see her sitting on her front step, reading the *New York Press.* I like girls that are willing to sit on steps and get their jeans dirty. The whole city's dirty, even nice parts like here. You can't fight it.

She rises to her feet, brushes off her well-defined ass and we do a quick kiss. I can pick up a tasty vanilla smell on her. We've just graduated from the cheek kiss hello to the lip kiss hello. It's not an insignificant step.

"Did you bring *Honey Bunny?*" she asks.

"Sure did," I say, taking *Honey Bunny's Happiest Birthday* out of my pocket and handing it to her.

"Oh—my—*God*!" she says, a warm smile taking over her face that makes me smile too. "This is the cutest thing I've ever seen."

Honey Bunny has a birthday hat on, its pointy top poking through his bunny ears. He's surrounded by his friends from Serenity Knoll. It *is* pretty fucking cute, I must say.

She stares at the cover and makes a face.

"By Sarah Appleton? Who the heck is that?"

"It's my *nom de plume*," I explain, exaggerating the French accent, as we head down towards Hudson River Park. "My editor at Green Mountain figured Sarah Appleton would have more credibility with the under-10 demo than Declan Coulter. She thought of the name. Says everyone trusts a person with a fruit in their last name."

"What about Darryl Strawberry? You trust that guy?"

"Good point," I say. "It's my editor's rule, not mine."

"Who's the old biddie?" says Haley, nodding at the 60-something school-marm in the author photo.

"Mrs. Slywotzky from 11B. She's my godmother, I think. She and my mom had this little wine club thing when I was a kid."

"I can't believe this."

"What?"

"I, uh, I don't know. Just look at you. And look at this book."

"Yeah?"

"You just don't look like the kind of guy who writes books about little rabbits," she says.

"That's why they use Sarah Appleton and Mrs. Slywotzky."

"I guess so," says Haley. "So how do I know it's really you that writes these books? What if I were, you know, a cynic, and thought you were making all this up to impress me?"

"You'll just have to trust me, I guess," I say with a chuckle. "I mean, I could show you the files on my computer."

"I believe you," says Haley. "You seem trustworthy."

"It'd be a pretty pathetic hoax. Even for me."

"Well, thank you for the book."

"No problem. I've got boxes of them."

"It's adorable. It really is. I have to bring it to class."

"Thank you," I say. "The designer did a great job on the cover. Check out the little mouse in the corner."

He also wears a birthday hat, and is eyeing a large piece of cheese on the table.

"Oh, God. That's adorable."

"That's Marvin Mouse," I say proudly. "He's from England. He's based on Shady Brady."

"Who?"

"Malcolm. Melanie's boyfriend."

"Oh, right. Shady Brady. Very good. So why a writer?"

"Why do I want to be one?" I ask as we cross Bleecker, which is teeming with pedestrians. We pass a cozy looking shop dedicated solely to children's books. I wonder if any of mine are in there. Maybe we'll pop in on the way back.

"Yes."

"Well, it gives you an excuse to be by yourself for long stretches of time."

"And that's a good thing?" she asks. "I *hate* being alone. I think that's why I went into teaching."

"It's a nice option to have," I say, concerned that I'm coming across as totally anti-social. I like people. Some of them, anyway. A few of them? "Ya know, if you're not in the mood to do something or go somewhere."

"Mmmm," says Haley. "I'm thinking about getting a dog. For company."

"Really? It's like having a kid, taking the thing to the dog-run every day, feeding it, all that stuff."

"It's not an *it*," she says with a laugh. "It's a dog."

"Yeah, I know. Don't get me wrong—having a dog would be cool as hell. But taking care of it—*him*—would be a pain. Takes a shitload of responsibility."

"That's not necessarily a bad thing," she says.

"I know, I know. Actually, there's another reason why I like being a writer. It's an excuse for, ya know, eccentric, irresponsible behavior. You can kind of act like a freak, and people just say, 'Oh, he's a writer. He's in that writer zone.' You get a little more slack than the average Joe."

"I suppose," says Haley. "You've always wanted to be a writer?"

"Yeah, I'm afraid so," I say. "Even as a kid, I'd do up little newsletters for our building. Called it 'View-point' because it was the Village View. Stories were all like, ya know, Mrs. Ortiz had twins, or old Mr. Pilowski's battle with pancreatic cancer was successful, or me and Jimmy Gulotta beat Luis and Reuben in wiffle-ball."

"Are you for real?" Haley asks.

"Sure," I say. "Luis and Reuben couldn't hit my knuckle-curve."

"How cute."

"Yeah, I suppose," I say. "Had another big scoop about this old lady who saw the Virgin Mary in her French toast. The *Post* was all playing catch-up on that one."

"Wow."

"How 'bout you? You always know you were gonna be a teacher?"

"More or less," says Haley. "Kinda like you as a young journalist—I'd play school all the time, and always had to be the one doing the lesson, giving the orders..."

"Being the boss," I say.

"Exactly. That was always my fort-*tay*."

"Your *fort*."

"Huh?"

"It's pronounced *fort*," I say. "It's French."

"You sure?"

"Positive."

"Then why does everyone pronounce it fort-*tay*?"

"I don't know, Hale. But each time, it chips off a little piece of my heart."

"Eek," she says. "Did I just commit a cardinal sin with you?"

I exaggerate a grimace.

"Let this be a warning."

"OK," she says with a smile. "My *fort*. Sounds so…imperial."

"How's the teaching going?" I ask, feeling foolish for correcting her pronunciation.

"Oh, it's good," says Haley. "It's maddening at times, but I love it."

"Summers off, huh?" I ask, then realize it was not the most inspired thing to say.

"Yes, summers off," says Haley. "That's certainly a perk."

"Nice kids?"

"They're great kids," says Haley with a smile. "I got it pretty easy. I mean, the school's about 12-grand a year, so it's not exactly a P.S."

"Must be some spoiled kids, though, huh?"

"Sure, a few," she says. "Rich kids, kids raised by their nannies, all of that. But I love 'em. Even the annoying little bastards… How's your volunteer work? With the needles?"

"Good. It feels good to, ya know, give a little somethin' back," I say with a straight face. "I know that sounds like a cliché, but I enjoy doing that kind of stuff, even if it's just one day a week."

"More than most people do," says Haley.

"Sad but true."

"Are you ever afraid of, you know, getting pricked?"

"Yes and no," I say, embarrassed to be slightly turned on when she says "prick." "I mean, we don't really *handle* the dirty ones per se. The dopeheads drop the dirty ones into the sharp box—that's what they call the needle garbage. We just hand them the clean ones. And we got rubber gloves on. So it can't really happen, unless one of the guys goes crazy and comes at you with the thing. That's a bit scary."

"It must be," she says.

SoHo's like an artsy Epcot, with its tidy streets and trendy shops and art galleries. It's packed; the beautiful day has successfully beckoned everyone out of their apartments and onto the trendy streets of SoHo. A power-shopping pair of well-tanned guys in matching buzz cuts, tight black shorts, tank tops and expen-

Michael J. Malone

sive wrap-around sunglasses has pushed Haley into me. Wearing a sleeveless white sweater, her bare arm brushes against mine, and I feel that jolt again as the goose-bumps rise on my arm.

"Sorry," she says.

"No problem," I say. "Assholes."

"Euro-trash," she adds.

The sun begins to drop behind the Jersey City skyline across the river as we sit in the grass at Hudson River Park, watching the boats go by and drinking the Rodney Strong Chardonnay I got from work. It's hot, but I don't want to take my shirt off—like a guy with bad eczema, I don't want Haley to see my fucked up tattoo just yet, and I'm not sure going topless would be appropriate date behavior.

"Saw DeNiro here once," I say. Everyone's impressed by my DeNiro story, and I have a moment of anxiety when I think I might've told her it already.

"In this park?"

Looks like I'm safe.

"Yup. Me and Gabby were sitting here about a year ago, hangin' out, and DeNiro walks by with some tall-ass black chick."

"No kidding," says Haley. "Sure it was him?"

I give her my best DeNiro-esque matter-of-fact look.

"Positive. Looks sorta nerdy, actually. Wearing these thick glasses, dressed in this dorky kind of Hawaiian shirt. The girl was a knockout."

"Of course. Probably a model," she says.

"Dude loves the dark meat," I continue, parroting what Gabby had said that day. "Check this out. Me 'n Gabby'd had a few beers, and we're sitting on that bench over there, and we see Bobby comin' down the path. So when he approaches us, Gabby stands up and says, 'Hello, Mr. DeNiro.'"

"No way!"

"I shit you negative. So DeNiro's sort of cool, sort of like, don't fuck with me, kid, not in front of my leggy black gal-pal. But he says hi and shakes Gabby's hand.

"So then Gabby says to him, all polite, 'Mr. DeNiro, if I may, I'd like to do an impression of my favorite actor.' And DeNiro totally takes the bait—he's all, 'and who might that be?'"

"Are you kidding me?" says Haley. "He's wearing a Hawaiian shirt, and he's being friendly. Robert DeNiro."

"I'm totally serious."

"Unreal. Gabby's got some serious nerve."

"Balls o' brass," I say proudly. "So Gabby does his DeNiro impersonation, which is spectacular."

"Taxi Driver? You lookin' at me?"

Haley's DeNiro is worse than mine.

"Nah, Hale. That's so... J.V."

Haley rolls her eyes and shrugs.

"*I make you laugh?*" she tries. "*I'm here to amuse you?*"

I smile. Those are Joe Pesci's lines, but I give Haley credit for giving it another go.

"No. *Cape Fear.* 'COUNSELURRRR!' Does this spot-on DeNiro thing, the one eye open wide, the smirk, head tilted. Everything perfect. Gabby crushes it."

"And DeNiro decked him," guesses Haley.

"No! Bobby was *diggin'* it! And the gal-pal was dying!"

"Oh my God," she says. "Probably because he did anything other than *Taxi Driver.* You must've been cracking up."

"Totally," I say. "It was really cool. DeNiro just laughed, shook his head and walked away."

"That's classic," says Haley. "*That's* a celeb sighting.'"

"Yeah. I don't really like actors, but that was cool. A real New York moment."

"Why don't you like actors?"

"I just don't. The whole living in the fake world thing, I don't know. It just doesn't seem all that...honorable. It doesn't seem like you've got to be particularly clever to pull it off. Screenwriting, on the other hand...those dudes are genius. How 'bout you? Any good sightings?"

"Not DeNiro."

"Anyone good?"

"Remember," starts Haley, "I grew up in Manhattan."

"Me too, me too," I say, though our respective versions of Manhattan may as well be opposite ends of the earth.

"Well, I actually did have a good one in this park."

"Really? Who?"

"John-John," says Haley wistfully.

"The Kennedy dude? The hot one?"

"Yup, a few years ago. Playing Frisbee with his buddies."

I make a quick sign of the cross, like Paula Coulter does every time someone dead is mentioned.

"Shirt off?" I ask.

"Of course," says Haley as she shuts her eyes, showing her long, beautiful eyelashes.

"Great body?"

"The best," she says.

John-John certainly had no half-tats on him.

"Him and DeNiro were neighbors," I say.

"I know," says Haley. "No. Moore Street."

"No. Moore John-John," I mumble to myself. "Are you one of those John-John girls?"

"'fraid so," admits Haley.

"My condolences," I say in a tone that allows her to either take it seriously or facetiously, whichever works better.

"Thanks. I was really upset."

"It *was* sad," I offer. I must really like this girl, commiserating about freakin' JFK Junior's death.

"I have a confession," says Haley.

"Whaddya got?" I say, intrigued.

"I… Oh, it sounds stupid."

"C'mon."

"Nah, not yet. Not til I know you better."

"I gave you a book I wrote about a bunny rabbit," I say. "It's your turn."

"If I tell you, will you read some of *Honey Bunny* to me?"

"I think that can be arranged," I say. It'll be good practice for when my big-people book comes out, and I have to do readings at Barnes & Noble. I *hate* reading aloud.

"I honestly thought I was going to marry John-John," says Haley.

"C'mon."

"I know, it's stupid," she says bashfully. "But when he moved here, I thought it was fate."

"Didja know the guy?"

"No. I almost did. I mean, my dad knows Senator Kennedy."

"The fat guy? The lady who drowned in Chappaqua?"

"Yes, Ted—the portly fella," says Haley. "And I saw John at a few parties and fundraisers and stuff. Never actually spoke to him, though. Just kind of admired him from across the room, like you would a museum piece. Which he is. Was. So, you know, things might've, could've worked out. Going to school up in Cambridge, you just sort of get caught up in the whole Camelot thing. It's stupid, I know."

"It ain't that bad," I say, patting her bare foot. Odd thing is, I can actually see John-John and Haley together. She's got that kind of look.

"I mean, I'm not the only girl who had a John-John crush. But I really thought we might end up together."

"His loss," I say.

"I s'pose. I'll probably end up marrying Joey Ramone, or something."

"Yeesh," I say. I'm better looking than Joey Ramone. "Haley Ramone. Wasn't he their drummer for like a week? Well, for today, you'll have to settle for me."

I mouth 'Haley Coulter' to myself. It's got a nice ring too. I bite my tongue.

"I could do worse, I guess," she says with a smile. "John-John never wrote children's books."

She hands me *Happiest Birthday*.

"Start reading, bub," she says.

I take a deep breath and lick my lips.

It was a bright, beautiful day in Serenity Knoll, I start. *As it always was. The glorious sun snuck its way into Honey Bunny's home, Warren #43, Serenity Knoll, and began to fill his happy hole with light.*

"This is...oh, I can't believe this," says Haley as she brings her hands to her mouth. "I... Too damn cute."

"Oh, it gets better."

"Honey Bunny!" sang his mom, Mommy Bunny. "Rise and shine! It's someone's birthday!"

Lying in his little bunny bed, Honey Bunny shook his sleepy head. It was his birthday! A big, happy smile spread across his face. He was having a birthday party today!

Haley shifts to put her head in my lap. It's by far the most significant physical contact we've had to date, even better than the hello kiss on the lips. I'm not thinking of Tisa right now, and it feels great.

"How's my birthday boy?" asked Mommy Bunny, coming into Honey Bunny's little bunny room.

"Great, Mommy Bunny. It's the best day of the year."

Mommy Bunny set down a plate full of all Honey Bunny's favorite foods: green leaves of lettuce, long blades of grass and a bright orange carrot with a red bow around it.

"Thank you, Mommy Bunny."

"You're quite welcome, my son. And later on, we'll have your party, and you can open your gifts and eat some sweets!"

Party! Gifts! Sweets! Honey Bunny's floppy ears perked up excitedly. Yesterday, he'd gotten all his chores done, so Mommy Bunny told him he could plan a party. He hop-hop-hopped around Serenity Knoll, handing out party invitations to all his friends: Marvin Mouse, Blue Jay, Jane Doe, even mean old Sigmund the Snake. All the animals in Serenity Knoll were his friends. And they'd all be coming over today!

"Heard enough?" I ask Haley, as a sailboat lazily drifts by on the Hudson, "Idyll Worship" painted on its rear.

"No, go on!" she says. "I wanna hear about the party."

Dead Bolt

Gabby wants me to meet his new chick. Either that or, more likely, he just doesn't want to be alone with her. We're in the Whiskey Bar in the Paramount Hotel. It's a fucking ridiculous place: snotty, expensive and crowded, my three least favorite things in a bar. Heck, it's probably not even a bar, per se, but a *lounge*. At least there's no pool table here. Still, I'd trade the hottie waitresses in cat suits for Christine's wrinkled old mug at the Homestead any day. But Gabby's new chickie wants to meet him here, so here's where we go.

I must admit—I'm *dying* to see the bathroom. I make a mental note of each toilet I use in restaurants, bars, department stores, even friends' apartments, and store them all in my mental database. This often comes in handy, because it's important to always have a good bathroom nearby in which to do your business.

The public bathrooms in New York fall into a number of different categories. At the top of the heap is what you'll find at some of the fancy hotels in midtown—a couple of stalls that have proper doors that extend all the way to the ground, with a dead bolt locking you in. The bolt is fool-proof; it's going to do its job every time.

You can't say that for the knob lock—not the Yankee who can't make the throw to first, but the kind of lock you either push in or twist. It may work or it may not. Depends on how old it is and how much abuse it's taken.

A bathroom with two stalls is the next best set-up, though they're pretty rare, due to the city's space constraints. Some hotels, or maybe a really big restaurant, have them, but not many.

Third best is the single stall. You get decent privacy, but you never know when someone's going to be waiting for you to finish up, some burly outer-borough bruiser asking you if you're up to the paperwork yet, and sometimes you just don't want to move that quickly.

Last is the bathroom either with no stall or one that's there, but is not really usable, one that's just waiting for the Health Department to slap their brightly-colored death certificate on the door.

If I'm at my job at Avatar, I generally go to the Radisson a block away to take care of business. It doesn't happen that often, but sometimes I need to bang *Honey Bunny* out at work with a deadline coming up, or sometimes I'm just so fucking bored that I need a little excitement. So I go to the Radisson.

The Rad's usually pretty chill—as long as you're white, which I am in spades, and you don't look homeless, which I usually don't, you just stroll right in past the bellhops and security guards. Sometimes I'm feeling kind of cheeky, as Shady might say, and I say hello to them, like I'm one of the fuckers paying $350 a night for the privilege of staying at the Rad. The last thing they're going to do is bust my ass. It's a hotel, and they're all about service, so they don't want trouble. And I'm pretty respectful. I go into the stall, snort up my stuff and reflect on life for a bit; flush, if necessary, leave the can, get a free cup of mocha latte from the machine in the lobby, grab an apple from the fruit basket—it keeps the doctor away—and I'm on my way. No blood, no foul. Right?

The bathroom at the Whiskey Bar is a two-staller. I was in there once, laying out my dope on the shiny metal toilet paper dispenser. I rolled up a dollar bill— yeah, high roller, I know—and was about to give it a big ol' toot, and someone walked into the bathroom. Sure enough, he pulls into the stall right next to me. It's kind of an unwritten rule of the Guy Code that you don't use a stall next to one that's occupied. But this guy really had to go. So I check out his shoe, which is about six inches from mine, which is tapping away nervously. It's a black Reebok high-top. I'd been going to the Radisson long enough to know what the black Reebok high-top is all about. Security. Fake shoes. No one else would be caught dead wearing them. And I'm sitting there with a dollar bill jammed up my nose, just about tickling my brain, and a fat line of Harry Potter powder sitting on the dispenser. Me and him side by side: Security and Insecurity. I can't wait to hit that line, and the heat plops down next to me. What an exercise in patience that was, holding my breath and tapping my foot, waiting for the fucker to flush.

But I wasn't a guest there—not a paying guest, anyway—so I suppose I wasn't in a position to complain.

"Betcha drinks are like $8," I say as Gabby and I approach the bar. The Whiskey is dark, with a blue neon glow. A bunch of short tables and fancy stumps for sitting on dot the floor.

"Reguluh drink? $9," says Gabby with his usual self-assurance.

"Betcha," I say.

"You're on."

"Whaddya havin'?" I say.

"Gin & tonic. Make sure it's Bombay Sapphiyuh."

The bartender is a gorgeous brunette whose comic strip-heroine figure is accentuated by her skin-tight outfit.

"Two gin & tonics," I say to our meow-mixologist as Gabby stares at the scenery. It's the kind of bar where you're afraid to order a beer, because the waitress will look at you like you're some sales guy from Wisconsin that's wearing white sneakers. I'll usually order a beer in this kind of situation, just to make a point, but the warm air outside has me in the mood for gin & tonics.

"What kinda gin?" she asks.

"Don't matter," I whisper.

She slinks off to make the drinks.

"$16," she says upon her return.

"Hah!" I say to Gabby. "It's on you."

"Muthahfuckuh," he grumbles, pulling out his wallet, which is attached to a chain. "Must be happy oww-uh."

We find an open table. A waitress frowns when she sees we've already got drinks.

"So what's this one's name?" I ask Gabby.

He sips his drink, then catches a piece of ice in his teeth.

"Sonja," he responds after spitting the shard back into his drink. He pulls hard on his Winston and bares his teeth like a hyena. "With a j."

"Haven't heard about Sonja with a j. Girlfriend?"

"Nah, man. Two dates, is all. It's chill."

"Where'd you meet her?"

"Bunch of us from work went out to the Gramercy Hotel for happy oww-uh, and she was there meetin' one of the girls I work with. Her and I just got talkin'. She's a designer too, so we had some shit in common. Now I gotta pretend I hang out in hotel bars all the time cuz she's a classy broad. Shit gets *expensive*."

Gabby waves sheepishly, offers the object of his gesture a rare, awkward smile, and Sonja with a j is in front of us.

"Hey-ya!" she says in a southern accent as she pulls up a stool to join us. Sonja is thin and long—the word "willowy" comes to mind—with long black hair and long legs in leather trousers that look real. She's sexy; not in the easy way that Haley is sexy, but in a way that likely takes her some effort each day. I tend not to like my friends' chicks, but ol' Sonja hasn't really given me any reason to dislike her, except maybe that she's got too much makeup on, and her accent is funny. And she's my best friend's chick.

"Wassup, Sonja?" says Gabby. "This is my man Declan. He had nothin' to do, so I brought him along."

"Hi," I say, lifting my butt a foot above my seat in a half-assed show of politeness. "Actually, I chaperone Gabby on his first coupla dates. Then, he's on his own."

"Gaah-bee?" she asks.

"Sorry. Paul," I say.

She forces a smile.

"Nice bar, huh?" she says cheerily.

Michael J. Malone

"S'awright," says Gabby. "Far as hotel bars go, not my favorite, but it's cool. Whaddya havin'?"

"Um, your *geee-in* & tonics look good," she says. "Tanqueray."

Gabby signals the waitress and orders her drink.

"So, Deck-laaan," she starts. "What do you do?"

"The recycling business," I answer. I keep a straight face, but Sonja gives me a hearty fake laugh.

"I'm totally serious," I say. "Ain't glamorous, but it pays the bills."

Sonja laughs again, though not as heartily. Gabby chuckles as well.

"And what kind of recycling do you do?" she asks warily.

"Cans, mostly," I say. "You'd never believe what kind of crazy shit you find in people's garbage."

"Ahh can imagine," she attempts. Her *geee-in* & tonic shows up.

"Not all cans, though. Bottles. I do tin, too. A bit more money in that. Old couches—anything pleather. Refrigerators....radiators...old Atari cartridges... spent Chap Sticks."

"Mmmm," she utters, sipping her drink sheepishly. Gabby bites down on a smile.

"Stuffed animals," I add. "Can't forget those."

"Declan's too embarrassed to say he works for a shitty wine magazine," says Gabby. He must really like Sonja with a j.

"Oh," she says, relieved that the game of Monkey in the Middle has apparently ended. "*Wine Enthusiast?*"

"Nah," I say.

"*Wine Spectator?*"

"Actually, *Cork & Bottle*. The other one."

My employer is the third tenor whose name no one can recall.

"Ahh didn't know there was another one," Sonja says.

"And what do you do?" I ask.

"Actually, ahh'm in the magazine biz as well," she says.

"No kidding."

"Yee-up. I'm an editor over at *Lilith*."

Lilith is this hip new chick mag that's much more about cool music and sex than beauty tips and cute boys. The editor pops up in Page Six all the time, where she's referred to as an *editrix*.

"They bust yer balls over titles at Lilith?" I ask. "Like, good people get stuck on associate editor because they're unwilling to kiss the right asses?'

"Damn right they do," she says. "Ahh came in at senior editor, and basically ahh have to wait for the editor-in-chief to die before ahh git promoted. And she's, like, 28. Any idea where ahh can score some arsenic?"

I muster a fake guffaw.

"10th and C," I say. "Ask for a dude called Buzzsaw."

She smiles.

"Where do you live, Declan?"

"Avenue A. 6th Street."

"Ahh love the East Village," she says.

"Actually, it's the Lower East Side."

"6th and A? That's not the East Village?"

I've explained this a million times but no one seems to listen.

"There really is no such thing as the East Village," I say. "There's Greenwich Village and the West Village, but 'East Village' was just kind of made up by some smart-ass realtor type. It's the Lower East Side."

Sonja with a j frowns.

"Ahh think of, like, Chinatown when ahh think of the Lower East Side. Or Ludlow, or down below the Manhattan Bridge. Ya know—way down there."

"Yeah, well—that's the Lower East Side, and so is 6th Street and A, and so is 14th Street and 3rd Avenue."

Sonja with a j sips her drink.

"Ahh think all the city's neighborhood names are just nicknames," she says. "Ahh mean, none of them are official names, right? They're just what people call them."

"I live on the Lower East Side," I say sternly, wondering why I get worked up about this stuff.

We have one at the Whiskey and then Sonja with a j says she wants to meet some friends at some joint called the Firebird Café a couple blocks up. She throws in that she used to do "a little cabaret" there before she settled into her "workaday routine," and suggests the next bar in a way that excludes me, looking at Gabby—sorry, Paul—all the while, her way of saying the threesome ends *now*. I think the Firebird Café sounds like some cheesy burger joint on the Jersey Shore and I tell her as much, but Sonja says it's a beautiful old Russian townhouse. She offers a lame last-minute invite. I decline. They leave and I'm by myself.

So it's a Monday night and I'm sitting alone in the Whiskey Bar. People eye me with annoyance, as I'm taking up a table, and legitimate two-, three- and four-somes are forced to stand. A football game is on over the bar, the sound turned off. I'm pleased to see that the Scottish Claymores are up by a touchdown. We got this weekly football pool going at work, and it's down to me and this girl in accounting. Not only does Avatar Publishing do a pool for the NFL season, like most offices across America, but we're so addicted to gambling that we bet on European football league games too. Oh well. Wasn't my idea—I'm just playing along, putting my fiver in each week, hoping for a little found money.

Michael J. Malone

I picked the Claymores over the Barcelona Dragons, because the Claymores have a kicker that used to play rugby for Scotland. If the Scots win, or lose by less than 6, I win the pool. If the Dragons win by more than six, the pot goes to Tricia in accounting. None of us knows shit about this ridiculous World Football League; we just know it's another excuse to bet.

Ever the selfless soul, I give up my table to a nervous couple that looks like they walked all the way from the Midwest. After standing like a dork for a few minutes, drawing funny looks from a few of the waitresses, I seek out the head, which is in the lobby of the Paramount. Hotels mean one thing to me—well, two, if you count ridiculously overpriced drinks.

I walk through the lobby and into the bathroom. Man, what a find—the marble floor spreads out before me, the chrome shimmering in the soft white light.

"Evening, sir," says a man in a black waistcoat and bow tie. He works here. In the bathroom. He smiles as I pass him en route to one of the two stalls.

It's bigger than some studio apartments I've been in. I spread my arms and twirl around, and don't touch a wall in any direction. There's a full-size door that reaches the floor, and the lock is the dead bolt; it's pretty much your own all-enclosed, completely secure little world for as long as you want, the rarest of luxuries in New York. I couldn't be happier.

For all its efficiency, there's something scary about the dead bolt, more than just the creepy irony to the name. I mean, situations like this, you love that you're bolted in. But somewhere in the back of your head, you think, jeez, if this roll comes up snake eyes, the planets are aligned just so and my number is called, that dead bolt's going to keep anyone—waistcoated bathroom attendant included—from getting to my convulsing ass. Can't help but think about it, especially with all that super-strong shit, that Body Bag, going around the city. I mean, I *can't* die yet; there are so many things I haven't gotten around to. I want to be able to play something besides "Free Fallin'" on the guitar. I want to do it with an Australian girl. Well, I sort of got some oral from a New Zealand nanny in the can at Swift's once, some chick the Kiwi brought out...man, that was a sloppy night... Anyway, you get my point. I need to talk to Tisa, and also have to patch shit up with Ma. And there's Haley.

I can't die yet.

Oh well. I bolt the door. Roll the dice, move your mice.

I got this rule, just a little something I do to keep my less-than-healthy enthusiasms in check. I can't buy dope with my own money. Honey Bunny's not paying for my dope. *Cork & Bottle's* not paying for my dope. My stash has got to come from found money, extra money, gift money, money I didn't really earn. This batch I got with some of Victor's money. Victor runs the liquor store on 4th and A. I get these bottles in at work for the wine review, more than I could ever review, so I sell some of them to Victor. When Ma and I were speaking, we'd go up on the roof with our beach chairs and pop it open, our own little rooftop Riviera. But mostly I sell them to Victor for a fiver or so. That's how I bought this little bag of Slim Shady, which burns like a mofo going up.

I'm not happy to admit this, but the Muzak being piped into the bathroom actually sounds pretty good. Haven't really paid Muzak much attention of late, but they certainly seem to have spiced up their playlist. There's a pleasant instrumental version—well, I guess they're all pleasant instrumental versions, really—of, get this, "Born to Be Wild," followed by some of the crap you'd expect, you know, Loggins & Messina and then Loggins solo and Bread and shit, before they play a version of "Since You're Gone," by the Cars. It sounds great. I close my eyes, and when I do, the Cars have been replaced by a Muzak version of Eminem's "Slim Shady." *Will the real Slim Shady please stand up? Please stand up.* Is this really happening? Can it be? Rap is short for crap, Gabby likes to say—either playing the part of a redneck or actually being one. *Please stand up.* I'm tempted to stand up and ask the bathroom steward for confirmation.

My eyes are jerked open a bit later when someone pulls on the doorknob. I clumsily scramble to my feet, mumble some nonsense and slap a little color into my face, then remember there's a dead bolt protecting me from the outside world. I sink back to the bowl, close my eyes and enjoy the moment. *Please sit down.* The would-be interloper tries another door.

The Muzak is now onto some old hit by either Vanilla Fudge or Three Dog Night or Cat Stevens, I can't recall which, and I decide it's time to move on, maybe get some fresh non-restroom air, perhaps get a bite to eat. I remove the dead bolt; escaped another one, though I honestly don't envision myself learning any new songs on the guitar any time soon, and nor do I have an Aussie chick lined up to bed.

"Evening, sir," the attendant says again. *How long has it been?*

"Hey," I mumble with a smile. I wonder if he has a business card, and if so, what it says.

I walk over to the beautiful marble bank of sinks and splash some water on my face. The cold wakes me up a bit and sends a little jolt of energy through my body. I check my face in the mirror and it looks, well, it looks like me.

Black Jeeves hands me a towel, and I thumb through my wallet for a dollar. The smallest I've got is a five, which stays in the wallet.

"Night, man," I say.

"Night," he sniffs. I take a peppermint candy from the basket and jiggle it around in my hand.

Shuffling into the lobby, I sense the late hour, though I can't really confirm it. There's an abstract clock above the check-in desk, where rich guys await their room keys as their wives or *gumars* look impatient, but I can't figure out the time on it. On another wall, four more clocks give the times from various cities across the globe: Tokyo, London, Frankfurt and Tel Aviv, but none pertain to me. I step outside, into this night on Earth and taste the cool breeze and the warm air, Times Square's white glow beckoning me like a moth to a candle.

Hitting Broadway, I pass a line of people waiting to enter the World Wrestling Federation restaurant—guys in mullets and long denim shorts, and the women who inexplicably love them. I look up and take in the urban canyon, enormous mountains of varying sizes made of steel and glass. It's breathtaking and, as such, I take a breath, my first in, jeez, Jeeves, an hour, or perhaps all night, probably. I pop the peppermint into my mouth, pep the poppermint, and savor its sweetness. My eyes open wide, I smile. I get it! I understand Times Square and its allure for the first time in the 29, almost 30 fucking years I've lived here and passed through it. An enormous screen showing "Jerry Springer" features two female combatants—one white, one black, both 30 feet tall—scratching and clawing at each other as burly guards gamely try to subdue their flailing appendages. On another screen, Drew Carey wears a dress, and on another, an ad for Hot Jobs trumpets the merits of the dot-com world. A gorgeous woman with a washboard stomach lies on her side and offers up a coquettish smile in the name of Jockey underwear. I take in the NASDAQ score, though I've never owned a stock in my life. My body temperature soars at the sight of an enormous Lipton Cup o' Soup, steam rising from it, then cools as I regard the 40-foot bottle of Budweiser nearby. A feast for the senses. A wire report flies by on the ticker, telling all the world that a brick-wielding madman has been incarcerated. Daffy Duck guffaws at the breaking news.

For the first time in my life, I'm sympathetic to the tourists fixing cameras on this sensory explosion, the glass forest and steel mountain range all around them. I see the football game hovering on a screen a hundred feet in the air, its players big as Godzillas. The Claymores are still up; there's about three minutes left and they're ahead by 7. So the Barcelona Dragons, favored by a touchdown, can tie it up, and they can go to OT, and Claymores can lose in sudden death by 6. But the Claymores still beat the spread, and I still win the pool. $65. I could use it. C'mon, *Sshkuttlin*. Damn, Gabby does such a better Sean Connery than me. *SHHKOOT-lin!* You got it or you don't.

I consider watching the rest of the game from my little camp here in the canyon, but, getting jostled by sky-gazing tourists, I decide to head home. With no available cabs in sight, I duck into the subway station at 42nd and Broadway, the sensory smorgasbord reduced to a piss-flavored stairwell and sobering light.

At the bottom of the escalator, there's a man whirling around a life-size puppet in a passionate tango, as the crowd cheers him on and throws change into an inverted snare drum. On the platform, a crowd of seemingly drunk Fleet Week sailors in white uniforms approach a teenage girl with a fold-up scooter.

"Ya know," says one in a wide, flat Midwestern accent, "ya don't need no subway if ya got *thaaat* scooter."

I see the dual purpose of her smile—politeness at our armed services guests in the big city, and a clear message he'll have to up his game several notches if he really wants to approach women in Manhattan. I get everything. I chuckle before taking my place on the platform, waiting on that damn R and N—the Rare, the Never—but I'm in no hurry, the platform's heat surrounding me in a sticky embrace. I think of that enormous bottle of Bud and would trade a limb for one. Two rats skitter along the track, taking turns nipping at each other in what is either an antagonistic or playful way, though I can't be sure, as rats always have that same determined expression.

There's a guy playing guitar. It's a beautiful blue acoustic with the back like a turtle and its rich sound surrounds the platform; I can see the notes filling the air, clanking sabers with the sticky heat and ultimately winning the fight. Music conquers all. The troubadour's got long red hair cut in a Prince Valiant and a red beard fashioned into a creepy Abe Lincoln. He sings in a nasally, monotone voice; like Dylan, but with a better voice and, needless to say, inferior songwriting skills. But not bad. He's doing a song about a breakup; he talks about having his ex's fingerprints all over the apartment. The song makes me think of Tisa. Will we reschedule our summit? Does she want to get back together? I quickly wipe her fingerprints from my mind.

I think I'm hearing rain, but I know it can't be, because it never rains inside a subway station. I look around for the source of the noise and see a guy tearing at the plastic that sheaths a new CD he's bought, a blood-red Virgin Megastore bag under his arm. I squint and peer intently, desperately trying to learn what disc it is. He keeps ripping at the tricky plastic, fingers feeling for an opening. Every time I think I can make out the type on the disc, the fucker moves it, the name escapes me and I'm back at square-one. I stroll over for a better look. He feels my presence and attempts to freeze me with a glare.

"Whatcha listenin' to?" I ask with a smile.

He's got thick glasses with marbled brown frames, and chestnut hair that nears his shoulders, stemming from a regrettably high hairline showing hectares of forehead. The classic fivehead. He's got the going-bald version of the mullet: the skullet. I titter. The two long-haired guys left in New York are both on this platform.

"I'm not *listening* to anything," he hisses.

"Well, whaddja buy?"

My persistence incenses him, and amuses me.

He stares, hoping an endless five-second delay will negate further interrogation. I hold my ground.

"Beastie Boys," he allows.

"Mmmmmm," I say, staring. He doesn't look up but he knows I'm there.

"Beastie Boys," I repeat.

"Mmmmm," he says.

"*You gotta fight!*" I shout. He stays quiet.

"How is it?" I ask.

"It...looks...well-made," he says. "A perfect circle. Shiny, with a hole in the middle. The way I like my CDs."

I've got no retort to that.

"*...to parrrrtaaaaay!*" is the best I can muster.

He shakes his head and finds another area on the platform in which to stand, one without me.

The train finally shows up. I take a seat, my sore ass telling me I was on the can in the Paramount for longer than I thought. The A.C. is cranking, and it gobbles away at the beads of sweat on my back like Pac Man munching blue ghosts. The sailors sit across from me, adjacent to a not-unattractive girl reading *HTML For Dummies*.

"Ya know," starts one sailor, as the girl warily raises her eyes above the book, "HTML's gonna be a thing of the past. Ain't no use in learnin' it now."

He must be an officer. She smiles and returns to her book. I chuckle, and the sailor looks at me. He's about to say something, but stops before he utters a sound. Soon, he and his buddies are joking around and clapping each other on the shoulders.

I open my eyes and I'm at 8th and Broadway.

I'm wondering if the football game is over as I walk along St. Mark's, looking for a good bar to watch the end of it in. Each place I peer into, something freaks me out about it; probably just a chemical-induced case of paranoia, I tell myself, though it doesn't appease me enough to actually duck into one of the places.

After 10 minutes, my legs are like jelly and I'm dying for a beer, and 7A's off on the horizon is a friendly place that seems to offer everything I desire. I enter and take a seat at the bar. Sure enough, the game's still on, and some talking head bereft of neck is going on and on about the revitalized Scottish Claymores and some hotshot quarterback they got who couldn't cut it in the NFL, but loves life in *Edinburrahh*. In the background, the crowd sings "Flower of Scotland."

I realize the news is good for me, bad for Tricia in accounting. My beloved Claymores have won, and so have I. $65! I celebrate with a pint of Anchor Steam, which I take over to the window that looks out onto the street. It's been a good day.

I take a sip of the beer—Anchor Steam's got a beery taste, even for a beer—hoppy and yeasty and, well, *beery*. My mouth is dry, and it tastes wonderful.

I stare out the window and dig the groovy day I've had. A few leaves blow down the sidewalk. Across the street, a plastic Key Food bag floats about 20 feet in the air, gently up and down, left and right, diving and lifting, dipping and rising. I'm rapt by this weightless bag. It looks like it could stay suspended in this vortex all night and, dammit, I could sit here all night, sipping my beery Anchor Steam and watching it, maybe capture its gossamer grace with pen and paper. Use it to kick off my long-awaited, as yet unnamed and unstarted, second novel. I'm transfixed by this beautiful image, this Key Food dervish.

But something about this image is familiar. I've followed its aimless progress before, though I can't figure out how, or when, or why.

It hurts my brain to think. "Sugar Magnolia" comes on the stereo. I think of my old pal Jimmy Gulotta. After his glam rock phase, but before he went punk, he was into the Grateful Dead. Then lots of people seemed to get into the Grateful Dead at the same time, and he stopped. He played that stupid Dead tape in his stupid boombox that whole summer. It was called "American Beauty."

I realize I just saw this same image, that bag floating like a lifeless leaf, in that movie me and Haley saw, the one where Kevin Spacey is all hot for his daughter's friend.

The bag disappears from sight, leaving Leshko's Diner in its wake across the street.

If any place sort of sums up the new Alphabet City, for better or for worse, it's freakin' Leshko's. Used to be like the rest of the Russki diners—Eastern European waitresses with dumpy bodies and lumpy faces, bad coffee, even worse lighting that made you wonder if you looked as sick as the people you were with. Me and Ma used to go there a lot when I was a kid; I remember her brother, my Uncle Joseph, coming over from Derry, and we went for lunch there once. Man, I could never understand what that cat was saying.

But they remodeled Leshko's—put in modern furniture with agreeable lines and huge windows that let in all sorts of light, piped in soothing classical music like what you hear in commercials—and now you see it in the gossip pages, in boldface, in the same sentences as the famous people that eat there now. Trendy types show up for brunch, sit next to the windows and squint in the sunlight, before moving to a table away from the light, where they sit and explain their emotional struggles in car trouble terms like "breakdown" and "bottoming out."

But the reason why I haven't been back there has nothing to do with the harsh sunlight or insufferable posers. It's where I met Tisa. In retrospect, it's hard to imagine a snotty chick like her working in the service industry, but she had ulterior motives, as always. She knew that being a good looking hostess at a trendy place like that meant you were going to get lots of attention from potentially important people. Folks just assume a hot hostess or waitress is an actress on the side; chat up the right director or something, and you weren't hostessing or waitressing for long. Tisa knew she was slumming, and she also knew that if she kept her headshots under the stack of menus and played her cards right, she wouldn't be for long.

I take another sip of my Anchor Steam, which I can feel traveling through the pipelines of my body, to my hands and feet, bringing life into my limbs along the way.

Anyway, it was years ago, and I was there with ol' Jimmy Gulotta. Last I heard, he was locked up at Sing Sing for something related to the drug trade, or maybe it was underage girls—he dug both. Too bad. He was Lower East Side tough, Village View tough, but I don't think he's Sing Sing tough. Starting when he was about 15, Gulotta would assume a different rock star identity for about a year or two—outfits, hair, everything. He was Elvis Costello, then Bowie, then Keith Richards. Guess he's Tommy Lee in the slammer now. But that Sunday afternoon, he was Johnny Rotten and I was me and we were hung over as shit, getting food and killing time until the football game was on. Tisa'd sat us, only I didn't know her name was Tisa, and I couldn't take my eyes off her. She had her hair pulled back in a ponytail and a real pretty face, like it was made of china or something, and she was wearing a black short-sleeve turtleneck and black silk slacks that flared at the bottom, with a flowery design on them that you could only see if you were staring at her ass real hard.

They used to give you free Bloody Mary's with brunch—we called it Lushko's—though I'm sure they charge Whiskey Bar prices for them now. It was one of those times where you're so hung over that one drink makes you feel real good, and by the second one, you've bypassed drunk and are just a mess—not making any sense, faces in front of you melting into surreality, that sort of thing. Then you order another without even realizing you did.

Some chick next to us was blathering to her friend, a dude in a wispy beard and wool ski hat, about how she wanted to elevate DJ-ing to an art form, but was frustrated by spinning for drunk people all the time. And Gulotta's going on and on about some shit—fixing elevators, banging underage Latinas in our building, whatever the dude would rap about—and I just kept staring at Tisa, waving her over when she caught me staring, making up something I needed—jelly for my eggs, non-dairy creamer for my pancakes, that sort of thing. I remember that lunch with my Uncle Joseph, him asking for non-dairy creamer, and me making some ridiculous joke about people from Derry not being allowed to use it. Stupid, I know. I was a kid. And Ma really let me have it, creamed me with a backhand to the head, even though Li'l Declan was just trying to be funny for Uncle Joseph from Ireland.

So at first Tisa was being a good sport, smiling back at me and asking the waitress to fill my request, and then she said, kind of in a forced polite way, "I'm a hostess, not a waitress."

Well, I somehow hadn't noticed the English accent before, and that shit just kills me. I was smitten. I asked her where she was from and she said, "Somerset" or "Somerville" or "Somershire" or some Somer-y place that sounded beautiful and quaint and picturesque, like her accent. I told her I did a hazy semester in Liverpool and she smiled politely, and I realized saying that was kind of like when people in Liverpool would tell me they had a cousin in Boston, was that near New York, perhaps I knew him? She said she'd never been to Liverpool and didn't have much desire to go there, and I told her it wasn't as bad as people said. Jimmy, he'd never been out of the city, I don't think—his first time out of town was probably in shackles, on a rickety bus headed upstate—so he just sat there, sippin' his Bloody, hoping the convo would swing towards something he knew about, like banging elevators and fixing Latino chicks.

I asked her how work was going, and she said the new Leshko's didn't permit smoking—the old one was like a bloody opium den, she'd said—so her workload was cut in half.

"You see," Tisa'd started, "the role of the hostess used to be 'Hi, how many?' and then, 'Smoking or Non?' Now, it's just 'Hi, how many?'"

I asked her what she did with all the freed-up time, and she said she spent it studying her hostess manual, figuring out better ways to master the art of hostess-ing, so she could be the best damn hostess she could be. Her way of telling me how she was above the job, I guess. A fly kept buzzing around her face, a holdover from the old Leshko's searching for his buddies, probably. He was looking to land and she kept swatting him away, keeping the airspace clear without ever losing her cool. I was impressed. I wanted her there and then. And if not there and then, then at least in the refurbished Leshko's bathroom during her cigarette break, pound home the dead bolt and pull down those silk pants.

We talked a little more and then she smiled and said she had to get back to work. I had another Bloody, waved her over again and asked her out as Jimmy Gulotta slurped his Bloody, and she said no.

But I didn't quit there. No, I was young and optimistic and foolish—fool enough to have been carrying around a stamped envelope containing a Visa bill that I'd been meaning to drop in a mailbox all freakin' day. The check came and the server's name was Skye and I wondered if that was the lovely hostess's name. I know they don't normally put the hostess's name on the check, but she was just so above this Earth, so otherworldly, and I was drunk on Bloody's, that I figured she was Skye. Jimmy wanted to stay and drink more Bloody's but I wanted to get the fuck out of there, get some air, so we split the check and stood up. I smoothed out

Michael J. Malone

the wrinkled Visa bill and slipped it onto my chair, thinking she'd find it and see my name and look me up in the phone book, and we'd fall in love. Hah.

I take another sip of my Anchor Steam, which is no longer bringing life to my limbs. Now it's just making me sleepy, and I wish I could crawl under the window here at 7A's and sleep for a few hours, until I got the energy to walk the two blocks home. I put my head down on the cool wood for just a second, gather my thoughts, think of my book and Haley and what she's doing and fuck Tisa and
. . . .

"Hey ho!" sings the bartender, giving my shoulder a firm but friendly shake. "Y'awright, buddy boy?"

I slowly lift my heavy head up and get him on my screen. Hipster dude, soul patch, tight black t-shirt that says "Fender" on the chest in ornate cursive.

"Yeah, man. Long day."

"Hey, no worries, dude. Same here. Can't letcha spend the night, though. Heh heh."

"No problem," I say with a smile. I sip my beer—it's warm now, and the warmth brings out the hoppy, delicious taste—and think of that plastic bag floating toward the heavens. I wonder if there are any beautiful images left that haven't yet been claimed. I figure there are. I wonder if I'm capable of claiming such an image. That I'm not sure about.

But at least I won the football pool.

Found money.

Garlic, Green Pepper, Olive Oil

"I'm chopping broccoli," I croon over the Bob Dylan playing on my stereo. "I'm choppin' broccol-*eye*."

The phone rings. I put down the knife and grab it.

"Yeeoohhh," I yell to the receiver, trying to sound casual but fearing the worst: Haley's calling to cancel, and I've wasted half an hour chopping broccol-eye and laying ricotta on strips of pasta, just how ol' Paula instructed me. Northern Irish lasagna.

"Yo, Deckie," says Gabby.

"Heyya, buddy boy. Whaddya got?"

"Damnnn, man," says Gabby. "Turn that shit *down*."

The stereo's loud. I shuffle off to the living room and turn that shit down.

"Sorry."

"Shit," growls Gabby. "What the hell was that?"

"Dylan," I say. Gabby hates Dylan as much as he hates "donkey music" and other turbo-Irish trappings.

"*Time Out of Mind*," I say. "Came out a few years ago. Won him a Grammy, I think. Dylan's good inspiration."

"Inspiration for what?" asks Gabby.

"I, uh, I'm cooking for the girl," I stammer. "Dylan's a good reminder that you don't have to be a natural at something to do it well."

I can see Gabby's look of bewilderment, perhaps disgust, through the phone.

"Is this really something you thought about?"

"Nahh, man," I lie.

"You think too much," he says. "I mean, most of the time you don't think enough, if at all, but it's times like this that you think too much."

"Fair enough," I concede. "Wassup?"

"Not a lot. They're showing Australia versus England at MacLennane's. Mick says it's three dolluh Guinness for all the boys. You wanna go watch? I'll buy first pint."

"The Wallabies versus England," I repeat. "At Twickenham or Down *Un-dahhh?*"

Gabby does such a better Aussie accent than me.

"Twickenham," replies Gabby. "A replay from Saturday. Great match. I won't tell you what happened."

"Shit… I can't, man," I say. "I told you—cooking for the girl."

"Uh, Haley?"

"Of course," I snap at him, annoyed that my best friend would think I might be cooking for Tisa.

"Whaddya makin'?" asks Gabby.

"Lasagna. *Meat* lasagna."

The meat modifier takes some of the wussiness out of cooking for the girl.

"*Cooking for the girl,*" he taunts nonetheless. "That's…interesting."

"No, it isn't," I argue. "There's nothing interesting about it. I, uh, lost a bet. And if dinner goes well, maybe tonight will be, ya know, the night."

"You haven't banged her yet?"

"No. So how 'bout you? You cook for…that girl…with…the long legs… yet?" I've forgotten the name of Gabby's new chick. It's hard to keep them straight. "Leather Tuscadero?"

"No way, bro'," says Gabby. "Leathuh cooks for *me.*"

I can hear Gabby snapping his fingers and clapping his hands like Leathuh Tuscadero through the phone.

"Really?"

"Well, it happened once. Just fajitas, wasn't all that. Sonja's got a rad pad though."

Sonja. That's it.

"Duplex in Tribeca, some building with a name," he adds. "Starts with 'The.'"

"No shit."

"Anyway, Deckie, if she cancels, meet me up at MacLennane's. Shady's gonna be there, Flyboy, maybe Ghetto Ron and a few uthuhs. Did I mention the three dolluh pints?"

"Yes, Gab, you did. She ain't gonna cancel," I say, wondering if Haley will indeed cancel.

"Well, if anything weird happens, you know where to find me. Shepherd's pie. Guinness."

"I'll keep that in mind, man," I say, and hang up.

"Garlic, green pepper, olive oil," I'm muttering as I wait for the light to change at 4th and A. *"Garlic, green pepper, olive oil."*

I glance through the window at Two Boots for a look at the clock. I've got an hour. It's cool. *"Garlic, green pepper, olive oil,"* I repeat as I cross A and head into Key Food.

I repeat my mantra as I traipse down the aisles. *"Garlic, green pepper, body oil..."*

Something...someone's caught my eye as I pass through Produce. She's cute, with a great body that shows undeniable definition amidst baggy overalls. Jesus, she looks familiar, I'm thinking as I select garlic cloves. She's beautiful. Her wavy head flies past me in a flash. Happens every day along Avenue A. Someone I've probably gaped at before, maybe even got shot down by in a bar. I shrug and trek onward.

The Key Food on A is great—this neighborhood did not have a real grocery store until it opened a few years ago—but like any good thing in New York, the lines are killer. The guy in front of me pisses me off without even saying a word: Soul patch, spiky mod hair poking out from under a tattered wool cap, Airwalk sneakers, droopy jeans, messenger sack resting oh-so-casually on his hip. One goofy Sunday at MacLennane's, Me and Gabby dubbed those dudes WHIS kids—Wool Hat in Summer a-holes. But that shit I can deal with; hell, you live in Alphabet City, you have to deal with Alphabet City hipster types. What I can't deal with are the 12 items in his basket, when the Express sign clearly states no more than 10. That shit sends me through the roof. Two Elio's frozen pizzas, cinnamon buns, a package of sliced turkey, a bag of bagels, peanut butter, American cheese. It's a white-trash smorgasbord. Pepperidge Farm cookies, double chocolate. Advil. Two types of mustard—a condiment connoisseur! A sixer of Sam Adams, and I'm counting that as one. Man, that's 12, minimum. I look at the items in my arms—two cloves of garlic, three green peppers, one bottle of olive oil, a pack of condoms. I'm playing by the rules. Normally, I'd say something. But I've got a date and some food to cook. The poseur doofus will live to see another day. Attractive girls have a good effect on me, I think as the line plods along, its laborious pace due in part to scofflaws such as the slacker jackass in front of me.

I turn back to a far more favorable image, the hauntingly familiar rotini pasta curls on the head in the line next to me, the overalls and ratty cardigan and funky Adidas sneakers, blue with white stripes, that brought me such pleasure a mere moment before. My produce paramour very well might be Violet Oppenheimer.

At Art & Design, boys subscribed to two temples of worship. Either you were a guy who dug Katherine DiSorto, or you grooved to Violet Oppenheimer. If your vote was for Katherine—blonde, lean, preppy, wholesome—you likely combed your hair, wore Izod shirts and played a sport, or would if your levels of dexterity, athleticism and self-confidence would've permitted it. If you were into Violet Oppenheimer—naturally kinky brown hair, breasts like ripe peppers and surprisingly ample for such a diminutive figure, ass like the best onion in the bunch over in the produce aisle, hip, and actually pleasant to boot—you dressed a little funky, or wished you did, you didn't mind girls who went to more than one Duran Duran concert per multi-night Madison Square Garden stint, and if you weren't into REM, you would be soon. Call me biased, but Violet was the thinking man's crush.

I remember well the early days of high school, and on its soundtrack, besides way too much U2 and Ramones, was that typically overwrought Sting song about Russians, the one I believe he titled, with a most uncharacteristic simplicity, "Russians." There was a verse that went something like, *"How can I save my little boy/From Oppenheimer's deadly toy."* God, how the back half of that couplet rang true to me. I desperately wanted to be Violet Oppenheimer's deadly little toy. Sting went on about how we share the same biology, but Violet's genetic makeup was of another world. Of course, the song was about devastating nuclear bombs and kids suffering their merciless mayhem, but Violet's power over me—and the enlightened contingent among Art & Design's young males—was no less awesome and destructive.

Anyway, back to Earth and the Lower East Side. And freakin' Violet Oppenheimer—God, I hope that's still her last name—is in the next line over. I swear it's her. I mean, it's been…probably 12 years or so. I'm sure I haven't seen her since the Art & Design commencement ceremonies, and that was… yup, a dozen years ago. Wow. But it's *gotta* be her.

I stare at her purchases, feeling naughty and getting a small but not insignificant infusion of sexual energy from this grocery store voyeurism. Romaine lettuce, green peppers—just like mine—and a vegetable I can't identify. Cashew nuts and Lady Mitchum deodorant. I'm inside Violet's cupboard; it's warm and it's wonderful.

I clear my throat, slip the condoms in my pocket, and clear it again.

"*Garlic, green pepper, olive oil,*" I say, *sotto voce,* by way of "Testing, 1-2-3." It comes through clear. It's time. I'm on.

"Violet," I say slowly, confidently.

Her head whips around and, with it, a shock of kinky hair—*naturally* kinky hair—the rotinis tumbling into the colander, slo-mo, like in a commercial.

There's an awkward pause. The Express line karma transgressor in front of me turns around to cadge a glimpse at the nascent drama. I turn him back around with a stare, and return my gaze to the lovely Violet. Recognition has enveloped her face in a warm embrace. It suits her well. Hell, the two-skirt, three-tank-top look, *a la* Madonna 1985, suited Violet Oppenheimer well. She's that kind of girl.

"Declan… Coulter," she coos. "How have you been?"

"I'm fine, thanks for askin'," I say in a voice I temper with a bit of Tom Waits rasp, to let her know that my last 12 years, if not exactly a dirty dozen, have at least been spent in dark bars with edgy miscreants. I have stories to tell.

"And you?" I volley back with a smile.

"Oh, I'm well," she says. "Living on 7th between 1st and A. For today, anyway."

"Really?" I say. "I'm on 6th and A. Village View."

"You always were an East Village native, weren't you?"

"'fraid so," I admit, not bothering to go into my no-such-thing-as-East Village diatribe, but disappointed that a Manhattan native would succumb to the silly neighborhood nickname. "I'm an urban local. A hick. I can't seem to leave."

"Why would you?" queries fair Violet. "And what do you do, Declan?"

"I'm a writer and an editor."

"Really?" She's suitably impressed. "What kind of stuff?"

"Well, I work full-time as an editor for a wine mag—"

"*Wine Enthusiast?*" asks Violet.

"Nah, the other one. And then I do some fiction stuff on the side. Some kids' books that get published and some big-people books that don't...yet."

"Really? That's excellent. What kind of children's books?"

"A series called *Honey Bunny*," I say. Other men might be embarrassed by this admission. I'm proud as hell.

"Good for you," says Violet.

"Mmmm."

I picture me and Violet lounging on the beach, her putting sunblock on my half-a-tat. Tisa is a million miles from my mind; Haley, 500,000. The Express line hits a standstill as the cashier checks the price of the doofus's cinnamon buns. No worries.

"And how 'bout you, Miss Oppenheimer?" I ask.

"Oh, this and that," she says. Apparently, her name is still intact. "I'm an actress, though that of course means busting your ass on the side in far less glamorous pursuits. I've been bartending at Veruka down on Broome for two years or so."

Great. Another actress.

"Nice," I say. "That place always pops up in the gossip pages."

"Yeah, I feel like I've been pouring drinks for Leo and his boys for the past six months."

Leo Sayer? Leo Durocher? Seinfeld's Uncle Leo? I don't ask.

"What sort of acting do you do?"

"Off Off-Broadway, a few indie movies. I was in the stage version of 'Bright Lights Big City' at the Theatre Workshop. Did you see it?"

"I meant to," I say.

"And the indie films—nothing you would've seen, I'm sure. Small-time stuff."

"I'll look for you," I say. And I will.

"You wanna, uh," Violet starts, negotiating the intent of my purchases, "go somewhere with, uh, better ambiance? Go for a drink, maybe?"

Did she... Is she... Is this really happening?

"This lighting's killing me," I say, looking skyward. "I'd love to. Let's pay up and get out of here."

My line moves a bit quicker than Violet's, so I wait for her by the door. Finally, she's paid and bagged, and gives me a smile. I put my hand on my hip, offer her the crook of my arm like a cheesy squire, and she threads her arm through. The physical contact is like electricity.

"Shall we?" I say.

"Let's," she agrees, and we gambol toward the automatic doors.

"How about Niagara?" she suggests. Damn. Bad memories there.

"Sure."

We head toward the exit.

BAHHHHHHHH!!!!!!!!!!!!!!!!!

Wrong answer, according to the anxiety-inducing buzzer. The condoms in my pocket don't sit well with the electronic sensor that stands sentry at the doorway. Over hustles a security guard, a man with skin black as ink, pockmarks on his cheeks and a flat nose that looks like it's had the cartilage removed.

"Ya got me," I say in a tone that tells the man it happens all the time, that my Goldman Sacks ID or Visa titanium card always triggers the alarm. I smile and raise my arms like a busted perp.

The guard looks in my bag.

"Garlic, green pepper, olive oil," I sing.

He looks me in the eye.

"Go 'head, mon," he says in a lilting accent. "Happen all dee time."

I have two thoughts in my head as we exit Key Food: I'm going for a drink with Violet freakin' Oppenheimer, and I forget the other one. Unfortunately, the bag containing garlic, green pepper and olive oil has not clued me in to another important thought—that at that moment, Haley was likely applying a dab of that perfume she wears that makes me think of that nap you take after the beach to her neck and preparing to head towards my apartment for dinner, an invitation which had surely surprised and impressed her immensely.

It's drizzling, a steady breeze is blowing and it's considerably cooler than when Violet and I ducked into Niagara for a drink. The rain taps repeatedly on my head, like a mother reinforcing to a child how stupid he is, as I watch Violet hustle down 7th Street.

Damn, I could feel the ghost of Tisa all over Niagara, guarding the door like a huge black bouncer who hates his job. It had been a few weeks after I first saw her at Leshko's, and I'd popped into Niagara for a beer before heading over to MacLennane's to meet the boys. There she was, sipping a drink by herself near the bar, looking around nervously. It was early-ish, the bar not yet full. I felt my heart explode, just like it did the first time I saw her. I slowly composed myself and walked over towards her. What was that name on the check? Earth? Sun? Moon?

"Skye!"

No reaction.

"Skye!"

Nothing. I moved a few feet to the side, closer to the direction she was facing.

"Getting off work?" I'd asked, as she turned to find the source of the statement. She looked at me and just kept looking for a few moments, a polite smile buying time as she tried to figure out who I was, what I wanted and how she might dispose of me.

"Leshko's," I added, nodding towards Avenue A. She was wearing a tight baby T with a kid's crayon drawing of the sun on it. The sleeves were short and it was cut to show her midriff, and she had pure white skin that you desperately wanted to touch, to lick.

"I don't work there anymore," she replied. That accent! I'd forgotten how rich it was. "Did you used to work there too?"

"Nah. Eat there now and then. Drink there too."

"Thank God I'm not there anymore," she said. "That was the most miserable two months of my life."

"I can imagine. Where are you working now? No shortage of diners in this neighborhood."

"I'm an *actor*," she spat.

"Aren't female actors called actresses?" I tried.

She coolly sipped her drink.

The rain picks up a bit as I make my way down A and turned at 5th, the unseasonable gusts blowing in my face. I wish I had a freakin' jacket. The breeze and the booze join forces in a tag team effort that almost makes me lose my balance, but I steady myself by raising my arms, one arm with a bag containing a few cloves of garlic, three green peppers and a bottle of olive oil hanging from it. Usually pints of Guinness do well to warm me up, but I think my persistent chill has more to do with Violet telling me she's leaving for L.A. in the morning than the weather. "I've beaten the bushes in New York," she told me, the message crushing but the choice of words titillating, "and I haven't attained what I'd consider a comfortable living as an actress. The prospect of living in L.A. appalls me, but I know the work is there, much more than it is here. I've got to try to make it work."

Needless to say, the prospect of her living in L.A. appalls me too. Violet Oppenheimer in fucking Los Angeles. Who the hell buys a full head of Romaine

Michael J. Malone

lettuce the night before they move to Los Angeles? It doesn't make sense. Nothing makes sense. Violet dropped that on me and my thoughts immediately turned to Haley. I fucked up big time. I feel terrible. I've skipped past drunk straight into hung over. I didn't think I dug Haley this much until I lost her, which I'm positive I did tonight.

"I'm Declan," I'd said to Tisa that fateful evening. "It's Irish."

"I know," she'd replied. "I'm Tisa."

Tisa. It was like a chick from Queens saying "teaser." But the only Queens in this girl's life wore crowns and drove their daughters-in-law to eating disorders and fatal car crashes.

"Tisa," I repeated. "Who's Skye?"

"Skye?"

"That was the server's name on the check. Did you work with Skye? I've never known a Skye."

"Oh, right. Every check at Leshko's has Skye on it. I never knew any Skye there. They do it to sound trendy. Plus, I was the hostess. Not the server."

"Can I buy you a drink?" I asked.

She was quiet for a moment, then nodded and turned toward the bar, revealing a moon tattoo on her lower back. It was just a sliver of the moon, a crescent.

Tisa told me later that the only reason she let me buy her a drink was because she was done with hers and out of money, waiting on her delinquent friend to show up. She asked for a bourbon and coke, specifying the bourbon (Jack) and the coke (Diet). I leaned over to the bar and, out of earshot, ordered a Beam and coke, because it was cheaper, and a Jameson's on the rocks for me. I handed her the drink and threw down a tip. She took a sip.

"Is this…," she started through an unhappy face, "regular coke?"

"Diet," I said.

"It's awful sweet," she replied. I grabbed it from her and sipped through the straw, then made a face similar to hers.

"Ecch," I said before handing it back to her. "That's diet, alright." Tisa made another face and dropped the straw on the floor.

"What sort of acting do you do?" I asked.

"The-*ay*-ter," she responded as her cell phone rang.

"Where the fuck are you?" she yelled at it, the curse sounding out of place amidst her elegant inflection.

"I'm here," she continued, looking up at me and rolling her eyes. "Bloody hurry."

"Friend?" I said as she slipped the phone into her purse.

"Soon to be ex."

"Ex-boyfriend?"

"No, ex-friend," she said, and my heart beat faster. "I told Shan half-nine. It's...9:50. Bloody hell."

Bloody hell. That's how you felt after a long, boozy brunch at Lushko's.

"Do you live around here?" she asked.

"Yup," I said sort of proudly. I used to be ashamed. Now the neighborhood was considered cool. "Two blocks down."

She pushed across a smile and we were quiet. I wondered how long we had before Shan rushed in.

"I...," I began, like a singer trying a do, a re, a mi. Here it goes. "I think we should, ya know, go out some time."

She was big with the silent pauses.

"And why do you think that?"

"I just do," I said. That response wasn't going to cut it, and Tisa's look told me as much.

The wind still in my face, I pop into a pay phone at the corner of 5th and A and try Haley's number, which I know by heart for the first time. The phone rings and I'm desperate to hear her voice, to confront the issue and express my contrition for missing our date and being, well, an asshole. It rings and rings; seven, eight, nine times. We're past ten. She's gone...and presumably took her machine with her. Maybe Haley's moving to La La Land as well. *Haleywood.* Fuck.

Tisa stared at me for an answer.

"Cuz we got good chemistry," I tried.

No dice.

"Cuz I want a tattoo and I'm nervous and you could tell me all about what to expect. Does it hurt?"

A tattoo was just about the last thing I wanted.

"It's a man jabbing needles into your body. Of course it fucking hurts."

I winced and almost let my Jameson's slide out of my hand.

"Ouch," I croaked. "Well, yours certainly came out beautifully."

"Thank you," Tisa said, throwing out a hip and twisting at the waist so we could both get a better look. I impulsively went to touch it, like a child would some shiny trinket, and she shot me a look but didn't say anything. I petted the quarter moon gently and felt my knees weaken.

"It's beautiful," I repeated.

"Ta," she responded. "What are you thinking of getting?"

What the hell would I get? I never thought about it. A rugby ball? A pint of Guinness? My *fookin'* Ma's name?

"A dolphin," I said, and Tisa started cracking up.

I approach my building, fumble with my key, and it eventually slides into the hole. I exit the rank elevator, enter my apartment and flick on the lights, my eyes

Michael J. Malone

immediately shooting past the neglected tray containing graying ricotta cheese atop a lonely bed of flat noodles, like mortar on brick, toward the answering machine. I pray for the blink and get my wish.

There's hope. It's Haley. Or it's Tisa. Or maybe it's Violet—she's changed her mind and is back in Niagara, done with insipid, shallow and culturally bereft L.A. before leaving, coming to her senses and staying in New York with the rest of the cool chicks.

"A dolphin!" Tisa had shouted. "That's absurd!"

"A fucking dolphin!" I insisted. Who was she to make fun of my dolphin?

"You must've loved Sea World as a child."

I remember Ma taking me to Florida when I was a kid, driving us down in that shitty old Duster, and balking at the ticket prices for Sea World, just like she'd done at Disney the day before. We ended up at some cheesy aquarium down the highway a bit called Shark Park.

Tisa looked at her watch again.

"Fucking hell," she said.

"How long's a tattoo take?"

"Thirty odd minutes, depends what you get. Though I'm not sure how long your *dolphin* would take."

Her cell rang again.

"Hold on... Hey-ya. 7th and A, Shan, same as before...For *fuck's* sake."

"Sorry," she said after hanging up.

"Why is the moon so significant?" I asked.

"That's really none of your business."

"Ya know, you wear the fucking thing on your body, people are going to ask about it. Wear a shirt like that, it's everyone's business."

"I don't think I want to tell you," Tisa had said.

"Fine."

"Fine," she shot back, glancing past me.

"There she is."

"Alright," I said. "I'll leave you two alone. Don't let her off easy."

"I don't plan to. Nice meeting you, Declan. And thanks for the drink."

"No problem," I said as Shan approached us. "I didn't get your number yet."

There was that deadly pause again. The bar was filling up, the DJ spinning stacks and perfect silence between me and this Tisa chick.

"6-3-1-8-5-2-6."

She said it fast, and I sent it to memory immediately. "6-3-1-8-5-2-6," I whispered to myself. I nodded and walked toward the door. 6-3-1-8-5-2-6. 6-3-1-8-5-2-6.

54

"Bloody *hell*, Shan," I heard as I approached the door. 6-3-1-8-5-2-6. I was out of there.

I shooed a mouse away from my lasagna and hit the Message button on my answering machine.

"Hi Declan," it said, *"it's Haley. You're gonna kill me, I'm soooo sorry. I can't do dinner. Got hit with a major lesson plan thingy—this field trip we were going to do, then not do, and now we're doing it—and I need to have this dino stuff, Cretaceous versus Jurassic, Paleozoic versus Mesozoic, blah blah blah, what did they say on 'Seinfeld,' yada yada yada? Anyway, I need it for tomorrow morning. I'm pulling an all-nighter—feels like college all over again. I'm so sorry to do this, but I couldn't get out of it. I'll be online most of the night, but please try to call. I reeeeaaally apologize. You're so sweet to make me dinner. I'd love a rain check. I'll make it up to you, I promise. Okay, I'm babbling. Gotta get to work. Talk to you soon, sweetie."*

I put my Key Food bag on the counter and take a seat. My elbow props up on the kitchen table and my forehead eases into my hand. I'm a fucking idiot. I wonder if Gabby's still at MacLennane's. I haven't eaten yet and shepherd's pie and a Guinness might make me feel better.

Julio y Marisol

His is a vibration; hers is a sound. So his I feel, and hers I hear. Wish it were the other way around. Wish it didn't happen at all.

The Greeks took care of the damn ceiling fan above the diner across the street—I guess they got tired of Ma yelling out her window about the *fookin'* thing. So now I just have the vibration and the sound emanating from next door to bother me. It's always something. He's got a low voice, so I feel the vibration of his moans through the wall: *"Mmmmm. Mmmmm."* She's a clipped, staccato screamer: *"Eh! Eh! Eehh!! Eehh!!"* They screw, and I lay there in bed, feeling Julio's vibrato moans and hearing Marisol's stunted shrieks. That's what I've dubbed them, after the comic strip featuring the hot Hispanic couple on the subways, arguing about safe sex. It's a fucking opera, complete with changes of pace, highs and lows, and finally, the crescendo.

Then the second act.

It's at least twice a day: once in the late morning, and once at night, just after midnight. For most of the morning sessions, I'm laying in bed, often hung over, Julio and Marisol acting like convicts on a conjugal visit.

Kind of like how I am today. And I have to meet Haley at Bendix Diner in an hour. Her idea, of course. What self-respecting guy would plan a *brunch* date? She feels bad about missing the dinner date at my place last week, and offered to take me out to brunch. I picked Bendix. Seemed like a good idea at the time, but little did I know that I'd be at Swift's the night before, the boys lucky enough to happen upon a team of marketing reps for a Scottish beer called Belhaven that they're introducing here in the States. It's a creamy ale, like a Boddington's or a Caffrey's, and man, it's good. I didn't even have to pay for one—and we were there until 5 in the morning or so. Swift's must have something worked out with the cops that allows them to stay open so late. So my head's pounding. As are my walls, to the vibrations, and sounds, of Julio and Marisol.

I'm a few months shy of 30. This is my life.

"Lookit your eyes," says Haley, as we sit across from each other in the jam-packed Bendix. There's probably a higher concentration of diners on the Lower East Side than anywhere else in the world. We've got Greek diners, Ukrainian diners,

Michael J. Malone

Polish diners, Russian diners, even a few American ones. No Irish diners, thank God. I wouldn't be surprised if the diner was *invented* somewhere along Avenue A. But Bendix over on 1ˢᵗ Avenue is the best; as Zagat's might say if they reviewed diners, it's the Thai-influenced comfort food, non-pareil coffee, casual ambiance and peppy wait staff. And they play cool music most of the time—comfortable garage rock-y stuff at a low volume. Smart neighborhood people know all this. Judging by the crowd in here today, they're not the only ones.

"Good God," she adds. She's got on a black leotard top that clings to her fit body—unlike me, she actually uses her gym membership—and faded, flared Levi's that she wears down low on her hips. A black velvet band holds her blonde ponytail in place.

We're not at the point where Haley can chastise me for being hung over; at this stage of our brief tenure, my libertine behavior and its short-term effects are more like endearing other-side-of-Broadway character traits to her than anything else, a welcome change from the antiseptic preps she's dated before. If we stay together, that'll change, of course. Tisa certainly didn't find my unique capacity for alcohol very endearing.

"I know," I admit.

"My God, Declan, what time were you out til?"

"Late."

"Like, what time?"

"Please, Haley, don't break my balls," I say, rubbing my temples. "Not today."

I was shocked to find the 48-count bottle of Advil I'd bought two weeks ago empty this morning, and hard-pressed to figure out both how I finished it and why I chose to leave the empty bottle in the medicine cabinet.

She seems to back off, but I say it anyway.

"You stood me up for dinner, remember," I add. It just slides out. I was going to cash that chip in at a more strategic moment, and can't believe I just wasted it.

"I'm not *breaking your balls*," she says, "and I apologize for *standing you up*. I'm just curious how late you were out. I haven't closed a bar since college, or maybe the year after college. I'm sort of...envious."

She gives me a cute shrug. I'm guessing Haley's last closed bar was indeed college, not the year after. College was Radcliffe and, if I remember correctly from when the Vipers trekked up there to play the Boston Irish Wolfhounds, Massachusetts bars close at 2. The year after was New York, and I just can't picture ol' Haley fighting the good fight until 4, drinking straight from the pitcher and air-drumming to the little "Hotel California" *duh duh duhm duhm duh* solo on the juke box.

"How's your writing going?"

"Slow," I say.

"Still working on the novel?"

I cringe. I shouldn't have told her I was doing a novel. It was going well for a bit and I thought I'd have the damn thing done in a few months. Then I ran into a wall, and now it's a short story at best.

"Sort of," I say. "A short story popped up, and I've been dedicating my efforts to that."

"How 'bout Honey Bunny?"

"Mmmm. Got *Enchanted Meadow* due in a few weeks. Haven't really started it, to be honest."

"How long's it going to take you to write?"

"Once I get into it, it's no problem," I say. "It's just a matter of getting in the right frame of mind."

"Getting into Honey Bunny's head," says Haley.

"Pretty much."

I don't tell her that getting into Honey Bunny's head is all about getting something into *my* head.

"I can't wait to read it. You'll show it to me when it's done?"

"Yeah, sure."

"Great."

We're quiet for a bit as we sip our coffee, and I sing along to the song playing on the stereo.

Feeling like a hundred bucks, exchanging good lucks, face to face
Checkin' his stash by the trash at St. Mark's Place.

"What's that?" asks Haley.

"The Replacements," I say. "Haven't heard this song in years. Man, I wore this record out growing up. Every time I pass by St. Mark's, I get it in my head."

"It sounds cool," she says. "What's the name of it?"

"I forget. Something weird, some dude's name or something. They're from Minneapolis."

"When they say, 'St. Mark's,' are they talking about this St. Mark's?" she says, pointing her head toward 8th Street.

"Yup. Right around the corner…Alex Chilton—that's who it's about. That's the name of the song."

"Wow."

"Yeah. There's a huge rock and roll history on St. Mark's."

"Like CBGB's?" Haley asks.

"Yeah, well, sort of. That's over on the Bowery. More like the old community center where the Velvet Underground used to play way back when."

"I don't know them."

"You know Lou Reed, right? 'Walk on the Wild Side'?"

"Of course."

"The Velvets were his band when he was, like, a kid."

Haley absorbs it all with a polite smile.

"Hey! Speaking of famous people, you'll never guess who I saw today."

"I have no idea," I say, spiking a hash brown with my fork. There's a frowny lesbian couple at the table next to us, no more than eight inches away. When I squeezed in between tables, my ass knocked over their syrup, contributing significantly to both their general consternation and my hangover anxiety.

"Oh, c'mon, Declan. Play the game, will ya'?"

I'm certainly not in the mood for games. Hash browns, yes. Really strong coffee, yes. Games, no. Haley's tilting her head sideways. I sip my coffee and play her silly game.

"DeNiro," I offer. She makes a face. I break into my DeNiro impersonation which continues to suck. My left eyebrow is up, neck bent to the right, lips in a scowl and head back on my shoulders. Just like Gabby does. But something's off. I've done it in front of the mirror. It's...it's...just off.

"Ah yooo tellin' me DUH—Neero's a baaad guess?"

It's a hopeless DeNiro, but Haley laughs anyway. One of the lesbians is talking about how movies shot in 16 millimeter look fine on video, but come apart on the big screen. "Look at *The Brothers McMullan*," the one with a buzz cut and a steel rod through her ear lobe says. "Mmmm," says the other, a mousy, almost cute blonde with black-framed glasses—*publishing* glasses—and a big, silly straw hat that threatens to brush against my neck and irritates the shit out of me.

"No, I didn't see DeNiro," Haley says, the playfulness back in her voice. "Guess again. Think quirky. Think *films*. Think charming second bananas. I saw him on Greenwich, just east of 7th Ave."

Haley's a film chick. We went to the Angelika to see some flick about a little French boy who dresses up as a girl, and she knew the people working in the café there. She couldn't believe I'd never been to the Angelika before. I told her it was too far from my apartment, but she noted that MacLennane's was just as far, and that didn't prevent my few-times-a-week visits.

"Hint," I say. "All I got is quirky, second banana and West Village. I need more."

"OK, fair enough," says Hale. "Cute, but a different kind of cute. Not obvious cute, like, say, Leo. *Subtle* cute."

Who is this Leo guy?

"Subtle cute," I ponder. I'm not enjoying this game. "The little guy from 'Spin City.' With the shakes. *Back to the Future* dude."

"No!" she shrieks. "He's so...no."

"I dunno, baby...Matt Modine."

"*Matt Modine?*" says Haley, looking at me with a gaze that makes me feel foolish. I sip my coffee.

"Ya know, *Vision Quest*," I say, by way of an explanation. Gabby and me rented it the night before the match against the Long Island Rovers. Haley cracks up; she thinks I'm being funny. That's cool.

"Matt Modine's gotta live somewhere. Why not on Greenwich, just east of 7th?"

"No, I didn't see *Matt Modine*," says Haley with a smile. "And I think it's *Matthew* Modine, anyway. OK, you give up."

"I give up," I shrug. Guess I'll get some Turtle Wax for my efforts.

"Paul Rudd!" she says with a satisfied smile, like she's accomplished something meaningful. She then waits for me to acknowledge her accomplishment.

"Who the hell is Paul Rudd?"

"PAUL RUDD!" Haley says louder, as if the decibel boost will clue me in to this guy's identity.

"Paul Rudd," she adds quietly.

Nothing.

"He's big," says Haley, clearly disappointed that her star-sighting is falling fast. "He's been in lots of stuff. *Clueless, The Object of My Affection.*"

"With the chick from 'Friends'?"

"Yes. Jennifer Aniston was in that one.'"

"Those don't sound like very *quirky* films."

"He did other stuff," says Haley with a shrug. "*Romeo and Juliet*. Some other stuff. Plays a gay guy sometimes."

I shrug. I just don't know the dude. And he doesn't sound so cool, either.

"I'm sorry, Hale… Did you talk to him?"

Then Haley got some granola or something stuck in her throat and started choking. I grabbed for a glass of water, but miscalculated the distance and knocked it over, causing its contents to gush down the gap in between our table and the lesbians. The lipstick one went to pick up her Sunday *Times* that was getting doused on the floor just as Haley decided to thrust her arms in the air in an effort to stop choking. Haley caught the chick under the chin with a backhand, causing the silly straw hat to fly off, and the buzz cut one reflexively leapt to her wounded partner's defense, rocking but not upending their table. Buzz glared at Haley, Farmer's Daughter returned her chapeau to its rightful place and my date's coughing eventually subsided. We all settled back to our meals.

"Coffee?" asks the waiter, a tiny Asian man with rings in both lobes and shiny black hair pulled back in a ponytail.

"No," grumbles the foursome in unison.

Michael J. Malone

"Y'awright, babe?" I say, patting Haley's knee under the table. She looks a bit shaken.

"Yes, I'm fine. Sorry."

"No worries," I say as my heart grudgingly returns to its normal pace. In a weird way I kind of dug this peculiar diner drama. I watched Haley make a face that I hadn't yet seen her make, and it's sort of fun to see a heretofore unseen side of someone you're dating. We still haven't had sex yet, so I haven't gotten to see *that* face, but the whole thing sort of turned me on, warmed me up, and I knew then that this hangover could be beaten. Maybe I'd get something done today. Maybe sit down in front of the new computer and work on *Enchanted Meadow.* Maybe get the novel going.

"Where were we?" I continue, feeling better.

"I forget," she says meekly.

"The cute guy."

"Right, Paul Rudd," Haley says.

"We'll rent one of his movies soon, huh?"

"Sure."

"Cool," I say, and sip my tepid coffee.

Friends and Family Day

Which brings us back to Friends and Family Day.

It's a home game, against the Bayonne Barbarians, on Randalls Island. Randalls is located between Manhattan and Queens, under the Triborough Bridge. We like to refer to as "Viper Park" to make us feel important, but to others it's just "The Rock." They don't call it The Rock for nothing; the fields are like cement, with a few blades of grass when the season starts, and none after a few weeks. Most New Yorkers have never been there, except maybe if they went to a Lollapalooza concert, or the Fire Department Academy, or if they play for the Village Vipers.

We were supposed to play this touring team from Wales last fall, but they took one look at the field and wouldn't play us. We were all psyched to play those Welsh bastards—they were called Glyn something-or-other—so when they backed out, we decided to play against ourselves, since we had the field and a ref and all. The Welshies, who just wanted to go to MacLennane's, start drinking, and chase New York women around, couldn't believe their eyes when we chose up sides and ran onto the field; I think they were pretty embarrassed. Good. Fuck 'em. We had a blast. Probably just as well they welshed on us, though—they 'were big, ugly bastards, and probably would've beaten us by 50. The field really isn't *that* bad; I mean, your knees lose their skin and you take some lumps, but at least there are no needles on it or anything.

Unlike our practice field over at East River Park 125 blocks south of Randalls, a forsaken strip of weeds and rocks in between the FDR Drive and the river. We have to fight with soccer, Frisbee, baseball and flag football for space, not to mention the Avenue D projects kids and the junkies. We're all fighting for East River Park, which really isn't worth fighting for, but it's all we got. We practice in the rocky, grassless outfield of two baseball fields, balls raining all around us like mortar fire, just missing our heads. You throw the big rocks off the field, but they somehow keep growing back. Unlike Central Park, there are no wealthy neighbors contributing to some endowment that will plant grass and trees, clean the park and put in new benches when the homeless bust up the old ones for firewood.

In the summer, salsa fills the air at East River Park, as the Latinos from all the nearby projects barbecue. Some lady sets up a pot with a tarp strung around it like a shower curtain, and charges 25 cents for the "Baño." She does OK, as the

Michael J. Malone

Parks & Rec closed the bathrooms because the junkies were OD-ing in the filthy toilets. The pit bulls run free, raised nasty and hard by the local teenagers who see them as power and a lift in status, a semi-legal assault rifle. The kids wrap bricks in bandanas and put them around the dogs' necks, and beat them with bats to make them mean. Sometimes two packs of kids will let their respective pit bulls spar, and they scream and howl as the dogs try to get that locked jaw in place on the other's jugular, the bout's instant win card. Eventually they pull them apart, and the dogs are just overflowing with adrenaline, like two guys right after a bar fight, and you think the mongrels—the dogs, that is—are going to come for us when we're running laps, and you're going to have to climb the fence and just hang out until one of the punk kids gets a leash around the dog's neck. Assuming, that is, the kid doesn't want to hang out and watch the scared whitey in the dumb striped shirt whimpering and clinging to the fence for dear life.

The dopeheads love East River Park too. The place where I volunteer is just a few blocks from the park, so the junkies get their needles, score their drugs and come to the park for a little picnic. When I'm giving the grimy bastards their shiny new rigs, I'm always tempted to tell them to keep out of East River Park, or at least throw their needles in the fucking garbage cans. Nothing worse than playing rugby and wondering if you're going to get stuck by a dirty needle when you get tackled. Like the game's not rough enough.

We were hoping to get tons of chicks out for Family and Friends Day, but today there's just a handful of them, along with Mental Ben's German shepherd. The boys usually do all right. Most of the guys are single—playing rugby in the city pretty much prevents you from taking any of life's serious steps—and when we're working on that post-match adrenaline buzz, mixed in with alcohol, we're actually quite charming. For every ten chicks that turn away in disgust—*"those rugby guys,"* they say with disdain—there's one that digs us. And she's usually with a few others.

We played Bayonne last spring at their field, which is in a surprisingly nice park on the water, definitely the best part of their scruffy Paddy immigrant town. We gave them a good match, losing like 21-18, but they look bigger this year. They're scrappers, those Bayonne guys. It's in their blood. We're sons of architects and investment bankers and lawyers and the occasional psychotic West Belfast nurse, but these guys' pops built bridges and skyscrapers and highways.

Gabby's talking to the ref and the Bayonne captain, mostly nodding and grunting, because Gabby doesn't say much before games, and I'm wondering if I got time for another piss. There are no bathrooms anywhere near our field—no Baño for hire either—so we just run over to the high grass by the creek that separates Randalls Island from the Bronx. I decide I have time, so I run off the pitch. Shady Brady yells, "Yo, Deckie," but I wave him off. My guys know how much I piss before games—they call me Sir Piss-a-Lot. It's my eighth so far today, and it's only

64

1:00. Sometimes I think I'm obsessive/compulsive about it, but my bladder always seems to produce. I figure, with one piss for every beer I'm going to have tonight, I'll have gone 24 times by the time my head hits the pillow. Whizzing every hour, on the hour—that *can't* be healthy.

I'm a freakin' nervous wreck before games. It starts on Friday morning at work; I start tuning out my boss Ken, focusing on the match, on making my tackles, on the feel of the ball's bumps on my fingertips, on the club playing well. Not necessarily even winning—we never win—just playing well. For a few minutes I can't think of anything else and I can't hear anything around me; I just think about the match. I start to shiver and get this weird tingling in my fingers and my back gets coated with a clammy layer of sweat and I just want to get the game over with. I'm pretty useless at work on Fridays during the season; that happens to be the day we do our weekly editorial meetings, planning for the upcoming week, so I'm probably going to get my ass fired one of these days.

It's sort of silly that I'm so nervous, but that doesn't stop me. The Vipers play in Division III, which means that we play in the lowest division in a country that hardly plays rugby. By definition, that makes me one of the world's worst rugby players.

With all the anxiety, I sometimes wonder why I play at all, but then the match is over and I made some big hits, knocked some guys on their asses, had a good run or two, maybe juked a guy and made the boys on our sideline howl, and then I put on the outback hat that Haley got me on a whim at Urban Outfitters, sit on the barren grass and drink a beer. Euphoria. People who don't play sports don't get that shit, and people who play non-contact sports only get part of that shit. People who play contact sports other than rugby—hockey dudes, those lax guys—have an idea, but not the whole picture.

The piss comes out slowly. I crack my neck and say a quick prayer. I got crunched against the Bainbridge Bruisers a few years ago, the nasty Irish fuckers out of the North Bronx, and I still feel it in my neck. It's kind of embarrassing—I was trying to make the tackle and this big Paddy with a flat nose was bearing down on me. I ducked at the last minute, like you would one of those monster waves at Rockaway Beach, and he caught me square on the top of the head. I got what they call a stinger—sounds kinky, but it's the furthest thing from it. It's a weird vibration throughout your body where you think you're paralyzed. I sure thought I was. It's not that you can't feel your fingers and toes—they just feel weird as hell, like they're asleep and they ain't waking up.

So I was on the ground for a few minutes, and had to be helped off. Ended up cracking a tiny piece of my vertebrae, up in my neck. Never told ol' Paula. She would've freakin' flipped, not just because I was seriously hurt, but because I got hurt playing *that fookin' Pommie poofter game.* It scared the shit out of me and I figured my little rugby career was over, but I took a few months off, let it heal, and got the old jones again.

That was the only time I had to leave a match due to injury. Up until my knockout today.

I'm down in the Randalls Island dust, a ring of vaguely familiar faces surrounding the sun. Dr. Demento has just given me the 5th degree, all sorts of stupid questions about my name and my girl's name and the day and the month and other bullshit.

"Pardon me," a polite English voice cuts in. I look up. It's the ref, who looks like John Cleese, only squashed down about a foot.

"Are you alright, lad?"

"Yes, sir." I remember to call the ref "sir," like you're supposed to.

"Well, I hate to treat you like a piece of meat," he continues, "but we've got to get you off the pitch. Can you get up?"

"We'll get him up," says Demento.

Goose and Ghetto Ron each grab under my arms, and Demento supervises the whole affair. He's still shaking his head because I can't think of my girlfriend's goddamn name. Slowly, they lift me up, and the world around me spins wildly.

"One second," I say, and we pause. I take a deep breath. Moments later, we start toward the sideline.

"Tisa!" I yell.

The guys are silent. I scan the sidelines for her, suddenly desperate to see her. My head pounds.

Someone brings over a beach chair for me, and the boys ease me into it. Demento hangs over me.

"Alright Coal-turr, what month we in?"

Jesus. Here we go again. The correct response sits on the tip of my tongue, ready to come out, then slams it into reverse. It swirls around in a vortex of month names—a jumble of 'uarys and 'embers and the rest of them, before sliding down a black hole. *Whoosh.*

"July," I say with authority, as if my confidence will convince them a wrong answer is right.

Demento shakes his head.

"Damn," I mutter to myself.

"You're going to the hospital," he says. "Soon as the game's over. We got Bayonne's ass to kick first."

I nod, then sit back and watch the game. The big dude, our captain with the sideburns, hauls the ball into the teeth of the other team's defense and sets a ruck. The enemy pack swarms him, knocks him down, and someone gets him with a boot in the ribs. You always want to get a good shot at the other team's captain when he's down, like gunning for the opposing general in a war, maybe put him out of the game.

Who the hell are we playing?

"Tracy, you got room for Coal-turr?" says Demento as he walks me over to Tracy's truck, guiding me from behind by the shoulders. Demento gave up a bright future in neurosurgery to play rugby with the likes of us, and ended up in the ER at Kings County out in the ass end of Brooklyn, in a neighborhood without a name. He says it's the busiest, bloodiest hospital in the city. "He's got to go to St. Vincent's. So does Flyboy—I'm gonna drive him down on my bike."

"No problem, mon," says Tracy. He's from Jamaica—the island, not the crappy section of Queens. His real name eludes me at the moment, but he looks just like Tracy Chapman, short little dreads and all, so we call him Tracy. Tracy's with his girlfriend, who looks like Courtney Love. Her name eludes me too.

"How you feelin', Deckie?" he says.

"I'm fine, man."

I do feel fine. Why is everyone treating me like their batty great grandmother?

"Beth can sit in the back," Tracy says. "You oughta sit in the front."

"Nah, I'm fine back there," I say, nodding to where the boys are piling into the back of Tracy's truck. "Let your girl sit up front."

"You sure?"

"Yup."

"Alright, Coulter. Here—wear this."

He tosses me a scrum cap—those flimsy padded head things some guys wear because they think it will prevent their brains from being scrambled at the bottom of a ruck. I take off my outback hat and put the padded cap on.

"Protect ya from the bumps," he says.

Shady Brady helps me into the pickup bed, and invites me to use him as a cushion for our ride into Manhattan. I would've hoped for a beefier buffer zone—he's about 160 pounds, or "11 stone," in his words—but Shady is kind to offer himself. I lean back onto Shady, like how Tisa used to lean back onto me on the playground whale.

"Comfortable, Deckie?" he asks in that fancy BBC accent.

"Yeah, I'm fine. What happened?"

"You took a shot to the melon. We'll take ya to St. Vincent's just to be safe, but I think you're OK."

I check my head for bruises. It feels fine.

"Where's Tisa?" I ask, turning to face him.

Shady looks at me crazily, the corners of his Chelsea smile pointing downward.

"Tisa?"

"Where is she?"

"How the fuck should I know?"

Tracy pulls the truck away.

"What about Haley?" Shady asks. "Statuesque blonde?"

Haley. *Fuck.*

"Where's Haley?" I say.

"My missus said she was going up to Vermont for the weekend."

Haley.

"What is she doing there?"

"No idea. The things you American lot do in Vermont, I reckon. Something to do with syrup?" says Shady, shoving a can of Bud in front of my face from behind, then pouring it in my mouth. "Maybe this'll help ya remember shit."

"Are we still together?" I ask as I wipe spilled beer off my chin.

"Far as I know, mate. My missus says it's going good between you and her."

Well, that's good news. Or is it?

"How good?" I ask. "Like, engaged good?"

Shady hesitates like he's thinking about fucking with me. We head toward the Triborough Bridge, up the labyrinth of ramps.

"Not that good, mate," he says with a laugh. I see the blight of industrial Harlem across the river.

"Where we going?" I ask.

"You, my good man, are going to the hospital. We are going to MacLennane's."

"What happened?"

Shady takes a deep breath.

"Ya got your bell rung, Coaltah."

"Damn."

I must look like I need a pick-me-up.

"Ireland beat England," Shady adds.

"No shit!" I say. Ireland never beats England.

"Right as rain, mate. 20-14. Just this morning."

"Fuckin' A. How'd the Vipers do?"

Shady is silent.

"Bloody brilliant match," he says. "They were up by a try with about five minutes to play. One of their guys took a swing at Flyboy and knocked him out, just knocked him out cold. The mother of all cheapshots. All sorts of *aggro* after that—we damn well sorted the ponce out. Ghetto Ron got him with the boots, and

Gabby grabbed hold of the guy's facial orifices like a bowling ball. We marched down the pitch, must've been 10 or 12 phases, quick rucks, clean ball out to the backs."

I follow excitedly. Did we actually win?

"...but Goose knocked on on the goal line. The try was on. He just...dropped it."

In other words, we lost. Again.

"Wow," I say.

"It was a memorable match," says Shady. "The boys played their balls off. Bayonne will be feeling it tomorrow."

Wish I could remember any of it. Flyboy got knocked out? Ghetto Ron sorted their thug out? Goose coughed it up on the goal line? I wonder if Goose's chick was there to watch it. We call her Mother Goose.

We pass the giant sign for the History Channel in the South Bronx, which promotes a show about the underground railroad.

"Where's Haley?" I ask. Shady shakes his head and pours more beer down my gullet.

We exit the FDR Drive at 23rd, and traffic is crawling down 2nd Avenue. But, like a kid awaiting confession, I'm in no hurry to go the hospital. Maybe if it takes long enough, my memory comes back, and I won't have to go. I sit back and see the sun going down over the Empire State Building on a cloudless blue Saturday. I see the U.N. to the left. The back of the truck's a fucking U.N. summit—a New Zealander, a Brit, an Aussie, a Paddy, an Argie, a Welshie and a Mick-Yank from Avenue A, passing around beers and a flask, singing, trading barbs with guys in cars next to us at lights, trying to flirt with the ladies. It seems like an hour has passed by the time we get to the Village—our Tracy Chapman at the wheel certainly wasn't the one who sang that "Fast Car" song. Instead of letting us out in front of MacLennane's, Tracy stops the truck at St. Vincent's. I look around the truck, but no one seems in need of medical attention.

"Your stop, mate," says Shady.

"Huh?"

"Into the ER, pal. I'll go with you. Get off me."

"Huh?"

"The knock. To the head."

Shady illustrates the point by knocking on his head.

Oh, right.

"What month is it?"

Shit. What's with Dr. Demento and his calendar obsession? It's warm. I'm perspiring.

"August."

Demento hangs his head.

"June, Coal-turr."

June. How can I remember this for next time? June is the…one-two-three-four-five…new hand…sixth month. I wear #6 on my jersey. Five fingers and my thumb. Easy enough.

"What happened?" I ask. Demento takes a deep breath and explains it to me. I look around the ER. There are about 10 other people on beds, some surrounded by curtains, some not. Across from me, an old lady in bright new running shoes gives me the thumbs-up, and I reflexively return the gesture.

Our captain with the sideburns walks in. Good to see a familiar face.

"Hey, man," I say.

"Hey yo, Deckie," he says. "How's he doing?" he asks Demento.

"Hey Gab," says Demento.

Gabby. That's it.

"About the same. How's Flyboy?"

"He's pretty fucked up. They moved him upstairs. Says they gotta do some surgery on his face."

"'s what I figured," says Demento, shaking his head. "Orbital bone, I'm sure. Dirty fucking bastards."

"Would've been nice to beat the fuckuhs," says Gabby. "Goddamn Goose."

What happened with Goose? None of this rings a bell, though that's not to say I didn't have a bell rung today.

"Ireland beat England too," says Gabby. "Damn donkeys came up huge."

"No shit!" I exclaim. Ireland never beats England.

"Yes, suh. 20-14."

"Where am I?" I ask.

"St. Vincent's," says Demento.

"Who were we playing?"

"Bayonne Barbarians," says Gabby. "Cheatin' fuckuhs."

I look down at my sheets. Something's not right.

"St. Vincent's in the Village, right?"

"Yup."

"Down the road from MacLennane's?"

"Yup."

I point to the sheets like there's a giant cockroach crawling on them. Light blue stenciling says "Beth Israel Hospital." It truly does.

Demento and Gabby shrug.

"You're at St. Vincent's, Coal-turr. Trust me," says Demento. "Maybe the laundry got crossed up. Don't worry about it."

"Where's Haley?" I ask. God, I wish she was here, wish she was holding my hand, wish she could walk me home. I'm confused. I feel like crying here in the middle of St. Vincent's or Beth Israel or wherever the fuck I am.

"She's away," says Gabby.

That's not good.

"Are we still together?"

"Jesus, Coal-turr," begins Demento. "It's fine with your girl. Stop asking about her before we have to resort to surgical tape."

I wonder where she is, but I'm afraid to ask. If Demento says we're OK, I guess we're OK. After all, he's a medical professional.

"Doc says you got a contusion, basically a brain bruise," says Demento, who's wearing a purple and gold rugby jersey with a patch bearing a court jester on the chest, a souvenir from our trip to Mardi Gras, and a layer of Randalls Island dust on his face. "Take it easy tonight and make sure someone is there to watch you when you go home. You might have a headache tomorrow. Doc's gonna come by in a few to check you again, then I think he's gonna let you go."

"St. Vincent's," I say. "How long we been here for?"

Demento looks at his watch.

"'bout three hours."

Three hours?

"What's the month?" asks Demento.

I sense that we'll all be in MacLennane's as soon as I provide the answer. It's...it's...it's my jersey number! Pleased with myself, I twist around to read it, but see only my bare white back and humiliating half-a-tat poking through a hospital gown. I'm on my own.

"July?"

Demento lets out a loud breath.

"I'm gonna check on Flyboy," he says.

"It's June, dude," says Gabby.

June.

"Where's Tisa?"

Gabby walks me over to MacLennane's, and the combination of elapsed time and the night air helps to clear my head. Facts and figures seem to be sticking in my brain now, instead of just passing through. We played the Montclair Vikings, I think, or maybe it was the Danbury Hatters. We almost beat the bastards. Ghetto Ron got laid out by a sucker punch, and unlike me, he's still in the hospital. Or maybe it was Goose.

Mental Ben and Spartacus are walking towards us on Greenwich Avenue. We stop in front of the candy shop that sells gay porn.

Michael J. Malone

"Deckie!" says Ben. "You still on Queer Street?"

"Doin' better."

"We're heading in to see Flyboy," says Spartacus.

Flyboy got knocked out.

"Dude's fucked up," says Gabby.

"No shit," says Spartacus. "Hopefully this'll help."

He pulls two bottles of beer out of his front pockets.

"I'll be up there in a little while," says Gabby. "Just gonna walk Mr. Short-Term Memory over to Mac's."

"See ya up there," says Mental Ben.

"You oughta take it easy tonight, dude," Gabby says.

"I know."

"Like, coupla beers, and that's it. Home."

"Right."

"And Demento says someone should watch ya tonight. With Haley bein' away, you got someone? Yeh muthuh?"

"Yeah, man, no problem."

Now there's a quaint notion, a mother taking care of her injured son.

"Cool. Call me if you need someone there."

We approach the bar, and I hear the Bayonne guys doing a raucous version of "S&M Man," sung to the tune of "Candy Man."

Who can take a cheese grater? sings one, and the chorus echoes him. *Strap it to his arm...*

I know it's their guys and not ours, because "S&M Man" is lame, and our songs are more sophisticated than that. Not that "sophisticated" is really the right word for songs like "Bestiality's Best" and "I Used to Work in Chicago," but "S&M Man" is just so...freshman year in college. To be honest, some of us wouldn't mind slugging a few of their guys for what the bastards did to Flyboy, but it's rugby—that final whistle blows, and we're all brothers in arms.

I realize I haven't pissed since before the match, at least as far as I can remember, and head downstairs for the bathroom. I'm relieving myself for all it's worth, and it feels great, shoots a warm shiver throughout my body. Shady Brady pulls up in the urinal on my left.

"How's the head, mate?" he says as I hear his stream slapping against the back of the ancient urinal.

"Much better, man."

"You weren't making much sense before."

"I know. I'm better now."

"That's good. Ya know, Ireland beat England today."

"No shit!" I say. Ireland never beats England in rugby, or anything.

72

"Yeah, mate. Two tries for that kid O'Driscoll. Big bastard just *shredded* the England centers. 20-14."

Shady starts belting that Irish song about a prison ship waiting for the young Irishman who stole corn to feed his family in the face of British oppression; it sounds funny in his posh English accent. It makes me think of Ma taking me to the Catskills when I was a kid—some pasty Paddy troubadour tuning his guitar by the pool, that night's entertainment at the Shamrock House.

Shady and I finish at the same time and head out of the bathroom. He opens the door for me and puts an arm around my shoulders as we start upstairs to the bar. I can hear Shane MacGowan growling out of the juke box, guiding me to the bar like a dark guardian angel.

Hoooraaahhh! Ya fuck!!!, the song goes.

Come hell or high water

Arm in arm, me and Shady join in. We like this one.

I might've fucked your missus

But I never fucked your daughter!

I see a table of women, three blondes and a brunette, and they look young and pretty, maybe NYU girls. Our boys are all over the place, drunk and still riding the adrenaline rush of a hard match several hours later. The pretty Irish girls that work at MacLennane's are bringing out trays full of shots for our guys. It's fucking V.J. Day. You should see us when we actually win.

"Up for a shot?" asks Shady.

"Sure, man."

I smile and walk toward the bar.

The juke box goes quiet and Irish George starts a tune. We gather around.

I played the wild rover for many a year

And I spent all me money on whiskey and beer.

And now I'm returning with gold in great store

And I never will play the wild rover no more.

His voice is clear and strong, and surprisingly high-pitched for a burly guy who plays prop. George swings his pint glass like a conductor's baton. We sing along with the words we know, and mumble the ones we don't. The Paddies from Bayonne join in too.

And it's No, Nay, Never

No Nay Never, No More!

We sway in unison like we're on a ship on rocky seas. Beer spills. The singing gets louder. Everyone knows the chorus, even if they don't know the verses.

Will I play the wild rover

No Never No More!

Michael J. Malone

The lights in MacLennane's are swirling around and the juke box is back on and the music's loud and it's smoky as shit and they told me to take it easy and I did, definitely didn't drink like I normally would, even had a few sips of water, but when do the girls ever give us free shots, and Flyboy is gonna be OK and Ireland won, fuckin' A, and maybe it wasn't a good idea and the lights just keep swirling and the smoke and the music is just pounding from within my stomach and my skull and...

Outside, it's a different story. I see couples dining on the sidewalk and it's a manageable dose of sensory stimulation. I take a deep breath. Quit while you're ahead, I tell myself, and take in a second gulp of air. Make sure someone keeps an eye on you tonight, the doc at St. Vincent's said, or maybe it was Demento, or Gabby, or someone else. I'm out of commission for a few weeks, but I should be back in time for the big match with Bainbridge. Make sure someone keeps an eye on you...

I walk toward 7th Avenue and head uptown. My steps are a bit wobbly and my bearings aren't quite what they were earlier today, before the match, but I know what I'm doing.

Her place is probably a ten minute walk from here, 15 at my wobbliest.

The light pries its way into my eyes.

The pounding is just relentless, like a construction crew excavating my brain from my skull, ordered to use the heavy machinery and the explosives. Jesus H. Christ. It's like I took a blow to the head and then went out and downed a bunch of shots, some of them silly free bar mixes and some Irish whiskey, and a handful of beers on top of it.

Fuck.

The bed is soft and warm, and I never want to get up, never want to put my head through anything more rigorous than just lying motionless on the warm, fuzzy pillow. The apartment is smallish and tasteful, and I've never been here before.

Tisa's face smiles down at me from the side of the bed. Her hair is longer and straighter than the last time I saw her, like she's a long-lost *Friends* character. Her long, shiny, shampoo-commercial hair was always her best feature. Almost didn't recognize her in the smile. Earl is next to her—it must be him—and he's smiling too. Beyond them is an impossibly green field dotted with sheep. He's got a square jaw and white teeth and stylishly tousled hair. He looks like an Earl. I chuckle and it hurts my head.

I lay the picture frame face-down on the nightstand.

I'm naked. My knees are covered with dirt stains, some that extend onto the crisp white bedsheet, along with a bit of blood. Despite my head's feverish protests, I push myself up on my elbows. What the fuck? There's a framed print across the room that says Pas De Deux, and shows a ballerina flitting about. I check the sheets for stains other than dirt and blood. Nothing.

What the fuck?

My rugby shorts are in a pile next to the bed. I scan my brain for clues. What's the last thing I remember? Me and Gabby out Friday night for dinner, taking it slow at Telephone Bar on 2nd Avenue, cheeseburgers and one pint apiece, resting up for the match. Saturday? Who were we playing? How did I get up to Randalls? My face feels sunburned. Did we win? Yeah, right—like we ever do. Jesus. No idea. Between the shorts and the dirty knees, I know I've been playing rugby. By the headache, I know I went out after. Get the headache every time after rugby. But fuck, never like this.

My hand goes up to rub my head, and a silver glint catches the sunlight.

Hospital bracelet.

St. Vincent's.

An old lady in running shoes giving me the thumbs-up.

What the fuck?

Nausea takes over, and I run to the bathroom and toss up everything I've eaten since adolescence into the toilet, slowly sinking to one knee like a sword-stabbed thespian, one hand on my gut, the other on my pounding head. Next to the toilet is a garbage can; once I'm done being sick, I search through it for clues—a spent condom, a wrapper, a firearm, maybe a minute-by-minute account of the past 24 hours. My hand feels something slimy and hairy, like a wet rat, and I barf again.

I drop back, my ass cold on the tile floor. Tisa let me in. That's great. Or was it? Did we… Could I take Earl in this state? Hell, could I take the old lady with the running shoes and the thumb pointing to the heavens right now? What the hell was she so optimistic about? I wonder if there's some sort of morning-after pill for guys—I'll have to ask Demento about it.

Fuck.

The pounding of my head is the only noise I hear. The hospital bracelet. There is no sign of damage to any of my limbs; actually, the soreness is way less than normal for after a rugby match. Judging by what I've just offered up to the toilet, I didn't get my stomach pumped either.

What the fuck?

Tempted as I am to fall back into that warm, beckoning bed, I put my rugby shorts on and pull my t-shirt over my head. It smells like a thousand men played rugby in it. I go to the window and don't know what to expect—a fiery red surface, like Mars? A desert? The fucking ocean? I see a city street and tree tops and a Middle Eastern man idling in a yellow cab with NYCTA on the side. That's good. Wherever I am, a subway token will get me home.

I take one quick look around Tisa's apartment, not really sure what I'm looking for, and get the hell out of there.

Found Money

Found a fiver on the subway platform today, and boy, did I earn it. Been taking that goddamn N/R train every motherfucking day for as long as I can remember: up to 42nd Street en route to City College for almost four years (My resume says I *went* to City College for four years, not that I graduated.), up to 57th during my just (dropped)-out-of-college days at the freebie paper, a few jobs in between, right up to 49th now for Avatar. I'm freakin' sick of the N and the R; who wouldn't be?

Determined to change my life, I tried the F today. It's no quicker; in fact, the ride has one more stop than the N/R, but it's closer and, more importantly, it's something different. I'm not going to leave New York—when you're born here, leaving is simply not an option, no matter how much you hate it—and changing the default font on my computer did not have its desired effect. So I'm changing my subway...or at least trying out a different one. A new perspective. A new vantage point.

It's Monday morning, and I entered the F train station at 1st and Houston, and BAM! A $5 bill, staring up at me: wrinkled, dirty, in dire need of a warm wallet. I looked around the platform and saw lots of people who would've killed for the fiver. The F is presumably greasing my palms in an effort to gain my business, and that's just fine with me.

On this particular day, the F's not winning my patronage based on its merits. I'm waiting a good 15 minutes or so, and I can hear my boss Ken yelling at me from midtown. He's a fat prick; his gut stretches out the golf shirt he wears every day, hanging low over the edge of his Dockers. Ken tried to grow a goatee to look hip, but he just looks like a dork. Guys over 40 should not be allowed to grow goatees. We just had a talk last week about me "mailing it in" at work, according to Ken, so I guess I'm on some sort of unspoken probation. To tell you the truth, it doesn't mean shit. Ken isn't going to fire me because I've got more talent than any of the editors there, and I make him laugh. Well, more talented than everyone except Becky. She's our intern and a student at Columbia, and her father's some publishing big shot. If Ken does sack my ass, I'll finally give the freelance thing a full-time whirl. Crank out twice as many Honey Bunny books, maybe start a new series;

chipmunks are bound for a comeback. Work on my novel. Yeah, fire my ass, Ken. Bring it on… Actually, don't.

C'mon, F train.

My fired ass is becoming more and more likely as I look down the empty tunnel in vain. The platform fills up and my anxiety starts to bubble. Finally, after 20 minutes or so—inexcusable on a work day, in the busiest damn city in the world—I see the flicker of yellow light on the distant tunnel wall. The train is pulling in. But it's blaring the horn and it's *moving*, and any New Yorker knows that means the train is going express. The crestfallen commuters, all fearing a tongue-lashing from their respective Ken's, retreat from the edge of the platform. I'm done with the first side of Steely Dan's *Aja* on my Walkman—coffee and the Pogues on my Walkman gets me way too keyed up in the morning, while Steely's nice and mellow…*languid*, as Donald Fagen would write—and I'm not even out of the Lower East Side.

I suddenly find myself nostalgic for the N/R.

This is not good, I think, as Side 2 starts. I was planning on writing a good chunk of *Enchanted Meadow* today, because my editor Sally wants it by Thursday. Sally's cool—basically lets me write what I want, and does very light edits. Ken don't know shit about Honey Bunny; he thinks I live for *Cork & Bottle*, like he does.

It's cool that they made a sales guy the editor-in-chief at the magazine; Ken's got no freakin' idea how long it takes to turn these releases into articles. (After he got promoted to the boss, we ran like three issues in a row where he was listed on the masthead as "editor-and-chief," instead of "editor-in-chief," before we caught my dumbass boss's error.) He walks by and sees me working my ass off, and has no clue I'm doing Honey Bunny at Serenity Knoll, at Enchanted Meadow, etc., and not my feature on the Carmel Wine Expo, or some other advertiser, which will take me about 45 minutes to crank out. Sometimes, when Honey Bunny's not exactly flowing, Ken'll see me with my head down on my desk, taking a little catnap, and he'll slam his hand on my desk. Of course, if I was a senior editor and had my own office, none of this would be a problem. He was ripping into me for this a few months ago, and I ended up spinning this whole tale about how I was in a band and we played at CB's until the wee hours the night before. The yarn was just spewing out of my mouth—I had no idea where these details were coming from. I figured the fat fucker would dig that—he's one of those guys who lives his entire life through other people; all his stories are about some guy he knows. He asked me the name of my band and I did a quick scan around my cube, saw a case of Pindar chardonnay, and told him Green Glass Bottles. He was like, "Super cool, Coulter," in that effeminate way he speaks. "I'll have to check you guys out some time." Of course, he'd sooner go to Iraq than go below 14th Street, so I don't have to worry about that. Ken brings sales dudes over to meet me, saying I'm in this hotshot band—his connection to street cred. So being a part of Green Glass Bottles has earned me a little slack at Avatar. But not too much, and probably not for long.

Within moments, another train shows up. But, surprise surprise, this one's packed. It stops and opens the door, but there's not enough room for even a single new passenger. A few riders exhale audibly when the doors open, thankful for the momentary decompression of flesh and a gulp of piss-flavored subway platform air.

I thank the Lord I'm not hung over; I'm trying to be more positive about stuff, at Haley's suggestion. Mercifully, another train shows up a minute or two later, and it's pretty packed, but I'm able to squeeze inside. Of course, the train is so full that the doors won't shut. *Baaaa-Buuum*, goes the warning bell. They close halfway and open again. *Baaaa-Buuum*. Same result. "You's in the back," bellows the conductor on the intercom—it's always the jackasses in the back—"stand clear the closing doors." They pay no heed. *Baaaa-Buuum*.

"*C'monc'monc'monc'mon,*" pleads the man next to me, a short, portly guy in a too-long suit with gray hair and a salt-and-pepper mustache, *Financial Times* folded under his arm. "*C'monc'monc'monc'mon.*" *Baaaa-Buuum*. It worked. The doors find each other and we creak away from 2nd Avenue.

It's slow going; more of the same at Broadway-Lafayette, with the doors opening, shutting and opening again, and the guy in the mustache pleading "*C'monc'monc'monc'mon*" from a downtrodden face that wants no part of this city. His B.O. is really starting to kick in. A Latina woman with a baby stroller is barking at a guy whose golf bag keeps hitting her baby. Unbeknownst to her, the baby playfully reaches for the fuzzy tassels that protect the heads of his clubs. The guy shrugs indifferently at her, his mind clearly on his golf game.

Golf. Haven't swung a golf club in forever. I remember the last time I did, that postcard of a summer day a few years back, when Tisa and I went to Chelsea Piers and hit balls on the four-story driving range they have on the river. *Tisa.* Jesus. My head pounds and I think of Friends and Family Day. Did we...is she...Are we...*Shit*.

She'd never swung a golf club before, and I'd only played a few times up in the Catskills many years previous, with the bartender from the Killarney House when I was about 17, so we were quite a sight to behold, I'm sure. Tisa loved the way a fresh ball automatically popped up out of the ground every time you slugged one off the tee. "Bloody American ingenuity," I remember her saying with a shake of her head.

I was trying to teach Tisa how to swing, standing behind her, enveloping her body, both of our pairs of hands on the club. I was guiding her arms through the full cycle of the swing, emphasizing the importance of the follow-through, as my old Little League coach with the Eat At Joe's Cardinals used to stress to me and Jimmy Gulotta and the rest of the team. We'd watch the ball either fly from our third-story level toward the Hudson off in the distance before nosediving to the fake grass floor below, or simply dribble off our perch toward the floor. My chin resting on her shoulder, Tisa smelled like the Botanical Gardens up in the Bronx, when you catch it on a nice day. I was up against her ass and I had a pretty good view down the front of Tisa's shirt—not that I didn't get to see them whenever I wanted back then—but it got me going nonetheless, the faint tan lines intersecting in between her breasts. One of us made a dirty joke; me, I'm sure, and we both cracked up.

Well, Tisa being Tisa, she thought she could give it a go all by herself, so I backed off. She brought the iron back real slow, which gave me time to duck, then snapped it forward with a Gary Sheffield-esque eruption of violence. The club struck the ball and, as she followed through, we watched the silver club fly from her hands off towards the river, rotating in slow motion and glimmering in the sunlight before plummeting to the floor below. She turned around, hand to her mouth like a horrified girl who's just dropped her mum's china on the kitchen floor. I guess Tisa thought I'd be angry, but I thought it was hysterical, and eventually, she did too. I had to go down to the ground floor, make an announcement to all four tiers of golfers that our club had gotten away, then skitter out to grab the wayward wand as the annoyed golfers held their fire.

Well, that was enough golf for one day, we'd reckoned, so me and Tisa grabbed a beer at the bar—a much safer pastime, something we're good at, I remember her saying. We ordered our drinks and I caught the score of the Met game on the TV above the bar. They'd beaten the Braves and moved into first place; I think it was the only day all season they held the top spot. We grabbed a table overlooking the river, alongside the little marina with all the expensive boats parked there. The one in front of me had "Esperanza," Old Saybrook, Connecticut, painted across the rear, along with a picture of a blue dolphin. *Esperanza*, I remember saying to myself, over and over. Didn't know what it meant, but the word had a beautiful flow to it.

The sun was just beginning its descent, and we sat there sipping glasses of amber ale, watching the boats parading past. I waved to a goddamn Circle Line boat chock-full of tourists; man, what a dork I was. And they waved back. I'd just started at *Cork & Bottle*, I was 50 pages into my first novel, Tisa had just gotten an agent and the Mets were in first. We were the couple you find in a new picture frame.

"To us," she'd said, as we clinked our pints together, the glass huge in her little hand.

"Esper-r-r-ranza," I'd replied, rolling the r as well as an Irish kid might.

The irate Latina woman with the baby stroller is rolling her r's at the pasty white golfer guy, who's pulled his visor low on his face, as if to hide. There's little progress on the F train. We experience a period of about three minutes when the train stops in the black of the tunnel, throwing my anxiety into overdrive, before lurching ahead just as Side 2 of *Aja* fades out. But these all are minor annoyances, really, not criminal activity, which the conductor mentions when the train rests at 14th Street.

"Due to criminal activity," he says, "this train will be making no further stops."

There's the requisite collective groan from the luckless F train contingent, as they reluctantly shuffle off the train.

But they get their first break all morning, as an express train is pulling in across the platform. It squeaks to a stop as we stave off tinnitus by jamming fingers into our ears. That doesn't prevent me from hearing Ken's voice of doom off in the distance: *Coulter!!* The doors open and it's packed. No one gets off. No one gets on. I'm tempted to throw the fiver back on the platform in an attempt to reshuffle the cards that seemed to be stacked against me on this particular morning, but reconsider.

It's found money. I can do something fun with it.

"It'll take ya 20 minutes," I say to Gabby as we sit in the playground. "Over and out, you're done. I buy your drinks."

Gabby leans back on the purple concrete whale, hands folded behind his head, looking up at the dim stars. He's got on a tight wife-beater and grubby chinos. I don't like him sitting on me and Tisa's whale, but I don't say anything.

"No fucking way. How's the head?"

"It's fine."

Then again, maybe I can use it as an excuse why I can't do my reading.

"Glad to hear it. We could use ya in the pack. Serenity's more of a hooker than a flanker."

Serenity is this Scotsman on the Village Vipers—this positively insane red-haired guy who gave up drinking some time ago. Every time we go to MacLennane's, he asks the girls behind the bar for tea, and it sounds like "Serenity" in his crazy *Trainspotting* accent.

"Jesus, Gabby, what's the big deal? Just read the fucking thing."

"Why the fuck can't *you* read it?" says Gabby. "You wrote the thing."

"Cuz I find it hard to read after getting dinged."

"You just told me you were fine."

I don't see what the big deal is. I mean, the whole thing is good. Good news. Good break. Got my short story chosen for a reading at Troika. It's called "The Apathy and the Ecstasy," and it's sort of about Tisa, only I called her Liza to protect the guilty. As always, my priorities are a bit askew; my Honey Bunny deadline was coming up, and I get an idea for a short story and work on it instead. Smart. But Sally cut me a little slack, and gave me a few weeks' grace. She just wanted to know it's in the works, and I assured her it was.

Troika is a scruffy old bar on 4th Street, a dark third-floor place you'd never see from the street. Supposedly Troika used to be a covert hangout for Communist sympathizers back in the day. It's a classic Lower East Side dive now; dim red lighting, local guys with creative facial hair wearing Che Guevara t-shirts, wallet chains and thrift store slacks, chicks with tattoos in strange places, all sorts of drugs sold over the bar either by or to sleepy-eyed bartenders with names like Gus and Tripp. They do literary readings there each Sunday, and they've had some pretty big-name people, mostly all published authors. I dropped a story off kind of on a whim, and wouldn't you know it, mine got picked. Only problem is, now I have to read the fuckin' thing. Unless I can persuade Gabby to do it.

"C'mon, man," I plead. "I *hate* reading aloud."

It's true. I just never got the hang of it. They used to make us read out loud at sunday school over at St. Brigid's on Avenue B, and I'd stare up at ol' Jesus on the cross in the front of the classroom, just like the one hanging in Paula's kitchen, and beg the man to not have Mrs. McDermott (who always called me "Dee-clahn"—an

Irish lady who somehow could not pronounce "Declan") call on me to read. I can't *stand* reading aloud.

"You're an edituh and a writuh," counters Gabby, sitting up straight on the whale to look me in the face. "You deal with words for a living. You should be able to *read*."

"You got such a better reading voice than me," I try. "You got that...timbre."

"You're the one who went to the fancy college," says Gabby.

"Yeah, fucking City College. 'Cultured' is the word that comes to mind. That, and 'leafy.' They say Harvard is the City College of New England. And it's not like I graduated...yet."

Even though he never went to college, unless you count a three-week stint at Pratt, Gabby's actually better read than any English degree-flaunting, publishing glasses-wearing people I know. They know him by name—Paul, not Gabby—over at St. Mark's Books. He won't even set foot in that new Barnes & Noble on Union Square.

I'd thought about asking some of the other guys to do the reading, but they all had something wrong with them, whether it's their voice—Shady is too British, Dr. Demento is too redneck—or they stammer or look funny or, for whatever reason, aren't quite worthy of bearing the "Declan Coulter" name in front of a discerning literary crowd. Gabby, on the other hand, is perfect. He's rough, but he can hold his own with the book people. And he's like an original hipster, even though he'd punch you in the nose if you ever called him one.

"You'll do fine," says Gabby.

"I won't *do* anything. I'm not doing it. That's it."

"Whaddya mean, that's it? This is a huge opportunity. They publish an anthology each year from the Troika readings, don't they?"

"Yeah," I say. "Doesn't mean I'd necessarily be in it. They're almost all published authors. *Real* writers."

"No, but it's still a fat opportunity."

"Please?"

I'm giving Gabby the hangdog look now. I hate this.

"I just don't get why you can't do it," says Gabby.

"I just can't," I say. "I just know I won't get through the whole thing without pissing myself, vomiting on myself or running out weeping. To be honest with you, since my knockout against the Barbarians, reading has been...a challenge."

"Maybe you should quit rugby," says Gabby. We both smile at that; that ain't happening.

"Deckie, man up," he adds. "Show a little confidence."

"Fiction's tough. You're...exposed."

"So ya wanna expose me instead," says Gabby. "Thanks. Damn, man. You wrote the shit. If people hate it, I ain't gonna incur their venom."

Gabby's using power words like "incur" and "venom," but he's not giving me an outright "no," like he was before.

"Just think about it, Gabby. Give it a few days."

"So you'll play rugby with that crack in your neck, with your freshly scrambled brain, on the fucking concrete fields of Randalls against 250-pound wreckin' machines, but you're afraid to read a little story to a buncha wanna-be hipster, pseudo-intellectual tools."

"Right."

"How 'bout you give me the story to look at?" says Gabby. "If I hate it, you're shit outta luck."

"Alright," I say, my hopes perking up. "I got a copy back at home. I'll send a messenger over to your work tomorrow."

The whole messenger concept is one thing I love about the professional world. I sent one over to Shady Brady's place for a bag of weed last week.

"If—," starts Gabby, "and we're only at the 'if' stage right now, and I mean that. *If* I do it, you're gonna owe me big-time. Not like, do me a favuh some time in the future, or buy me a beer. I mean like, I name a favuh for right here and right now, and you cough said favuh up, no questions asked. Dig, Deckie?"

"Yeah, man," I say. "Anything. We'll work something out."

That's Gabby, always looking for something in return.

But he's going to read my story.

"Whaddya wanna do tonight, anyway?" he asks.

"Don't know. Was thinking of maybe heading up to Paddy Reilly's. Black 47's playing."

"Damn donkey music," he says. "Count me out."

"Yeah, whatever," I say. "They're cool. The singer dude's creative as shit—it's like a short story or a history lesson in every song."

Gabby shakes his head.

"That dude's voice," he says. "Lay off the helium, pal."

I look up at the stars, exhale and smile. I have a short story at the Troika readings, and I don't even have to read it. I'm going to sit in the crowd—well, the collection of 25 or so of Troika's hipper-than-thou types—and take in their reactions. Their laughter. Their heartbreak. Their amazement at my literary precision, insight and skill.

"I'm fine with just hanging out," I add. "Save a little dough."

"Mmmehehemmm."

It's the resonant throat-clearing of a big man, which Mr. Snow certainly is. We're at Gotham, a place off 5th Avenue that I'd never in a million years be able to afford. But, if Haley's folks are buying, well, I'm game.

"So," starts Mr. Snow. He's got slicked back hair that's surprisingly dark for a man his age, which appears to be around 60. Haley told me he played basketball at Columbia, back when Columbia was a national power, and white guys dominated college ball. Mr. Snow looks like he could still post up and go strong to the hole, or chase down and pummel the boy who screwed over his daughter. He's some high-powered entertainment lawyer, and I've seen his name in the gossip pages before.

"Haley tells me you went to NYU," says Mr. Snow.

I'm about to correct him, then realize it may be what I told Haley.

"Uh, yes, sir," I say in a voice I reserve for court summonses, job interviews and meeting girlfriends' parents. "NYU. Not far from here."

"We used to play 'em in basketball," he says. "Believe it or not, both NYU and Columbia, where I attended, were among the strongest basketball schools in the nation."

"No kidding," I say. "Academics have certainly surpassed athletics at both institutions."

"Indeed."

"Haley says you're in publishing," says Mrs. Snow.

"Yes, ma'am," I say. "I work as an editor for a wine magazine, writing features about, well, wine—new wine releases, wine expos, wine country and wine people, and overseeing a wine review."

I don't elaborate; my job sounds more interesting the less I say about it. And I leave "associate" out of my title. I edit. Therefore, I'm an editor. Actually, if you're to boil my job down, I'm a typist—I rewrite press releases for winemakers that advertise in our magazine. More accurately, I give the releases to our intern Becky, and then cruise job websites and dream about a better tomorrow. I'm always nice to Becky, because she's smarter than me, and I realize that my brighter tomorrow might possibly be linked to her.

"Wine Enthusiast?" says Mr. Snow.

"No—."

"Wine Spectator?" guesses Mrs. Snow.

"No, *Cork & Bottle,* actually. We're a little younger and less stuffy than the others."

By less stuffy, I mean less ads.

"And I've written a few children's books as well," I add. "This character called Honey Bunny." They look at each other and force a smile; they seem to like the wine magazine better than Honey Bunny. No problem.

Michael J. Malone

"Interesting," says Mr. Snow.

Mrs. Snow, who has streaks of silver in her straight blonde mane and makes me think of the word "proper," nods in agreement. They're a classic middle-aged New York couple: attractive, well-dressed, an air of culture and wealth about them. He looks like he's been to more than one party at the Dakota, and she looks like she's got a funny Woody Allen story to tell.

"I've never met a Declan before," says Mrs. Snow. "Am I saying it right?"

"Yes, ma'am. There aren't many of us."

"That's Irish?" she asks.

"Yes. Irish mom, English dad."

"That's uncommon."

"Yes, well, they didn't get along, as you might guess."

"And where do they live?"

"Uh, mom's here in the city, dad's probably back in England."

There's an awkward silence, as everyone sifts through my family's dirty laundry.

"So, where's the world's best wine made?" Mr. Snow asks. It's the one question I'm asked every time someone over 40 finds out what I do for work. I press PLAY on autopilot.

"Well, Mr. Snow, there's always France, of course," I start. "And I like what they're doing down in the Southern Hemisphere, most notably South Africa and Australia, what with their Shiraz/Syrah, and they've got a nice array of Cabernets as well. Honestly, though—"

This part I love.

"I've had California wines that are every bit as good as the rest of the world's. Any Mondavi Cabernet is exquisite, Benziger out of Sonoma makes great stuff and a little guy up that way called Imagery is sublime."

Americans are always elated to hear that the U.S. of A is competing with, even surpassing, the rest of the world. Reds, whites and blue. Mr. Snow gives a satisfied nod and Mrs. Snow pumps her fist. Haley smiles at me. It's going well. Next they'll demand I pick out the evening's wine.

"Well, I guess we'll have to insist you choose our dinner wine," says Mrs. Snow with a smile. "It'd be a shame not to use a resource like you."

I beam. I'm a resource!

The waiter breezes through the specials. There's a pumpkin ravioli in pesto and pine nuts, and a salmon with penne and lots of other things that sound good, especially with the Snows paying.

Haley squeezes my knee under the table. She's got on a sleeveless black turtleneck and a long black skirt. It's a lot of black, and on some girls it might look morose or Goth, but on Haley, offset by her long, straight blonde hair, fanning out

86

at her shoulders like a veil, it looks wonderful. She was nervous about asking me to meet her folks, and seemed so surprised when I agreed to come along. I told her she was selling me short, measuring me up against a guy stereotype she got from sitcoms. Of course I'd like to go for a free meal at Gotham! Of course I'd like to see the creatures that house the cells from which she was spawned! And yes, I'm ready to admit to her, her folks and, most importantly, myself, that I'm willing to take this next step in our relationship.

And maybe we'll finally have sex.

I order a bottle of Jekel, out of Monterey, from 1995. It was a good year. A *very* good year. It was before I met Tisa.

"She had all this energy as a kid," says Mrs. Snow who, after three glasses of Cabernet, has requested I call her Lydia. So I do. We're at the stage of the dinner where they're telling stories about Haley's childhood, much to her mortification. Of course, I fan the flames with probing questions, about her bad haircuts, Shaun Cassidy fetish and things she had irrational fears of as a kid—shopping carts, a purple frog rocking toy on a playground near their Upper East Side apartment.

"I swear, she'd just fly about the living room, crashing into things. That's why we called her 'Haley,'" says Mr. Snow. "She was like a comet. Still is."

"That's where the name came from?" I ask with genuine surprise. "I thought—"

I don't want to say I thought Haley was her given name, even though I'm surprised to learn it's not.

"I thought it was a college nickname."

"I never told you?" asks Haley.

"Nah. Never. So what's your real name?"

There's a moment of silence; each of the three Snows figures the other one will tell the story.

"Meadow," spits Haley.

"Meadow!" I exclaim with much more vigor than I intended. It dawns on me that I've recently attained a fairly serious relationship milestone with a girl named Meadow. I feel so...*earthy*.

"Meadow," says Haley, as her parents look bashfully at each other. I'm trying to picture Lydia and Jack Snow in their hippie days—muddy, hirsute, naked—but I can only muster a vision of them in the urban finery they have on tonight. I can't even picture them outdoors.

"Meadow," I repeat. Maybe it's the Cabernet, but I'm starting to like it.

"Who wants dessert?" asks Meadow.

Michael J. Malone

We get dessert. I have a flourless chocolate cake, warm in the center, while Meadow gets a raspberry torte. We all order espresso and drink it at a comfortable pace.

When the check comes, I make a weak move to grab it, but Mr. Snow snags it like it's an offensive rebound. He drops an awesome black credit card on the silver check dish, and then we stand outside the restaurant for a considerable amount of time, making painless small talk on the warm night.

"Well, Declan, it certainly was a pleasure meeting you," says Mrs. Snow.

"Likewise, Lydia," I say, delicately shaking her hand as she leans over for a kiss.

"Nice meetin' you, Declan," says Mr. Snow in a fraternal, if stern, tone, giving me a firm handshake. "Take care of our Haley, will ya?"

"Yes, sir," I say, flattered to be saddled with the responsibility. I have a vision of me, Haley and a dog in some house in the woods, seeing the Snows off after a visit. Not sure who's paying the mortgage, but hell, dare to dream. I hardly even think of Tisa.

"Of course," I say. "Thank you for dinner."

Mrs. gives a final wave as Mr. flags down a cab.

We're walking down 10th Street back to Haley's place. It's a beautiful block—townhouses, carriage houses, places with huge windows that taunt everyone on the street who lives in a rent-stabilized tenement on the distant east side. Sometimes the residents sit in plush chairs in the window, smoking pipes and reading books by long-dead authors, looking down at you as you gaze up, rubbing it in that they have an unthinkably pleasurable living situation, and you very definitely do not.

Walking hand in hand, neither one of us is speaking, but it doesn't feel awkward. Dinner with Haley's folks has gone really well, no doubt about it. Haley clears her throat and I know what she's going to say, something like, "Well, that went well."

"Eleanor Roosevelt lived there," says Haley, pointing to a gorgeous brick townhouse with a stable door.

"Really?" I say, scanning my brain for any facts I might have about her that I can bring up. Married to a crippled president, face like a horse. Neither is worth sharing.

"Yup. After FDR died," says Haley. "Supposedly she had a female lover living with her."

"No shit?" I say. "Really?"

"You won't see it confirmed anywhere," Haley says, "but it was common knowledge. The press left those things alone back then."

I try to picture the *Post* exhibiting such restraint.

"Well—," starts Haley.

"—that went well," I interrupt, smiling and giving her hand a squeeze.

"Yes. It did. I'm glad."

"Me too," I say, leading her toward 6th Avenue.

"Take your shoes off," Haley says from the kitchen as I sit on her black leather couch. She's got Ethan Allen, and I'm just graduating to IKEA. The significance of the shoe-removal command is not lost on me; I've never been invited to take my shoes off at Haley's before. I have a flash of anxiety as I consider the state of my socks—there was little to no forethought as I dressed this morning. I examine them and they thankfully appear OK.

Haley's got a classic West Village one-bedroom—a vintage walk-up on a block with lots of trees; it's how I picture Paris. She's got exposed brick on one living room wall and a fireplace that doesn't work, but just sits there like an open mouth that can't speak. Her hardwood floors are shiny, with a white throw rug in the middle. There's a dark wood coffee table in the middle of the living room, and on it is a video called *The Locusts* and a book entitled *The Girl's Guide to Hunting and Fishing*. I had no idea she was such an outdoorsperson, my little Meadow.

A purple candle makes flickering shapes along a white wall, and she's put on some groovy jazz that's either Miles Davis or John Coltrane. I have no idea which because I don't like jazz.

She comes back from the kitchen with two glasses of port, and hands one to me.

"I didn't know you knew so much about wine," she says.

"I, uh, I know how to stretch my limited knowledge out pretty good."

"Well, it was very impressive."

"Thank you."

"I got you a gift," she says.

"C'mon!"

"Something small."

"What for?"

"No reason," she says. "Just a little gift."

I feel bad for not getting her anything, but how was I to know we were exchanging presents? She opens the drawer of the end table and pulls out what can only be a CD, wrapped in shiny silver paper.

"Thank you, Hale."

"Open it!"

I do, and see Keanu Reeves in a football uniform, kissing some girl. It's the soundtrack for a cheesy football movie called *The Replacements*.

"It's that band you like!" she gushes. "From Minneapolis! The song about St. Mark's Place!"

"Rigggghhhht," I say, turning it over. There's a song by Young MC and a bunch of other stuff by hip-hop sounding acts I never heard of.

"Thanks," I say, leaning over to kiss her. "You're very kind."

"No problem. Maybe you can tape it for me."

"Sure...Meadow," I say, and she recoils slightly.

"No," protests Haley.

"No more Meadow?"

"'fraid not."

"My new Honey Bunny book takes place in what I've titled *The Enchanted Meadow*," I say. "Coincidence, huh?"

"I'm surprised you didn't make a joke about the daughter on 'The Sopranos,'" says Haley.

"Whyzat?"

"Her name is Meadow."

"I don't have HBO," I say. "I must say, though, I'm a little surprised with the name. I mean, your parents just don't seem like the types to name a kid 'Meadow.' What's your sister's name, Forest?"

Haley takes a sip of her port, which sends a flush of color throughout her pleasantly pale face.

"Brooke," she mumbles.

"C'mon."

"I'm serious, Declan," she says, giving me a look that reinforces the statement. "I wish I was kidding. *God*, I wish I was kidding."

"Brooke!"

"Yup. And she's still a Brooke. At least I had the good sense to run around like a lunatic and get a nickname."

"Brooke and Meadow," I say. "That...just...blows my mind."

"I know, I know. It's...fucked up."

Haley never curses. The swear sticks out like a wine stain on her white throw rug.

"Like I said, I just don't see your parents as the hippie types."

"They're not," says Meadow, who I promise I'm calling Meadow for the last time.

"I sense a story coming on."

"I'd rather not," says Haley. "Maybe when I know you better."

There's a flirty tone to her protestations, so I lean over and kiss her.

"*I met your parents...*," I tease.

"You really wanna know?"

"Yes."

"It's fucking stupid."

Apparently Haley only curses when talking about her family's fucked-up, fucking stupid names.

"Go on," I say. "I'll tell you something stupid about me."

"Okay," she says with a laugh, taking a healthy slug of wine and beginning the story. "When my parents were first married, they had no money."

"They look like they were born rich."

"Yeah, they play the game well," explains Haley. "Sort of like you and your wine. Anyway, for the first few years they were married, they had this crummy little apartment out in Long Island. Sorry—*on* Long Island, my father always corrects me. It was my grandmother's house, and they rented out the basement. The ceiling was about six feet high, and my dad's, ya know, a pretty big guy, even bigger then. I went back to see the place once. It was heinous.

"My dad was working in the city," she continues, "as a runner on Wall Street."

"Runner?"

"Lowest life form in the business. You literally run around and place orders for brokers."

"Ouch."

"Yeah," she says. "A real bottom feeder. He was doing that and going to law school, and my mom was teaching. My dad would get home late, and Mom had to get up early, so they didn't have much time for each other. But almost every night, when it was warm, they'd get into my dad's old car and drive down to Jones Beach. Back then, they didn't have any kind of security there, and you could just sort of walk onto the beach. My dad didn't get home til 9 or so, and there wasn't usually anyone there by the time they got there, so they'd throw a blanket down and—"

"Screw!" I blurt. I'm an idiot.

"No," laughs Haley. "Well, maybe. I never thought about it."

Obviously, it was the first thing *I* thought about.

"So they'd hang out there every night. Once they had me and my sister, they never really got much of a chance to go back, at least not on their own. And after my dad started moving up and making, you know, more money, they bought a place in the city. He became an attorney and that was the end of their quiet nights of watching the waves."

"Nice," I say, and it does sound *nice*. It's a *nice* story.

But wait. It's not over. It *can't* be over. Something's missing.

"What about the names?"

"Oh!" yelps Haley. "I almost forgot. This is the stupid part. They used to take the Meadowbrook Parkway to the beach. And those nights were always such special memories for them. So I got Meadow, and Brooke got Brooke."

"Wowwww," I say. "So they *were* screwing on the beach."

"I guess," says Haley bashfully.

I'm with someone named after a highway. I have something in common with Eleanor Roosevelt.

"You should get a toll-free ride every time you're on the Meadowbrook," I suggest lamely. She laughs anyway.

"It's free for everyone."

"Well...you should get your own lane, or something."

"I'm not on the Meadowbrook very often."

"Maybe we'll take a ride out there when it gets warmer," I say. "Go to the beach."

"That sounds wonderful," says Haley, putting her glass on the coffee table and resting her head against my chest. I can smell the ocean in her hair.

Miles or Coltrane is wailing away, positively *wailing*, as Haley turns her head up for a kiss, and I like jazz for the first time in my life.

And those tunes just go on and on. He's *still* wailing when we get to our feet a bit later. I don't think Haley's going to call me on sharing something stupid about my life, and I'm grateful for it; it would be hard to pare down my list. I shake a little life into my sleepy limbs and head; this all seems to be happening in a dizzying, surreal fashion. Haley leads me by the hand towards her bedroom, like a tow truck pulling a car with a blown engine. On the Meadowbrook.

Rules of Engagement

"Haley," says Gabby.

"Goin' good," I say. "Thanks for askin'. I mean, I don't know if we're really what I'd call ideally suited for the long term, but what the hell, I sort of dig her. Yeah, I do. How 'bout you? You got anyone goin' on? Leather Tuscadero? She seemed...nice."

"Nah," says Gabby through a mouthful of Monterey Jack cheeseburger at Paul's Place off St. Mark's. None of his relationships, if we can call them that, last any longer than his time at Pratt did. He's much worse than me.

There's a miniature mechanical man up on the ceiling over our heads. He rides a little unicycle back and forth along a high-wire. Paul is apparently going for the juvenile set, though you never see kids in the neighborhood. More likely, he's just catering to stoners with the munchies.

"What happened?"

"Just a bad match, man," says Gabby, taking a pull on a bottle of Rolling Rock. He puts the bottle down on the tile table kind of hard, and some foam comes shooting up over the rim. I think of sex with Haley. We're close.

"You guys didn't seem, ya know, logical," I offer. "She was kind of a classy broad, and all. And you...you dine at Paul's."

Gabby glowers and looks up at the high-wire act.

"A cynic might say the same about you and Haley."

"S'pose," I allow. "So who broke up with who?"

"Didn't even happen," he says. "It just kinda...died."

"Sorry," I say, though you don't really say things like "sorry" to Gabby, unless he's about to beat your head in or something.

"Yeah, whatever. Wasn't meant to be, I guess. Plus, those hotel bars were drainin' my finances."

"Mmm," I say. "So we got the Bainbridge Bruisers this weekend, huh? Dirty Paddy fuckers."

We despise the Bainbridge Bruisers. They're ugly, broken-nosed, foulmouthed louts from up on Bainbridge Avenue—a real disgrace to *Eire*, as Ma might say. Plus, they've got this gorgeous pub up in the Bronx for post-game parties, which makes us despise them even more. Matches with Bainbridge always end up in a big punch-up; it's never if with them, it's when. I'd like to call the Village Vipers versus Bainbridge thing a rivalry, but I'm sure the nail would like to call that thing it has going with the hammer a rivalry too.

"No shit," says Gabby. "Donkey bastards. It's their Friends and Family Day. They scheduled us as their fucking homecoming opponent. Could use yuh out there, Deckie."

"I'll be out soon," I say.

It's been more than two weeks; I'm probably cleared to play again. I'm just afraid of…I don't know what. I sort of lost my nerve. Broken bones don't scare me. The scrambled brain does.

"Haley," says Gabby again, looking at me in a weird way, kind of like he's doing his DeNiro.

"Yeeeeaaahhh?" I query, wondering what he's on about. I try to read Gabby's expression. He's scrutinizing his burger, wondering where to make the next bite.

"That's what I want for reading your story."

"You want me to drag her by the hair over to your cave, Gab?"

"Uh, yeah."

I've got a mouthful of steak and cheese sandwich, and I can feel the fatty food grow cold in my mouth.

"What the fuck are you talking about?"

"That's the trade, man," says Gabby. He keeps staring at me, looking me in the eye in that creepy way that makes my skin crawl. "I said there'd be a favor involved for reading yuh story."

"You want the deed to the girl I'm seeing."

I'm trying humor. I'm not optimistic it's going to work.

"I wanna *do* the deed with the girl you're seeing, is more like it."

"I, uh, I find your proposal indecent at best."

If Gabby gets the movie reference, he's not letting on. The thought of his big, grubby hands, the knuckles strewn with a roadmap of scars, on the fair Haley really turns my stomach. I look down at my sandwich and the grease has soaked into the roll. I can't eat anymore. The mechanical man whizzes back and forth overhead, oblivious to the anxiety below him, which seeps out of me like grease from one of the giant Paul's burgers as it's squeezed between the spatula and the grill.

"Then read your own stupid story," spits Gabby, taking a wolfish bite on his burger. I still can't tell if he's fucking with me or not.

"So, what, I'm gonna tell Haley to sleep with you?" I say, anger rising but still not level with my anxiety.

"Yup."

"Man, *I'm* not even screwing her yet."

"Huh?"

"Well, if you must know, and I really don't think you must, we're doing everything but. But, ya know, we haven't closed the deal yet."

"Jesus Christ," says Gabby. "She must be dying for it. Enter Gabby."

My teeth clench and my jaw aches.

"What is this, some after-school special, when the star quarterback tells his girl, 'well, if you love me, you'll sleep with my friends'?"

"Nothing like that," says Gabby. "Just mention to her that I'm sorta diggin' her, and then get us all into a situation where it can happen. I'll take care of the rest."

"What, a fucking threesome?" I say, picturing Gabby's hairy white ass. "She ain't Jennifer Jameson, ya know."

"*Jenna* Jameson, dumbass. Me 'n her, man. Yuh make yuhself scarce."

Smug motherfucker, I think but don't say. He takes another greedy bite. Gabby's table manners are atrocious.

"Speakin' uh Jameson, a little neat whiskey actually sounds good," he adds.

I agree but don't say so.

"And how long have you been *sorta diggin'* my girlfriend?"

"Now she's your girlfriend?"

"Yeah."

"Not that long."

"Really."

"You just said you guys weren't suited for the long term."

"I said I don't know if we're suited for the long term. Who knows?" I say with a shrug. "She certainly has her...attributes."

"Just one time," says Gabby. "That's all I want. Unless, of course, you get a book deal and have to do an author tour. And we have to negotiate something long term. But we'll worry about that then."

"Smug motherfucker."

Gabby shrugs and takes another ravenous bite. I can't get over how big the burgers here are—his never seems to shrink after his sharklike rips. My sandwich is not shrinking either, but that's because I'm done eating it.

"Did you, uh, like the story?" I ask sheepishly.

"'S'awright," says Gabby through a full mouth, shrugging. "It's a little... derivative, if you ask me. And that title...c'mon, dude. You call yourself a writer?"

Michael J. Malone

Usually I catch one of them on 6th and B, or thereabouts. They usually hang around this old school on the corner. Made of red brick, the school has a bunch of steps out front, so it's a decent place to sit, hang out, be young. I know—me and Jimmy Gulotta used to go there to look at his older brother Stanley's stroke mags when we were kids. And the cops rarely come that far east; Alphabet City is essentially self-policed, which means non-policed. Which the dealers and junkies, needless to say, appreciate.

This school is huge, extends all the way to 5th Street. But it's not a real, functioning school, at least not in the traditional way. Don't know what they do with it. There's a mural of a globe on the side of the school along B, and it says "The Earth School" on it, whatever that means. The yuppie basketball leagues play there, and I'd heard the Transit Authority holds classes there, teaching the citizens of New York to mumble misleading subway information into squawky intercoms and deal tokens without expression or sound.

I see a guy doing the junkie stagger along the community garden between 5th and 6th. He has his shirt off, and periodically stops and buries his face in it. He bends over, hands on his knees, his head almost scraping the ground, then rights himself again. He keeps heading uptown, tiptoeing along the curb, threatening to plunge into traffic. He stops again, drops to a squat and nearly topples over. People walk by and give him a prolonged stare, then ignore him. A few feet away, an iron fence separating them, people plant flowers in the garden—bright purples, pinks, yellows. The man is a master of the fiend lean. No one thinks to help the guy, who will die today, tomorrow, in a few weeks, a year. Why should they?

Tonight, the dealers are nowhere to be found. They're everywhere when you don't need them, when you're trying to show your girl from the other side of town that the neighborhood's not that bad. The presence of drug use is everywhere, in the faces of the dirty white kids with multiple facial piercings, rooster-heads or shaved skulls, ripped jeans, often with rows of safety pins holding them together, combat boots, Wite-Out messages of nihilism and well-rehearsed despair on their leather jackets. Children last seen on milk cartons. I'm walking by them and saying hi, which explains my intent pretty clearly. No one says hi in New York, so if you do, you're looking for dope or sex.

"Yo, share that 40-dog, Fluke!" yells a guttersnipe girl with a grimy, pierced, pretty face.

I got my hair buzzed short recently, which I do at the beginning of every rugby season. All the guys do it—I guess we think it makes us look hard. My hair's about two millimeters long and fire-engine red, and that's part of the trouble. The kids think I'm a narc or something. They look at me warily, but hey, junkies look at everyone warily—at least when they're well enough to note the presence of others on the planet. I don't take it personally. I score so damn infrequently, because I use

96

so damn infrequently, so I don't exactly have preferred customer status over here. No free bag when I get my card punched for the 10th time. Bummer. You never exchange names, anyway, so I got no one to ask for. I see a few regulars from the Harm Reduction Center, but I look away before they recognize me. Not that they ever would; I could smack one of them in the face at the Center, then come out here that night and ride a unicycle around naked or something, and they still wouldn't make the connection.

This part of the neighborhood was so fat with drugs when I was growing up: Avenue A and 6th, where my best friend in 4th grade, Frank DiPietro, lived; B and 8th, in front of St. Brigid's; all of Tompkins; C and anything. I'm scoring dope—*trying* to score dope—about 200 yards from my childhood home in the most sophisticated city in the world. If you live on Central Park West, you play soccer in the park. How could one grow up here and not at least *dabble* in the local fare?

I'm walking from 6th to 7th along B, right up to the corner of Tompkins, crossing the street, then back down to 6th, then back up again to 7th, saying hi to everyone that looks like they might know an alternate meaning for the term "Body Bag." Nothing. Thank God I'm not an addict, I'm thinking. Imagine the anxiety then, having to score and being unable to. At least I'm only looking for fun. It's the truth—the last time I used was more than six weeks ago. I just enjoy it now and then, and the fact that I only buy it with found money keeps me in check. Football pool money, poker winnings, change I've rolled up, money from Victor and the wine scam, money I find on the subway platform, and money I find in Subway sandwich shops, like on the way home from work today. Subways have been very good to me of late.

I dropped into Subway on St. Mark's, feeling bad about the creepy talk with Gabby about Haley, hoping one of those foot-long subs would take my mind of it. And there it is, sitting on the ground, crumpled but clearly recognizable. Honest Abe, sitting amidst a sea of Skechers, Airwalks and Vans. I couldn't believe no one saw the fiver—the Lady Godiva, as Shady Brady might say—they're pretty hot commodities east of Broadway. So I casually bent over and grabbed it. Two five-spots in two weeks: dig it. Kind of like that Win for Life lottery game.

With this embarrassment of riches, I'm now permitted, according to the Declan Constitution (flawed as it may be), to buy myself a bag. So here I am, standing outside of 7Bs, waiting for something to happen, to see some guy I recognize as a dealer, or someone who recognizes me as a customer. That Velvet Underground song pops into my head:

> I'm waiting for my man
> $26 in my hand
> Up to Lexington, 1-2-5
> Feel sick and dirty, more dead than alive...

I swear, if I have to go up to 1-2-5 and Lex to score, I'm quitting this extracurricular activity for good—especially if dime bags start costing $26. *"C'monc'monc'monc'mon,"* I try. I saw it work on the subway once.

I watch a girl in a short purple denim jacket and high heels stumble up B towards me. She's wearing a black skirt that hangs limply on hips that're having a tough time holding it up, bare legs, the crack of her bony ass showing. She's got the unmistakable look of a junkie—pockmarked grayish skin, concave cheeks, feet tapping to some arrhythmic beat heard only by her. She asks me for a quarter and I'm tempted to go into the bodega and buy her a candy bar or maybe a plantain, for the potassium, but I simply hand her the coin. She walks over to a pay phone and dials, then does a half-circle lap around the phone, as far as the cord's tether will allow. It's the same half-circle—frontwards, backwards, frontwards again. Finally, she hangs up and crosses Avenue B in the middle of the block, against the light and into the teeth of traffic, making like Frogger, as the self-preservation department in her brain has been closed down due to lack of funding. Fortunately for both of us, she gets across unscathed. She sets off down 6th towards C, and I follow her.

I don't know whose idea it was to put a sports bar on the Lower East Side, but someone evidently sunk a lot of money into this one. I see it gleaming across 1st Avenue like a shiny new Cadillac in a junkyard, with a gaudy sign that says BACK PAGE over the door and a black scoreboard below it with orange electronic type jetting across the screen, giving up-to-the-minute scores, coaches' hirings and firings and injury updates. Right smack in the middle of the Lower East Side. A jazz joint, maybe; a coffee shop, probably; a Tibetan gift shop most definitely. But a sports bar? Jesus, no. *New York Press* was going to *crucify* this one.

I'd already read a review of the place in *Time Out*, and they weren't gentle. One thing I did remember from the article was that each bathroom stall had its own TV hanging above it, showing various college basketball games, trout fishing, NHL action, tractor pulls or whatever vaguely sports-esque programming they could muster up to fill out the schedule. I decided I had to try it.

So, with my hard-won dime bag burning a hole in my pocket, I'm crossing 1st Avenue to check out the Back Page. For me, doing dope in your own apartment is like drinking a 12-pack while sitting on your couch. It's hard to justify spending $60 to get drunk in a bar when you can do it at home for $10, but you pay to satisfy your craving for stimulation—chance encounters, people watching, pretty women slumming it in Alphabet City. I'm occasionally a social guy, and I get even more social when I'm doped up—that's how I know I'll never be a real junkie, sitting in some abandoned building by myself or with a bunch of zombies. According to Dead Bolt Theory #1, I'm scared to death of doing a little too much with no one around. I'd like to be found while I'm still breathing, not three days later. Plus, unlike downing the 12-pack, there's no going downstairs and heading outside after doing up a few lines. So I prefer to do it out, dig all the weird shit around me, maybe have a beer and gradually make my way back to the safety of my place.

Tonight I'm actually staying out, meeting Haley at Tile Bar a few blocks down 1st. We're on for 8:30, having a drink at the Tile and then heading over to 11th and 3rd to the movies. We're going to see *Cider House Rules*, which looks long and boring, but Haley wants to see it before it goes to video, says it looks "inspiring," and I'm trying to be agreeable. So I have to keep a casual eye on the time, and, of course, only do a little bit. She's taking me out to celebrate me getting picked to read at Troika.

It's barely 7 now. I'm cool.

"Hello, Sir. Welcome to the Back Page," says a tall, well-scrubbed, muscular black man who looks like he averaged 15 points and 10-plus boards in college.

"Hi."

Man, it's odd in here. It's cavernous. I can't picture what was here before, even though I've lived here my entire life. What could have possibly filled this space? They've got TVs everywhere. Big screen. Bigger screen. Basketball. Two hockey teams I never heard of. The hoop team with two white guys versus the team with one white guy. Golf. Tennis. Soccer from a place where they call it "futbol." Sports everywhere, though, of course, no rugby. They're even piping in sports trivia and some dreadful jock rock: silly sports ditties, the Chicago Bears' eminently forgettable "Super Bowl Shuffle," Gary Glitter's "Rock 'n Roll Part One," better known up in the bleachers as, simply, "Hey!" Each employee cheerily says "Hello," and "Welcome to Back Page." Clean-cut people of all colors fill the tables and the bar. They're most definitely not from the neighborhood and, by the looks of them, not even from the city. I feel like we've finally lost the neighborhood—we don't own it anymore, they do. The Lower East Side has indeed become the East Village.

I walk in slowly, ready to bet my meager savings I'm the only one in here with a deck, as they say on the news but never on the street, of dope in my pocket. Call me Deck-ie. Three, four, five men fill out what appear to be job applications at the bar. Everyone wants to be a part of the Back Page.

Me, I want to be part of its new but no less mythical restroom. A sign points to the can, and I head past the bar. The bartender, wearing a referee's stripes, catches my eye and says hi. I nod and keep walking, escaping a penalty flag.

One door is marked "Sir," and the other, "Madame." Strange choices for a sports bar bathroom, like the manager desperately tried to think of something sports-y and clever, like "Meatheads" and "Butches," or something, and just came up empty, opting for Elizabethan instead. Like the bar, the bathroom is cavernous; roomy by Midwestern standards, colossal for New York. Music is piped in here as well, and there are trivia questions in between songs, about Ted Williams winning the Triple Crown but losing the MVP, and Wayne Gretzky scoring 200 points four years in a row. There's a framed poster of the '27 Yankees, looking tidy and clean-cut, and another of Don Shula's undefeated '72 Dolphins, all mutton chops and fluffy porn-star mustaches.

I duck into the furthest stall.

Oh, this is good. The commodes are spotless and ergonomically stellar; from a seated position, I can rest my head, or at least my nose, on the toilet paper dispenser. I've got jock rock—"We are the Champions"—and trivia. And the personal TV screen, looming over my stall like "SportsCenter" from the heavens.

I cut the bag into two lines with my Avatar work ID. That's all you get for a dime bag, but the wacky Paki shit out there these days is off-the-hook pure as snow, pure as Haley Snow, and about the same color, even when you buy off some skell you don't know. Volunteering over at House o' Needles, my smack-jackin' customers say the Colombians are now involved in dope, and they don't know shit about how pure to make it, and it's fucking *strong*. Just a little bit is more than enough to put me in a good mood, without zonking me out for my date with Hale tonight. Just a little one-man happy hour at the Back Page, is all.

I bend over and inhale a line off the dispenser, and the shit burns like a firecracker stuck in my nasal cavity. I always forget about that part. Well, beats the fuck out of playing doctor and jamming yourself with a needle. The work ID is still in my hand. I look at the kid in the picture: young, naive, ambitious, stupid, likeable, ugly, well-meaning. I hope that, somewhere in the Village View, Paula Coulter's proud of him. Though I'm not sure why she would be. And I hope Tisa's having the mother of all Declan flashes. Putting "Tisa" and "mother" in the same sentence gives me anxiety. Thank God I don't get Tisa flashes.

I do up the other line, which burns less, close my eyes, hum silently and feel the all-over tingling that I also sort of forget about each time. I mean, I remember the tingling, but never quite how fucking wonderful, how *tingly,* it is. It's like the bath water's *perfect*, for once, hots and colds joining hands in harmony, singing "Hallelujah"…the Jeff Buckley version, not Leonard Cohen. My stomach gets the funny, happy, cheerful little bubbling in it that tells the rest of the body that everything's just dandy; the doctor has arrived, the United Healthcare card was approved and I get a lollipop to suck on.

I shut my eyes and…*just…start…to…*

Tisa had no dough; it was before any of her pilots went on to not get aired, before any of her commercials ended up running at 3 a.m. during "The Robin Byrd Show." She was paying big-time rent for a place down on West Broadway, right off Spring, and her pops back in Jolly Ol' was kicking in serious scratch, but he finally decided he was gonna cut her off, hoping it would get her to move back to Blighty, away from my broke, sorry, Irish ass. So she wasn't able to make rent and, me being a gentleman, I move her into my place. I'd been sort of hinting that we move in together, so I was totally happy, and ended up looking like a good guy in the process.

So we were kind of sort of like a married couple for a few months, and I dug it. I mean, it wasn't perfect, but it was adult-like, and it felt good. Proper meals, proper bedtime, actually waking up at a decent time and not feeling half bad. Then Ma calls one day and tells me to *get the fook* down to her apartment, all pissed off, so I tell Tisa my mom needs help moving furniture around, and bolt down the stairs. Ma's freakin' out when I get there, telling me how the *little coont's fookin' around* on me, how she saw Tisa with some tall guy walking around the West Village hand in hand, not kissing or anything, but hand in hand and looking all kind of couple-y, in the part of town over by Eleanor Roosevelt's place where you only go to with someone you care about. Man, I felt my heart drop into my stomach, and then my stomach got real heavy with the heart in it, so it was leaning on my bowels, and I had to run to the can and take care of intestinal matters.

Sitting on the john, I was thinking, Tisa's a friendly chick, an actress, an emotional kind of girl—there's a total explanation for this. So I went back to the living room and told Ma, sure, I knew about the guy, name's Will, he's doing a show with Tisa, they're linked on stage and they're just getting into their parts. Running lines, I think Tisa used to call it. 'Course, Ma didn't buy that for a second—Tisa's the thesp, not me—and I remember her bony finger pointing at me all witch-like as I left her place, tell me to *get yer wee head outta yer arse*, to *wake the fook up*.

Well, I kind of sat on this bit of info for a bit, not sure what to believe, hoping it would just go away. I mean, Ma hated Tisa from Day 1, because she's a Brit, naturally, and *really* didn't approve of me shacking up with a chick, Brit passport or not, so I figured it was possible that Ma was just looking to bust us up. So I decided to sit tight for a bit, sort of check out Tisa's moods, be a little skeptical, see if I could figure anything out.

So me and Tisa went on living together for a few more weeks. We had this old computer, this big, honkin', shitty thing that I bought on the sidewalk on 2nd Avenue for 40 bucks that made the Commodore 64 look rad. Me and Tisa shared an AOL account. This is kind of embarrassing, but our email address was DecTis@ aol.com. Tisa said she didn't like that address much, thought it sounded too much like "Dicktease." I think she just didn't like to see our names that close.

Well, Tisa used to go online at night, check the *Back Stage* listings and email her mum, and about a month after Ma told me about what she saw, I found out that she was logging on as a guest, with her own separate screen name: NYCityKitty@ aol.com. If you ask me, *that* sounds a lot more like Dicktease than DecTis does. So she'd go online, and when she was done, she'd replace GUEST with DecTis. And I never noticed; how would I?

But one time, she left GUEST clicked on in the window. She was out at rehearsal, or so she said, for some Off Off-Broadway show over on East 4th Street. I was gonna go online and check my email, so I turn on the computer and see GUEST selected. I click it and, lo and behold, NYCityKitty comes up, and it asks me for my—her—password. Well, I knew ol' Tisa pretty damn good, and it only took me one guess: T-I-S-A. Bang. I'm in. And man, did I find some shit there.

There were about three dozen emails from Leanandhungry@mindspring. com: *Tisa, I can't wait to see you again. Tisa, I hear an English accent on the street, and feel a stirring throughout my body. Tisa, talk dirty in that lovely accent. Tisa, we must move it up to 7:30—I simply cannot wait til 8.*

Dammmmmnnnn.

I just sat there shivering, freezing, sweating; motionless for about an hour. I couldn't speak, couldn't think, couldn't move. She came home, walked in the door, saw my face and she just knew. She started putting on the show of her life, babbling about how they're in a play together, they're getting into character, it's me she loves, *blah blah blah.* Tisa tried that for about a minute, me sitting all quiet, staring hard, then gave it up. I kept asking her who the fuck Leanandhungry was, and she said I didn't know the guy. But I needed a name, and she finally coughed it up: Earl. That made me laugh. *Earl.* An Earl, but not an actual *earl.* Who cheats on a Declan with an *Earl*? Should be the other way around. And I told her Leanandhungry sounded like some new Jenny Craig line of meals, but Tisa said it was *Shakespearean* in that condescending way of hers.

So Earl came into our lives; well, into *my* life. He'd been in my girlfriend's life…and pants…for who knows how long. And still is.

We had one more dreadfully long week together at my place, alternately sniping at and ignoring each other, before she moved in with Earl. Man, I could feel Leanandhungry between us during that week. We were still sleeping in the same bed, but we both clung to the opposite edge, like we were making room for him. He sure took up a lot of room, for a Leanandhungry type.

I'd see Ma on Avenue A and around the Village View, or reading her Maeve Binchy books in Cooper Square before work, and she'd say to me, "Did ya kick the wee tramp out yet?" and I'd tell her we were working shit out. Soon after that, Ma wouldn't even bother speaking to me; she'd just clench her teeth, turn her face away and walk right past me. So my gal was—is—banging some bastard named Earl, and my mom wasn't—isn't—talking to me.

Had a good talk with Gabby about it; we went to Milano's down on Houston, loosened ourselves up with a few happy hour Guinness, and the floodgates just opened. Not tears, mind you. Just words. Man, I told him everything, and Gabby was great, totally out of character. Told me to get the bitch out of my life, stay off women for a while, dedicate myself to rugby, get in shape, hang out with the boys, because the boys don't dick you over. "Rugby's all about support," I remember him saying, scoffing at the turbo-Irish shamrock carved into the head of his Guinness as "Ring of Fire" came out of the juke box. "Use yuh boys." We came out at about midnight, sloppy, stumbling into the darkness. I felt lighter.

So I'm not exactly sure how I ended up walking out of Moishe's Diamonds on 47th and Broadway the next day, down my life savings and up a shot of whiskey from a proprietor with Hassidic curls, an engagement ring bulging like a third testicle in my jeans pocket. A Hail Mary pass to show her how serious I was about us—about DecTis, I guess.

Me and Tisa were hanging in the playground at the Village View, her on the purple concrete whale, me on my knee. And she laughed at me. Not like, laughing in my face, but laughing at the absurdity of me proposing after all the shit that happened. Either way, you don't laugh at a man that's on his goddamn knee in front of you with a diamond ring. You just don't.

The next day, Tisa moved her stuff out.

Never told a soul about the proposal. Except Moishe, that is. He was cool—gave me my money back, minus $200 for what turned out to be a 48-hour rental of the ring. "You pick them more careful, my friend. You find good woman someday," he said. Moishe threw in another shot of the dusty bottle of Laphroaig he kept under the counter for celebrations and emergencies, and wished me well.

Fucking Tisa. We need to meet up. If nothing else, my anxiety level would go down a bit upon finding out what happened that strange night of the memory loss. Then again, my anxiety could go through the roof, depending on the news. Either way, I think I could deal with seeing her for an hour, have a few drinks and get the fuck out of there with my dignity and get on with my life. I think. At this point, I'd rather fail than not do it. But it's on her to call.

I'm not one for premonitions, but I know she's pregnant. I try to picture our kid. Do we raise the fucker together? Do I pick him up on Sundays and take him to the latest Disney movie, bring him toys and Irish wool sweaters from Ma? Was I man enough to spend my dough on toys instead of beer? Would Ma even acknowledge the little bastard?

I lean back to watch basketball. There's a player for N.C. State named Sir Vincent something or other. That's his name, I heard the announcer say it, Sir Vincent Hayes, I think, and then I saw it, *I fucking saw it,* on the screen. Sir Vincent. His given name. Who would name a kid Sir Vincent? The audacity! I love it. I wonder what his siblings are called. White people's names suck. Tisa and me's kid is going to be Sir Vincent. Sir Vincent skies for a board over some typically doofy white guy from Duke. Sir Vincent converts the alley-oop. N.C. State is *trouncing* Duke. The crowd goes wild! This is so much more enjoyable than anything Tisa-related.

The speakers are cranking "Talkin' Baseball," that cornball homage to our national pastime. I close my eyes and appreciate the silliness of the song: *Willie, Mickey and the Duke.* My brain is moving fast, just flying about. It's soon filled by another tune that only I can hear, one which tickles my nerve endings with a far superior touch. Seems that all these alley-oopin' Sir Vincents and doofy white guys from Duke and silly baseball ditties about Mickey and the Duke and bathrooms marked "Sir" have all sort of jumbled together to somehow, in some indecipherable but no less wonderful way, get Stevie Wonder's sublime "Sir Duke" piped straight into my head from the biggest, baddest, bestest Radio Raheem ghetto blaster in the world.

You can feel it all o-o-o-ver, You can feel it all o-o-o-ver, people, sings Stevie, and I do, and it's perfect, it's so much better than Willie, Mickey and the Duke, or trivia about halfbacks from Army, back when Army produced world-class football dudes. I shut my eyes and take it in some more: *Music is a world within itself, With a language we all understand.* Damnnnn. I can see what Stevie sees; I can taste the richness of his tenor and smell the sweet stench that stems from deep inside the cavity of his piano, its hammers blissfully, efficiently striking taut wires. I remind myself, *plead* with myself, to buy a Stevie Wonder disc in the near future, one with "Sir Duke" on it. I open my eyes and Sir Vincent is juking and jiving, duking and diving upcourt. His body is rigged to the tune of "Sir Duke"; he swerves and shimmies to the beat as Stevie wails away. His ball control is *masterful.* I shut my eyes again and lean my head against the stall's back wall. I can feel Sir Vincent dribbling the ball through-out my body, as it strikes the hardwood in Charlotte, North Carolina, goes up the coast, into the TV, through the bar that holds the TV in place, through the ceiling, then the wall behind my head, then my head, then my heart, then every...little... nerve...in my...body, caressed by Stevie, Vincent and Sir Duke.

Say hey.

I can feel it all over.

He's poking me with a mop.

He's a little guy, a Mexican, I think. Black mustache, black t-shirt that says BACK PAGE over the pocket. He's only slightly taller than me sitting on the can. And he's poking me with a mop. How did he get in here? This stall could use a dead bolt.

"Amigo," he says. "Get up. Stand up."

The Marley reference is unintentional. He's working, not playing. And stand-ing...sitting...in the way of his work is me. I look at him and decide the little fella's got a fair point, that I should be getting up, standing up. My legs, however, don't share my enthusiasm for his suggestion.

"Amigo!" he implores. "Get up. Get up!"

Yeah, I gotta get up. Don't give up the fight. It's sinking in. He's got the Back Page shirt on. I'm in the fucking Back Page can. Party's over. I got it.

I nod a weary nod to let him know that I plan to cooperate, and he extends his mop handle like an olive branch. I grab on and attempt to pull myself up, and my ass, stuck on the toilet seat for...hours? days?...gives up its adhesion reluctantly. I'm erect for a split second before falling forward, straight onto the butt end of the man's mop, as it catches me smack in the solar plexus. I'm momentarily impaled on the mop, wind knocked out of me, throat screeching for lubrication, until the man pushes me back onto the toilet with the mop.

"Amigo," he says. "You drink too much!"

Recognizing a good plea bargain when I see one, I nod and slowly rise to my feet. I'm wiser this time, shaking a little fuel into my somnambulant lower regions. I look at my watch; it's nearly 10. *Fuck.*

"Too much," I whisper, and follow him out of the bathroom. He's got "All the Brews That's Fit to Drink" on the back of his Back Page t-shirt. The grammatical liberty appalls me, and I know I'm back on Earth.

Michael J. Malone

The Cooper Diner's no Bendix, but it's OK. To be honest, if the Cooper were on 10th, and the Bendix just a block-and-a-half away from my place, I'd probably never go to Cooper. There's nothing that stands out about it—no pierogies, no Thai influences, no all-you-can-drink brunches—except that it's close. The food's decent. The coffee's decent, the standard-issue Eastern European waitresses are decent. It's all…decent.

Me and Haley have a brunch date again, and again, I feel like hell. She's being over-the-top nice because she thinks I'm going to break up with her. Actually, I don't know if it would even qualify as a breakup, as I don't know for sure that we're officially going steady. But I've met her folks and we're, ya know, intimate, so I figure it's something. And no, I don't want to break up with Haley, though I don't know if it's a bad thing for her to think I might. Haley feels terrible to have missed me on our Tile Bar-and-a-movie date last night, especially after canceling on me when I was going to make my special Northern Irish lasagna.

Tile Bar's been there on 1st Avenue for as long as I've been old enough to notice bars, and it's a good little joint. The real name is WCOU, like a radio station, but everyone calls it Tile Bar, because there's no sign out front, and no indication of a name anywhere, and nothing distinctive about the place except the black and white tile floor, and that when Tom Waits's "Jockey Full of Bourbon" plays on the juke box, you get the reverb off that tile floor, the flamenco guitar riffs and the funky bongos and of course Waits' junkyard dog growl, and it sounds better than anything. But The Bar Where Tom Waits' "Jockey Full of Bourbon" Sounds Great Bouncing Off the Tile Floor takes too long to say, so people just call it Tile Bar.

I was going to tell Haley to meet me at Tile Bar, but I figured, in case she forgot the address, she'd never be able to find it. So I said to meet me at WCOU. That way, if she had to look it up in the phone book, or call Information, they'd tell her where to go. As soon as I said it, Haley was like, yeah, I been there, no problem. So I left it alone.

Well, the owner also has a place called KCOU over in the West Village—not to mention XCOU uptown, which I've never been to, seeing as it is north of 14th Street and all—all with these radio themes. Living on Charles Street, Haley knows the West Village bars, and KCOU's on Hudson Street. So poor Haley sat there from 8:45 until about 10, trying not to look bored, fighting off advances from hornball suits and lusty lesbians alike, waiting for the likes of me, while I was leaning back on the can, sitting in a haze, watching N.C. State annihilate Duke, and Sir Vincent running the floor like a caffeinated dervish… Uh, I mean, I was sitting in WCOU, throwing bills in the box, playing Tom Waits and Johnny Cash, waiting on my dear Haley and looking forward to the movie.

106

"Please," I say, showing Haley my palms. "No more apologizing. Totally honest mistake, Hale. I should've been more clear. I should've picked a place that didn't have these sister places all over town."

"It's *totally* my fault," she says, looking flustered. Elementary school teachers are big on accountability. I put my hands up again.

"Don't," I say with an understanding smile. "I'm not mad. You buy me brunch, you come and pick me up in a limo for our next date so as to avoid any confusion, wear that slinky black top I dig, and we'll call it even."

She laughs.

"OK," Haley says, flashing her super-white teeth. Exonerated, she rubs her hands and dives into her feta omelet. Man, she's a good girl. I feel terrible about standing her up again, even if she thinks it's her fault, and I feel even more awful about what I did with Tisa that other night, whatever I did with Tisa that other night. Just being there was wrong. I know she's tormenting me, keeping me in the dark. She called the other day, left a message at my place at 11 a.m., telling me "we simply *must* meet up." Like I might not be at work at 11. She *has* my work number. God, please don't let her be pregnant—that kid would be the devil spawn for sure. I'll do volunteer work for the rest of my life, and be nice to Ma too. *Please*.

"Sooo," I start, taking a sip of my coffee. "Whaddya think of Gabby?"

Haley shrugs and makes a face that explains she's buying a few seconds to swallow her mouthful.

"I *like* Gabby."

"You sure?"

"Yeah. Gabby's interesting. He's crude and he's kind of dark, but I think I get him. In a city full of posers, he's authentic. A real New Yorker, accent and attitude and all. I approve."

"I'm not looking for approval."

"I know it's important for guys to have their best friends get along with their...girls they date."

"I wouldn't say he's my best friend."

"Besides Malcolm, he's the only one of your friends I've said more than two words to," says Haley with a shrug.

"Whatever. So...you think he's, ya know...good lookin'?"

Haley does that shrug-pause thing again, only her mouth is empty this time.

"I dunno, sort of," she says, and I feel a burn of jealousy. Gulping my coffee, I'm starting to sweat. "I mean, I could never go out with someone named 'Gabby.'"

"I'm going out with someone named 'Meadow,'" I point out. "That's pretty open-minded of me."

She rolls her eyes and gives me a look that says she's not going to dignify my comment with a rebuttal.

Michael J. Malone

"No more," she says.

"Okay… So Gabby's no Paul Rudd."

Haley chokes on her coffee.

"No," she responds once her throat is clear.

"Would you, ya know, sleep with him?"

Haley's eyes get as big as fried eggs, sunnyside up.

"With who?'

"Gabby."

"What're you talking about, Declan? *Why* would I sleep with Gabby?"

"Just curious," I say weakly. "I'm…he's going through a little…crisis of confidence. He thinks girls dislike him."

"He could probably treat them a little better, if you ask me, and it wouldn't hurt him to learn to speak in full sentences. But you didn't, so I'll keep it to myself."

"So on a scale of 1 to 10—"

"New topic," protests Haley, more bored than annoyed.

"Just trying to figure out your type, I guess," I try.

"My type is you, without the stupid questions," says Haley. She smiles and I feel anxiety bubble out of me like shaken champagne. The French toast at Cooper is every bit as good as Bendix's, and the coffee's great too. The waitress comes over to refill me; I shoot down what's left in the cup to make way for reinforcements.

"So it went well with my folks, huh?" says Haley.

"You tell me."

"What's that supposed to mean?"

"Nothing," I say. "I mean, did they think it went well? That's what matters."

"It's not all that matters. I care what you think too. But since you asked, they thought you were a gentleman."

"A *gentleman?*" I say with a laugh. I'm playing it cool, but I'm pleased to hear this. It may be the first time in my life someone has called me a gentleman.

"Yes, a gentleman," confirms Haley. "*I* thought things went great, for what it's worth."

"It's worth lots," I offer. "Tons. A buttload. Your parents are nice. I'm psyched it worked out."

She smiles a big smile and we both are happy.

"So—," she starts, and I cringe. Haley wants to meet ol' Paula now. I have to tell her.

"Yes?"

"Tell me about the new *Honey Bunny* book. In the *Happy Meadow*."

"*Enchanted Meadow*," I correct. "I haven't really written it yet. Honey Bunny goes around sort of righting the wrongs in the Enchanted Meadow."

"Is it, like, autobiographical?" Haley deadpans.

"Sometimes. Very astute of you to ask."

"So what goes on in the *Enchanted Meadow*?"

"Not a hell of a lot," I start. "As you can guess, things are pretty happy there, crime almost nonexistent, unemployment right around 100%, but no one wants for food or shelter. So Honey Bunny happens upon the animals and plants in the Enchanted Meadow, but realizes there's not much work for him to do. Sorta like a Jedi with no one from the Dark Side fuck—...messing with him, ya know?"

"Mmm."

"So he's gotta sort of refigure his purpose in the universe...or at least in the Enchanted Meadow. It's about...calling audibles."

"Audibles?"

"Like in football," I explain. "You go to the line of scrimmage and you don't like the defense, so you call a different play. You call an audible."

"Got it," says Haley emphatically, like an eager employee on the first day of work. "And how's rugby?"

She's the first girl I've dated that hasn't referred to rugby as soccer, football or lacrosse. Even Tisa, who grew up in a country where they play it.

"I'm still on the mend," I say, knocking on my head, which is healed by now. "Maybe I'll get a few games later in the season."

"Are there audibles in rugby?" she asks.

I laugh.

"No," I say. "Well, come to think of it, it's one big audible. It's football in improv mode, without the helmets. And the huddles. It's like jazz. They pass to you and you run with it until you can't run anymore, so you pass it to the next guy."

"What's so funny?"

"Nothing," I say. "You just...it sounded like something my mother would ask."

"So when do I get to meet your mother?" asks Haley.

I carve off a corner of French toast and dip it in a pool of syrup, then chew as slowly as I can. Nice work, a-hole.

"You really wanna meet ol' Paula?"

"You met my folks."

"Ma's crazy, Hale. I mean, your folks are good in any social situation. You're never...embarrassed by them. Paula? She's a loaded gun. You don't wanna meet Ma."

"Why don't you let me decide that?"

"You can meet my mom if you want. But, I'm telling you, she's crazy."

"I don't care," says Haley. "You're pretty crazy too."

I stick my tongue out and wag my head around like a crazy person. Haley smiles and shakes her head.

"We'll meet my mom out for dinner," I say with a borrowed air of confidence. "Next coupla weeks."

I have to end this Cold War with Ma; if nothing else, at least to prove to myself that I'm not as stubborn as she is. Fuck, as far as family is concerned, we're all each other has, not counting Uncle Joseph in Derry and some asshole absentee dad named James Garrison bumbling around London. Me and Ma live in the same goddamn city, neighborhood, building. This is ridiculous.

I signal the waitress for more coffee. It is silent between Haley and me. We simultaneously offer up awkward half-smiles.

Haley Gets Painted

The hangover is just...jeez, the word eludes me. I'm too hung over to think of the right adjective. The hangover is...insurmountable...insufferable...inscrutable? Well, it's certainly proving to be indescribable. The alliteration actually hurts my head.

Lying in bed, I'm afraid to move. It's noon and this is the third time I'm trying this. I attempt to piece together the night, which I find myself doing more and more of. Ace Bar with Gabby. Very drunk at Ace Bar with Gabby. I remember starting to not remember much, and remember thinking, man, you oughta go home. Remember what happened at Tisa's place, I told myself, even if you don't remember what happened at Tisa's place.

I roll onto my back, giving my brain and body a moment to adjust to the new settings, and try to think. There was something up with Gabby last night—there's *always* something up with Gabby last night. But something about whether or not he'd read my stupid story at Troika next week. Jesus. I can't remember what we discussed. Gabby'll do it? I don't remember. I have no fucking idea. What the hell happened? That's it—no more rugby, no more booze. I'm going to need this brain when I grow up.

I look around my bedroom for clues. Jeans and shoes—both Skechers, right and left, a good sign—on the floor. No vomit anywhere. Good. Half-eaten plate of fries alongside a coagulated pool of ketchup, cigarette butt sticking out of the mess like a flagpole. Since when do I smoke? Not so good...though not exactly felonious. Maybe those fries soaked up some of the alcohol and have actually prevented me from feeling more miserable. No, I'm pretty rock-bottom. The thought of my brain—veiny, gory, gray matter-y—swimming in alcohol has made me queasy. I involuntarily look at the foul ketchup and have to be sick.

Jumping to my feet with a swiftness that pounds my boozy, bloody brain like a mallet, I stop for a second to stop the throbbing, and feel the bile ascend in my throat. In a few seconds I'm in the bathroom.

Sick.

It's a tough spot to be in. The hunger is gnawing away at my stomach—the apparent fries at some unknown hour were presumably not enough—but I'm too nauseous to eat. I figure, take a walk over to Broadway, get a little air and duck into Duane Reade, buy a few different types of painkillers, and walk back to Teresa's Diner—another winning Lower East Side diner, its strength being Eastern European food like blintzes and pierogies, and a bit of space between the tables—on 1st Avenue. By the time I make the round-trip, hopefully I'll be able to eat; if not pierogies, at least a bagel—a bit of butter, if the gods are smiling upon me today—and some coffee. It's a plan.

In the shadow of Cooper Union, taking baby steps, I pass the triangular parkspace of Cooper Square, curious to see if Ma's there, buried in a book, though I generally only see her on weekdays. New York's got this art exhibit thing across the city for the whole summer called Cow Parade, where all these artists have been commissioned to paint life-size cow statues in whatever fashion they want. The things are all over—Times Square, the West Village, Grand Central, Cooper Square—though none, of course, in Alphabet City. This guy in the Cooper Square park is named "Diverse Moo York," and has all kinds of positive messages painted on him: black kids shaking hands with white kids, a guy in a Met hat shaking hands with a guy in a Yankee hat, even the Statue of Liberty curtsying before the Empire State Building.

I cross Astor Place, reach Broadway and enter Duane Reade. Despite its size—it used to be a Modell's and it's *enormous*—it feels like the walls are closing in around me. Nothing's going right; every aisle I choose, every turn I make in this cruel maze, sees me bump into someone. I mumble "excuse me," even though I don't think it's my fault, and we do the excruciating Care to Dance? routine, my head pounding.

I finally reach the "Pain Reliever" section, across from the curiously titled "Ethnic" section, way down, way to the left, probably in the West Village by this point. Duane Reade's choices are vast, and I have no idea what's good. All the aspirin I've ingested, and I still have no clue what works best for my hangovers. I should start a spreadsheet, though that would mean figuring out Excel. I alphabetize the selections before me with surprising clarity, check my wallet—there's a $20 in there, another good sign, and the messiest nest of singles you ever saw—and opt for the first three in alphabetical order: Advil, Aleve and Anacin. I make the mental note to take the Bayer and the Bufferin for a test drive next time.

Two registers are open, and one line feeds into both. The woman on line in front of me looks 40-something and normal, a demographic group that's almost as poorly represented in this neighborhood as little kids. She's white, with straight blonde hair clipped neatly at her shoulder line, and is wearing tan Capri pants and a sleeveless white top. The word "suburban" comes to mind. She eyes my triad of aspirin, and I give her a shrug. She smiles a mirthless smile to no one and looks away.

What the hell happened with Gabby, I'm thinking still. This is important. I mean, if he doesn't, *didn't*, agree to read my short story, then I've got to work something else out. I'd love to just sit in the crowd, treat myself to a Jameson's on the rocks, taking in the laughs of an appreciative literary gathering. Or maybe I'll just blow the damn thing off entirely. Hell, the story got selected. That's good enough.

I remember Gabby going on about Haley again, telling me his "fee" for reading my story. And I didn't know if he was fucking with me. That's the weird thing about Gabby—he's not a bad guy, but he wants you to think he is. So he's prodding me and I got pissed off...yeah, I remember that. *Majorly* pissed off. Threatened to break a pint glass over his head, I think. Ouch. His eyes kind of gleamed when I said that, like he was thinking, give it yer best shot, man, and I'll *still* kick your ass. Why do I hang with this guy? But then Ghetto Run, or maybe it was Flyboy, got between us. Gabby smiled and told me he was messin'. Yeah, it's all coming back to me now. Said he liked the story, despite a few "reductive" parts, something about Bukowski's fingerprints being all over it, and said he'd read it. *That's* why I hang with the guy. Said he just had two requests. Of course, I tensed up when Gabby said this; I'd been there before. Said the title, "The Apathy and the Ecstasy," sounds too Gen-X. Fair enough. And he wanted me to buy us both a shot of Bushmill's for every page he had to read. Gabby made it Bushmill's to bug me, I'm sure; that's the Northern Ireland whiskey, whereas the good Catholic boys in the Republic drink Jameson's. The story runs about a dozen pages. That's when it got fuzzy.

I feel a bit better as I wait on line. It's taking forever, but the night's events are coming back to me, and it all seems good. At least I've lined up my reader for Troika, much as I can recall, and Gabby's hopefully done asking weird questions about my girl. There is only today to worry about, and the aspirins seem to be doing their thing through osmosis.

But then a teen girl with caramel colored skin—not quite 5-foot, an NFL-sized ass swelling the confines of her acid-washed jeans—has popped up from out of nowhere and walked right up to an open register, completely ignoring the five of us on the line.

There's mumbling, but no one is willing to speak up. I give my line-mates looks to see who's on board with a counterattack. The cashier, a Middle Eastern woman with her hair in a bun, eyeglasses chained around her neck and a name tag chock full of vowels, prepares to ring her up.

I flash back to that Express line-transgressing hipster condiment connoisseur on Avenue A. I need to live somewhere where there are no lines at the drug store, like Wyoming. Or where people actually let those who arrived on the line before them go first, like heaven.

Someone's got to take a stand.

"Hey," I say. I try to say it purposefully but it comes out weak and thin, like the horn in a Hyundai that's been cut off by an enormous SUV. It's my first word of the day and it is, understandably, shaky on its feet.

"Hey!" I try again, with more feeling. The transgressor turns around with a look that says she's ready for battle.

"Hey *whahht?*"

"How 'bout waiting on line like the rest of us?"

My line-mates support my salvo with a faint chorus of *mmmm's* and *yeah's*.

"Fock *yooo*," she replies, spinning around, a full-blown Hoochie-Momma Head Shake just for me.

It sparks a physiological maelstrom in my body; bile has risen from stomach to throat, heart is cranking out blood in double-time, most of it to my head, which demands reinforcements for its increased pounding, bowels are finally rejecting last night's French fries/Marlboro mix, adrenaline floods my muscles. I'm a chemistry experiment conducted in combustible conditions.

I lash back at her, forcefully, and immediately wish I could reel it back in.

The word sits between us like a big pile of barf on the tile floor.

Silence.

More silence.

Stares. Glares. Too far.

The one guy on line, in a denim jacket with Les Miserables on the back, the painting of that waifish little boy-girl, a black velvet t-shirt and black and white mottled trousers made to resemble a cow's hide—Jesus, there're cows everywhere in Manhattan these days—lets out a slow, pained whistle.

Clearly, "cunt" was too much.

I've lost the support of everyone on line. I'm a man alone—a vulgar island of lusty, foul-mouthed miscreants. I'm Australia.

"She cut the fucking line!" I howl. "That's bullshit!"

Two of the women on line jump behind the controversial register. The grand experiment—the one-line-feeds-two-registers scheme that requires a level of human decency—is over.

"Why don't you calm yourself down?" suggests the suburban looking woman. "Maybe count to 10."

"Fucking *bullshit*," I say to everyone, to no one, to myself. "She cut the line. It's fucking *wrong*."

I consider tossing the bottles in the air and walking out—the right thing to do, the *only* thing to do—but I desperately need them, and the nearest Duane Reade is...they sure seem like they're on every other damn corner when it's a pub or an ATM you're looking for, but I can't actually think of another nearby.

"This place sucks," is the best I can offer. The offending girl has gotten her change and walks by with a smirk.

"*Pendejo*," she spits.

I don't know what it means, but I pretty much do. I'm simmering, shaking, shivering—too angry to speak. Knowing a convincing defeat when I've been dealt one, I seethe, giving ample ammo to my embryonic ulcer.

I'm finally next up and walk to the register. I drop my clutch of aspirin bottles noisily on the Formica counter.

"That was all your fault," I hiss at the worker. "You never fucking shoulda' helped her."

"So angry," says the woman, whose name I can now read is Saandeepi, in a tone that could almost be described as kindly.

Saandeepi gives me my change and I exit the store, feeling my fellow customers' wrathful eyes like darts in the back of my head as the aspirin bottles make like maracas in my bag.

Devoid of saliva, and not having possessed the forethought to buy a bottle of water, I've got two aspirins—both Advil, if you're scoring at home—stuck in my throat. They're half up, half down: stuck in an esophageal purgatory that does nothing for my headache, only fills my mouth with a putrid taste. Mercifully, Advils are covered with a sugary coating, unlike their other 'A' colleagues. It's a minor break.

I'm walking towards a hot dog vendor on 8th and Broadway, fixing to buy a bottle of water to force the pills down, when I'm struck by the woman walking towards me. She's not beautiful—not even that pretty, really—and neither thin nor fat. A solid 7. But she's wearing a skin-tight tank top, made out of a sheer material more typically found in lingerie. It's pink and essentially transparent, quixotically attempting to sheath a woman with, far as I can tell, nary a speck of modesty. A steady breeze blows down the stretch of 8th Street between Broadway and Astor Place, river to river.

The breeze grabs me, pushes me down 8th Street, westbound in her wake. It's the opposite direction of my home, but, well, this decision appears to be out of my hands.

She traipses across Broadway as the DON'T WALK sign flashes, then goes still, daring my defiance from the other side of the street. With a cat-like quickness that belies my sorry condition, I attempt it—bolting across the wide avenue as taxis blare their horns and whip around me. I've beaten the throw and have successfully stolen Broadway, getting myself into scoring position. She's just a few feet ahead of me, heading west on 8th. I can smell her perfume: flowers, wine, a little baked apple, some musk. My blood is pumping. The aspirins slide down my throat. It's the best I've felt all day.

Michael J. Malone

Broadway to University, 5th Avenue and then on to 6th. With her dark sunglasses and CD Walkman on, she never notices me.

There was a moment of distress between 5th and 6th Avenue when I lost my pink paramour, and had to peer into several stores I passed. Tannery Shoes, negative. Couch Potato Video, no dice. Krispy Kreme's expansive interior took a few moments of scanning, and God, did it flirt with my olfactory region, but to no avail. A gander inside the Korean-owned Lucky Man Deli revealed the object of my desire, my hangover-busting babe, buying Parliament menthols from its grinning proprietor—the little dude gleefully eye level with her chest. Lucky Man, indeed.

At 6th Avenue, she turns downtown and, alas—enters a building half a block south of 8th Street. I stop on the sidewalk and watch a doorman address her, as he makes a visible effort to keep his eyes north of her shoulder line, and thus retain his job. I stand dumbfounded, heart pumping double time, shooting blood to all corners and recesses of my body, alternately unsure what to do and feeling the entire day opening up in front of me like an expanse of highway through a lonely stretch of the American West.

"Declan!"

I whip around.

Huh? Who? Waahh?

"Wassup, babe?" I say, giving Haley a kiss. She looks happy to see me.

"Look at those eyes," she says, shaking her head.

"Yeah, well…"

"You're 30! Time to start taking care of yourself!"

"Right on, Mom," I say with a smile.

"What're you doing over here?"

"Jest…walking around. Enjoying the beautiful day."

I feel a fat drop of rain on my head.

"The wind blew me west," I add.

"Pleasant surprise," Haley says. She's got on a white tank top, short black skirt and black sandals. My x-ray vision sees right through the clothing. She's beautiful. My blood boils. Again.

"What are you doing around here?" I ask.

"I live around here."

"Well, sort of. I wouldn't necessarily call this your *immediate* neighborhood."

"True," says Haley. "Just met a friend for brunch over at TJ's Luncheonette. Corn Flake French toast. Yum."

"And what's your friend's name? Anyone I know?"

"No."

"Name?"

"It's, uh, Paul."

116

A dude. I feel a burn of jealousy. The hangover pulls itself up to its feet again. My throat burns where the Advils were stuck.

"College friend?"

"No."

Pause.

"Co-worker?"

"No...just...a friend."

This can defeat me, or I can crush it. I stomp the hangover into the ground again, actually raising my boot and bringing it back down on the sidewalk.

"Let's go to your place," I say.

"I'm being painted," she says.

I picture Haley's angel-white body naked, except for some red paint. A tiny bit.

"My place," I say.

I hail a cab and open the door. There's a moment of indecision. I look at Haley and she reminds me of the chick in one of those '60s TV shows about the innocent girl in the big city. All she needs is a silly *chapeau* that she can throw skyward. She dutifully climbs in.

"Don't you want to get to know me first?" says Haley as my hands greedily grope.

"I know you fine," I say as I lift off her tank top. She's got some spaghetti strap bra/tank thing on underneath, breasts like children hiding under a sheet.

"My hopes, my dreams, my desires."

"Yeah, baby. All that stuff."

"You often pick up strange girls on 6th Avenue?" she says in a southern tone like out of a Tennessee Williams play.

"You don't seem strange to me."

"OK, you often pick up normal girls on 6th Avenue?"

"Ya ain't that normal either. And not often enough," I respond in the gruff tone that seems suited for the part. I can feel the sultry summer heat pouring into our Mississippi manor house. *Her* Mississippi manor house; I just work the grounds.

"D as in Declan," she says, fingering the stupid half-harp tattoo on my shoulder. I wince.

We descend onto my bed before I can drag down the moment with witless improv. I'd pictured our first time with flowers and wine and soothing music and billowing white curtains in the frame, but this will do. I quickly grab an issue of *Juggs* from under my blanket and throw it under the bed. Haley notices but doesn't seem to care. I sense the presence of an angel and a devil perched on either of my shoulders, the devil hanging over my half-a-tat. The angel reminds me about my

Michael J. Malone

Tisa encounter, and that unprotected sex with Haley is bad for everyone involved. The devil is making greedy grabbing motions and smiling a demented smile that makes me think of Shady Brady.

I climb on top of Haley. The angel falls to his knees and weeps.

Within seconds—no, not that—my reverie is jerked from Mississippi plantation back to New York tenement. Marisol is yelping through my cheap-ass tenement wall.

"*Eh, eh, eh,*" she moans in that clipped fashion I've come to know all too well. "*Eh, eh, eh.*"

And I know what follows. When there's smoke, there's fire, and when Marisol is moaning, Julio's vibrations can't be far behind.

"*Mmmmm,*" he goes, as I feel the rumbling through the wall, into my stomach. "*Mmmmm.*"

"Declan," says Haley.

I wonder if she notices.

"Yeah, babe," I say as I'm about to enter.

"Do you have...condoms?"

"Uh, yeah," I say as I climb off her and shuffle through my top drawer. The angel is on his feet again, giving me two thumbs-up.

We begin again, as Julio and Marisol continue their yelping and moaning. Instead of enjoying me and Haley's own encounter, I'm immersed in theirs. I'm hit with a pang of inadequacy: Nearly 30, I live in this crummy apartment where you can hear your hot-blooded neighbors having sex through the walls. I feel worse for Haley; she goes out with the guy who lives in that crummy apartment. I speak a bit to try to drown out the Latino lovemakers, but all you can really come up with in that situation is dirty talk, and I don't feel up for it. I can do a little southern plantation fieldhand, but I don't do porn star.

Amidst the distraction, it's difficult to perform; I think of Mike Piazza stepping out of the batter's box at Shea Stadium as a plane making for LaGuardia zooms overhead. But the moans and hums soon quiet, I calm down and the sex is OK—good for me, and somewhere between adequate and mediocre for Haley, if I'm reading her correctly. As we lay together afterwards, our bodies finding a natural fit, there's a peaceful quiet in the room.

But that's soon punctuated by Julio and Marisol. You think they're done, and then they just start up again, her with the "*Eh, eh, eh,*" and him with the "*Mmmm, mmmm.*"

Marisol's *ehhhh's* escalate to a crescendo, as they always do, culminating in a harmonious litany of *aaaahhhhh's* that give way to a satisfied silence.

I sense envy from across the bed.

"If Brady's late, we ain't waitin'," growls Gabby. "We ain't missin' part of the Yankee game because fucking Shady Brady's watching fuckin' sockuh. It ain't American."

Gabby ain't waiting. They're his tickets, so who am I to argue?

Shady said he'd meet us at this bar called Stan's right across from the Stadium, because he was watching England play Holland in *footie*. We're standing in Stan's, and I'm feeling just a little jealous. Covered in Yankee memorabilia, Stan's is a dive that fills up with Yankee fans before games. I hate the Yankees—no regrets there—but the Mets have nothing like Stan's, just miles of parking lot around miserable Shea Stadium. In *Queens*, no less—everyone's fourth favorite borough. Don't know what happens here when the Yanks aren't playing; can't imagine anyone would come up to the South Bronx to pay $5 for a beer, even if some savvy real estate agent renamed the neighborhood SoBro.

I order two Bud bottles and hand one to Gabby, who nods his acknowledgement.

"What's the word?" I ask.

"Nothin'," he says, back to the bar, looking into the crowd, away from me. He's wearing battered plaid pants that're cut in a low-slung, Fifties style, and a black pocket t-shirt with the tickets in the front pocket, just begging some Bronx punk to try to steal them.

"Still wanna leave New York?"

"Yeah," says Gabby. "I mean, I ain't moving on the idea or anything. It's just something that I think about more and more."

"How's business?"

"Totally got my hands full," says Gabby. "That's good."

Gabby's time at a dot-com, doing design for a high-end nut distributor called NetNuts.net, went bust. He got a fat severance, collects unemployment and does freelance design now. One client, some dot-com called Urban Fetch that will deliver anything short of drugs and guns to lazy New Yorkers, gave him the Yankee tickets.

"Where the fuck is Brady?"

"Dunno," I say, scanning the opening of the bar.

"How's the head?" he asks gruffly.

"I'm as clever as I was before," I say.

"You gonna be playing again any time soon? Season doesn't last forever."

"Yeah," I say. "Just bein' lazy, I guess."

"You runnin' at all?"

"Nah."

"Surprised you're not getting fat," he says. "If anything, your ass is skinnier."

"Fast metabolism."

Michael J. Malone

"Wish I could say the same," says Gabby, patting a belly that hangs 1 ½ inches over his pants, and slugging on his beer. "Fuckin two-and-a-quartuh."

"Jesus, you fat bastard. Who ya got this weekend?"

"Listen to you," says Gabby. "'Who *you* got' instead of 'who *we* got.' You're still part of this club, Deckie. This is the mob, brother. You don't ever quit the Vipers."

"I know."

"We got the Hoboken Harlots. Out there in Jersey."

"Their field's a dump," I say.

"They're all dumps. And they're all better fields than we got."

"True. You guys...*We* oughta be able to handle 'boken."

"Hope so. They got that Aussie flyhalf who just slaloms past people. And that's all they got. Get a few good smacks on his bony ass early on and their offense goes nowhere."

"Right on."

"So what's up with Haley?" asks Gabby.

"Oh, Haley," I say with a smile.

"That means it's going good, eh?"

"Yeah, it's cool," I say. "I mean, I got no idea where it's heading, but I dig it. She's a good girlfriend."

"*Girlfriend*," repeats Gabby. "Wow. It's been a while now, huh?"

"Yeah, man."

I still get nervous when Gabby and I discuss Haley, but he seems genuinely interested in how we're doing.

"How long?"

"Good question. Since I met her, or since we started dating?"

"Since ya first banged her."

"OK, none of the above. We took it kinda slow at first. Rebounding, ya know?"

Gabby shakes his head. "Heard from the Teaser lately?"

"Nah," I say, swallowing hard. "Still supposed to meet up, but I ain't chasin' her down."

"Miserable bitch. She still acting?"

"Yup. Was out in L.A. for a bit. Did some cheesy movies you never heard of, and some pilot that never aired. Back in New York now."

"Kickin' ass, huh?"

"Oh, yeah. She'll be hosting the Emmys next."

"She married yet?"

"Maybe," I say. "I honestly don't know."

120

Earl. I take a pull on my Bud. I'm trying to nurse it to buy more time for Shady Brady. Gabby's my best friend and all, but I don't know if I want to spend three hours with him alone.

"You call her?"

"Fuck, no. I ain't callin' her. Let her fucking call me."

"Ooo, still sensitive," says Gabby.

"Whatever. I ain't callin'."

"That's cool. So she could be married."

"Yeah. If she blew me off, I figure she's over me and her stupid Declan flashes. That's cool."

Gabby shrugs.

"With her bein' back in, ya know, New York, I am tempted sometimes to sort of pop in there. Like, if I got a few in me."

"Get that shit out of yuh head," says Gabby, whacking me in the forehead with his palm and attracting a bouncer's attention in the process. Man, what would he say if he knew I ended up over there after the Bayonne match? What would he say if he heard Tisa was, I dunno, maybe having my kid? I'd feel the full brunt of his two-and-a-quartuh right on the nose.

"I know, I know."

"Never liked her anyway," says Gabby.

"Me neither," I say. Gabby laughs and we clink bottles. He finishes his with a hungry gulp and burps loudly.

"Unlike Haley," adds Gabby, and I get that miserable feeling in my gut again. "Let's go."

We head out of Stan's and wait to cross at a light with scores of fans, the Stadium looming across the street. There are fathers and young sons wearing the same player's jersey. I picture me and little DecTis out at dreary Shea, in matching Mike Piazza shirts.

As the light turns, Shady Brady comes chugging up the street. He's wearing his England soccer jersey, typically trumpeting his English-ness in this most American of settings.

"Cheers, boys," says Shady with that demonic smile. "Sorry I'm late."

"How did England do?" I ask.

"Drew nil-nil. Holland played bloody keep-away the whole bloody match."

Gabby scowls at the mention of anything concerning England or soccer.

"Must've been tough for Holland in their wooden shoes," I quip.

"Sounds like a *cr-r-r-rackin'* match," Gabby says in mock Scottish as the crowd cheers over the ridge of the stadium. We're swept up in a mass of agitated humanity as we near the turnstiles. Gabby leads the way like he's hauling the ball into the Bainbridge Bruisers pack. "A 0-0 game. Can't figure out why that fails to catch on in America. Let's go. It's already unduhway."

"Hang on," says Shady, and Gabby scowls again. "Where can I get a pack of fags?"

The Yankee throng—burly, mustachioed, wearing long denim shorts and Paul O'Neill jerseys—turns and glares at Shady.

"They're fucking called cigarettes," spits Gabby, "and you'll do without."

"So testy," says Shady.

"Can't fucking believe they don't sell beer in the bleachuhs," says Gabby, head in hands, staring at the grime beneath his feet. "I mean, it's like…I dunno, how 'bout a metaphor, Writer Boy?"

"Like…," I start. "Like… I dunno. Without the beer, I'm useless."

"Typical writer," he says.

The gorgeous green of the outfield is spread out before us, Bernie Williams patrolling centerfield like a rich guy strolling across his estate. We city kids gaze at green grassy vistas like country folk gape at cityscapes. It will be like that when the Vipers schlep out to Hoboken for the Harlots match Saturday. But without booze, that novelty only lasts so long.

"I say we go back to Stan's," suggests Gabby. It's the bottom of the first.

"Nah, man," I protest. "We're here. It's 1:15 in the afternoon and the sun is shining. We can go without booze for a few hours."

Gabby and Shady look at me warily.

"Stan's," Gabby reiterates. "They got the game on the tube, and you can heah the fans across the street."

"No," I say. "I get to about two games a year. I agree that it's criminal to ban beer in the bleachers, but I'm not leaving. It's like…Christmas without egg nog?"

"Weak," says Gabby. Shady shakes his head. "Bloody 'ell," he adds.

"I know. I wanna stay."

"Shady?" says Gabby, throwing him the tiebreaking vote. Shady is staring intently at the game.

"It's the same as rounders," he says.

"Huh?"

"Rounders," repeats Shady.

"Whaddya talkin' about?"

"At Eton we played a game called rounders."

"You went to *Eton*?" I ask. I've heard of Eton—it's where sons of MPs and Nobel laureates go.

"Yeah, mate. Got thrown out when I was 15."

"What for?"

"Banged my maths instructor."

"What was his name?" asks Gabby.

"Simon," quips Shady. "Simon Buggerall."

We had a guy on the Vipers, Big Gay Greg, come out about a year ago. We'd bleed for the guy, same as we would any of our teammates. A few times, he's dragged us over to Uncle Charley's after we've had a few at MacLennane's, and we party with the other dudes in Big Gay Greg's life. I guess that's how we justify the gay jokes.

"Anyway," he continues, "we played a game called rounders that's just like baseball. Surely that's where baseball comes from."

The English assume they invented everything. I've heard this line of reasoning from Shady before: The modern pen, the lathe, the deep fryer.

Gabby is uninterested in debating baseball's genesis.

"You wanna stay, or go to Stan's and drink? Stan's only got Budweisuh, though."

"You wanna go?" asks Shady. "We just got here."

"You been listening?" asks Gabby. "They ain't sellin' beer."

"Well, why the fuck not?"

"Cuz some dickhead fell outta the bleachuhs last year and cracked his head open."

"Yanks," says Shady, though I don't know if he's talking about the culture or the baseball team. "Bloody ponce. I'm staying."

"Baseball's boring without booze," says Gabby. "Actually, it's boring with the booze, and excruciating without it."

The crowd erupts when Jeter rips a double off the fence in right center. Our bleacher mates express praise for the shortstop a dozen different ways.

"There's a strangely seductive quality to the sport," counters Shady, prompting Gabby to roll his eyes.

Shady pulls a flask out of his pocket. It's sterling silver, with the letters MMDDWSB engraved on it.

"This may help," he says. "Egg nog?"

"Christmas is saved!" I shout.

"Shit," says Gabby, striking his forehead, then reaching into his knapsack. A black flask emerges seconds later. "Thanks for reminding me. Packed it for the match against the Barbarians. Hope it's alright."

"What have you?" asks Shady. Bernie Williams has lofted one to right, causing Shady to momentarily forget about whiskey and leap from his seat in anticipation of a souvenir. We watch the ball drop into the rightfielder's glove, 20 feet shy of the warning track. It's the third out, and the Red Sox shuffle off the field.

"Oban," says Gabby. "Scotch whisky."

"Nice," says Brady. "What year?"

"Dunno. Older than you. Whaddya you got?"

"Black Bush."

"Prolly DeNiro's fave," I joke, but no one laughs. Haley might've liked that one. We can do dirty jokes now that we're...intimate.

"Damn donkey whiskey," says Gabby.

"You know," starts Shady. "Scotch whiskey is spelled W-H-I-S-K-Y, and whiskey from anywhere else has an E in the spelling."

"And the English invented it," I say. "Seriously...that true?"

"Right as rain, mate," he says. "Sound as a pound."

"That what they taught you at Eton?" asks Gabby.

"Yup. Ten thousand quid a year to learn such pearls of wisdom. No, actually my dah taught me that. He's Scots."

They reach in front of me and clink flasks together. I hang out with the class of Skid Row.

Shady offers me a pull, and I take a swig of the warm, burning whiskey. Through a scrunched-up face, I mumble, "smooth," as all guys are required to do after a sip of single malt.

"What's with the letters?" Gabby asks, nodding towards the engraving on the flask. "Roman numerals?"

"Initials," says Brady. "Mine. You know Camilla Parker Bowles?"

"Know the name," I say, trying to figure out why.

"Prince Charles' bird. The horsey face and the boxy arse?"

Gabby and I nod.

"I went to Oxford with her son Thomas...at least til he got thrown out for getting caught with hashish. I was in his wedding party. He bought us all flasks."

"Nice gift," I say.

"What's with the letters?" says Gabby.

"Malcolm Michael Dundee David Weir Simon Brady."

"Whatzat, the whole fucking wedding party?"

"Those're my given names," says Brady, slugging the Black Bush.

"Is there a hyphen or two in there?" I ask.

"Nah, man. Not so lucky...So how's your bird, anyway?"

"Haley's alright, man. Thanks."

"Nice girl, that one."

"Yeah, she is," I say. Shady Brady's right. Haley *is* a nice girl. Beautiful, too. I take another sip and look out onto the field. I'm exactly where I want to be. "Thanks for hookin' us up, man."

"No worries. Thank my missus."

"Here's to Lady Brady," I say, raising the flask.

"When you going to get your lazy arse out to training?" Shady asks.

"Soon, man. Just been busy."

Chuck Knoblauch has thrown one past first base into the seats, allowing the runner to take second. I wonder if there are knob locks in the bathrooms here in the Stadium. The crowd groans; we drink our warm whiskey in the hot sun.

Haley's New Friend

"Ever been to Jazz Fest?" I say to Haley.

We're sitting on the floor of her living room, leaning against her Ethan Allen couch, reading the Sunday *Times*, which is spread all over the floor. I've just finished a story about the festival, which is in New Orleans. It's food, booze and music—and not just jazz either, as I've just learned.

"The New Orleans one?" she asks.

"Mmmm."

"Naahh," she says. "I mean, I love jazz, but I don't know if I could deal with a few straight days of it. It would probably make me sleepy. I'm not that into jazz."

"It's not all jazz," I say. "There's lots of mainstream acts—Van Morrison, Dave Matthews. It sounds like a blast, actually."

"I wouldn't have pegged you for the Dave Matthews type. You're more like, Ramones and Replacements and Shawn MacGowan."

"Shane MacGowan."

"Oh, right."

"I actually can't stand Dave Matthews," I say. "Just making the point that it's not all jazz. And you walk around and try all these crazy foods, po' boys and beignets, hear lots of music and everyone gets loopy on Hurricanes. And then you go out that night in freakin' N'awlins."

I hope I pronounced "beignet" correctly. Rhymes with "Ben Gay"...right?

"Mmm, doesn't sound bad," Haley says. "Have you ever been to New Orleans?"

"Sorta."

"What do you mean, sorta?"

"Kind of a long story."

"It's always a long story with you, isn't it?" Haley says with a laugh.

"I s'pose. The Village Vipers went down there for a Mardi Gras tournament. Some of us got in trouble and got escorted out of the city. That was after a few nights in jail. I think it was a few nights—they had us in this underground cell that was like a dungeon, and I totally lost track of time."

"What did you do?" asks Haley sheepishly.

"Sat there and waited to get out," I say. "Sang a bit, carved up the wall with a screw I found on the floor. Tried to train a mouse. Not much else I could do."

"No, I mean, to end up in the dungeon."

"They said I assaulted a cop."

"Did you?"

"Depends who you ask. I call it self-defense. Either way, it was stupid stuff. I was a kid."

"How long ago was it?"

"Coupla years."

"Mmm," says Haley, taking it in...taking *me* in.

"Let's go to Jazz Fest," I say.

I'd been thinking we might be ready for a weekend away, but was thinking more along the lines of a one-nighter out in Montauk or something. Jazz Fest just kind of slipped out.

"When is it?"

"In the spring. And if we wanna go for next year, the article says we gotta hurry. Stuff gets booked fast."

"Next year?" says Haley. "As in, 365 days from now?"

"Give or take a few, yes. Let's go to New Orleans."

I figured I can save the money by then.

"NOLA!" I say. "The Big Easy!"

"Mmmm."

"As in, mmmm, yes?"

"I don't know, Declan," she says, staring at the paper. "It's a long time off."

"So it's a long time, as in, you might have something going on then, or a long time like for you and me to still be going out?"

"I don't know. Both."

She puts down the Arts & Leisure section and picks up Business. Maybe she's looking to see if her dad is mentioned.

"Whoa," I recoil. "You...don't...think...we'll still be going at it in a year?"

"Going at it? You make it sound like a couple of monkeys copulating."

"OK. You don't know if we'll still be *dating* in a year?"

"I don't know. Nobody knows. Maybe. Hopefully!"

"But you're not confident about it?" I ask. She stops reading the Business section and looks at me.

"You don't *date* for a year," she says. "It's got to, ya know, progress."

"And you're not confident it will?"

"I don't know. Are you?" Haley asks.

"Well, if I'm talking about going to Jazz Fest with you, yes, I'm relatively confident we'll be going strong in a year."

A pair of birds sings a cheery tune outside her window. Where I live, it's the listless bleat of pigeons.

"But not confident enough to introduce me to your mother."

Silence.

"Is that what this is about?"

"No, not really," says Haley. "I'm just saying, who knows where we'll be in a year? It's not like we talk about it or anything. I have no idea where we'll be in a year."

"But it's reasonable to expect that we'll be together. I mean, I'm very into you, and I'm not seeing anyone else, and I don't really have the urge to, either. Not to make too big a deal about it, but that's kinda big for me. You're...special."

Haley looks back down at the paper.

"I'm glad," she mumbles.

"How 'bout you? What's your take?"

"I don't know," she says, looking up at me and shrugging. "Dunno."

"You're not committed to this, are you?"

I can hear our hearts beat. Separately.

My stomach slowly leaks into my intestines. I assumed that deciding whether or not there was a future between us was pretty much up to me. *I'm* the one coming out of a relationship, even if it's been almost two years. *I'm* the one who's supposed to take it slow. I'd been pretty good—haven't cheated or anything, or least not that I really, truly know of. And if I did, it certainly wasn't under ordinary circumstances. Why wouldn't Haley see us together in a year?

"I am, I think," starts Haley. "I'm just not sure *how* committed...at this point. Right now."

"Are you happy?"

"Yes. I mean, most of the time."

She picks up the Book Review and taps it on the floor like a news anchor. I feel like ripping the fucking thing out of her hands.

"When are you not into it?"

"I don't know, now and then."

"Anything I do that gets in the way of, ya' know, us?"

"Not really," she says. "I mean, you're not all there sometimes, but part of me likes that about you. And the thing with your mother sort of bugs me, but it's not that big a deal."

"What thing with my mother?"

"Like, me never meeting her. Like, you actively working to keep us from meeting."

I have to patch this fucking thing up with ol' Paula. This is ridiculous.

"So, if you meet my mother, we're cleared to go to Jazz Fest next year?"

"You're missing the point."

"Well, do you wanna, ya know, talk about anything?" I ask.

"No."

Can't say *I'm* not keeping the lines of communication open. We sit there and not talk, pretending to read our respective parts of the paper—me with the Sports and the cursed Travel section, Haley now onto the Styles section. I read the same opening paragraph about why the Mets will never win anything with Piazza behind the plate, but none of it is sinking in. This goes on for about 10 minutes. I timed it.

It is Haley who breaks the silence.

"Declan, I have to tell you something."

This can't be good. Suddenly, I long for that awkward silence we had seconds before. At least there was hope then. Whatever it is she's going to say, I'm losing Haley. Sometimes a guy just knows. Even a thick-headed motherfucker. We won't attend Jazz Fest next year, or ever. No Bendix. No Leshko's. No *Cider House Rules*. I stare at her hard, try to see through her.

"I've ...sort of...ya know, met someone."

Gulp. Breathe.

Choke.

"A guy," I say with a calmness that belies my frenetically racing brain and roiling stomach. I reflexively think of Gabby.

"Yes."

"That you...like."

"Well, yes."

"And you're seeing him."

"Uh..."

"...Sort of."

I want to cry. I can't speak, afraid my voice will not just crack, but *break into bits*—a pint glass slipping from your hand outside the bar and smashing into the sidewalk. I can't believe a girl other than Tisa has been able to make me feel this terrible.

I take three long, slow breaths to keep from passing out. I want to use her bathroom, but decide to wait until I get outside and can hit some diner. I think of this fucker's hands on her and it makes me ill. I picture him and he looks like an actor. Handsome, in a way even a guy can appreciate. Dark hair, classic features. *Actorly.* Nice manners and good speaking voice. I wonder if Haley's met his mother. His normal, socially acceptable, probably even charming mother.

Red cheeks contrasting her porcelain complexion, Haley too looks like she's going to cry as she yanks at the ends of her pony tail to tighten the elastic band. I desperately want her to cry—that would validate what we had. Not because I want to see her in pain, but because it would show me that our little relationship warranted tears when it ended; there would be comfort, however small, however perverse, in that.

But none are forthcoming. And when she spoke, Haley's voice sounded strong.

"I'm so sorry, Declan. But we never called ourselves boyfriend and girlfriend, ya know? We never said we were…exclusive."

I open my mouth and nothing comes out. I try again. Air.

Third time's a charm.

"But I called you my girlfriend."

"Not to my face."

"*I* was exclusive," I croak. Wasn't I?

She's quiet, like it's the first she's hearing of this.

"Well, you didn't have to be."

"That's fucking bullshit," I say. Sadness is giving way to anger.

"Why the fuck did you introduce me to your parents?"

"There were times when I felt we were, ya know, on course," she says. "To be a couple, to be more than just *dating*. And it seemed right to take the next step. But other times—"

She lets that hang in the air. It sits on my chest like an elephant.

"On course," I echo. "Who's the fucking guy?"

"It doesn't matter, Declan."

"Actually, it does. If it didn't, I wouldn't fucking ask."

"He's an actor," Haley says quietly. She looks scared.

"Like, he has headshots and hangs out with people who sit around reading *Backstage* all day and tells impressionable girls he's an actor?"

"Don't be mean," she says in a slow, measured way. "He's a working actor."

I have this crazy thought: She's two-timing Tisa with Earl. It cheers me up, however slightly.

"What kind of stuff does he do?"

"What does it matter, really? He's a fucking actor and I'm fucking seeing him!"

That hits me like a hard tackle to my midsection, some broken-nosed Bainbridge Bruiser flanker fucker's construction job-hardened shoulder connecting with my solar plexus and leaving me unable to breathe. I can taste the Randalls Island dirt, see the Empire State Building across the river, looming like a concerned parent.

"Movies? Commercials? The-*ay*-ter?"

For some reason, I feel it's necessary to gather as much info on this asshole as I can, then sort through all the data and let all of its jagged edges rub against my open wounds, and keep on doing it for weeks or months or years, until I've felt it all. Then I'll know the worst of the hurt is over. I want to know his face, his height,

Michael J. Malone

his build, his body of work, his neighborhood, his measurements on the tag of his Levi's. I want to hate the whole of him.

"He's a movie star," Haley mumbles, looking down.

"A movie *star?*"

"Well, yes. Sort of."

"Porn?" I joke, then pray the answer comes back negative.

"Fuck you, Declan."

Thank God.

"All I'm saying is, 'star' is a strong word. I mean, is he a household name?"

"Depends on the house."

It is slowly sinking in. My girlfriend is seeing someone who signs autographs, who turns up in glossy magazines.

"Have I seen him before?"

"He wasn't in *Vision Quest*, if that's what you're wondering."

Now she's just being mean.

"So what's he been in?"

"You really wanna know," says Haley.

"Yes, ma'am."

"Well, Paul's done lots of stuff, some of it sort of big Hollywood stuff."

Paul. He has a name. And it's Paul.

One letter different from my mom. *Paul.*

Same name as Gabby.

"*Clueless,*" she says.

"Well, why the fuck don't you try one on me before you fucking call me clue-less?" I yell. "No need to be nasty."

"That's one of his movies."

"Oh," I say, and swallow an apology. "Never saw it."

"He did *Cider House Rules.*"

"Never saw that one either. You blew off our date, if I remember correctly."

She grimaces.

"*Object of My Affection.*"

"Never saw it."

"*Romeo + Juliet.*"

"Was he...Romeo?"

"No. That was Leonardo. I forget his character's name. I saw it before I knew him. It wasn't a big part though."

"I thought you said he was a star."

Haley shoots me a look.

"And how long's it been going on with *Paaaul?*"

132

"I don't know, it's sort of hard to measure it. I mean, I met him and I ran into him again and we went out for coffee and it was not really a date and I ran into him again. Then we made a date."

"And when was this first 'date'?"

"About a month ago," says Haley.

"How many dates, exactly?"

"Like, three. Three and a half."

"And there's enough there to break up with me?"

"I don't know," says Haley, as she puts the Sunday *Times* back together by section. "I didn't say anything about breaking up. It just seemed wrong to plan for next year."

"So if it's between me and *Paaaul*, then our handsome actor—our movie star—friend gets the nod."

Jeez, I think I know the answer to that one. The dashing thesp prince, or the associate editor at the other wine magazine who writes bunny books and blows off dates when a pretty girl has turned his head or said head is filled with booze or dope. Haley still hasn't cried, and I feel I need her to before I can leave. And once I stop playing Detective Sipowicz, I can bawl myself. Til then...

"I don't know," says Haley once again. "I don't really want to decide."

"It's all on you, Haley. Nice spot to be in."

"It doesn't feel nice. It feels...kind of...icky, to be honest with you."

We're silent for a moment, looking at each other, then looking away.

"Who was I kidding," I say with a pathetic croak. "A beautiful, classy West Village girl. And me."

She looks at me with big, sad eyes.

"Don't do that."

"So you're thinkin' maybe me and you still can, ya know, *see each other*, until you and *Paaaul* figure out what ya got."

Haley is silent. I was hoping she'd say yes and then I'd shoot her down, call her a bitch—the stronger terminology is reserved for Hoochie-Momma line cutters and Tisa, who I just might be calling today—make her cry and then be free to leave. Now she's undoing the *Times*, section by section. She's somehow ended up with my Travel section. Maybe she's rethinking Jazz Fest. Maybe she's thinking of going with *Paaaul*. I bet he'd pay for everything—the flight, the hotel, the beignets.

"I think you should go," says Haley with a crack in her voice. She's doing all the things that accompany tears—looking away, rubbing her eyes, sniffing, blinking—but I don't see tears. "I apologize for not handling this better."

It's finally starting to sink in, and I feel empty. It's worse than empty—empty sounds like you feel nothing inside, and there's an unmistakable heavy, jagged slab of granite in my gut. And the granite is sitting upon these super-long tendrils inside me that extend from my tear ducts, down my throat, into my gut, under the granite block. I'm not sure if that jives anatomically—I'll have to ask Dr. Demento—but that's how I feel. Every time I move, I can feel the tug on the tendrils, sending a wave up my body to my tear ducts. They can't take much more. I try to sit still but I'm shaking. If I look at Haley, it's all over. I look down at the paper. Piazza should move to first base. Strawberry is finding his groove again in the Bronx. I stare at the door and don't take my eyes off it until it's behind me.

The Haley chapter of my life is over. I think of the times when I felt that hint of a good, happy feeling. I think of how much I loved coming to this urban paradise west of Broadway. It was nice to forget about Tisa for a while. But now that's over.

"Hey-yah, you've reached Tisa's cell. Please leave a message, and I'll ring you as soon as I can. Ta!"

I hung up the phone with equal parts relief and disappointment.

Sometimes you stand on Avenue B for an hour, and end up following some waste-case chick with the pockmarks and hoarse voice towards C just to score. Sometimes you do a single diagonal walk through Tompkins Square, from the southwest corner at 7th and A to the northeast corner at 10th and B, and you've got a bag in your pocket by the time your feet hit B.

Like today. My editor Sally has been way cool about extending my *Enchanted Meadow* deadline, but she needs some Honey Bunny real quick, and I gotta hop to it. No big-people novels. No short stories. No haiku, no sonnets and no quadrameters, either. I have to produce a manuscript or my bunny money is done. So I scored a dime of this new shit Chicken Run that's going around. I bought it on Found Money-cred-it—meaning, next time I stumble on found money, which hopefully won't be long, I have to spend it on something other than dope, or put it in the bank. That's my rule.

It was weird—I thought I saw Haley like three times during my park walk, and Tisa twice. Not like either of them would ever be caught dead east of Avenue A.

I'm sitting in my apartment, doing this ridiculous little pre-writing drill that I do. It consists of doing every possible preparatory thing imaginable: cleaning my room, getting a beer, laying out a notebook and pen, putting Shane Mac-Gowan on my stereo for inspiration, switching Shane for Tom Waits after a few songs, searching for just the right mood, and back to Shane, thinking about calling ol' Paula, not doing it, thinking about calling Tisa, doing it, before finally sitting down in front of my computer to write. I guess I still have anxiety about the writing procedure—scared to death that one day I'll sit down and start to write, and nothing will come out. Then I'll have to stop calling myself a writer and get a job digging graves, or selling derivatives, or something like that. So I tend to put the actual writing off for as long as possible.

Every writer has some sort of elixir to deal with this anxiety; for me, a little East-of-A fairy dust always seems to grease the skids and get the words moving. I cut the bag into a few lines and lay them out on my desk. Of course, dope has an anxiety all its own—shorting out your system after doing a big, fat hit, and being locked in this apartment with no one to check in on you, since you've severed ties to most of the people that were close to you. But that's just something you kind of, sort of, eventually get used to. Occupational hazard, I guess. Safer than being a deep-sea fisherman.

The line burns, and it's a pretty intense pain. It feels like it's going to burn a hole right through my nose, and then the pain caravans north to the brain. A sharp shake of the head seems to disperse the hurt a bit, then it turns into a good ache, then just a good kind of...everything. The tickle in the stomach.... The giddy tingling in the shoulders, the fingers, the ass, the thighs, the stomach, the kidneys, the pancreas. The waking slumber that soothes the soul. My eyes are closed and I put my forehead upon my keyboard for...a moment or two. *The pain gonna make everything alright, alriiiii-hiiiight.*

I lift my head up moments later, which takes a fair bit of effort, and stare at the screen, which is full of the letter "h." Must be hundreds of 'em, all perfectly identical. H for happy, h for horny, h for hungry, h for Honey Bunny. H for dope. God, this stuff makes me productive—I started writing without even knowing it.

I drag the cursor over all the h's except for the first. That one I can keep. The rest I throw back.

Shane is singing about Nancy Whiskey casting her spell on him.

As I went down through Glasgow City, just to see what I might spy.

What should I see but Nancy Whiskey. A playful twinkle in her eye.

I focus my eyes on my monitor. H. The writing process has begun. The words bounce out like a bunny across a meadow.

...oney Bunny sat in the cool grassss as the sun came up, wondering what this summer day held for him. It hsd been one week since Honey Bummy's mother had died, and the hurt had not gone away at all, not even a little. Honey Bunny knew that Mommy Bunny was old and sick, and Mommy Bunnies don't live forever. Nothing does! But it hurt his heart so bad when he woke up in their home, Warren #43, Serenity Knoll, and Mommy Bunny did not. Honey Bunny gently prodded his mommy, sinking his paw into the sofft fur on her side. But Mommy Bunny did not open her eyets.

Hunney Bunny knew he could not stay in Serenity Noll anymore. Sure, he'd spent his entire life here, scampering around the meadow on his big, furry feet with the other rabbits as a baby bunmy, running away from mean old Sigmund the Snake, playing hide-and-seek with Jane Doe, Blue Jay, and the other residents of Serenity Knoll. Except for a few visits to see his cousins in Pleasant Plain, he'd never been outside Srenity Knoll. But it held too many memories of Mommy Bunny.

So Honey Bunny burieds her in their warren, along with a picture of himn with his hair combed neatly and his floppy ears pinned flat. He wrapped up his belonging in a tattered piece of red cloth that he tied around his bunny tummy, and set out for the Enchanted Meadows..

It being early, HoneyBunny thought he could sneak out withouyt saying good-by to all his friends. He'd already said a painful good-buy to his mother, and that was enough good-byes for one bunny in one day!

Hopping about, Honey Bunny ran into Marvin Mouse, who usually went to sleep when the sun rose. Marfin came to Serenity Knoll from a faraway place called London many years back on an ocean liner. Marvin had a funny way of talking, always drank tea and ate cheeze, an used funny words like "Cheerio."

"Hellooooo, Honey Bunny," said Marvin in his funnmy voice. He was wearing a flannel niteshirt and a flannel nitecap that had a funzzy pompon hanging from it. "What do you have in that tattered piece of red cloth? Perhaps a piece of cheeze for your old friend Marvin Mouse?"

"No, Marvin Mouse, I'm afraid not,"said Honey Bunny. "This tattered piece of cloth holds my belongings: my Babar book, my bloo marble, my pillow and a photograph of Mommy Bunny. I'm afraid I amleaving Serenity Knoll."

"Andwhere do you reckon you'll go, Honey Bunny?"

"I'm off to the Enchanted Meadow."

"I've heard its' lovely," replied Marvin. "Honey Bunny, you were the first one to greet me upon my arrival at Serenity Knoll. I would attemp to talk you into stayingh, but it appears your mund is made up. I will miss you trenendously and promise to think of you often."

"Thank you, Marvin," Honey Bunny said sadly.

He continued walking.

"Oh, Honey Bunny," said Marvin, and Honey Bunny turned around to face his old friend, his floppoy ears perking up. "Mommy Bunny was a sweet and kind bunny. My own motther is back in London, and Mommy Bunny always felt like a mother to me."

"Thank you, Marvin," said Honey Bunny, a tear rolling down his fuzzy bunny cheek. "She was very kind."

"Cheerio, old friend."

"Good-bye, Marvin."

As Honey Bunny hop-hop-hopped to the edge of Serenaty Knoll, he took one final look back. He saw the blue jays flying about, deer running and jumping and other bunnys playing in the high grass as Serenity Knoll came to life. They'd been his friends for his entire life, even mean old Sigmund the Snake. But it was time to move on.

Surely there would be lots more nice freinds to meet in the Enchanted Meadow.

Hop-hop-hop, he went.

I push myself back from the computer and exhale, as if I've been holding my breath the entire session, afraid that breathing out would interrupt the flow. God, weeks of anxiety over, what, 20 minutes of work. *Enchanted Meadow* is half-done. Sally will be so psyched to get the first part in her hands, and that'll buy me another week or so. Easy money. I grab a grubby sock from the floor and wipe the sweat from my forehead and neck.

Clicking on the printer icon, I request two copies: one for Sally and one for Haley, both of whom I'd promised one to. Paul does vapid movies for mindless teens. Declan writes thought-provoking books for impressionable young minds. As the printer kicks into gear, I put my shoes on. Got a fucking great head on right now, a burst of energy and a big dopey smile on my face, the first in weeks. I'd love to extend it: sit in a beer, drink a bar or two, put some songs on the juke box, shit the shoot with some pretty ladies, walk along A and, well, just see what the fuck's out there. Or maybe just lay my happy, heavy head down on one of the benches outside, big, fuzzy stars hanging overhead and, well, just mellow out for a bit. Right on. But first...

Michael J. Malone

"Hey-yah, you've reached Tisa's cell. Please leave a message, and I'll ring you as soon as I can. Ta!"

I get to Troika at about five-to-eight. The readings start at 8 and run until 10. I called Gabby to reiterate what we'd discussed before the Bushmill's shots kicked in, and Gabby again agreed to do the reading. Thank freakin' God. I typed up a new cover page, based on Gabby's suggestion—I can't believe I'm taking editorial directions from freakin' Gabby, though I'm not in a position to oppose him—and headed over to his place on St. Mark's and A to drop it off. You have to pick your battles, especially with that Neanderthal. He thought of "Angeles Ashes," which I actually think is kind of brilliant, though I wouldn't ever tell him so. But the story doesn't feature a strong-willed Irish mother; I told him I'd use that title for sure when I write my memoir. Then he suggested "L.A. Fadeaway," which is probably just as good a title as "The Apathy and the Ecstasy" anyway.

A graphic designer who comes up with useable headlines—the dude is downright dangerous.

I hit St. Mark's and got that stupid Replacements song in my head. I arrived at Gabby's place and rang buzzer #3C, Paul McMenamin, and nobody answered. I didn't really give Gabby a time that I'd be stopping by, so I'm not totally surprised that he wasn't home. But it still worried me a bit. I sat on his front steps for about 15 minutes, my back killing me from sleeping on the bench the night before, my anxiety starting to bubble up over the reading. Across the way I saw the tattoo and cappuccino shop in which my work-in-progress ink began; reliving that dreadful day added to my anxiety. I couldn't wait to be sitting in Troika with Gabby, a cocktail in my hand.

Gabby didn't show, so I slid the envelope under the building's front door. He'd likely see it when he got home, or someone else who stumbled upon it would see his name and could just slide it under his door. That's not expecting too much, even in New York. Even if Gabby never got it, I had another copy on me.

To get into Troika, you go up a flight of stairs, past a dusty little theater advertising off-putting productions ("Cannibal Cheerleaders on Crack" graced the little marquee on this particular day), up another flight, and bang a right into the darkness. As I duck in, the sun is just starting to disappear under the concrete skyline to the west. Troika is dark, but not dark enough to hide the pallor in the faces of the boozers and chemically-enhanced hipsters inside.

"Readings going on tonight?" I ask the bartender, who's got an eyebrow ring and a black Sun Records t-shirt.

"Yeah, mate," he says in a cockney accent. "Coupla minutes."

"Great. You make Bloody Mary's?"

"Sure, mate."

I put a forearm on the sticky bar and look around. Gabby's freakin' making me nervous—when is that fucker ever *not* making me nervous? That's his goddamn purpose in life. There are about 20 people scattered about, none whom I know. That's good; I hadn't considered what would happen if someone in attendance actually knew me.

The bartender produces my Bloody, which I'm elated to see is a pint, with a big stalk of celery. Dinner is served. I tip a buck, which earns me a perfunctory "Cheers, mate."

Fuckin' Gabby. I head out to the pay phone, which is at the top of the stairs. I drop a quarter in and dial Gabby's number, 725-5375. For the first time, I realize 5375 spells JERK. No shit. No answer. His message comes on. "Leave a message, if yuh feel yuh must," he spits in his Rockaway accent, as my anxiety nears the boiling point.

I take a seat and start thinking. OK. It's 8:00. Gabby could be running late. They probably have four or so people read. So as long as I'm not first, we should be OK. Even if I am, I'll just speak up and say that I just spoke to Declan Coulter, yes, I'm his agent, and he's running a bit late, can they move Mr. Coulter to the back of the line—back of the *queue*, better yet—thank you very much.

A man in an ancient Johnny Thunders t-shirt, plaid sport jacket and grimy khakis rises at the front of the bar.

"Hello, folks," he begins in a cheery tone suited for Up With People. "I'm Peter Alderson. First off, thanks for comin'. And if you're not here for the readings, well, thanks also for comin'. Seriously, if you're here to talk with your friends, you might wanna finish your drinks and relocate, as we'll be starting our readings in a few minutes, and doin' our thang for the next two hours or so. But, if you wanna stick around, we've got some good stuff tonight, as we do every Sunday. Copies of *The Troika Reader* are available at the bar for a most affordable $10. We'll be underway momentarily. Thank you, and enjoy the readings."

He places a lamp and a pitcher of water on a table near the front of the bar, and we're about to start. *Fucking* Gabby...

People hustle from the bar to their seats, drinks in hand.

I stare at a red poster of a flexed arm holding a steel hammer, the bicep bulging. "Strength" is all it says.

Actually, the bastard's right, for once. I *can* do this. I wrote the damn thing, I should read it. I've been reading since I was, what, five? "The Apathy and the Ecstasy" is a good story. If not warm, the crowd at least seems too indifferent to get nasty. I just need a little support.

On a whim, I run out to the pay phone again and dial Haley's number, 924-6477. I see that 6477 spells MISS. Miss Haley. I miss Miss Haley. I sure missed my chance with Haley. Her phone rings. She'll inspire me. I have no idea what I'll do if she picks up, but each successive ring decreases that likelihood.

"You've reached 924-6477. We're not here to take your call..."

We're? Who the fuck is *we're?* Is she freakin' living with Paul already? Could that fucking be possible? Or has her machine always said that, perhaps a plan to dissuade stalkers for a pretty girl all alone in the city? I don't remember. I just don't know. I hang up. I didn't need that, not now.

The negative thoughts creep back in. I was sitting on Gabby's front step. Staring at Gabby's buzzer: Paul McMenamin, 3C. *Paul.* Jesus Christ. Can't be. Whoa, slow down, Declan. Haley's Paul is an actor...or so she says. I know how completely irrational all this is, but still let it fester in my brain. God, I would do anything to walk back into that bar and see Gabby sitting there, ready to read, not in bed with Haley.

Of course, he's not. An angry looking man with Buddy Holly glasses and a thin moustache is preparing to read. I take my seat.

He clears his throat.

"My name is James Soderbaugh," he says. "First off, thanks for skipping 'The Sopranos' to come out tonight."

Two guys at a table look at each other, shrug and hustle out of the bar.

"This short story is called 'Breaking the Camel's Back.' It has nothing to do with quitting smoking."

There's polite laughter from someone who must be friends—coworkers?—with James Soderbaugh.

"This story appears in an anthology called *Angry America*. It's put out by Sour Apple Press, and they have it in St. Mark's Books, but not *Barnes & Noble*."

Soderbaugh says "Barnes & Noble" in a way that indicates he would *never* shop there, much less let his precious little book be sold there.

"Thanks for listening," he growls, and begins.

Steven Murchison looked at his wife of 24 years, sleeping in the bed next to him. In six months, they'd have been married for a quarter-century. It was a vastly hackneyed adage, he knew, but the time sure had gone by fast. They'd gone through much in those 24 years: his failed attempt at screenwriting before settling into an unsatisfying but solid job in his father's picture frame business, her slow but steady ascent in academia, her brief affair with a faculty colleague at the leafy liberal arts college they lived at a decade before, the 18-year-old son Ethan they'd raised.

On the surface, June 25th looked like any other early summer day. But there was much more to it than was immediately available to the eye; there was an unidentified, unnamed beast lurking beneath the surface of Steven Murchison's psyche.

So Murchison eventually got out of bed, drove to work, got pissed off when an SUV packed with teenagers with a Limp Bizkit sticker on the rear window cut him off and the kids gave him the finger, and then he sort of went crazy or something at his stupid picture frame job. I can't be sure, though, because Soderbaugh lost me after the first few paragraphs. Not because his story sucked—at least something *happened*, unlike most of the stories in these pretentious little salons—but because I was obsessing about Haley and Gabby and, to a lesser degree, this freakin' story I'm supposed to read. What was I thinking dropping it off here in the first place?

After 20 minutes or so, Soderbaugh finished to modest applause, and thanked his audience for their time. Peter then got up to introduce the next reader. I held my breath. I've got to piss. Even if I wanted to read, I couldn't.

"Thank you, James," says Peter. "Certainly a story to make you think. OK, we'll take it in a different direction for our next story."

Shit, "The Apathy and the Ecstasy," or "L.A. Fadeaway," or whatever I called my damn story, is a different direction. Here's a fresh take on taking it in a different direction—I can sprint out of the bar. Or I can sit there and look surprised like everyone else when Declan Coulter proves to be a no-show, and some jokester in the audience breaks the awkward silence with "He moved!" No one knows who I am.

"Ladies and gentlemen," continues Peter, "Phoebe Berlioz reading 'Night Defeats Day.'"

A dour woman of about 40, looking like a woman trying to look French, approaches the reading table. She's wearing a tightly wrapped, flowery sarong, clunky black glasses and a black leotard top that reveals saggy cleavage.

"Sank you," she says. "Zis is a story about lesbians."

A few people snicker, and Phoebe Berlioz begins her story.

A few tables away, I spy a guy about my age by himself, with a tuft of red hair on his chin and a woven rasta hat containing his bulbous dreads. I ease into the seat next to him as he sips a whiskey, causing him to eye me warily.

"Hey," I whisper.

"Yeah?" he replies.

"I need a favor. I'll give ya a hundred bucks."

His eyebrows jerk north. A Benjamin still buys a lot of contraband in Troika. A few people look back at us, giving us the visual *shoosh*.

"What up?"

"Can you read this?" I whisper, handing him my story. "I wrote it, and they're gonna call on me, but I can't read it."

More stares and more *shooshes*, a few of them audible.

"Why the heck not?"

"I... I'm dyslexic."

"You're scared, is what you are."

"I'm *fucking* dyslexic. And you shouldn't even be asking for money to do this."

"You offered me money."

At this point, Phoebe Berlioz delicately places her finger on the page and looks up.

"Nobody considers dyslexia a serious disease."

"Show me the money," he says.

I check my wallet. I've got $34, which I give to him.

"Take this now, I'm good for the rest. *Please.*"

He stares at me and scrunches up his face.

"It's like *Cyrano de Bergerac,*" he says.

"Yeah, whatever."

"I'll do it."

I smile and excitedly hand him my story.

"'L.A. Fadeaway'?" he says.

I snatch the story back from him. I cross out the title and write "The Apathy and the Ecstasy" and hand it back to him.

"Much better," he says.

"It's from a Rogue's March song. Irish band. Plays over at Paddy Reilly's."

"Like...the Pogues?" he asks.

"Exactly."

"Right on. My mom's grandma is from Ireland."

"Cool. So...you'll read it, yes?"

"OK."

"Thank you. I really appreciate it."

We shake hands and I return to my seat. I take a satisfied bite of celery, which prompts more dirty looks.

I slink back to my reader friend and ask him to hand the new title page to Peter the host, which he does.

Phoebe Berlioz continues her story: set in St. Charles, Louisiana, it's a noir-ish thing, and, from what I gather, not half-bad. There's a stolen painting, and a massive flood, and someone who might be a vampire. When she's done, people applaud enthusiastically, and Phoebe Berlioz replies, "Sank you, sank you."

Then Peter rises.

"Thank you, Phoebe," he says. "Certainly a few things to think about with that one. Folks, just a reminder—please try to keep silent while the readings are going on. Be courteous, please."

Of course, everyone looks at me.

"And next up, it's Declan Coulter..."

I jerk upright in my chair and feel my heart rise up in my throat. I can still bolt, and no one will know.

"...reading...'The Apathy and the Ecstasy.'"

The name does sound stupid, Gabby's right. My new friend gives me a solemn nod and rises. He approaches the reading table, sits, cracks his knuckles, clears his throat and takes a sip of his whiskey.

'The Apathy and the Ecstasy,' he starts.

Timing never was my for-tay.

"Fort!" I yell, turning heads everywhere. There's an uncomfortable silence as everyone looks at the man who inexplicably yelled "Fort!"

"It's pronounced 'fort,'" I say sheepishly, prompting Phoebe Berlioz to nod in agreement. My gun-for-hire shrugs indifferently and continues.

Fort, he says reluctantly. *I chuckled to myself as I composed a To-Do list on an index card at work. I'm big on both To-Do lists and index cards; both permit me to believe that there's structure to my life.*

Someone laughs; not a 'that's funny' laugh, but more of an, 'I think that's moderately clever and deserves some sort of utterance' laugh. Anxiety drips out of me. It's the best I've felt in days.

Liza's photo stared back at me, my reader continues, mumbling a bit. *Her brown eyes teased, flirted, beckoned and cajoled. The way they always did.*

"Louder, please," I yell. My reader shoots me a dirty look, and continues, louder.

Such a peculiar stroke of fate, he reads, and I mouth the words along with him, surprising myself that I know them all, like a prayer you learned in CCD, or the lyrics to the first album you owned. They sound pretty good. Of course, there's the self-consciousness, like with hearing your voice on tape. And there are times when my anxiety makes it too difficult to listen, and I have to plug my ears and recite the words to one of the few songs I know all the words to, from the first album I owned—Styx's "Too Much Time on My Hands"—over and over to drown out his voice.

...being assigned to write a short magazine feature, my reader continues, *about an up-and-coming actress that happens to be the woman who stole your heart ...*

"Too much tiiiiime on my hands, tick tick tick tick," I whisper.

Your first love, he reads, *the one who rendered you incapable of love and healthy relationships up to this very day, smiling up at you in her fancy haircut in her fancy studio headshot.*

"Too much tiiiiime on my hands, tick tick tick tick."

You remember loaning her money—never repaid, mind you—to have the shots done. "Do them right this time," you advised, "and you won't have to do them again." There's a press release that lists her various achievements. I noticed that "breaking Tristan Geary's heart" was not listed among the indie movies you've never seen and television pilots that never aired.

"Tickin' away, tickin' away from me..."

Michael J. Malone

Some chick and her boyfriend in the corner are talking; actually, Chatty Patty is talking to him, and he's merely nodding. She's got the nerve to talk not 10 feet from me.

I get up from my chair and, squatting, do a duck-walk over to their table. A quick rap on the table gets their attention, and they stare incredulously at the man squatting next to them. I point to Cyrano at the reading table, and punctuate that with a jerk of the head and a scowl. They get the message and clam up.

My reader continues and, once I started to relax, or at least came as close as Declan Coulter can to relaxing, I actually start enjoying it. Sure, the title's a dud, and there are some clunker lines. But for the most part, the writing's good, the story moves, my reader doesn't stumble too badly, and the audience seems to be into it. I wish Haley...my mother...Tisa...hell, a number of people...were here to witness it.

And so, my story ran, concludes my reader about 15 minutes later.

It was a small article, two up-and-comers to a page, and I told the world what a star Liza Francine—not her real name, of course—was going to be. That's the beauty of the phone interview—she never knew it was me. Unlike me, "Liza" did not have a fancy head-shot of the person on the other end of the line in front of her. With her faux graciousness in her preposterous English accent, she thanked me for my "indulgence," told me to look her up if I ever was in L.A. in that coquettish tone she can flip on at any moment, and we both hung up.

Look her up in L.A.? Who knows? Maybe I will.

There was silence, then applause. A fair bit of it too; more than what James Soderbaugh got and about the same as Phoebe Berlioz. Of course, I was clapping like a lunatic; so was the couple I'd shooshed, who kept looking over at me uneasily. Who needs freakin' Gabby? My reader smiled proudly and bowed like a diva, basking in his borrowed glory, then walked back to our table.

"Great work, man," I say, pumping his hand with near-violent enthusiasm. "What the hell's your name, anyway?"

"Jed. No problem. I actually enjoyed it—it's a neat story. Chick Liza's a bitch, huh?"

"Big-time."

"Wish *I* could write," he says through a lopsided smile.

"Well, maybe we'll keep our partnership going," I reply.

"Keep writing, man. I'll keep reading."

"Let's get you some money," I say, wondering how much I have in my account.

"Wait til they're done, man," says Jed, nodding towards the reading table, where a guy with a pompadour and a soul patch was preparing to share his "exurban parable about chastity."

"Right, right," I say, smiling broadly. "Hey man, can you buy me a drink?"

144

Some people start dreading work on Sunday night. For me, it's Sunday afternoon or, more likely, Sunday morning. It starts within seconds of me waking up. My brain slowly turns on, fights through the cobwebs, and starts to recall the sad state of my life—recently broken up with, living in a miserable dump—and my body fills with dread. Then I think of Haley waking up across town with her handsome actor friend, as he serves her fresh fruit, croissants and Sumatran coffee in his boxers and abs.

Then I think of work.

My job is entirely unsatisfying crap. The pay is shit; if my place wasn't rent stabilized, I don't know what the hell I'd do. I can't seem to leapfrog over this goddamn "associate editor" tag that hangs around my neck like an albatross—sorry about the mixed animal metaphors. If I can make the jump to senior editor at *Cork & Bottle*, I go in at another magazine with that title. More money. More prestige. No more doing assistant crap like photocopying, mailing and dropping off Fed Ex's—business and personal—for dickheads like Ken.

But I'm getting desperate; I'm starting to think I'll try to find a new job without making senior editor, even if it means the dreaded lateral move. Starting at a new place would be totally helpful toward me getting my mind off Haley. You know, the whole clean slate thing. Toward that end, I'm in at 8:00 on this Monday morning, ready to send out five resumes to jobs I've starred in yesterday's *New York Times*.

Buying the Sunday *Times* was a real bummer; it was the first time I bought it since that stupid Jazz Fest article broke me and Haley up. I'm afraid I'll always think of her and her sweet apartment and the ill-advised N'Awlins suggestion every time I see the damn Sunday *Times,* its contents spilling out like an overstuffed sausage. But my need for a new job outweighed this anxiety, and I coughed up the $2.50 for the paper.

I set my large coffee down at my desk, in the cubicle amidst this ridiculous rabbit warren we have here (senior editors get offices). I pry the lid off the java, take a sip and play back my voice mail.

"Declan, it's Sally at Green Mountain. Please call. Thank you."

Speaking of rabbit warrens. Guess she read *Enchanted Meadow.*

By 8:30, I've got four of the five sent out. I've typed the addresses on the envelopes, slapped free work postage on them and slipped them into the mail slot out in the hall, where they plummet five floors to a waiting basket, out of sight of any Avatar higher-ups. I have to get out of this place. There are about three people that make it bearable.

"Morning, Declan," I hear from over my warren wall. It's Becky, our intern. One of the three.

Michael J. Malone

"Morning, Bex."

She pops up at the mouth of my tiny cube and leans against the opening. She's wearing tan Levi's cords, a white tank top and a brown cardigan—total prep, until you get to the black skull on her shirt. It dawns on me that she wasn't even alive when corduroy pants were unironic.

"You're an eager beaver today, girl."

"Mmmm," she coos, closing her eyes. "I love it when you talk dirty, Declan."

I blush, and curse my pallid complexion.

"Sweetie, there's laws against talking dirty to underage girls."

"I'm quite sure there're laws against calling them 'sweetie,' too, though this place seems to have its own rules regarding harassment."

"Sorry, Becky. Seriously—you're in early."

"I'm here every day at this time," she says with a smile. "It's you who's early, smart guy."

She's right, as always.

"Sending out resumes?"

"Yup."

"What kind of jobs?" she asks. Becky's ten years younger than me, but acts like she's older. But never in an irritating way; she's just smarter than me.

"Couple of men's mags, a weekly paper out in Queens, a sex mag."

"You'll never last out in Queens," she says. "Not with all your friends meeting in Manhattan for happy hour. Not with the extra half hour you'll need each morning to get to work. Something to keep in mind. Manhattan natives like you never fare very well off the island."

"I don't really want the job," I say. "I'm just applying for it."

"Which skin mag?"

"Doesn't say. Just says, 'must be comfortable handling adult material.' I can handle adult material. Been doing it since I was 12."

She makes a face that's half amused and half grossed out.

"Someone's testosterone appears to be nearing the brim this morning. Rough weekend?"

"Don't ask."

"Just make sure you're cool with having the skin mag on your resume for the rest of your life," she says.

I'm getting career advice from a 19-year-old. Stranger yet, I'm listening.

"Good point," I say. "We'll see if they even get back to me. The money's good."

"Better than here," says Becky.

"No shit."

"I'd be sorry to see you go, Deckie. You're one of the normal people here."

146

That tells you a little something about Avatar.

"How was your weekend?" I ask. I feel small, looking up to her from my desk as she looms above me like a parent.

"Oh, same old, same old. Went out downtown Friday with the girls."

"Where?"

"East Village, of course. Sorry...Lower East Side. I know how you get about that."

I smile. I still have trouble dealing with the fact that where I live is a destination. "Whereabouts?"

"Some place on St. Marks."

"Which one?"

"Oh, some trendoid hangout. Like 8th and A. Vixen, I think."

"Right," I say with a nod. "It's been like five places since it was Downtown Beirut. None of them have stuck."

"Downtown Beirut sounds much more my speed than Vixen," she says.

"It used to be a scary place," I say. "If you needed the bathroom, the bartender had to buzz you in from behind the bar because there was so much drug use going on in the can. Now it's got the velvet rope and the bouncer. Man, all the skells that hung out there before, and they never needed a bouncer. Bet pints cost the same as pitchers used to. You didn't wait on line, did you?"

"Hell, no," says Becky. "Too many damn bars for that. Life's too short, Coulter."

"Attagirl. How's your ID?"

"Not bad," she says, taking out her wallet. "This dude Siddharth at school was making 'em in his dorm room. $50 a pop."

It's a New Jersey license with Becky's mug, but the name is Lucinda Ellersbee, and she's 24. I wish Becky was 24, though she probably wouldn't talk to me then.

"So I s'pose Jersey was cheaper than the rest of the states, huh? The Garden State Discount?"

"That's all he had," says Becky, taking the license from my hand. "Whaddya gonna do? I'm Lucinda Ellersbee. My boyfriend's name is Christuphuh."

I look at her blankly.

"'Sopranos'?" Becky says. "Hello?"

"No HBO," I say sheepishly. "So Vixen was fun?"

"Yeah, I guess," she says. "Got drunk, flirted with one cute guy, got hit on by his dorky friend, kissed a third guy in their group, got bored of the place, had pierogies and some Ukrainian moonshine at Kiev and was home by 3. The usual. Sorta psyched for school to start, I guess."

Becky shifts to part-time here once the fall semester begins.

"Tough life," I say.

"Yeah, I know. How ya' holdin' up, anyway?"

"Whaddya mean?"

"With the girl. Can I say her name?"

"Sure."

"Harley?"

"Haley."

"Haley. Y'awright?"

"Yeah, Bex. I'm good. Thanks."

"You deserve better, Declan."

It isn't true, but Becky is sweet for saying so.

"Same goes for working here," she adds.

"I know, I know," I say. "I'll get some breaks. Thanks... Ya know, I never knew a smart girl named Becky before. Seems like such a...bimbo name."

"Not sure if you're insulting me or complimenting me," says Becky. "If I were smarter, perhaps I'd understand your logic. Then again, I'm just a Becky."

"I'm just saying you've got the smarts of a girl with a different name. A Heather. An Anne. A *Susan*."

"Stuck in a Becky's body, I'm afraid."

"You were born a Rebecca, I assume?"

"I was actually born a Becky. My grandma's last name was Beck."

"Like the rock star?"

"Her last name, you jackass."

"Easy."

"Sorry. This place just puts me in a foul mood."

"Me too," I say with a smile. "So you'll hire me when you make it big, yeah?"

"Of course. Work habits like yours are hard to come by. In at 8 on a Monday morning...That's dedication. That's a company guy."

"I'm a hard worker," I protest.

"That's true," concedes Becky. "What you're working on, I'm not always sure, but you are capable of working hard."

"On that note, I better get this resume out before fucking clueless Ken gets in. Another freakin' Monday at Avatar. Same shit, different week."

"Hopefully one of our last. Need help?"

"You're not busy?"

"I've got a thrilling day of filing, smiling and fetching Captain Ken's coffee," says Becky. "I've got time. Whaddya need?"

"Wanna throw postage on this?" I say, handing her my final envelope.

"Sure," says Becky, taking it from me and reading it. "Cunning Linguist Publishing?"

"Yeah, that's the skin mag."

"I figured it wasn't the weekly paper in Queens," she says.

"Figured it was worth 34 cents of Avatar's money."

"Job's a job," says Becky. "Unfortunately, not all mags are about Guinness, Shane MacGowan and lacrosse."

"Rugby."

"Right," she says, turning on her heel. "Well, two outta three ain't bad."

"Thank you, Bex."

"Right on, Coulter."

I hear her singing "Two Outta Three Ain't Bad" as she disappears from sight. Somehow, Bex makes Meatloaf sound cool.

Day of The Locusts

No Haley.

No Tisa, no Ma and no Gabby. *Bastard.*

I ain't got much. I got Shady Brady and I got Honey Bunny. I seem to do well with those whose names rhyme; maybe I can catch Ralph Malph on Nickelodeon tonight. Shit, even the rabbit's tenuous. Sally ripped me a new one about the story I sent in—told me kids would be crying their eyes out and parents totally freaking, wanting their money back if we published *Enchanted Meadow* the way it was. Sally says *Honey Bunny*'s got to be a happy story. Sorry, I'm just not feeling too happy, Sal. Being totally, completely alone'll do that to you.

It's a Friday night, and I'm in this new video store on 1st Avenue, in between Mickey-Ds and the Homestead. Its arrival means I don't have to schlep over to Kim's Video anymore, where the workers are sniveling little film school snobs who never made it to film school. Whatever you rent, it's wrong. Something that came from Hollywood, and you're *so mainstream*. Anything indie, and you're a *poser*. Videos arranged by director…like that's making life easier for anyone. I'm *so* psyched to never have to return to Kim's.

I whip out my index card:

The Object of My Affection

The Locusts

Clueless

Romeo + Juliet

I find *Object* right away, because the Romantic Comedy section in this cynical corner of Manhattan has about 10 vids, and *Romeo + Juliet*—the dude's boyish, even girlish, mug on the box—doesn't take much longer. *Clueless*, however, is nowhere to be found.

"Excuse me," I ask the man stocking the shelves. He's an Asian guy, tall and reedy, hair in a flip down over his eyes, wearing a t-shirt that says Mean People Suck, Nice People Swallow.

"Yes," he says with a treacly-sweet smile.

"Know where I can find *Clueless*?"

"Ooo, good one," he says, confusing my query concerning the tape's locale with a request for a review. "You'll like it."

He skips over to the computer and taps it in.

"Ooo, out," he says, daintily shrugging a shoulder. "Sorry."

Perhaps another man recently rendered single by a certain versatile actor has his hands on it. Leonard freakin' Maltin studies the two tapes under my arm.

"Paul Rudd fan, huh?" he says.

"Eh, ya know," I say. "Just doing some…research. Writin' somethin'."

"He lives here in New York," the man says.

"Yeah, I know."

"He's great-looking, but a quirky kind of great-looking," the man says. "He wears these great little glasses in *The Locusts*. You ought to check out the Paul Rudd discussion group on Alta Vista."

"Where do I find *Locusts*?" I ask impatiently.

"Bottom shelf on the left," he says, pointing to the Drama section.

It's a Friday night and, needless to say, I have nothing planned. The rest of the boys are taking it easy for the match tomorrow—playing up on Randalls Island against the Morris Mud Turtles (I have to get my ass out running and get in shape to play again)—and there's no chick to go out with who's eventually just going to break my heart. It's just me, a six-pack of Bass and a few videos.

It's just about as hot at night as it is during the day, the thick, soupy air smelling like urine and garbage. With fall around the corner, you start jonesin' big-time for its month of crisp glory. And the start of fall means my big 3-0 birthday as well. Fucking great. If it were today, I wouldn't have a soul to share it with. Maybe Becky will take me out for a sympathy beer. And I *have* to work on my novel. Tomorrow.

I enter my apartment and instinctively look at the answering machine, which blinks optimistically. I flick on the lights, pop open a Bass and sit next to the machine in case it bears big news, like word of my pending fatherhood. I hit 'Play.'

Hi Declan, it's me.

She sounds pregnant. The bottle slides through my fingers and crashes on the floor, spilling beer everywhere. Nice move, buying the expensive sixer with money I don't really have. What kind of father will I be? Can't do worse than my own father. The nerve, referring to herself as "me" after all this time.

Listen, we really must talk.

Can a person *sound* pregnant? She sure as hell does.

I know we keep missing each other, but please try me again on my cell. Please. Hope you're well. Ta!

I get to my feet, grab another beer and make room amidst the spent shells of failed novel first chapters and index cards that litter the couch before dumping the videos on the coffee table.

I take in the squalor at my feet and all around me. The spilled beer continues to spread like an oil spill in the Arctic, the smashed shards of bottle little chunks of ice across the amber landscape. Nearly 30, I think to myself, and this is my life. My brain scrolls through its database for an inspirational quote, but none is forthcoming.

This has to change.

Everything has to change.

I peel four cards from the stack and write "Ma" on one, "Tisa" on another, "Haley" on the third and "Gabby" on the fourth. I lay the four cards out in front of me on the coffee table and take a greedy gulp from a new bottle of Bass.

I blow on the shiny ink of Ma's card. My guy at Art & Design, Mr. Wooden Eye/Glass Leg, always stressed the virtues of index cards, said they were essential to effective organization. Glad to see I learned something in school.

Ma.

She's a crazy Mick from Northern Ireland, that accent that brings to mind tenuous treaties. She lives downstairs from me. You'd think we'd be close, living in the same building and all, but we're not. I pass by her on the stairs or out on the sidewalk or when she's sitting on a bench in Cooper Square before walking over to NYU to work, reading a gigantic Maeve Binchy novel from the library just above St. Mark's Place, and she just looks up from the book and glares at me, giving me a chill no matter what time of year it is.

Ma would kill me if she knew I was talking to Tisa. Beat me with the Binchy book, kick me, call me a *fookin' eejit*, that's what she'd do. I wish. If she were to somehow find out, Ma would either glare at me or, more likely, turn her head away, just walk on by and pretend not to see me, like she's done for the past few years.

They say there's the Irish temper, but I think the Northern Irish temper is even worse, because those people have been fucked with big-time. They've been fucked by the Brits and, in Ma's case, she fell for a Brit and had a kid with him, and then he *fooked* off back to England, like she—and I—never existed. So she's been both figuratively and literally fucked by the Brits, with me as a constant reminder.

I'll pop in to Ma's, or I'll call, maybe offer to make her dinner, and I'll tell Ma I love her and miss her and want her in my life again. How's a mother going to say no to that? Even if she does, I'm no worse off than I am right now. We'll go out to the Homestead and have a pint or two, and she'll tell me she loves me, and all will be cool again. She's my mom. I'm sure she wants it that way.

Tisa.

Yeah, we're talking, or at least leaving messages on each other's voicemails. I mean, we didn't speak for almost as long as me and Ma didn't speak—because *I* said so, mind you—and then all the sudden, about four months ago, she was back in my life. Said she was getting, uh, married and wanted to meet up and talk. But then, true to character, Tisa leaves me standing at the alt—...leaves me hanging, blowing me off for our big summit, blowing me off a few times after that. For all I know, she's married, she's hauling my kid around in her belly from the night after the Bayonne Barbarians match, who knows? I really despise her, which I find sort of empowering. She broke my fucking heart like no one ever will again. This whole Haley thing smarts like a mofo and all but, compared to the Tisa breakup, well, it doesn't really compare. I mean, Haley's a better person, but me and Tisa had *history*...

All my misery stems from Tisa: she fucked it up between me and Ma, which mucked it up between me and Haley.

I put Tisa's card first, and Ma's second.

Haley. I've called a few times, and she hasn't returned my calls. I'll be trying again, just not right away. If not out of mind, it might be wise to have her out of sight for a bit; maybe I'll stop thinking I see her every time I spy long blond hair in a crowd. She hurt me bad, but I think it was just a severe sprain, maybe a hairline fracture, not a clean break of the heart. I mean, how well did we truly know each other?

I put her card third.

Fucking *Gabby.* I've asked the bastard for about three favors in all the years I've known him, and he totally left me hanging at Troika. But he's a guy; guys don't mean anything by their shit. A rugby guy would walk on burning coals for another teammate, and that code may be the only one Gabby lives by. He flaked on me at a fairly crucial time, but he'll come through next time around, I'm pretty sure. And he's not the kind of guy you just confront and have it out with...not sober, anyway. I'll see him soon enough, maybe even tomorrow at MacLennane's after the Mud Turtles match, and he'll apologize and buy me a beer, or we'll act like nothing happened. He's still a dickhead. But I knew that.

I put Gabby's card fourth.

I rap the stack of cards on the table like a blackjack dealer. Time to play the hand life dealt me. I lay them out on the table.

Tisa

Ma

Haley

Gabby

Each card stares back at me, as if they bore the person's face. Each one gets a week to address. Then I turn 30. Yes, index cards give my life order—thank you, Mr. Glass Leg/Wooden Eye. I slip Tisa's card into my back pocket, stack the remaining three into a neat pile and turn my attention to the video boxes to figure out which to watch first.

The Object of My Affection looks cheesy, pretty much how you'd expect a romantic comedy box to look: happy, well-scrubbed couple dancing, him impish, her insouciant, him dipping her, her being dipped. "Written by Wendy Wasserstein," the copy reads, "this rollicking romantic comedy..." yeah, yeah, yeah—whatever. *The Locusts* looks better, with the perpetually sexy Ashley Judd and the lady from the second *Raiders of the Lost Ark*, who I think is married to Francis Ford Coppola. And I've got yet another remake of *Romeo + Juliet*. It's got Leonardo DeCaprio, and the truly cute guy in the film—yes, our buddy Paul. It's a fucking Paul Rudd Filmfest.

I kick the broken glass out of the way and pop in *The Locusts*, which gets first billing due to the prospect of seeing Judd or Coppola's wife nude. I grab another Bass from the fridge and make myself comfy on the couch as the credits come up. I recognize the guy from *Swingers*—Gabby and me snuck a 12-pack into the theater on 12th and 2nd and saw that one. I liked it and Gabby thought it should've been better. It's the studly actor guy, the tall one—think his name's Vincent Vega or something.

The movie makes me miserable. I want to study this Paul Rudd cat, freeze his image on-screen, watch it, absorb it and picture Haley with it, kissing it, *right this fucking minute*, across town, which I'm positive she is, til I'm ill. I want to keep doing that to get it all out of me, deal with it, get past it. He's pale, with dark hair and these really freakin' blue eyes. He's an OK looking guy, a mediocre-at-best actor.

But I can't deal. I go from pausing the tape when he's on to fast-forwarding through all the scenes he's in. I just can't deal with this guy; not yet, anyway. I look at the stack of Paul Rudd movies—sorry, Haley, *films*—and regret having wasted the $10.50 that would've been better spent on, oh, anything. I can't fucking hang in my apartment on a Friday night, sit here and be ill while Paul and Haley are sitting in a French bistro on a leafy, picturesque West Village street, him ordering for the both of them and pronouncing everything correctly, after all the time he's spent in Paris, winning over the disdainful French waiter—the first American ever to do so—with his mastery of the language, his grace and charm. Then they'll leave the place arm in arm, people passing on the sidewalk thinking, man, what a nice looking, happy couple, and they'll go to a little Bleecker Street coffee shop named for an artist for cappuccino and canolis, and the waitress will tease them about how the two of them should really make a child, if they haven't already.

I wonder if he knows about me.

I wonder why the hell I wondered that.

I'm sitting in my apartment, pizza box on the coffee table, broken glass under my feet, smell of spilled ale seeping up into my nose. Don't know where Paul lives—don't know why the fuck he doesn't live in goddamn L.A. with the other fucking *ac-tors,* and just leave me and Haley alone. But I know where Haley lives. And I know it's a third floor place that faces the street, offering up a pretty good view of the living room from Charles Street.

I stop the video, put my shoes on and head outside.

There're two cash machines at the Ukrainian bank on Avenue A between 3rd and 4th, and one person waiting for each. I take my place on line. The machines are covered in a mosaic of spent bank receipts; while the rest of the city is paranoid that some Albanian street swindler will get his hands on their receipt and somehow figure out a way to tap into their life savings, the Alphabet City residents prefer to display their bank slips for all to see, a Gen-X expression of poverty-chic in which they dare the world to tap into the $242 they have to their name.

A homeless guy in dreads down past his chest rattles a cup of change. "Change for the strange," he sings. "Change for the deranged, for the insane."

I ask the machine for $100.

"Gimme some cash, help me get smashed," he continues. "Add to the collection, so's I get my injection. Help me get high, I'm a nice guy."

The machine serves up my money and receipt. I pocket the money and plaster the receipt to the wall: $12.43 in Checking. Don't even ask about Savings.

I walk past the homeless guy and head up A, past the Pyramid, where about 50 kids wait to get in. Becky told me they do some '80s Night thing there on Fridays, playing all kinds of Billy Idol and "99 Luftballoons" and Thompson Twins and stuff, and few in the line look like they're old enough to have heard the stuff first time around. Nonetheless, they're stoked to get in, passing 40s around, smoking butts and blunts, guys staring at and mumbling "Hey baby" to the tattooed chicks in tight tank tops and trampy micromini's who walk by. A girl in a red and black tartan miniskirt and torn fishnets hangs a flyer on a telephone pole. I stop to view her work; it advertises a band called Heavy Flo that's playing at Brownie's. She's got an eyebrow ring, red hair to match her skirt and a real pretty face. I try to think of something to say to her, maybe use the fake *Shhkuh-issh* accent to make a joke about what clan she was from, and then realize I haven't tried a line on a girl in months, and my Scottish accent sucks. I keep walking.

Banging a right on 6th, I head towards B. There's a couple old Latino guys sitting at a card table in front of the bodega on the corner, flipping dominoes and drinking malt liquor. There's that crazy-ass sculpture, gotta be 60 feet high, of carousel horses and stuffed animals and Mother Mary statues and plastic reindeer and ventriloquist dummies, coming to a point with an American flag on top.

A gaggle of young homeless punk kids mills about on the steps of the school across the street, smoking cigarettes, a pit bull at their feet. There's a poster on the door that shows a young Asian girl painting at an easel. "Who ate at school today?" the poster says. "I did!" There's a Drug Free School Zone sign on the door too. "Violators will be prosecuted," it admonishes to deaf ears.

A guy walks by and asks the gutter punks how old their "pit" is, and they converse briefly about how big the dog's going to get. About 10 feet from them is a dude on a cell phone, lurking in the shadow of the school, back to the street, wearing a white wife-beater and black jeans. He's thin and has a wolf tattooed on his shoulder. I head towards him.

I give him a quick nod and a grimace. He puts his cell phone in his pocket and turns his head sideways to look at me.

"Whaddya got?" I ask.

"Huh?"

"What's good, man?"

"Whaddya mean, what's good?"

"Ya know, whaddya got? What's good?"

He looks at me blankly.

"Free beer. Sunny days. Easy women. It's *all* good."

"Let's party, man," I say.

"You want to...party?"

"Yeah, bro."

"And whaddya want me to do? Suck yer dick?"

"Ya know. Give me sumpin' to party with."

"You want money?"

"No."

"Drugs?"

He looks around nervously. It is the world's lamest drug deal.

"Uh, yeah, man."

"You think I'm a fucking...dealer?"

"Nahh," I say, backtracking.

"I look like a motherfucking dealer to you?" he barks, turning to face me.

"Nah, man. You look normal. You look sorta hip, sorta urban, so, ya know, ya could be a dealer, maybe, but prolly not. Or maybe ya know one."

"Fuck you," he says, bumping my shoulder as he walks past.

"Ahh, fuck off," I whisper when he's out of earshot.

I head further east on 6th, toward the East River. While Alphabet City is hopping east of Avenue B, this is still a damn dead block—pretty creepy, if you ask me—few people sitting outside, and no bars to draw in the party people. A few Latino kids sit on the front step of their building, bouncing a basketball back and forth, but they look too young to sell. Still, I give them a little nod, just to give us

Michael J. Malone

both a chance, see if they're in the business and let them know I'm in the market, but they don't look up from the basketball.

At the corner of 6th and C, a cop car approaches from uptown and drives by slowly, the passenger-side cop getting a real good look at my face, his expression telling me he's on to my game, that, despite the neighborhood's gentrification, a white boy has no purpose being this far east of the numbered avenues after dark. When it comes to this business, I'm not hard, I'm not weathered. I don't have thick skin, and I'm tempted to go home and just forget about it, maybe drink myself to sleep. But something propels me uptown on C.

Three Latino kids, maybe 17 or so, walk towards me on the sidewalk, yet another pit bull, this one unleashed, leading their way. As the dog nears me, he growls angrily and juts his head in my direction, causing me to let out an effeminate little yelp. The youths emit a satisfied chuckle; surely they've trained the dog, who they call "Mato," to growl at skittish white dudes. I'm happy to put them behind me.

As I approach 7th and C, a cop car again passes by, again real slow. I see the driver, black, mustachioed and mean, and get a quick glimpse of his partner, the same guy I saw just a moment ago. I don't remember seeing cops east of A ever. Maybe there's a killer on the loose. I check to see if the moon is full, but I can't find it amidst the tall buildings. They pass by doing about 10 m.p.h., throwing me the worst vibes imaginable. 'We know your story,' their eyes bellow. 'We know your every dirty secret.'

The cops turn left at 7th and C, so I follow them, thinking they might know where the action is. They speed up a bit and I see their tail lights approach Tompkins, then they turn left onto B. The cop presence has cleaned up Tompkins pretty good, unfortunately, but there are usually some unsavory types lurking on the perimeter.

I pass a few folks along 7th, see some people drinking 40s on their doorsteps, and I nod to everyone, the friendliest guy in Alphabet City. You nod to score the damn stuff, and then you nod all night after you score it. It's enough to give you a stiff neck—especially if you cracked the damn thing playing rugby.

Unfortunately, all my nodding's doing fuck-all for me tonight. I again ponder heading home; it's not like I need the stuff, I just feel kind of crappy. A few slugs of bourbon should get me to sleep, then I've got a 12-hour or so break before I have to deal with my shitty freakin' life again. Don't get me wrong: it's going to get better. I've been through break-ups before—well, one—and each day you're working towards being all good again. And those index cards—as Ken at work would say, I'm being "proactive" about my life. Yeah.

I'm leaning against the front of 7Bs, or Horseshoe Bar, or Vasac's, or whatever you wanna call it, bricks cool against my back, wondering if I should go in for a drink, or just head home and pour one there. Across the street I see St. Brigid's

158

Church; it's where Ma would walk me to pre-school when I was 4. I thought I was going to "priest school"—it was in a church, taught by nuns—and I found out my error years later. Priest school was cool by me; if Ma wanted me to be a priest, so be it. Mighta saved my ass.

The Ramones' "Sheena is a Punk Rocker" spills through the open window of the bar. *Sheena is…a punk rocker.* I sing along. *Haley is…a Rudd fucker. Paul is…a cock sucker.* They got this great amber ale called Watney's on draught, only place I've ever seen it. I'm about to pop in and have one when I hear a voice behind me.

"What you need, big man? Talk to me."

I turn around, and there's a streetlight over my man's head like a halo. *Yeeeeaaaahhhh…*

Yeah, fuckin' proactive is definitely the key word there, thanks, Ken…Be proactive about shit, shit's gonna work out. You can either sit on your fucking couch and cry about shit, or go out and make shit happen, make yourself feel better, take life by the horns or the short hairs or the balls, or whatever other clichés you come up with. *Proactive…* Shit's gonna work out.

I'm back at my place, because the West Village just seemed like the other side of the world, Broadway like a vast river, and I ain't got money for cabs, or a gondola, so it's probably for the best. So I'm done with *The Locusts,* and halfway through with *Romeo + Juliet. Locusts* was decent—were decent? I dunno. Ashley Judd played this chick Kitty, and she's pretty damn hot, and there's a slow kid in it too, and the mental kids are always compelling to watch, 'specially when you're a little looped, and kinda get a feeling for what's going on in their little brains. *Romeo + Juliet,* decent too. Leo plays Romeo. He's real cute, almost pretty…Had a job when I was 19, after I got fired from bein' a doorman, swear that Mrs. Barrows got my ass fired, she was a piece a' ass, even at her age, tennis dress, bitch got me fired but even today I know she *wanted* it, then I was a security guard for some chocolate shop on 5th Ave, some fancy-ass place… Ma worked with some lady at the med center whose boyfriend was a guard there, too, guy useta eat cottage cheese an' apple sauce sandwiches, fucker was a freak, an' they got me in. Believe that one, a freakin' security guard for a place that sold *candy?* Not like I was really a security guard—I was just a kid in a blue blazer, makin' $5 an hour, checkin' out the hot tourist chicks as they looked for Prada, takin' their pictures for them, jokin' with the dudes lookin' for the Playboy building, and smiling at people when they walked in. But next door was this jewelry shop, and they had this young guy, this good lookin' kid 'bout my age, to stand outside and look official, sorta like me, and chicks dug him so much that they'd be taking their picture with him and shit… So that was his job—stand there and look handsome, and lure women into the shop. Not security, not selling anything, not even dusting the merchandise. Paid to be cute. And that fucker looked just like this DiCaprio cat. Fuck was 'is name? Brett or somethin'…Brad?

Locusts was kinda fucked up, but in a good way, and not what I expected. Oz Luhrmann directed it, and Ashley Juggs is in it, playin' this chick Kitty, and she's fuckin' hot as shit, and there's a retarded kid in it too, which always makes me kind of emotional, knowin' what they're knowin'... I think I was out for a part of it—actually, I *know* I was out for part of it, just not sure for how long, long enough to drool a bit on my chest, long enough to have a few holes in the story, few holes in my shirt where the cigarette hit it, some of them gaping, some small, but mostly it was cool and weird and shit. And *Romeo + Juliet* is, like, pretty easy to follow, since we all know the story, couple just doomed from the get-go—now there's a plotline I'm familiar with. It's set in the modern era, in the States, which makes it easier to understand.... And the chick that plays Juliet is pretty decent looking. Seen her before, in other shit. That show about the girl in high school with no friends.

Stepped on some goddamn broken glass on my floor—man, that'll fuckin' wake yer ass up...and it's starting to hurt like hell... Had some napkins laying around from when I got the pizza the other day, so put some bourbon on a napkin and cleaned the cut, like I was in a western or something. Just give me a bullet to bite on. Man, that mofo stung. It kept bleeding so I took my sock and wrapped it around my foot, and eventually the bleeding stopped. Reminded me of going into a ruck against those straight-off-the-boat Paddies from Bainbridge Avenue and cracking my head against some Mick's bony hip. Not too much got on the floor, which is good. I should get up and put a Band-Aid or some tape and shit on it, get this ridiculous sock tourniquet off it, but this fucking couch has absorbed me, just gobbled me up. And the movie's pretty, ya know, engrossing. So I sit.

Rudd fucker...

Man, me an' this kid from Art & Design used to go to this place Fuddrucker's that was over on 7th Ave. Cheesy fucking place, totally for tourists and shit, but we were kids and wanted to go to bars an' none of the real bars would let us in, an' the fake IDs we bought off some shady black mofo on Times Square for 40 bucks each, after some other fucker played us like suburban kids an' ripped us off, so we made it back in Three-Card Monte, got out while they were letting us win, setting us up for the big loss, walked away with their dough, them yellin' all sortsa shit at us, game ain't over, no it ain't. The fake ID's worked there... So we'd go to Fuddrucker's. Isn't that just the stupidest name for a bar? Fuddrucker's. Who gave *that* name the green light? So we'd go there, because we could get in, me 'n that fucker from Art & Design, that fuckin' tall kid with the zits, the what the fuck's his name, the rumor about him doin' his dog, the freakin' tall guy. Zits... Bill! Dollar Bill, Dollar fuckin' Bill, they called 'im, never had dough, always had to buy him beer and smokes and shit. Man, that kid had nothin'. How'd the fuck he ever get in to Art & Design? Shit, how the fuck did *I* get in? Oh yeah, Ma worked with a lady who knew a guy. Why did I hang out with him? I was working as a doorman up on Lex'n makin' lotsa dough, like eight bucks an hour, back in like '86 or so, when the Mets won it all, great year, and me 'n Dollar Bill'd go to Fuddrucker's, this real preppy-ass place, and sit on the upstairs deck—place had a nice deck, I'll give it that much, lookin' down 7ᵗʰ Avenue at the Twin Towers, hulking and square and shining like those Ukrainian boxer twins whose mugs you see in every Uke joint on 2ⁿᵈ Avenue—and drink Heinekens, which Dollar Bill always called "Heinies"— "Grab a Heinie," he'd say and laugh that stupid horse laugh like he thought of it first—and we'd hit on chicks from Jersey, those college broads from Fairleigh Ridiculous that one night... They'd look at me 'n Dollar Bill, an' wouldn't even turn us down, they'd just laugh. Like shooting us down was such a given that they didn't need to bother doin' it. That was fun. Dollar Bill ...

Rudd Fucker. That fucking quirky cute guy who stole my gal...

He's likeable in *Object of My Affection*, and plays this redneck farmhand in *Locusts*, which has Ashley Jugg, who always looks hot—wouldn't mind grabbin' her Heinie—and this special kid, which is always interesting to watch. Freakin' Dollar Bill... Fuck happened to that fucker? Dude *never* had any dough in his pocket...

Woke up sitting on my couch, slumped low on it, head hanging to one side like a man with a busted neck, my bum neck sore as shit and the foot bleeding like mad all over the sock tourniquet. Didn't know where the fuck I was, or what was going on, and this fuzz was on the TV like *Poltergeist* or something—*they're here!*— and my foot was just gushing. Well, maybe not gushing, necessarily, but bleeding pretty good. Last thing I wanted to deal with. Man, I was out of it. A few slugs on a mug of coffee I'd left out from the other day, milk seceding from the coffee and pooling in the middle, helped snap me out of it. I stare at the mug, which has "Dad" written on it in a million different fonts. Where the fuck did that come from? Who left that here? Have I always owned it? How do these things happen? I feel dread in the pit of my stomach as I dial the phone.

"Yeah-lo," comes back the Okie drawl.

"Demento," I mumble into the receiver.

"Yeeoohh, who's this?"

"Declan."

"Coal-turr!" Dr. Demento yells. "How's the head?"

"Better," I say. "Got something else for ya."

Demento sews up bullet wounds and knife gashes on gangsta punks all day out in Brooklyn. He says, if the kid lives, he'll surely see him again before long, when the kid's got another gaping hole that needs covering. And if the kid dies, his boys'll pour 40s of O.E. on the spot where he got capped or stabbed.

Demento's always getting knocked out—says it's easy to get a concussion once you've had a few, flicking his finger against his temple to demonstrate. Demento says everyone's got a "button", and if some guy from the Bainbridge Bruisers or the Long Island Rovers hits your button, it's Game Over. He's pretty liberal with the meds he gets at work—he's constantly jamming needles in his veins after matches and before the drink-up, booting up some concoction to alleviate the headaches and nausea. To him, it's like typing a letter, or opening mail—just a boring thing you do at work. I saw him get knocked out—*out*—against the Montclair Vikings, but that night, he was out at MacLennane's, drinking beer and singing that Cotton-Eye Joe song. He's a crazy fucker, Demento, but I'd trust him with my life.

Or my bleeding foot, at least.

"Whaddya got?"

"What're ya up to?" I say.

"Havin' my breakfast, gettin' my game face on. Heading up to Randalls in about half an hour. When you gonna get your ass out for rugby? You're cleared, motherfucker. No excuses!"

"I dunno. I'll be right over. Don't leave without me."

"You comin' to Randalls?"

"No."

"Well, whaddya want, then?"

"A very quick surgery. Like five minutes."

"Aw, c'mon," he whines. "I'm havin' my breakfast. Coal-turr, I don't come to you on game day and ask you to review a bottle of wine for me."

"I know, I know. I'm sorry. Just this one favor."

"Aw, fuck… I'm here."

"Thanks, Demento."

"Whatever."

I'm limping up 1st Avenue, approaching St. Mark's, and I'm freaked out by the normal people around me, good folks going to brunch and shopping for hardware and buying bagels, no one but me getting stitches in their foot from a guy named Dr. Demento because they stepped on glass, no one with an index card marked TISA in their back pocket, wondering if they'll be a father in the near future. I see people ducking into Bendix for brunch, and I wish I was one of them. The simple life. French toast and coffee. Scrambled eggs. Bacon! Rivers of coffee.

I pass Coyote Ugly and think of the last time I was in there. It was after Tisa had rejected my proposal like Sir Vincent stuffing some doofy Duke white guy's ill-advised lay-up, and I was looking for a place to get smashed in, and the Coyote just seemed perfect, with the chicks dancing on the bar, pouring shots right down your throat, sad country tunes on the box about guys getting dumped and a big ol' sign out front that said "Life got ya down? Try drinkin'!"

Well, the booze didn't do shit, just made me feel worse and less in control and just plain fucking miserable. Someone kept playing a song that rhymed "tequila" and "Sheila," and each time I heard it was like doing another shot of Cuervo. Tried telling the hottie behind the bar about Tisa, but she didn't give a shit, though to her credit she was generous with the shots of Jack, even did a few with me. I was tired of sitting there at the bar, hole in my heart the size of a baseball, looking around, trying to get girls to talk to me, ask me what was up, tell them my sob story and have them take me home and nurse me to wellness, but it wasn't happening. I was on my way out when I decided to give their bowling game a try, one of those games where you slide a silver puck down a waist-high lane toward bowling pins. There's sawdust all over the floor and I'm pretty bombed and I give it a good thrust, and my feet go sliding under me. Next thing I know, my head is crashing towards the game table, and then I'm on the floor. Some dudette in a cowboy hat helped me up and some chick put ice on my head and blew the sawdust out of the cut and brushed it off my clothes. I thanked them and got the hell out of there.

I remember walking down 1st Ave and some guy was walking up from where 1st hits St. Mark's, some black guy with dreads sprouting out of his head and an evil smile on his face. He was going, "Whatchoo want, bro, whatchoo need?" and I was thinking, the booze ain't cutting it, so I need something bigger and stronger, or at least different. Me and Jimmy Gulotta used to do a little coke way back, think it was during his Stevie Ray Vaughan days, the hats and the scarves, him a lot and me whatever he couldn't finish, which wasn't much. It always sort of agreed with me, though I could never afford it. Gulotta couldn't either, but that never stopped him…though Riker's eventually did. I gave the dude the nod and he nodded back and I may have nodded one more time and we walked around the corner to St. Mark's. As I patted the engagement ring in my pants pocket, he fished some shit out of a garbage can, and that Replacements song hit me real clear. I instinctively sang along:

Feelin' like a hundred bucks
Exchanging good lucks face to face
Checkin' his stash by the trash at St. Mark's Place

The guy nodded again and squawked, "Fuckers wrote that song about me. Didn't pay my ass a dime in royalties."

I paid him a dime and he threw me a bag, then tells me I oughta clean my head out. Seemed like a weird thing for a dealer to say—did I really look so fucked up that a *dealer* was telling me to get straight? But then he pointed to my forehead, where some blood apparently was still trickling down the side of my face, pooling and drying just south of my ear. I nodded one final time.

Then I was looking for a friendly place to drop anchor and do up a hit, let modern medicine cure my considerable woes. Walking downtown, I saw the Homestead across the street, and ducked in. Christine was working the bar, wearing one of her old housedresses, and her face went from happy-to-see-ya to good-freakin'-Christ when she saw the state of me. Even in my stupor, I could read the sadness in her face, the slo-mo shake of her head. She'd seen tons of neighborhood fuckheads like me and Jimmy Gulotta grow up, and few of us made good. I was yet another local kid sneaking into the bathroom, blood on his face, head full of coarse LES powders.

I nodded hello and beelined for the can, threw across the dead bolt and dropped onto the toilet. I could hear two guys yelling in Polish over a pool game. Don't know any Polish, but I think it had something to do with who had next. I poured a little coke on a paper towel I'd flattened on my hand, separated a line and took a hit, praying it would take my mind off that awful bitch.

JesusfuckingholyshitwhatthewhatmanohhhChrist.

I'd only done coke a handful of times, but sweet mother of Mary, that wasn't coke. I felt a whack of nausea and was thankful I could lean over the sink while sitting on the toilet, barfing up what looked like straight Tennessee whiskey and flecks of sawdust. That seemed to make everything better. I wiped my mouth and folded up the remaining powder and leaned back and closed my eyes and listened to the Polish guys arguing and the dude knocking on the bathroom door and Jimmy Roselli singing "Somebody Stole My Gal" and...just...simply...

The anxiety that had coursed through my veins since I was a boy, that was as much a part of my physiology as my blood and cells. Lifted. Gone.

And every Velvet Underground song ever finally made sense.

Some time passed. It may have been a few minutes, or an hour. Either way, it was pretty freakin' blissful. Eventually I mustered the strength to get up and leave the bathroom, where I encountered the doughy, pissed off faces of a few dudes waiting for the head. Christine waved me over to the bar, where she was holding a damp towel for my head, but I just floated right by her, desperate to get outside, get back to Village View and park it on a bench and check out the stars.

It's never been as good as that first time; each time, I think it's going to be, but it never is. When I'm thinking clearly, I know it's a waste of time trying to reach that high. But when my defenses are down, I forget that. Dope has a way of making you forget.

I finally get to 10th and 1st, where Dr. Demento has a small studio. You'd think a doctor would be able to live a little better, but Demento opted to work at that shithole hospital in Brooklyn, schlepping out to the end of the borough six days a week, instead of partnering in some cushy medical group on Park Avenue with a pretty receptionist. And the bastard makes almost as little as an associate editor for his efforts.

"Coal-turr, what's the problem now?" says Demento as he shovels a forkful of scrambled eggs into his mouth, chasing it with black coffee. He's wearing a black-and-red striped Oklahoma University rugby shirt.

"My foot hurts," I whimper as I waddle in. "I cut it."

"How the fuck did you cut your foot?"

"I stepped on glass."

"What're ya, walking around the streets barefoot?"

"It happened in my apartment," I say.

"Dumbass."

"I know."

"Man, ya get away from rugby for a few weeks, and your life falls apart."

I nod.

"You look like shit, Coal-turr. What're you up to?"

"Drinkin' too much," I plea bargain.

"Coal-turr, don't think you're foolin' me. Be careful. The East Village is full of temptation for the weak-willed."

"Tell me about it."

"You comin' up to the game?"

"Dunno," I say. The thought of going to Randalls Island seems akin to a trip to the Middle East: sitting on the subway for over a hundred blocks, waiting on 125th for the bus. *Up to Lexington, 1-2-5, Feel sick and dirty, more dead than alive,* I sing to myself, and feel a wave of anxiety. A trip to Randalls ain't happening. Challah bread French toast and coffee at Bendix, maybe; darkness and sleep, definitely. Watching rugby on Randalls, *not bloody likely*, as Shady would say, though it would be good to see the boys, watch them take down the Montauk Sharks.

"Maybe," I say.

"Lemme see your foot," he says, as I take off my shoe. I feel bad, flashing my dirty, bloody foot in Demento's face on his one day off—as he's eating breakfast, no less.

"Fuck, man. Good work."

"Thanks," I say sheepishly. "I did my best."

"Let me get my gear," he says with an exhale that's loaded with annoyance.

"You gonna use a needle?"

"How 'bout I use my fork?" he says, waving it in my face, a clump of egg stuck to it.

"Awright, awright."

Michael J. Malone

"Well, then, shaddup. And don't expect no lollipop from me, either, Coal-turr."

I sit in a clammy sweat and think about running out before Demento can jam me with a spike. But surely with my bum foot, he'll catch me and tackle me like I'm an opposing flyhalf headed for the goal line. Demento rummages through his cabinets. I'm hoping he leaves the room so *I* can take a turn rummaging through his cabinets—I know he's got some interesting shit in there—but no such luck. I concentrate on not passing out as he comes back.

It's 6 p.m., and I feel like I could sleep through the night, or at least past midnight or so. The pounding headache is gone and Demento's sutures have stopped the bleeding—I'm tellin' you, for all his quirks, Demento does good work, and I appreciate him not breaking my balls for boo-hooing when he stuck the needle in my foot.

The foot's better, but this feeling of general out-of-it-ness is persisting, like the world around you is a radio that's not properly tuned in. Of course, you sleep all day, you're not exactly gonna be ready to solve Advanced Trig when you get up. But I just can't seem to snap out of it—sitting up in bed for seemingly ever, trying to get my head sorted out. Everything feels kind of fucked up and it's all moving in slo-mo, my head heavy, full of trails and sound effects and all kinds of weird sensory enhancements that I wish would just go away—a hangover in jittery Technicolor.

I stumble out of my room, which is dark as a grotto, and head into the living room, where the sun streams in and forces its way into my eyes. There's crap all over the place—like a frat house after a big party. I've never been to a frat house, but I've seen *Animal House*. Thank God no one will be stopping by. I can just picture Haley popping in, tell me she's thought shit out and has decided I'm a better catch than that fucker Paul (yeah, right), but then she gets a gander at my apartment and screws off back to his resplendent West Village duplex.

I sweep up the broken glass and scrub the blood and beer off the floor, the stooping position making my head throb, but I get it done before the big headache arrives. I can feel my blood pumping, sending my senses creeping back into their rightful positions. Picking up my place serves to make me feel a little better about my life.

The VCR is whizzing away, as I rewind each of the three videos I watched last night; I'm really not in an economic position to be pissing away $1.50 in rewind fees. To be honest, I'm somewhat proud to have gotten through all three vids—it's a moral victory of sorts, and I feel like I'm on my way to getting used to sharing the planet with this Rudd fucker or Fudd rucker or whatever, and dealing with life without Haley. It's going to hurt like a mofo for a while, and it sure as hell did last night, but I soldiered on and got through all three. Romantic comedies are certainly

166

not the light-hearted romps the reviewers say they are when you watch them alone, without a real friend in the world, and your ex's new beau is the leading man.

I'm too embarrassed to drop off three Paul Rudd videos and rent more of the guy's *oeuvre* at the new place on 1ˢᵗ, so I just slip the vids into the slot and head over to the dreaded Kim's. Was hoping I'd never have to go back to that forsaken place, but this should hopefully be the last time.

Of course, I have no idea who directed *Cider House Rules*, so I'm shit out of luck finding the thing, and there's no asking any of the workers, because they'll just snicker at you, and I'm in no mood to be snickered at today. I'll end up hitting one of the little nose-ring weasels, make him bleed all over his Social Distortion t-shirt, and the way I'm feeling, I'll probably get my ass kicked by the little art school gnat, too. That would hurt.

Fortunately, there's a cyber café next door to Kim's, so I pay $3.50 to log on as DecTis (I *have* to get that changed) for five minutes, do a search for *Cider House Rules*, and find out it's directed by some chick named Lasse Hallstrom. Paul plays a guy named Wally. That's almost as bad as *Earl*.

Of course, I can't find this Hallstrom broad anywhere in Kim's. I end up asking some dork with an eyebrow ring and the Velvet Underground t-shirt with the banana on it where to find Lasse Hallstrom. He corrects me on my pronunciation—it's *Hall*strom, not *Hal*strom, and it's a he—and points to "Foreign Directors." I eventually find it, rent it and get the hell out of Kim's with my dignity and my sanity. Most of it, anyway.

Well, that's a sad freakin' movie. Thought I could get through it, and it's a *long* one, but it's all about orphans in this huge old New England house, looks just like the place you see from the train station in Montauk, that time Paula took me out there when I was a kid and she got in the big argument with the dude in the scary fisherman bar who had some half-baked opinions about the shit in Northern Ireland. The orphans line up when a car shows up, hopin' to look good and get their lonely little asses adopted. And this one kid named Fuzzy has respiratory problems and lives in this bubble that the doctor made for him, and he's just the saddest-lookin' kid in the world, worse than me, and the doctor calls 'em all Princes of Maine and Kings of New England and I just started bawlin' and missin' my girl and freakin' just acting like a goddamn idiot. Hardly even noticed the Rudd fucker—didn't need to. Thought the bourbon would help, but it didn't do shit 'cept make me more weepy and was hoping the dope I had left over from last night would do me right like it did last night, the 25-to-Life shit, and help me get through the movie, and I just kept thinkin' about those poor fuckin' orphans and *this* poor fuckin' orphan, this Pauper of the Lower East Side, and feelin' worse and was gonna go to the West Village and see if I could see Haley up in her window and try to look good on the street so she'd adopt me. That was sort of the plan, I guess, and it was enough to get me down to Avenue A, where I am now. And now I'm not sure how good an idea that is. I don't want to be alone and I don't want to be with anyone else, which is a tough spot to be in, though it's easier in New York. Here, you got cabs for hire all around, and they come with drivers, who pretty much satisfy both demands.

So I hail one.

I jump in and read the name on the panel that separates the front and back seats: Mammood Murdeshwar. I find the alliteration soothing. *Mister... Mammood Murdeshwar.*

"Where to, my friend?" says Mammood cheerfully. He's got brown skin and black hair and a t-shirt that used to be white.

"Hello, Mammood."

"Where to, my friend?" repeats Mammood.

It's an excellent question. Where the fuck to? I have no place to go. I reconsider the West Village mission, but in a rare moment of clarity, I realize there's nothing for me to do there, and it's only gonna make me feel worse. I could go to MacLennane's—I know the boys're there. But I can't let them see me like this. Maybe this cab thing was a bad idea.

"Just drive, please."

"I need place."

Don't we all.

"Head downtown."

"You are downtown."

"More downtown."

"You go somewhere?" says Mammood. "You tell me where."

"Mammood, please just fucking drive downtown."

Mammood is gripping the steering wheel hard, trying to shake it. I see the muscles in his brown neck tense. He needs a vacation, maybe a trip to the beach.

"Get dee heck out!" he says with a snarl.

"Okay, okay, I'm sorry. Please take me to—"

"Yes, where?"

I look out the window. 5th and A.

A black man in a wheelchair hits up a pack of girls in short dresses and heels for change. One of the girls, makeup dripping down her face, wobbles to catch up to the others.

"Jones Beach."

"Great Jones Street," he says.

"No, Jones Beach."

"Jones Beach?"

"Yeah, man."

"Out dare?" he says, nodding eastward.

"Yup."

"I no take you to Jones Beach. You no go to Jones Beach. You get out of my cab. You take train."

"Mammood, please. I need to go to the beach. I'm…meeting friends."

"Beach closed. You get out. You go home and get sleep. You *dr-r-r-unk!*"

"You have to take me wherever I want," I say. "It says so right here in the taxicab constitution."

"Anywhere in New York City," he says. "Jones Beach *not* New York City. It Long Island!"

Mammood knows the rules.

"Mammood, please take me to fucking Jones Beach," I plead.

"No!" he growls.

"I'll give you a hundred bucks."

"You show me a hundred bucks."

I get my wallet out. I've got two tens and two…three…four singles.

"I'll pay you when we get there," I say, but I know that ain't gonna work. "My friends got dough. At Jones Beach."

"You GET OUT!"

Anxiety is simmering within me; I feel my jaw jut out and my teeth clench. My entire world is about to crash down on poor Mammood's head. I know it's not his fault. It's like an out-of-body experience; I see Mammood getting hurt and I want to save him from this. But I'm powerless.

"You get out NOW!" he says.

"Mammooooood," I try, like a father attempting to get a baby to eat another mouthful.

"Get OUT!"

Mammood puts the car in park and sticks his head through the window in the panel like a one-man puppet show, attempting to get in my face and show me he's serious.

It was then that I belted him.

Demento was right—everybody's got a button, and Mammood's is right on his chin, front-row, center. I pull my hand back and massage the knuckles. The hand is *throbbing*. Mammood's head drops on the partition, then the weight of his body pulls him back to the front seat, where his body slumps to the passenger side. The fucker's *out*. Wow. And Gabby says I hit like a pussy.

You'd figure I'd be freaking out now, but I'm actually pretty cool, thinking with a surprisingly clear head. I'm thinking what a right cross I have, though knocking out Mammood was kinda like hitting a homer in tee-ball. When you're

15. I think my hand is busted; at least in a real fight you got your adrenaline flowing.

Okay, I can run and leave Mammood here, but some kids are going to throw his ass on the street and go joy-riding all night, drinkin' and goin' nuts in poor Mammood's cab, as he wakes up cabless, with a broken jaw in the gutter on A, cursing America. I got the fucker into this mess, and I'm getting him out. I could take him to the hospital, but they don't do shit for you when you've been knocked out, except ask you what the month is over and over. Believe me.

I jump out of the car, slide Mammood into an upright position in the passenger's seat and get behind the wheel. Haven't driven in months and, amidst all my fucked up New York City jobs, I've somehow never driven a cab. But I figure it's like riding a bike, though in this case, it's riding a bike without your dominant hand.

Mammood's got a photograph of what appear to be his kids taped to his dashboard. The girl looks to be six or so, and the boy is a few years younger. They've got big smiles, and a tiny tan terrier sits between them. The photo is wrinkled and its edges are curling.

I flip the radio on and it's some weird sitar *lada lada lada* shit, like you hear in the curry joints on 6th Street, so I switch to K-Rock. The Chili Peppers are on for a few seconds, then segue into a commercial for laser surgery for your eyes. I debate running upstairs for some tapes, get some good cruising tunes, maybe some Dropkick Murphys, and rule against it. I put my turn signal on, like I learned in Driver's Ed, check my sideview, look behind me to make sure, and pull up to the light.

There's tons of traffic coming into Manhattan on the Williamsburg Bridge, but heading towards Brooklyn takes just a few minutes. I get the hang of the cab-driving thing pretty quickly, and once I learn to turn on my off-duty light, I no longer garner the hails of Manhattan's hopeful revelers.

Mammood's got a deck of cigarettes with foreign writing on the package; I take one out and light it up. Something about smoking while driving seems enticing, seems *right*, though the cigarette is dry and makes me wish for a drink. I debate pulling over for a couple tall boys—road sodas, as Gabby would say—but decide not to.

The cab definitely has more juice than any car I've ever driven before, and I remind myself to keep it slow, take it easy, don't get carried away in the lights and the sounds and the air rushing in my window, get my sorry ass pulled over. Couple of times I kinda get lost in all that shit, and drift into the adjacent lane, and some Guido in a big Guido car blows his horn in my ear and throws me a vibe, mouthing the words "Muthuhfuckuh" when he flies by. So I take it real slow, do about 50, *stay focused*, like Coach might say. If I crashed, it would be mighty difficult for the white boy to explain the passed-out Indian guy in the passenger's seat. Now *there's* a

170

switch in ol' Cabbie-Land. Speaking of my passenger, not a peep from Mammood; he's a model passenger, the kind of fare he probably dreams about.

I'm not positive about the way to the beach, but I'm hoping I can piece it together. Ma used to take me to Jones Beach in her old Duster when I was a kid, her lone 8-track tape, some Paddy Reilly shit about the bombed out cars in the town he loved so well playing on the tinny AC-Delco stereo. If I let my instinct rule over my sense, I just might get there. It's gotten me onto the Grand Central, and then it's the Northern State, if I remember correctly, something else if I don't.

And finally the Meadowbrook.

I ease the cab onto the highway, slow down to handle the sharp curve and check out my new surroundings. It's a pretty road; the surface is smooth and there are these cool pine trees alongside it, and there's no one, not a soul, out here tonight. It's kinda eerie, it being Saturday night and all, the most crowded place in the world about 20 miles away, and only the crickets chirping and a lonely set of headlights coming at me every minute or so. It's eerie, but perfectly peaceful.

I roll down the window and am pretty sure I can smell salt in the thick, foggy air, so we must be getting close. I keep passing these beachy Meadowbrook signs featuring a lighthouse overlooking the sea, and a big 'M.' Each exit has the letter M in them: M1, M2, M3. M for miscreant, M for malingerer, M for malicious. M for Mammood. Poor bastard.

I look over at my passenger. He's starting to stir. *Shit.*

His eyes are open a full five seconds before he reacts.

"YOU MUDDERFUCKER!" Mammood yells, then clamps his jaw shut. His eyes bulge out like golf balls half-buried in a sand trap as he massages his jaw.

"Mammood, easy, man."

"Don't tell me be easy! You mudderfucker, you pull over and give me my car!"

I consider having a go at his button again, but don't have the heart or the energy.

"Easy, Mammood," I try again. "We're almost there. Then I'll give you your car back."

Mammood reaches for the wheel and the car darts left; fortunately, there's no one in the fast lane. I quickly straighten the cab out and unfold his determined hand from the wheel.

"You bad man," Mammood says.

"I know, I know. I'm sorry about hitting you and I'm sorry about stealing your car."

"You smoke my cigarette, too?"

"Yeah. Sorry about that," I say as I stub it out.

Michael J. Malone

He hunches his body against the car door and I hear the *beep beep beep* of his cell phone. I reach over and grab his collar, which tears a bit, and pull him close enough to where I can wrest the phone from him. He doesn't put up much of a fight. I slide it into my jeans pocket.

"Cock Mudderfucker!" he yells. "You go to jail!"

"No one's going to jail, Mammood. A few more minutes, we get there, I get out, you get your car back."

"What about fucking cell telephone!"

"Yes, Mammood, you get that back too."

Mammood opens his car door, allowing a noisy rush of air in the car. He considers the jump and roll, so I speed it up a bit and jerk the wheel left and right.

"No one's jumping, Indy Jones. Bear with me a few minutes, and then you get your car back."

"You owe me big money. $200."

"I owe you a little something, Mammood, but not $200."

"Mudderfucker!" he shouts. "You break my jaw."

I've got no retort to that, though I don't think it's broken. Maybe I'll send him to Demento for an examination.

We don't speak for a bit as we amble down the highway. I can hear high-pitched whimpers of anger and pain coming from him, as he mutters to himself.

"Should have bought gas station," he says. "Gas station safer."

"No, Mammood, gas stations are no safer. Those guys get held up all the time, and sometimes they get shot. You did the right thing."

"My friend Hasheem own Mobil Station in Middle Village. He never get robbed. He make good money."

"Mmmm," I say. "He'll get robbed."

We're quiet again.

"These yer kids?" I ask.

"Fock you, my kids."

"Mammood, c'mon. Are these yer fuckin' kids, or what? They're cute."

"My bruddah's kids. I uncle."

Uncle Mammood.

"No kids for you, Mammood?"

"Why you wanna know I have kids? Fock you, deeksucker!"

"Ah, fuck. C'mon, man. We've got a few more minutes together. Let's make the best of it."

"Mudderfucker," he mumbles. "My friends say no pick up people in Alphabet City. Bad people down there. Bad *white* people."

"Ah, c'mon, Mammood. Ya got me on a bad night. I'm not a bad guy."

"You mudderfuckerdeeksucker. You *hit* me."

"Mammood, I'm really sorry. How many times you want me to say it? I'm really fucking sorry."

I look over at my fare; he's shaking his head and rubbing his jaw.

"Where you from, Mammood?"

"Fock you, where I'm from."

"C'mon, I wanna know."

"Packy-stahn."

"Mmmm," I say, wishing I could share a single scrap of knowledge about Pakistan as a show of respect, other than it supplies New York with much of its cabbies and dope.

"Cool," I say. "Good food there, huh?"

"Yes, of course."

"You ever eat in the Indian restaurants on 6th Street?"

"No. I'm from *Packy-stahn.*"

We pass a sign for the Jones Beach exit.

"So we get to beach, you give me taxicab," says Mammood.

"Yes, my friend."

"Why do you go to beach at night? Beach closed."

"A girl."

"Ah, yes. And how do I get back?"

"Take this same road, the Meadowbrook, north. Stay on it until you see signs for the Northern State. Take that, uh…west, and then it's the Grand Central, I think, and you'll see the city."

"I no go back to the city. I go home. No more work. I sell taxicab."

"Ah, c'mon. Don't quit."

"I quit," he says wistfully. "Tonight. Tomorrow. Bad man."

I feel terrible.

"And where is home?"

"Not your business where my home is!" Mammood hisses.

"Just curious, man."

It's quiet for a bit. I take the exit, do the circle and pull the car over to the shoulder, where it seems safe to stop with no one around. The air is heavy with the sea. I can walk from here.

"Maspeth," he whispers.

"OK, this is the end of the line for me."

I take out my wallet. I've got $24. My thoughts turn to coffee and a bagel tomorrow. I give Mammood $22.

"Twenty two dollah!" he screams, then rubs his jaw again. "You mudder-fuckerdeeksucker! Twenty two dollah!"

"Mammood, c'mon, guy. This is all I got. I'm sorry shit worked out like this. I'll get you next time. I'll send the money to…Maspeth."

"I get YOU next time," he howls. "Bad man. I call police!"

That I expected. I'll have to keep my eyes open for them.

"That's all I got, Mammood. Thank you, and I'm really sorry."

I'm waiting for him to accept my apology, but none is forthcoming. We're quiet for a moment, just the crickets chirping outside the car. I finger the photograph on the dash.

"Yer kids're cute, man."

"NOT MY KIDS!" Mammood bellows. "And give me my cell telephone!"

I think about tossing it into the brush—he's only going to call the cops on me—but I don't have the heart. I hand Mammood his cell, hop out of the car and rap on the hood as I pass it.

"Mudderfuckerdeeksucker!" he yells, and I wave goodbye.

The air is thick and damp at the beach; I wish I'd brought a jacket. Didn't really expect to end up here—hell, didn't know where the fuck I was going—so I'm dressed in my old blue pocket T and a pair of jeans. My hand is still throbbing pretty bad. Can't go back to Demento to have him look at it; he'll know something's up with me, and he'll tell the boys, and they'll have a fucking intervention or something. You know you're at rock-fucking-bottom when the rugby guys have an intervention for you.

I run through the foggy air and down to the sea, where the surf progresses and retreats with metronomic regularity, and soak my sore hand in the water for a minute or so, flattening it like a starfish against the wet sand as the water soaks my Skechers. Walking away, I shake my hand dry, rub it on my jeans and put my arms inside my t-shirt, which does little to warm me amidst the unwelcoming sea air. But it's a comforting feeling nonetheless.

Standing atop the dunes, I look toward the parking lot. A rent-a-cop is driving around seemingly aimlessly, hoping to not see anything, smoking a cigar that I can smell from a hundred yards away.

Finding a spot on the sand, just beyond the dunes, I drop anchor and look to the sea. It's no wonder Haley's folks loved coming here—it's a beautiful spot. I'm totally alone; I can't believe the local kids aren't screwing on the beach, or at least drinking. It's a weird feeling. City kids don't get this totally alone thing very often. Most times I'd kill for it, but right now it just makes me even more depressed. The dope's worn off and I wish I'd brought booze and it's just me and there's not a fucking soul around, nothing, no one. Shit, this reminds me of the dungeon we got tossed in at Mardi Gras. I wish I was back in the City; at least the people, the lights, the buildings would give my brain something else to think about. I hate this beautiful spot. I think of poor Mammood, driving north on the Meadowbrook, rubbing his jaw, cursing America, cursing me. He's right—I am a mudderfuck-erdeeksucker. I deserve jail. Just not solitary. And please don't give me one of those roommates either.

So Haley's mom and dad would throw their blanket down and lay back on the sand, listening to the sea lap up on the shore, checking out the stars above and talk about their future. Mr. Snow would tell her that he'd eventually start making some real dough, and they'd move out of her mom's house and get some shitty little place in the Upper West Side, then he'd eventually save enough to go to law school, and he'd finish and get a job and an apartment like a house and they'd have their precious little girl, Meadow. I never saw Haley's baby pictures, but I've got one in my head: straight blonde hair in a pony tail held back with a red ribbon, red and green plaid pants like the skirt of the girl I saw hanging flyers on A, a white long-sleeve shirt with a sunflower on the front. Clapping her hands, big smile on her pretty little face.

I lay back on the sand and take in the stars. Despite the fog, they're huge—sparkling silver in the off-black sky. I roll over onto my side and curl into a ball. Past the dunes and through a wood-slat fence, I see two Nassau County police cars facing each other. They split up and do a quick circle of the lot, shining spotlights around before exiting. The waves create a gentle rhythm, lulling me toward slumber. I'm not going to say I cried myself to sleep, and I'm not going to say I didn't.

"Gabby, thank God you're fucking home," I say, trying to get comfortable with the phone in my left hand.

"Deckie?"

"Yeah, man."

"Wassssuuuuup?"

I grit my teeth.

"Not much, man. I need help."

"I been tellin' ya that for years. What made ya finally realize it?"

"Seriously, man, no bullshit. Do me right here, for once."

I kind of mumble the "for once" part.

"Y'awright?"

"Yeah, I think so."

"Where you been, man?"

Gabby blows off my Troika reading. Where *I* been?

"I just need a pickup," I say. "Can you score your bro's car?"

"I think so," says Gabby. "He's around this weekend. I'm sure his car is, too. Where the fuck are ya?"

"Uh, Jones Beach."

"Jones Beach? You hate the beach. Remember we all went to Rockaway Beach after the match against the Fishheads? You wouldn't even step onto the sand."

"I know, I know. Just sorta ended up here last night. Fell asleep on the beach, then next thing I know the sun's up and some kid's pouring sand on my head. Looked up and there were lotsa people around me. Felt like, I don't know, a fish outta water, ya know?"

"Dig it, man. You get some last night?"

"Uh, yeah. Course."

"Sex on the beach," says Gabby. "Pussy drink."

"Yeah, whatever. Pick me up."

"Awright, awright. Who was she?"

A man and a boy, the man armed with a metal detector, step onto the beach. The man gives me the eye, but looks away when his device starts beeping.

"Gabby, do me one favor."

I hate asking Gabby for favors.

"Actually, it's two," I continue. I hate this twice as much. "Pick me up, and don't ask me anything about last night. It's kinda fucked up and I gotta sort the shit out first. I'll tell ya when I'm ready."

"Oooh, someone hooked up with someone's missus," sings Gabby. "You shag Lady Brady? *That* would piss a few people off."

Gabby doesn't know me and Haley are kaput. Or does he?

"I didn't hook up with Lady Brady," I say. "How 'bout we just talk about rugby and shit."

"The Montauk Sharks are a buncha goons."

"They beat us?"

"Oh, yeah," says Gabby.

"Bummer. Thought we might win that one."

We still haven't won this season.

"Yeah. We coulda used ya, Deckie."

"Who's playin' flanker?"

"Flyboy and Ghetto Ron," says Gabby. "Me at eight-man. Gentle Ben at hooker."

I shake my head.

"Flyboy's got stone hands and Ghetto Ron can't tackle," I say.

"Neither can you."

"So what happened?"

"It was close with like 20 minutes left, like Montauk up 30-25 or something. Then Spartacus got sin-binned for a late hit on the flyhalf, total bullshit call by that ref with the mullet."

"That dude's awful," I say.

"Yeah. Then they got like five tries when we were a man down."

The automated operator asks for more money.

"Pick me up," I say. "Now. Please."

"Awright. Give me about an hour. Gotta walk up to Stuy Town to get the car, and there's gonna be traffic and shit."

"What time is it?" I ask.

"Almost eight."

"What the fuck you doin' up, anyway?"

"Just got in, man."

"No shit," I say. "Get a little?"

"Got a lot," crows Gabby.

"You OK to drive?"

I hear Gabby breath into his hand, checking his blood alcohol level.

"Yeah."

Please deposit 25 cents ...insists the recording.

"I'm at a big fucking tower, I think it's Field 4," I say. "Freakin' hurry."

"I'm on it," says Gabby.

"Thanks, bro."

I hang up. Well, that's one index card I can rip up. That was relatively easy; certainly easier than the rest are going to be.

Three to go.

Michael J. Malone

The goddamn bank machine's fucked up, I know it is. I know that beating the freakin' thing one, two, three, four times with my good hand is not going to produce a twenty, but I do it anyway. There's no way my account is empty; that just doesn't happen to gainfully employed people right around the corner from their 30th birthday. Fucking Sally's withholding my goddamn Honey Bunny advance until she approves the manuscript. Not sure what kinda bullshit that is. I mean, I got her something, not exactly on time, but not that late either; I've gotten her shit later than that. If she don't like it, it ain't my problem. And her telling me kids are going to be crying and shit when they read *Enchanted Meadow* the way it is, well, fuckin' A, it ain't all happy hops through the meadow, Sally. Sorry. This is life.

"Are you done, man?" comes the voice from behind me.

I whip around. A guy in a three-quarter sleeve baseball shirt with "American by Birth, Southern by Nature" atop American and Confederate flags is waiting for the cash machine. He's got his hair combed straight down over his eyes, like the guys from Oasis. He's not really a southerner, just a hip Avenue A guy going for that irony thing. Two girls wait on line behind him.

"Yeah," I say, putting my head down and heading outside.

It's a Sunday night, so there's not the usual nightlife crush choking Avenue A. A foursome walks into the screening room at Two Boots Pizza, and a couple of women holding hands walk out with a video and a pizza.

I bang a right on 6th and walk past Sidewalk Café, its outdoor tables full of bikers having drinks and keeping their eye on the bikes parked in the street. The school at 6th and B does not have its usual slacker throng on the steps; just one kid is holding down the fort. He's got a green sweatshirt on, the hood pulled over his head and tied under his neck.

I stop in front of him.

"Little Green Riding Hood," I say cheerfully.

"Sup," he says, not looking up.

"Not much, my man. What's up whichoo?"

"Uh, nothing," he says nervously. "Just sittin'."

"Ain'tcha got school tomorrow?"

"What're you, my p.o., or something? A *narc*?"

"Nah, man, just a concerned citizen," I say, taking a seat next to him, close enough so our sides are touching. I can smell cigarettes on his breath. He scoots over to put a few inches of moonlight between us.

"Whaddya want, man?"

"Just being friendly," I say. "They say people in New York ain't friendly, right? Just doin' my part to change that stereotype."

"That's cool," he says, untying his hood and yanking on the drawstrings, left, right, left right, like he's flossing his brain.

"Mental floss," I mumble to myself.

"Huh?" he says.

"Nothin', man. Just sayin', changin' stereotypes is important, I think. I mean, if I went with stereotypes, I'd say you were a junkie or somethin', sitting out here on Avenue B all alone on a Sunday, the Lord's Day, shivering here in the heat. Ya know, ya seem like a dopehead. But I ain't goin' with stereotypes."

"That's cool," says the kid, scooting over another inch. "I gotta meet my buddy."

He goes to get up, but I stick my arm out, like I'd jammed on the brakes and my kid was in the passenger seat.

"Wassup?" he says weakly.

"Hang out, man."

"I gotta go," he says.

I grab his upper arm with my right hand, which fits easily around where his biceps should be. I squeeze, sending a bolt of pain through my sore hand.

"What the fuck?" he pleads.

"Gimme your dope," I say. "You're better off without it."

"I don't have any dope."

"Yes you do."

"No I don't! I couldn't find any tonight. Streets're dry, man. It's *Panic in Needle Park* all over again. Fuck *off*."

"Don't jerk me around," I say, squeezing harder, ignoring the pain, feeling the grooves on his upper arm bone.

"*Uuuooooowww,*" he moans. "Oww, man. Leggo!"

"Fucking give it to me," I say in the clipped, tough-guy voice that I use on the rugby pitch, when the other guys are killing the ball in rucks and the ref's got his head up his ass and you have to take matters into your own hands. "Don't fucking jerk me around."

I'm hoping it doesn't come to violence, not because I couldn't take this runt, but because I've never thrown a left-handed punch before. I'll probably pull a muscle or something.

A respectable young white couple, the kind you see more and more of east of A, strolls by with their chocolate lab, which runs on ahead. The kid in my clutches cranes his neck to get their attention, but they're focused straight ahead, as they've learned to do until the neighborhood gentrifies entirely.

"Barney!" shouts the man. "Come 'ere, boy."

Then they're out of the picture. I can feel the kid's hope egress.

"Let's have it, then," I say.

"This is fucking bullshit," he says. "Get your own fucking dope. How old are you, like 25?"

Michael J. Malone

I squeeze his arm harder and try snapping it, but I'm not strong enough. Fucking wiseass.

"*Eeeeowwww!*" he squeals. "Alright, alright, fucking let go, you fucking thug."

I let go and his hand fishes into the enormous pockets of his cargo pants.

"It was my last fucking ten dollars," he says, handing me a bag with a court jester printed on it. "Hope you're happy, asshole."

"Thank you," I say. "I appreciate it."

"You're a bully, is what you are."

I shrug, secretly flattered.

"Are you, like, gonna kick me off the steps, too?"

"Nah, hang out, dude. I'm outta here. Hey man, I'll do you right next time I see ya, I promise."

"I'll be here waiting," he says.

"Awright, see ya," I say. I clap him on the shoulder and he winces. "You oughta get cleaned up, bro'. Move home and shit."

"Fuck you," the punk says, retreating under his hoodie like a turtle.

There's a newfound spring in my step as I gambol down 6th towards A. With no one around, I start singing to myself.

I am going, I am going
Any which way the wind may be blowing
I am going, I am going
Where streams of whiskey are flowing!

It's the happiest I've been all day.

Man, what a fucked up day it's been. Fucked up weekend, more like it. The Paul Rudd Filmfest. The cab ride—poor fucking Mammood. The beach—the metal detector, some kid pouring sand on me, saying, "Wake up, Mister" as I tried to make out my surroundings, his dad calling him back, slowly walk away from the freaky thing that rolled in with the tide. Jesus. Don't know how the hell I'm going to deal at work tomorrow; I'm going to be a mess. Oh well. Right now, it's about getting through tonight, and dealing with tomorrow, tomorrow. Just happy to see I'm feeling a little better.

The Back Page's bathroom, with each stall's individual TV, is certainly an enticing option, but it's another five blocks up 1st Avenue, while the Tile Bar looms just across the way. Thinking I'll get to sleep earlier by going to the closer bar, I dive into Tile Bar.

There's a smattering of customers, maybe eight at the bar, another 10 or so at tables. Zeppelin's "Kashmir" is on the juke box, the best little juke in all of New York. The bartender lady, wearing a cowboy hat and a buttoned-up vest with nothing on underneath, smiles coquettishly as I walk in. I nod toward the back, where the bathrooms are, indicating I'll be a fully paying customer once I take care of my business. She nods in return.

There are two single-occupancy bathrooms, neither marked with a gender, which is nice, because someone might try yours, find it occupied and will just try the other one. I enter and slide the dead bolt across, hear its satisfying click, put the seat down and lower myself upon it.

I separate the Ziploc clasps that seal the little bag and study the sinister-looking court jester on the front, laughing at all who dare ingest his evil elixir. The harsh white bathroom light shows the dope to be more brown than white. I pour a little into my hand, say as much of the "Our Father" as I can remember and snort away, waiting for the court's ruling.

Yeeeeeooouwww!

Oh, motherfucker. Fuck fuck FUCK—it's an ice cream headache times a million, jury's out on this one, just gotta…wait this one out…Zeppelin off in the distance, Page's guitar solo through the door, *Na na na, boom, na na na, boom…* Bonzo wailing, Plant keening, *Oooo oooo, yay-yeah…*

I'm staring at the stark white of the toilet's porcelain base, its little beads of condensation like the sweat on my forehead and back, a few squashed cigarette butts on the ground amidst a puddle of urine just inches away from my nose. I see the carcass of a roach, at least an inch long, on his back near the rear of the toilet. What a place to die. On the wall behind the toilet, inches above the floor and upside down, someone has scrawled "Writing this was very inconvenient." My head dangles limply between my legs, dipping closer and closer to the cigarette and pee soup. Nausea threatens; the earth is spinning, as I'm told it always does, but this time I'm spinning with it.

With no small degree of effort, I pull my head upright again, my vertebrae creaking with effort, my brains seeping through my neck and down my throat like a lumpy shot of tequila. My head is veering, listing, hydroplaning to the left, eyes shut, don't have the energy to resist it, it's like the Ouija thingee gliding across the board, spelling out the player's impending doom. Then my head reverses its course and, before long, meets the hard tile wall to my right. *Thwack!* That sort of hurt. My eyes jerk open. I'll be sick if I don't get some air.

Slowly rising, stepping out of the bathroom, legs like retreating soldiers below me, I see a woman waiting to use the head. She offers me something between a smile and a grimace, something that says she recognizes I was in there for a while, isn't happy, is trying to be nice. I can't believe the effort required to keep my head up; I never really noticed how much a head weighs before.

As luck would have it, Tom Waits is on the best juke box in New York, his boozy barroom baritone bouncing off the tile floor, off the mirrors behind the bar,

Michael J. Malone

off the bar's front window, his hard-won rasp surrounding the place in all its cen-
trifugal glory.

Sixteen men on a dead man's chest
I've been drinking from a broken cup
Two pairs of pants and a mohair vest
I'm full of bourbon and I can't stand up

I freeze for a moment, close my eyes and relax my body, which is happy for
the respite. I sway slightly to the song's punchy thrust. But I can't stay. I'm going
to Haley's.

The bartender spies me again.

"What're ya havin'?" she says.

I offer a slow smile and walk past her towards the door.

"Scumbag!" she yells as I slink out.

It's Mammood, I swear it is. He's pissed, and I guess I can't blame him. As I
tried to cross 3rd Avenue at Cooper Square, he got me in his sights and lined me up
for the kill. I saw him heading for me, and I froze for a moment—watching this cab
zipping towards me, another flash of yellow in a city full of yellow flashes, but none
as ominous, as here and as fucking *now,* as this freakin' cab heading towards me.
The brain kept sayin', man, *move!* and the body knew it was the right thing to do,
but the message just kinda died somewhere, put in an out-box, got stalled, got held
up, just ended up drippin' into the synapses or hangin' in the wind.

At the last minute, the cab veered to my right, so I thought it would be wise
to throw my body to the left. The cab clipped my hip, hipped my clip, hit my clit,
Rudd Fucker Fudd Rucker, Jeezus, however the fuck you wanna say it, it spun my
leg around like a graceless figure skater and knocked me on my ass.

So I'm laying in 3rd Avenue, checkin' out the fuzzy stars above me through
the soupy air, kinda enjoyin' it all in that split second between impact and conse-
quence. The cab is parked about 20 feet ahead and the cabbie is running towards
me, tossing a lit cigarette into the brush at Cooper Square. His door is open and I
can hear the radio, *lada lada lada,* yada yada yada, spilling out of his car.

"Mammood," I whimper.

"Are you alright?" he says calmly upon approaching me. A few other people
gather.

"Mammood, I'm so sorry. It was wrong. I deserve this."

"Do not speak," he says. He's wearing a brown faux-silk shirt, opened to
reveal gold jewelry around his neck and a shaved chest. "Just lie still and be quiet."

"I'm sorry."

"It is okay. You are drunk. You jump in front of my cab. Not smart, my friend."

"I'm so sorry," I repeat. The pain is taking hold.

"I am sorry too," he says. "I try to miss you. You in street, my friend. In traffic."

"Mammood," I say.

"Who is Mammood? I am Ekbar. You stay quiet."

His eyes dart nervously, left-right, left-right, as taxis fly by.

"I can get up," I say.

"Are you sure?"

"Yes, yes," I say, propping myself up on my elbows, traffic whizzing by, making me dizzy, more yellow flashes in the night. I close my eyes and the dizziness fades.

"Help me up, Mammood."

"It is Ekbar," he says, lifting me under my arms. "Maybe you lie still for now."

"No. I can get up. Help me."

"I help you."

Some chubby mook in a Hawaiian shirt pulls me up by my belt loops.

"Thank you, Mammood," I say. "I'm sorry."

"Ekbar!" says Ekbar. "You are okay?"

"I am okay," I say, rubbing the back of my head with one hand and my hip with the other, and limping slowly onto the curb, toward the tiny park at Cooper Square. I think of some rugby dude in California who died after getting two concussions in a few weeks, think he was from an army base or something. The league made us read about it. I can't split on my and Tisa's future kid like this. With no dad, he'll end up like me.

"You rest, my friend. You stay out of traffic."

"I rest," I say, easing myself into a bench.

"I go? That okay?"

"You go," I say. "You go."

He looks around, shrugs and walks briskly toward his car, reprieved from potential NYPD red tape.

"You sure you're alright, man?" asks the Hawaiian shirt guy.

"Yeah. Wasn't as bad as it looked," I mumble.

"Well, it looked pretty bad. Head OK?"

It's a loaded question. I touch my head. There's a bit of blood, but it feels OK.

"Alright, bro," I say, though he looks doubtful.

"Want me to call someone? An ambulance?"

"Nah, I'm cool."

"Good luck," he says.

Michael J. Malone

The pain starts up in my hip again. I lean back on the bench and exhale. My body is a mess. The hip, the head, the cut foot, the nearly-busted hand; I feel like I just went all 80 minutes against New Zealand. I'm down to one good appendage, so I wipe the blood from my hand and pour a little Jester into it. A quick hit, and I'm off to Haley's. She'll run the bath for me and make me chamomile tea and put a hot towel on my head and treat my sores like a kindly nurse taking care of a war hero.

Yeeeooooowwww...

Court is in session.

"Good Christ," I hear, but it's garbled, like I'm a million miles underwater, and it's faint, like I'm standing in Montauk, and this person's yelling across the ocean from Ireland.

"Oh my Lord."

It's a little clearer and a little louder, but still barely audible. My eyes peer open slightly, then stretch open wide in horror. I'm laying on my side on the cement, and a bull is poised in front of me, horns sharp and at the ready, head down, face contorted in a foreboding, bloodthirsty sneer. Fucking Gabby has talked me into running with the goddamn bulls. I'm laying in the Pamplona dust, and I can hear the frat boys whizzing by me, the sun bright, my body wracked with pain, a bull about to impale me. What a sorry-ass way to go. One Yank idiot gets gored every year, and this year it's me. All the guys back home are gonna laugh at this one, ol' Deckie gored to death in Spain. Warmth spreads over my groin.

My eyes focus and I see the words "Diverse Moo York" painted on my predator, and a painted white kid and black kid shaking hands.

"Can you hear me, son?" goes that tiny, wavering voice again. I roll onto my back to make out its source, triggering pain in the back of my head, the cement cool and firm under it. I see a white figure hovering over me, the sun framing her stark white face. It's a motherfucking angel. This is it.

"Declan? Declan?"

The voice is getting louder and my eyes are starting to focus.

"Son?"

A lone tear falls on me.

Good God, that's no angel.

184

23B

The bed is alternately comforting and foreign. It's softer than the one I'm used to, but it's not entirely unfamiliar. This waking-up-in-strange-beds habit has to stop when I turn 30. My feet spill over the edge and my arms hang over the sides; I feel like Gulliver. The locals haven't tied me to the bed, thank God, but my injuries prevent me from getting up. I wiggle my fingers and start pumping a little life into my hands and arms. I see a bruise the color of an angry sky on the middle two knuckles of my right hand, its sickening color spreading onto the neighboring knuckles. I touch my hip and recoil in pain. I feel my head for bumps, bruises, holes. It's sore but sound, and soaking wet.

My eyes adjust, and I begin to scrutinize the small room around me. There's a poster of the '86 Mets. Man, those boys could play. Straw, Mex, Nails, El Sid, Mookie, Dr. K, the Kid...Fuckin' A, they were a team. Had that swagger; other teams hated them. I loved them. Knew every guy in that team picture way back when, the year they won it all, even the trainers. Maybe I still do.

There's a bulletin board on the wall showing an array of certificates and medals. One certificate says ASHER LEVY MINNOWS SWIM CLUB on it, and another says EAT AT JOE'S CARDINALS, 2nd PLACE. They're both written in this half-assed calligraphy, and they're faded and curling at the edges. There are photos tacked all over the board, though I can't make them out from the bed. An ironing board is propped up against the wall and a sewing machine sits upon an antique desk, which has black steel legs and a red wood top, with a slot in the corner for an inkwell. Behind my head is a little shelf built into the headboard. On it is a rubber Great White with 'Shark Park' painted on the side and a Mets bobble-head doll, its demonic grin looking like a court jester.

Jesus watches over this manic menagerie from a giant crucifix hung on the wall.

I look back at the evil bobble-head doll's grin. It's Keith Hernandez. Whoa. The previous few days' events start coming back to me in flashes—the beach, the cabbie, the other cabbie—filling my body with dread and anxiety.

"Jayzus, don't know if 'how yeh been, son?' is really appropriate," says the voice in the doorway.

"Hi," I say weakly, my first word in...forever.

She walks in and stands next to my bed. It's the first time I've seen her close-up in a long time. The red in her hair is losing its battle with the gray. She looks thin and old, and it makes me sad. Someone should be around to protect her.

"How yeh feelin', son?" she says gruffly.

"M'awright," I lie. The words don't come easily. "Little sore."

I'm not sure how much she knows, what to lie about and what to come clean with. To be truthful, I'm not sure how much I know either. MacLennane's? Tile Bar? Shots with Gabby and the boys? Shit, I don't know. All I know is, I'm here.

"Och, thought yeh were fookin' dead when I found yeh," she says. "Yeh fookin' well shoulda been."

This isn't good.

"Mmmm," I utter. My brain is operating like the world's first modem. "Mmmm."

"Em, looks like we're both takin' the day off," she says.

I have no idea what day it is. Based on what she's saying, it sounds like a work day. Guess Avatar will have to get by without me. Hopefully Becky can cover my ass. Again.

"Guess so."

"Gave yeh a wee painkiller, which knocked yeh head over arse right 'nuff."

"Thanks."

"So how *have* yeh been?" Ma says, looking me in the eye for the first time. I can see the hurt, the heartache, the frustration, the disappointment in her eyes. This isn't how I pictured our meeting.

I ponder her question.

"I've been fine," I say. "Things're OK."

"Hmmm. Got yerself a girl?"

"Nah. I did. Not Tisa. But me an' the other one, the one after Tisa, we split up."

"Aye. That tall girl, looks like a Barbie doll?"

I never thought of Haley as a Barbie doll—her body's not quite as well-defined, but whose is? Yeah, I guess that would be her.

"Blonde girl, yeah."

"Pretty, that one. Seen yez around."

"Thanks," I say. "It's over."

"How 'bout that *ooother* one?" Ma asks. She still won't refer to Tisa by name. "Hear from *her*?"

"Her" oozes bile.

"Now and then," I say. "Not really."

"Em, now and then, or not really?"

"Heard from her a ways back, but haven't seen her."

Ma nods slowly.

"I think she's married," I add.

"Och, some other fookin' eejit's problem. Yeh still goin' to mass?"

"Sure," I lie. For years I would set foot, literally one foot, in a church at some point each Sunday, so I could truthfully answer that question in the affirmative when it inevitably came up. But I haven't done that in some time.

"Good. Job?"

"The wine mag. Still."

"Yeh make senior editor yet? I know that was yer bugaboo a few years back."

"Nah, not yet, Ma. Soon."

"Ah miss the free wine."

"Mmm."

"Yeh still playin' that Brit poofter game?"

"Little bit, not that much."

"Won't be playin' any time soon, is my medical opinion," says Ma. "Yer gettin' thin."

"Hopefully some of your lasagna'll beef me up again," I say.

She thwarts a hint of a smile.

"Yeh should probably sleep a bit more, sweat more o' that crap outta yeh," she says. "Once yer strong enough, yeh can go upstairs and get some clothes. But yer not stayin' up there. Yer puttin' that shite behind yeh, and yer fookin' stayin' here."

"Ma, I appreciate you...cleaning me up and all, but I'm gonna go home."

"Like fook yeh are!"

"Ma, I'm fucking 30 years old."

"Watch yer fookin' language," she hisses, her blue eyes glowing. "Yer not fookin' 30, and left to yer own devices, yeh won't be getting there, either."

"I'm not staying here."

"Yer fookin' stayin'! Now get some rest."

I'm not in any condition to argue; debating with Paula Coulter when you have all your physical and mental resources is hard enough. I'll stay for a nap, get my head sorted out and we'll deal with this later.

I ended up sleeping for another six hours or so, waking up every half hour, cramps in my legs and anxiety and dread all over and my heart racing real fast, sweating a lot, each of my nerve endings switched to hyperspeed, thinking I was having a heart attack and a stroke and, I don't know, typhoid or something, all rolled into one.

Never thought I'd be able to get back to sleep, but I did each time. Kept having this dream where I was in this enormous room filled with rats, rats on top of rats, and I'm naked except for a straitjacket, walking along a greased-up balance beam a few inches above them, hearing them squeak-squeakin' at me, nipping at my feet, hoping I'd fall and they could eat me, bones and all, for the next month or so, even after I spoiled. It was a stark white room with a high ceiling and nothing in it but rats, and their squeals created a cacophony that echoed through the room. I lost my balance and started to topple over, the straitjacket impeding the defense of my genitals, and Tisa somehow caught me. That was when I'd wake up. Over and over.

I'm sitting on the edge of my bed, debating my next move. Each movement seems to take forever: figuring out what to do, weighing the consequences in my brain, giving my body the signal to follow suit and finally carrying out the maneuver. I feel like I'm in a borrowed body—one found in a scrap heap that the dealer didn't have the nerve to ask the buyer to pay for. I have no idea what comes next. Stand up, put some pants on and get my ass home? The idea gets the thumbs-up, and slowly transforms into an action.

I limp my way into the kitchen. It hasn't changed since the last time I was here, years before. Jesus is hanging over the sink. The pope is on the fridge, blessing Ma's to-do list—return her Maeve Binchy book to the library, vacuum the family room, pick up wine. She's sitting at the table, smoking a Kool. She'd promised to quit smoking. Nothing has changed.

"Hi, Ma."

"Mmm," she says, not looking up from her gigantic hardcover.

I put my hands on the back of a chair for support.

"I'm gonna get going now," I start. "It's great to see you. We should, ya know, meet up. Maybe I'll cook ya dinner or something."

"Aye toldja, yer not fookin' goin' anywhere. Not yet, anyway. Adults live on their own, and children live with their Mams. I'm poottin' yeh in the latter category."

"Ma, as I said before, thank you for fixing me up. I had a bad night, a stupid night, totally embarrassing. I shouldn't drink whiskey, just stick to beer. I messed up. I'm OK now. I'm going home."

"Look in the fookin' mirror," she says, folding the corner of the page she's on and putting her book on the table. She looks up at me with moist eyes. "Lookit yerself. Yer not fookin' OK. Yer a fookin' mess, Declan."

Declan.

Ma rarely called me by my name, even though she gave me the damn thing. It's "son" or it's "laddie" or it's "fookin' eejit," or something else, but it's only "Declan" when she's damn-straight serious. There's a crack in her voice—a rare display of weakness, of humanity, of mortality—and I'm scared to death she's going to cry. My psyche is on incredibly thin ice to begin with, and that would just do me in. I take a seat across the table from her.

"Ma, I'm sorry about the last few years," I start, even though I don't think it was my fault. "I want us to be, ya know, friends again. I've been thinking about it a lot. I'll stop by every day, if you want, but I'm not staying here. OK?"

It's quiet for a moment, and Ma stubs out her cigarette.

"Smoking's gonna kill ya," I say.

Ma slams her palm on the table; I'm surprised how much noise her bony little hand can generate.

"Don't fookin' tell me about what's gonna kill me! Yer the one I found half-dead, passed out on the street like a common knacker, a fookin' itinerant. Like his fookin' Dah. Och, that's it, son, that's what I'm afraid of. Yer turning into yer fookin' Dah!"

She's glaring at me, her eyes glazed over. I prop my elbows on the table and rest my head in my hands; I can't look into those alternately burning and moist eyes anymore.

"Get yer fookin' head on straight," she says quietly. "Do it right this time, and yeh won't have to do it again."

We sit there, motionless and wordless. I can hear the kitchen clock ticking, the faint passage of cars on Avenue A and the sound of me forcing saliva down my throat. My head is pounding, my legs are cramping again and I seriously consider running out of there and finding a doctor who operates in the shadows of Avenue B. But that thought is too grandiose, too ambitious to earn support in the tenuous Congress that rules my body. I'm too weary to move.

I slide my hands under my chin and look at Ma.

"Can I go upstairs and get some stuff?" I say. I feel like I'm playing Mother May I?. I guess I am.

"Yes," she says quietly, giving me a look that *just dares* me to defy her.

"How long will I be staying here?"

"Until yeh show me yeh can make do on yer own."

"And then I can move back home."

"Aye."

"Mmm," I utter, wondering if there's any point in arguing.

"Aye can't babysit yeh while I'm workin', but you're to come home after work and be here for dinner every night. If you're to go out, I wanna know where and with who. Understood?"

"Yeah."

"And while yer upstairs, grab some proper clothing. We're going to mass tonight."

"What day is it?"

"It's Monday, and don't fookin' tell me yeh went to mass yesterday. Maybe yeh had your last rites read to ya by a passing priest as yeh were layin' there in Cooper

Square, but yer still fookin' goin' to mass. St. Brigid's has it every night o' the week, and you'll fookin' get well used to it, mister. It'll do yeh some good."

I nod my head and start out the door, wondering if it's the last time I'll get to leave 23B without hearing the beeping of an electronic device in my head.

My place is a mess, of course, and the state of it brings back my anxiety. But the blinking of the answering machine gives me hope. Someone has thought of me, has confirmed the rumors of my existence. I hit the PLAY button, and hear a familiar whiny voice.

"Coulter, Ken here, your boss at Avatar, remember me? I'm at work, and so is Stephen and Becky and Tricia in accounting and the rest of the crew. Except you, big guy. This was your last last chance, Coulter. If you come in at all, it's to clear out your desk. Better yet, we'll do it for you. Oh, and good luck with the band."

The news slowly sinks in, and I can't say I'm devastated by it. Of course, ol' Paula might not handle it quite as well, but what's she going to do, throw me out? I should be so lucky. I hope for the triple-beep that spells the end of further bad news, but there's another message. I shove aside some of the rubble on the couch and sit.

"Hello, Declan," it starts. *"It's Sally at Green Mountain. Haven't heard from you in a bit. We need* Enchanted Meadow *revisions ASAP, like, yesterday. We can't change the print date again. Please have it on my desk by Wednesday afternoon, or it's no go. This is your last last chance."*

Sounds like Sally's been talking to Ken.

Then there are messages from Gabby and Shady Brady, come out to Ma-cLennane's, missed ya Saturday, lost to Montauk, got the Rockaway Fishheads this weekend, pints of Guinness, boys askin' for ya, etc., etc., etc.

Ken can piss off, as always, but Sally's message really bothers me. I never felt anything for the stupid wine mag, but Honey Bunny I adore. I birthed the damn thing. I'm in no condition to crank out *Enchanted Meadow* now; even if my head was OK, with my hands shaking and beat-up the way they are, I don't even think I could type if I had something *to* type. Maybe I can take my beloved little bunny to another publisher when I'm up and about again.

I let out a breath that lasts an eternity. I should get up, but I'm enjoying a rare moment of respite. Me and Ma are speaking again, though that may change when she hears I've been sacked. I look out the window and see Avenue A's usual swirl of activity below. There's nothing to stop me from going out there. But something does.

I see Ma's index card on the coffee table and rip it up, throwing the pieces amidst the rest of the garbage on the floor—the broken glass, the Frisbee lid of late-night takeout, an old *New York Post*, even older spilled beer.

Two to go.

This is my life, I'm thinking as I sit at Ma's kitchen table, Jesus dying for my bottomless trove of sins above the sink. I'm three weeks shy of 30. Getting married? Nah. Paying a mortgage? Hell, no. Uh, working? Nope. I live with my mother. Well, if Tisa's pregnant, then at least I'll be doing one adult-type thing. I suppose this is what they call rock bottom. Jesus—yeah, you above the sink—I hope it is.

I feel like Ma hates me sometimes, but there's a strange comfort in that; at least she feels *something* for me. And she wouldn't have taken me in if she didn't care about me ... or so I keep telling myself. So it's warming a bit between us, the way the mercury sometimes creeps near 0 during a Siberian winter. We sit and talk over breakfast, then I walk her to work over by Washington Square Park, and then I promise to send some resumes out and have a productive day—the final Avatar paycheck will not last long—bid her farewell and not kiss her good-bye.

I read the Help Wanteds in the park for a bit, then head over to the community center on 7th Avenue. I get in a light workout, which is all my bruised body can really take. My membership runs out at the end of the month, so each time I go, I grab a few one-day passes for my supposed "guys at work." I've got a nice little stockpile that should last a few months.

When Ma gets home we go to Odessa Diner and get grilled cheese—her with tomato ("Jack-Tommy," the waiter calls her meal after she orders it), me without, coffee for both, and she smokes her Kools. Or she makes dinner, smokes her Kools and we talk some more. Then we head over to St. Brigid's. Never liked church, and I'm sorry to report that I still don't. I was surprised to see I still possess a skill I learned as a kid—the ability to completely zone out the second the priest starts talking, right up until he's done.

I look up at Jesus glaring down from his cross, and shrug an apology.

One might think that going's a waste of time if I'm not paying attention, but I walk through Tompkins afterwards with a good feeling, Ma at my side, making fun of *Fahder McGrier's wee belly*, or a fellow parishioner *with a nose like a rhinoceros*, or someone else in church.

I've also stepped up the volunteer work over at Needles R Us to twice a week. Hell, I've got the time. And I feel like it's a good penance for me, too. Damn, must be all that church-going, making me think of penance. If I start dwelling on my life and where I'm at—or not at—on the on-ramp to 30, I get the urge to bang a left on Avenue B and see what's what. But I keep my feet moving past B, onto C, turn right and check out the freaks lining up at the Harm Reduction Center for clean works. Those filthy bastards need me. Who knows? Maybe I need them too.

The rat dream notwithstanding, getting my *fookin'* head on straight wasn't seeing dead babies on the ceiling, like in *Trainspotting*. I mean, there's big-time anxiety, but that's nothing new. And the physical pain, well, between playing rugby on

Michael J. Malone

the forsaken New York fields for the last seven years and stealing some of Ma's meds out of the bathroom, it's been manageable.

You have to just fill up your day with stuff to do—exercise, read, write, talk to people, walk, people-watch, sleep—to get out of the habit of using to kill the anxiety and, even worse, the boredom, until you don't really think to do it as much anymore. Living where I live, the dope's never totally out of sight, out of mind, but I can feel it moving further back in the recesses of my head. And hopefully it'll keep sliding back until I can't call it up anymore. My head feels better, like the radio station has finally been tuned in correctly, or the owner finally coughed up the dough for a digital tuner.

It's not fair to your mother to fuck up when you're 30. That's what your teens are for, even your early 20s. But by 30, your ma should be able to sit back, relax and enjoy the effort she put into raising you, maybe bounce her grandkid on her knee.

Jesus. Tisa's next.

I look at Ma at the stove, her back to me, making scrambled eggs. I feel like me and Ma are all each other has. At least I'll have someone to take me out for my birthday, assuming I don't mess this up.

"So what do yez want for yer birthday?"

"My birthday? God, I haven't even thought about my birthday," I say.

"Aye, it's just eh few weeks off. Start thinkin'."

"I got what I wanted. I got you, Ma."

"Ah, fook off, yeh cheeky wee shite," she says, waving a spatula at me and sending a scrap of egg flying past my head. "I got an idea for yeh, if yeh can't think of anything."

"Whatzat?"

"Och, you'll see, son. What time do yez volunteer?"

"Two."

"Be home in time for dinner?"

"Yeah, yeah, of course," I say. "We eating in or out?"

"I figured I'd cook tonight—all this diner food's givin' me a belly. Whaddya in the mood for?"

Of course, what I'm in the mood for has little to do with what Paula can make. It's lasagna, or shepherd's pie.

"Doesn't matter—anything's fine by me."

"Em, maybe I'll whip up some lasagna," she says. "Or maybe some shepherd's pie."

"Either one sounds good."

"Alright, son. Ready to walk yer Ma to work?"

"Yeah," I say. "Lemme get my bag."

I shuffle off to grab it, and Tisa's index card as well.

So it's a lot of walking these days: over to the community center, back home to Avenue A, or over to C for volunteering, like I'm doing now. I like it—it keeps the blood pumping, gives me time to think. September is here, although the days still get pretty damn hot. But I like working up a sweat—it makes me feel like I'm still pushing all the bad shit out of me. Kind of like a reverse baptism.

When I'm in the West Village, I walk real slow, head on a swivel, keeping my eyes open for Haley. School probably just started, and sometimes I think maybe I can catch her on the way to or from work, or perhaps sneaking home at lunch to grab some forgotten lesson plan, maybe get a quickie from...nah, forget about that. Sometimes I do a little detour down to her Little Red Schoolhouse on Bleecker, and stand across the street like a lonely stalker. But I still haven't seen that pretty porcelain face. Oh well. Her index card will get its turn.

After grabbing a few gym passes on the way out, I schlep across town to the Harm Reduction Center, which takes a good 40 minutes or so. You're going from the West Village to the east side, and you really see the neighborhood change for the worse as you head east. Across B, it's projects, homeless guys in refrigerator boxes, short brown legs sticking out from under oversized sedans, radios cranking salsa, and old guys sitting contentedly on their steps, drinking beer from paper bags. There's a little neighborhood garden on 4th between B and C; if I'm a few minutes early, I'll go in and sit for a bit, taking in the smell of the trees, plants and wood chips, a welcome diversion from the usual potpourri of urine, dog shit, unattended garbage and malt liquor drying in the sun. The garden is sponsoring some sort of upcoming celebration, though the details are sketchy. "Pueblo-Batey invite's you to AREYTO, the Resurrection of the Spirit of Loisaida," the sign on the gate says. "From & dedicated to Generation (X)."

I pass the Bracetti Projects, which has about 20 flags from various nations, few that I recognize, hanging from poles in the courtyard. Making the turn onto C, I see the regulars hanging out in front of the Harm Reduction Center. They hang out there even when the place is closed; to them, it's a familiar place, one they associate with favorable responses from what's left of the pleasure centers in their brains.

I don't know anyone's name, but I recognize their faces. Two sit on a filthy discarded air conditioner, two more repose on a step and a few stand, doing that dopehead half-circle pace. Junk is an equally opportunity employer: there's a jittery black guy in a straw hat, a ferret-faced Latino man and white guys in the clothes they got addicted in. They speak in scratchy voices, walk with strange limps and chain smoke, asking passers-by for a light. Of course, they've got their own source of flame—what junkie wouldn't?—but it's that desire for contact with the real world, the yearning to sometimes interact in a non-criminal way with legitimate citizens.

Michael J. Malone

Before approaching them, I drop my bag at a pay phone and pop a quarter in. I now know Tisa's cell by heart. Don't know why she bought the damn thing—she never has it on.

It rings three times and I prepare my message.

"'allo?" a living, breathing entity states. My stomach drops into my bowels, and my knees get weak. It dawns on me there's no public restroom this far east—no hotel, no department store, no park with an unlocked bathroom. No wonder the sidewalks smell the way they do.

"allooo?" it says again.

"Tisa."

"Yes?"

"Declan Coulter."

As if she knows another Declan.

Maybe she does.

"Declan Coultah!" she says with all sorts of false charm. "We finally speak!"

"Not like you to have your phone on, Tis...a."

"Yes, well, expecting an important call."

For a second, I think *I'm* the important call, then realize it's surely some producer, some director, some agent.

"Thanks for letting me crash over your place," I try.

"Didn't really have a choice, now did I?"

"Uh, not really, I guess. I'm sorry. It was stupid."

"Yes, it was. Oh well. It *was* sort of good to see you, in a strange way."

"Yeah, it was good to, ya know, hang out."

"Well, I wouldn't exactly call it *hanging out*," she says with a laugh.

What the fuck happened? She's tormenting me.

"Right."

"Sorry I had to run out the next morning," she says. "Had to meet Shan for brunch. She was really amused when I told her what happened."

How 'bout fucking tell *me* what happened?

"Yeah," I say with a fake chuckle. "She musta been."

"So...are we meeting?"

"Definitely," I say.

"Grand. Well, I must get off the phone, but how about...a week from tomorrow? That work for you?"

I scan my mental day planner. As if I had *anything* going on the next few weeks.

"Perfect."

"OK, then. Let's speak in the next few days and decide on a place. I'm glad we're doing this, Declan. But I must run."

194

"OK, talk to ya in the next few days."

"Ta!"

"See ya," I answer, though she'd already hung up. I hang up the phone, grab my bag and walk towards the center, every bit as confused as I was before.

"Spike!" one of the Latino men hollers as I approach.

"Doctuh Declan!" yells another. My nicknames. Better than "Deckie."

"Gentlemen," I say. I'm always nice to them; these guys walk in with sharp, shining spikes dripping with sickness, and you're pretty much at their mercy if they choose to make life unpleasant for you. "How are we?"

"OK," comes the hoarse chorus. Waiting for the center to open, they've all got the wearily happy look of fathers-to-be.

"Sit, sit," says one of the men, a black guy with the shiny, sweaty, shellacked face of an addict, wearing gym shorts over blue jeans. He offers up his space on the air conditioner. It's grimy and foul and so are they, and I'd really rather not. But rather than be rude, I sit.

Across the street, there's a Fine Fare supermarket with cheery Grand Opening bunting all around—the Grand Opening has been going on for as long as I've been coming here. Two men are arguing about their place on line for the recycling machine. They're perhaps half-a-notch up on the hierarchy from the guys on our side of the block.

"What's the story, boys?" I say.

"Not much, man," says one guy. "Just waiting."

Waiting. It's what they do.

"What's the word on the street?" I ask. I look at their faces. How long before I would've joined them? Six months? Three months? Less? Shit. I shake my head to flush the thought out.

"Same old, same old," mutters one.

"Why you do this, man?" asks another. "Courts make ya do this?"

"Nah, just volunteer work," I say. "I do it on my own."

"Why?"

"Was gonna work with old people, but they creep me out," I say. I decide not to mention that I'm doing it to impress my ex, and remind myself to save up some mental images from volunteering so I'll have more stuff to talk to Tisa about when we meet.

"Yeah, me too," says the guy. "All shriveled up and shit."

A couple of kids from the projects wait to purchase ice cream from the Kool-Man truck, and an old Latino man pushes a trolley packed with groceries past us.

"And I thought you guys deserved some help," I add.

"Right on," says one.

"You guys hear about that chick judge the guy tried to kill?" asks one guy.

Michael J. Malone

I read about it in the *Post* yesterday.

"Yeah, man," says another. "Blonde bitch. She tried to jam me up once. Tried to hit me with 18 months for sellin' E.P.T.'s."

"What're they?" asks one guy. "Some kinda uppers?"

"Nah, man. Pregnancy tests. Stole a case of 'em from Duane Reade, sold 'em up at 125th for $5 a pop. Spent three fucking days in Central Booking, totally sick and shit."

"Ouch," says one guy.

"She's a bitch, man," offers another. "Can't say I wept over the news."

"What time ya got?" I say to the group, though, of course, they've all since sold or traded their watches. They shake their heads. One looks at the sun.

"Well, better be getting to work," I say, standing up and brushing off the seat of my jeans. "See you boys in a bit."

I enter the Harm Reduction Center, a grubby storefront room measuring about 10 by 12. There are posters on the wall of black role models—Martin Luther King Jr., W.E.B. Dubois, Langston Hughes—delivering positive messages, and anti-drug posters designed by neighborhood school kids. A printout hanging on the wall says "Women's Hours, Thursday, 2-4."

"Declan, how are ya?"

It's William. He runs the center. A tall, skinny black guy of about 35, William is HIV-positive. He assured me on my first day of work that he didn't get the virus from working at the center. He's pretty cool to the customers, actually takes time to talk to them, remembers where they're from and what their ex-wives' and girlfriends' names are. Some exchange places really enforce the one-for-one needle exchange, but with William, you throw a few in a box, he'll give you what you want.

"Hey, William," I say, shaking his hand, eager to show him I'm not afraid of his deadly virus.

"Some hungry customers out there, huh?" I continue.

"Yeah, the regulars," says William. "Better suit up and open up shop. Don't wanna keep them waiting."

"They got busy schedules," I say, and William laughs.

I take a set of rubber gloves from the box and pull them on, then clap my hands together. I like the sound they make. I look out the grimy window at the Loisaida Drugs & Surgicals across the street. It's closed down, but not to worry—our customers got the drugs, and we got the surgicals. I unlock the door and see the begrimed masks of weary anticipation turn into excitement, as our customers stand and begin to file into the center.

196

Unemployment with no end in sight means a few adjustments in your life-style, including doing your own laundry. When you're 30, or a week away from it, you should either live in a building where doing laundry in the basement is an actual option, or you should be dropping off your stuff—outsourcing it, as my former jackass, MBA-speak boss Ken might've said. No self-respecting man with three decades under his belt should be leafing through last May's *Time Out* in some depressing laundromat as he waits for his stuff to dry. Respectable people shuffle in after a long day at their respectable job, file past you with a look of disdain and offer up their winning ticket for a full bag of clean, fresh, downy-soft clothing carefully folded by loving Asian hands. I used to be one of them. Instead, I sit and read a cover story on ways to get drunk for less than $10.

But sitting in this sticky laundromat, the stink of old curry rising up from the guy from the Indian restaurant's cart full of tablecloths, actually serves a dual purpose for me today. I tried to sleep as late as possible, to gobble up as much of the day as I could, bring me that much closer to 2 o'clock. Told Ma I was sleeping late and not to wake me for breakfast. Got up at noon, and was going to eat at the diner, but figured my stomach couldn't hold it down. It's 1:00, and I'm starving and dizzy. I'd do just about anything to have it be 3:00 right now, be minutes away from ordering a big ol' cheeseburger and a beer, stand up, smile, say thank you, maybe shake hands and walk out of the place, have this goddamn unfinished business behind me. *Anything.*

Dismal as the laundry joint may be, it's better than doing it in the basement of my building, where the *abuelas* scrub the stains out of the kiddies' clothes and hog up all the dryers, which typically leave your clothes in a big wet ball. So I do it here, on 6th and 1st. I usually put my stuff in and bolt next door to the Homestead, where a pint still costs $4, order a Guinness from Christine and discuss her various battles with cancer. If I drink slowly, I can make my beer last until my stuff's ready for the dryer.

I'd kill for a beer today. But, it being 1:00 and me being virtually penniless, I can't let that happen. I need all the wits I can muster for this afternoon.

At least there's some hottie in here to take my mind, however briefly, off the afternoon's dreaded appointment, if only for a minute. Notably, it's one of the few times I've found myself attracted to a girl since I learned of the object of Haley's affection. This one looks like an NYU student: petite, tight tank top, proud little breasts gamely trying to be cleavage, stylish Converse flip-flops, heart-shaped ass in worked-over Levi's. We briefly make eye contact as I get $5 worth of quarters—the sound of them tumbling into the hopper always makes me think of Vegas, that rugby tournament the Vipers played in out there a few years ago, when Gabby broke that Southern California flyhalf's ankle and the pit boss's nose in the span of six hours—and I feel my body tingle. Laundromats turn me on, for some strange

Michael J. Malone

reason, probably because people are always hooking up in them in those old MTV videos, throwing their freshly laundered undergarments at each other.

I hang my Vipers jersey on a pole that extends from the table, like a flag representing a nation of fit, foul-mouthed, hell-bent dudes, so the girl can see it. I fold my clothes as she leafs through a copy of Kerouac's *Dharma Bums* in a way that tells me she's not really reading it, looking up my way now and then and turning pages faster than real reading would allow. They play Light 105 on the radio here, which attacks any amorous mood like new and improved detergent on tough stains.

Kerouac did *On the Road* in like a month. So I can do a novel in, realistically, a few months. I'll miss my goal of writing it by my 30th birthday, but will be done while I'm 30. I'm thinking about the plot—something about two guys, friends, a road trip, out west, something weird happens, a gun, and I'm lost in thought. I find myself singing along to the radio, that duet between Phil Collins and the other Phil, the black one, that "Easy Lover" song that came out when black and white duets were all the rage in pop music. I catch myself and quickly bite my tongue, then check to see if the NYU gal has caught me singing along to this '80s cheese.

I got away with that one.

As I fold, I work out the day's gameplan. I'm going to take my seat, sit up straight like a man, look straight ahead, smile the whole time and show that I'm impervious to pain. *Yes, hello to you to... Yes, it has been a while... It was very silly, yes, I know... Yes, I'd love to finish what we started... I know, I know, it hurts like hell but it gets better.*

Occasionally something good sneaks by on Light 105. Fearing the worst after Debbie from Rosedale wanted to thank Ruben in Corona for helping her find love when she thought none was to be found, I was pleasantly surprised to hear the soulful strains of "Sexual Healing," Marvin cooing *Baaayyy-beeee*, like only Marvin could. I close my eyes and fold my favorite black t-shirt, which will be my security blanket, my Rock of Gibraltar, in my moment of need today. I open them and the NYU gal is looking my way; our eyes meet, then hers jump back to her book.

I'm mortified to discover that I can't mouth the words to "Sexual Healing" in her general direction, as I don't know them. I mean, I know the chorus—every jackass does—but once the verses start, I'm fucking useless. I know both Phils' parts in "Easy Lover," but not a word of Marvin's seductive masterpiece. The NYU gal mouths "make love to me tonight," bobbing her head and staring down at *Dharma Bums.*

Deflated, I pack my clothes into my bag. Marvin ends and Fleetwood Mac's "Dreams" comes on. I know every goddamn word to that one—*Thunder only happens when it's raining*—because Ma bought the 8-track tape when the Duster's stereo ate her Paddy Reilly tape en route to the Catskills one year. But I don't sing along to

198

Fleetwood Mac. When I get my bag packed, I look up and the NYU gal is gone, a spread-eagle *Dharma Bums* saving her seat.

I have to be at St. Marks and A in just under an hour. I'm going to go home, put away my laundry, take a nice, long, cool shower, get dressed, go out. I picture myself as a boxer, saying his prayers in the training room, making the sign of the cross with his giant gloves, rolling his shoulders, body shivering under the satin robe, trainer telling him he's a wreckin' machine, getting ready to climb the stairs, face the crowd, enter the ring against a killer, and take his punches.

Walking up Avenue A, I'm taking deep breaths, feeling dizzy but careful not to hyperventilate, grateful for each sizable exhale I push out. I've walked a block and a half and my black t-shirt is sticking to me. I had a hunch the shirt would be lucky today, but black was not a good call for the sunny weather.

I see her up ahead, in front of Nina's Pizza, and my heart races up my gullet, creating a sound like happy pigs in a mud pen. She's waiting on the corner, just like she said she'd be. She sees me, and my fate is thusly sealed; there's no getting out of this, no feigning illness or death. I throw a right jab, left jab, right hook, left hook, go for the knockout with the right. Time to get in the ring.

"Barry fookin' McGuigan," Ma says.

"Hi," I squeak.

"Sure yeh can do this?"

"I hope so. I hope so."

"Happy birthday, son," says Ma, offering the closest she's come to a smile since our reunion. She takes my hand and walks me into Ink-a-Dink Tattoo & Cappuccino.

"Thank you, Ma."

"Getting it fixed is cheaper than getting the fookin' thing removed."

There are two vinyl dentist chairs the color of Gabby's brother's car, a dull beige. Both are empty. The walls are lined with tattoo art; one wall says "Dolls" and has all sorts of suns, rainbows, animals and other symbols of nature, while the "Guys" wall has cars, wolves, dragons and other emblems of virility.

A bear of a man in a Ramones t-shirt and black leather vest hovers between the chairs, wearing a long beard that's also kind of beige.

"Coulter?" he says.

I nod. He smiles demonically and waves me towards the dentist chair. I climb up, and my soaking-wet back prevents me from sliding in. I allow a weak smile and nod again, and the man pulls up a folding chair for Ma.

"By the looks uh yeh, I assume yer Big Jack?" she says.

"Yes, ma'am," the tat guy answers with exaggerated politeness. "By the sounds a' you, I assume yer the Scottish lady I spoke to on the phone."

Michael J. Malone

"Irish," she says with a glare.

"Right. Sorry."

"Aye," she says.

"You want cappuccino?" he asks.

"No t'anks," Ma says. "So you know what to do."

"Yes, ma'am," he says, pulling on rubber gloves. "How you feelin', big boy?"

Like a 10-year-old at the doctor's office, I want to say.

"Okay," I say in a pathetic pitch worthy of that 10-year-old.

I'm not going to ask my mom to hold my hand. I'm just not going to do it. My fingers dig into the armrests; both are worn through to reveal wood, like bone exposed by ripped flesh. Saw something like that happen to Ghetto Ron at the bottom of a ruck against Bainbridge—those Irish fuckers must've been filing down the studs in their cleats with their carpenter tools or something. Right through to his shin. Ron's tough as they come–grew up in the Jacob Riis projects along the FDR Drive, and ended up with the Vipers when he saw us practicing in the park from his window. That one freaked him out pretty good though.

"You gonna stick it out this time?" he says. I wince when he says "stick."

"Yeeeuhhh," I bleat, shivering.

"You wanna take your shirt off?"

I nod. It's stuck to my body, and I'm thinking, that's it, it ain't comin' off, gonna have to come back another time when the weather's cooler, thanks very much, Big Jack, here's a fiver for your efforts. But Ma helps me with it, just like she used to when I was a kid and it was bath time. For a second, I think Ma will take my hand in hers, but she doesn't.

"Lookie that," he says, staring at my half-finished tat. "A work-in-progress."

I wince again. Hopefully that's the last time I have to hear someone talk about the work-in-progress on my shoulder blade.

"What was that Dickens book," Big Jack continues, "the one where he died before he had a chance to finish it?"

"Dunno," I say, as he turns the gun on. My body tenses and a cold shiver goes throughout my body.

"Hold my hand," I whisper to Ma.

"Eh?" she says, leaning over.

"Please hold my hand."

"I'm not holdin' yer fookin' hand. Yer a big boy."

"Please," I whimper.

Big Jack looms over me with the gun, smiling wildly, poised and ready to rock.

"Fookin' 'ell," Ma says, brusquely grabbing my hand in hers.

200

"That Dickens book, what the hell is it?" says Big Jack. "Some guy's name in the title, I think."

He raises the gun to my shoulder. I think *Nicholas Nickleby*, but I'm too scared to speak. I feel the needles touching the surface of my shoulder and jam my eyes shut, hearing the gun's whir and picturing a jackhammer digging up a sidewalk, a drill cutting into bone. I gouge my fingers as far into the armrest as they'll go, and feel the wood underneath.

"FER FOOK'S SAKE!" screams Ma, pushing back in her chair, jumping to her feet and staring at her palm. Big Jack yanks the gun off me. "Och! I'm fookin' bleedin', yeh wee shite!!!"

"Ah, fuck," I say. "I'm sorry, Ma."

Big Jack emits a hearty guffaw.

"S'no way to treat yer mother, my man. She gave you life!"

"Jayzus, such sharp nails," she says, still staring at her palm. She takes a napkin out of her purse. "Do yez have some water?"

"Sure," says Big Jack, disappearing into the back room and emerging a moment later with a pewter stein full of water. "Big Jack, You De Man" is engraved on it. Ma washes out her cuts, sets the stein on the floor and goes back into her purse.

"Take these, Edward fookin' Scissorfingers," she says, sticking two—three?—chalky pills in my mouth.

"Whoa, hoa, Mother's Little Helper," says Big Jack. "Anything for me?"

"No," she says, freezing the big man with a stare. "Do yer fookin' job."

"We ready to go?" asks Jack.

"Yeah, man," I croak, as Ma, her hand wrapped in a napkin, takes my hand again.

"I'm tellin' ya, boss. Fifteen minutes, yer done."

"Yeah?" I say, feeling the first pin prick and moving my shoulder to accept the sting.

"Yeah, man," he says, with another pin prick. I jam my eyes shut again. Fourteen minutes and 45 seconds to go.

"Deckie Coultah!" I hear. I open my eyes and turn my head to where the voice is coming from. I see Shady Brady, his crazy Chelsea smile tilting up at the sides, wearing the shiny red jersey of his beloved soccer team.

"Shady. What the hell are you doing here?"

"Whaddya think, mate?" he says, showing his forearms, which resemble a roadmap of tattoos. "I said, if Arsenal won the Cup, I'd get another one."

I forgot—every time his "footie" team wins something, Shady gets another tattoo. By the looks of him, they've had quite a run.

"Shady, this is my mom. Ma, Malcolm Brady."

"Pleased to meet you, Mrs. Coulter."

"Nice to meet you, Malcolm."

"Where you been, mate?" Shady asks me.

"Just been busy, workin' and stuff. Heard about the Rockaway Fishheads match."

"Yeah, they're tough. Especially for a bunch of surfer dudes. Gabby hates losing to those lads. He grew up with a bunch of them."

"Who we got this weekend?"

"Forest Hills Irregulars, away," says Shady. "That mud bowl next to the Grand Central Parkway."

"Cool. Stomp 'em."

"Will do, mate. Our last chance to win this season. How's the head?"

"Better, thanks," I say. "I'll be out there one of these days."

"Good. The boys miss ya."

"Aye, he won't be playin' soon," says Ma.

"I miss them too," I say. "I'll be out there soon."

"Yer arse, yeh will," says Ma.

"Getting the harp finished, I see," says Shady, nodding toward my half-a-tat. "Wow. Never thought I'd live to see this day."

"Yeah, well, ya know, a birthday gift from Ma."

I'm aware of my mommy holding my hand in front of my rugby teammate, but realize I just can't get through this alone.

"Guess we'll have nothing to *harp* on you about after this, mate," says Shady.

"Believe it or not," I say to Ma, "this guy went to Oxford."

"Is that right?" says Ma. "Good for you, Malcolm, though I see you didn't study wit."

"Hey, then maybe you can help me," says Big Jack to Shady. "What was Dickens' last work? The unfinished one? Guy's name in the title?"

I think *David Copperfield,* but don't say it.

"*Edwin Drood*," says Shady.

"Bingo!!" says Jack, giving the needle a little extra push as I wince.

"So whaddya gonna get?" I say.

"A cannon," says Shady.

"A cannon? I thought it was gonna be an Arsenal thing."

"It is, mate. They're the Gunners. They started out as a munitions factory team during World War I."

"Gotcha," I say. Shady'll talk about Arsenal all day, if you're not careful. We like to joke that he puts the "arse" in Arsenal.

"Take me next, mate?" says Shady to Big Jack.

"Sure, man," he says. "Gonna get a slice after this, but 30 minutes or so, huh?"

"Right," says Shady. "Be back then. Ms. Coultah, a pleasure."

He shakes her uninjured hand daintily and bows his head.

"Nice meetin' yeh, Malcolm."

"Buy ya a pint o' *Harp* when yer done, Deckie," he says, nodding at me and Ma's clenched hands, and giving me a wink that says that will be our little secret, before skittering out of the store.

"That's Malcolm Brady," I say.

"I know," says Ma. "I just met 'im."

"He's Marvin Mouse."

"Yer bunny's little friend?"

"Yup."

"Grand."

"You don't like him."

"Aye like 'im fine!" says Ma. "He seemed like a perfect gentleman. He would-na' had the 38 tattoos if he was my son, but he seemed fine. Why wouldn't aye like 'im?"

"Just thought you wouldn't, ya know, like him, is all."

"Son, aye don't hate the English as a rule, if that's what yer on about. Only some of 'em."

"Like Dad."

She clenches her teeth, spawning wrinkles in her jawline.

"Yes, like yer Dah. Yer father was a scoombag. Not because he was English. Because he was a scoombag."

Big Jack's ears perk up a little.

"Do you miss him ever?" I ask.

"No," says Ma. "Do you?"

"No."

"Well, yeh fookin' shouldn't. Yeh never really knew him."

"I don't."

"Good."

"Good," I echo.

"So, Ma, like...Tisa," I start, emboldened by my bravery in the tat chair. Through my hand, I can feel Ma bristle. "You didn't dislike her because she's Eng-lish, but because she treated me...like shite."

"Aye, that's right, son," says Ma. "Her bein' a coont."

Coont. That's the word for Tisa.

"You'd have liked the one after her," I say.

"What was her name? The Barbie?"

"Haley."

"What kinda name is that?"

Michael J. Malone

"Actually, a nickname. Her real name is Meadow. Meadow Snow."

I somehow never put "Meadow" and "Snow" together.

"Sounds like a painting," says Ma.

"Never thought about it that way, but you're right," I say.

"Pretty, that one," says Ma.

"She was. *Is.* Nice girl too."

"What happened?"

"She met a movie star."

"Oh yah? Someone I've heard of?" asks Ma.

"Nah," I say. "Second banana type."

"Fook'im," says Ma with a squeeze of my hand.

"Fook'im," I say.

"That...should...just...about...do it," says Big Jack, and the hum of the gun ceases. The silence is golden; I release Ma's hand and the armrest and shake life back into my fingers, then rest my soaked head in my hands and take a deep breath.

"The new ink'll blend in with the old ink in a week or two," he continues. "How's it feel?"

"Feels fine," I say. "Sore, but it's OK. It's great."

"C'mere," he says. "Check it out in the mirror."

I look at my shoulder blade in the mirror. It looks like an Irish harp. A gorgeous, moist, shiny, *completed* Irish harp. I want to pluck the strings, hear it sing.

"It's beautiful," I say. "It's fookin' beautiful."

"Aye, lookit tha'," says Ma.

I wrap my arms around Big Jack and try to lift him off the ground, but he's too heavy and I feel a flash of pain in my lower back.

"Whoa-hoa, buddy. Easy there. Don't wantcha popping the ink out."

"Sorry, man."

"No problem, guy," he says. "Let's put some gauze over it and get you the hell outta here. I'm fookin' starving."

I flash Ma a big grin, and she nods coolly.

"Like yer man Malcolm says, yeh wanna celebrate with a wee pint?" Ma says.

"Yeah," I say. "Sounds delicious."

So life is almost back to normal—all that's missing is getting on the rugby pitch with the boys. I guess the head injury woke me up a bit, made me aware of my own mortality, jacked up my sense of responsibility to others. But I still want to play, even if Ma won't allow it under her roof. Not just because it's a *Brit poofter sport*, but because she thinks I'm going to kill myself playing. Had her out for Friends and Family Day a few years back, and man, that was a mistake. The Long Island Rovers

204

had some Samoan guy who was just going around cheap-shotting people, and we sorted the guy out nice, waited until he got caught in the bottom of a ruck and went freakin' Riverdance on his ass. Big brawl broke out, and that's when Ma went for a wee walk, shaking her head and walking towards the tennis courts to watch a more genteel sporting activity. *Yer gonna fookin' kill yerself, playin' that fookin' poofter sport*, I can hear her saying over a Budweiser and a Kool in MacLennane's afterwards. (The pub part she actually enjoyed.)

To be honest, it's a wonder I can compete in sports at all. I mean, growing up, Ma only wanted me to play Irish sports—as if my freakin' name wasn't enough to prove my turbo-Irish mettle—but finding another kid on the Lower East Side to boot the Gaelic football around, or give the slither a good whack with your hurley, well, that just wasn't going to work. Jimmy Gulotta sure didn't want to play Gaelic football or hurling. So Ma let me play her adopted country's national pastime, baseball. And when I was old enough to do things without ol' Paula's best wishes—a privilege, sadly, I no longer possess—I started playing rugby.

And I miss it now. I feel bad that I've been out of the loop, that stuff's been happening without me, and when the boys refer to some try that North-of-England Paul scored against the Morris Mud Turtles, some hit Mental Ben put on the Montclair Vikings winger, I wasn't there to see it. And it bums me out.

Well, I'm not going to start playing until I move back into my place, until I talk to Tisa and find out what's what, and until I get myself back into shape—I'm roadkill if I go out there and play all skinny and weak and out of shape. Bainbridge would eat me for Irish breakfast.

But I can still check out practice, show my sorry mug, say hi to the boys before the season ends Saturday. Told Ma I was volunteering the later session today, and I'm jogging over to East River Park, where the Vipers are practicing. Running in the gym's fine and all, and the girls in their little workout clothes make for some nice scenery, but the shit gets boring. And the damn treadmill, running all day long and not getting anywhere—well, that's a little too close to home these days.

It's been a while since I've been over to the park and, as always, there's new stuff popping up all over Alphabet City. There's a new French restaurant on 5th between A and B, and a trendy little lounge called Jewel Box next door. I see the strange school on B has a new coat of paint, and they've done up the area in front of it with an array of colored pebbles, like an old Jewish couple's house in Boca. Caught up in the scenery, I avoid a squashed rat at the last minute.

My lungs are burning and my legs feel like they're someone else's, like bad rental skates at the rink, but it feels good to be outside. Approaching the Riis projects on Avenue D, there're kids outside, kicking soccer balls, waiting their turn with the ice cream man, riding scooters and squealing in Spanish. The weather is perfect.

Michael J. Malone

I start climbing the overpass ramp that leads over the FDR, and see the East River gleaming ahead, its sparkling shade of blue pretty from the distance, belying the crap floating around in it. Industrial Brooklyn lies on the other side: big processing pucks like you see from the Jersey Turnpike, a Domino Sugar plant, a factory that makes staples. Up the river a bit, the huge Citibank tower stands erect, a one-man skyline looming over the ashy gray of Queens.

I see the boys up ahead, playing a touch version of rugby, aptly called "touch," that you do to warm up. I break into a gallop, pumping the knees high, like Coach has us do sometimes. In my mind I can hear Coach yelling "High knees!" and Gabby doing his best Butthead, or maybe it's Beavis, going, "heh heh, he said *hineys*," and I think of my old pal Dollar Bill saying, "grab a Heinie." The burn in my lungs grows even greater. It's good to be back.

I see Shady hit Flyboy on a perfectly timed skip-pass, Serenity caught flat-footed on defense, and Flyboy zooms down the sideline like he's piloting one of those fighter jets from his Air Force days. As the boys prepare for a kickoff, I enter their field of vision.

"Sir Piss-a-lot!" yells Spartacus.

"Out of retirement," says Flyboy.

"Back from the dead," says Ghetto Ron. "Hey man—what month is it?"

The game of touch has halted.

"Coultuh," says Gabby, giving me one of those handshake-hugs.

"Hey bro," I say. "Thanks for bailing me out."

"No worries, man," he says. "Buy me a beeyuh."

The Guy Currency.

"Up for a little touch?" asks Shady, juggling a Gilbert ball in his hands, demonic smile on his face, shiny new cannon on his forearm.

"Nah, man," I say. "Still letting the head heal. Just came to say hi. Next season—I promise."

The game of touch resumes, and it's fun to watch the boys. They've got real jobs by day—heck, Welsh Mike is an actual scientist—but out here, they're just plus-size children, laughing and running. Watching is not the same as playing, but I'm still enjoying being out there, tossing the ball to myself, feeling its bumps, softly kicking it in the air and catching it.

More and more guys show up, drop their bags on the turf with a thud, sit down, trade their work clothes for short black shorts and brightly colored jerseys. They lace their boots up, then take their place in the game. I see faces I haven't seen in a while, and some I've never seen. I feel like I've been away for years. I shake my head around. No trails, no dizziness. No problem.

You're not to play rugby, I can hear Ma. *Not while you're under my roof.*

What the hell, I'm thinking. It's freakin' touch—it's not really rugby. No contact. Five minutes, then Coach'll blow his whistle, touch will stop and real practice is underway. Long as I scoot out of here before they throw me into the scrum, then Paula's none the wiser.

Spartacus limps off the field, holding his hamstring.

"Pull it?" I ask.

"Nah, just strained a bit. Forgot to stretch."

"Dumbass."

"Hey Deckie," he says. "Heard they're making a movie about ya. Some guy that can't make short-term memories. *Memento*, or *Demento*, or something like that."

"I'll look for it," I say with a smile.

"You should."

"We need one," yells Shady to the sideline.

There's a moment of hesitation. I've been good. *Damn*, I've been good. Nah...

"Coultah?" Shady yells in his plummy accent.

Traffic chugs by on the FDR Drive on one side, and boats amble along the East River on the other.

"I'm in," I yell back.

Yeah, it feels great to play, to feel the dirt underfoot, to sprint, to throw a little juke-and-jive at the boys, nothing too hardcore, just a little shake-and-bake, let them know I can still smoke their ass, even on the brink of 30 and out of shape. I can't wipe the smile off my face. I feel like I'm 20. Or 10.

More guys show up, dress and jump in, until we've got 10 on 10. For once, inexplicably, there are no baseballs to dodge, no soccer guys looking to steal our turf, no ghetto kids with pit bulls to fight with. Oodles of space.

Shady's playing flyhalf and he's throwing all sorts of jukes at the other guys, freezing them with a dummy and dishing to us in support, and we're running up lots of tries. Hell, it's only a little warm-up, but it's still a nice feeling to make a little break, feel the defense on your heels, score a try, talk a little shit, shove each other playfully in the end zone.

He hits me with a skip-pass and I got Gabby in front of me. Gabby's surprisingly quick for his size. In close, he'll maul me. But with a bit of open field between us, he's no match. I've gone all kinds of Sir Vincent on his ass the last few times it came my way, and he's staggering like a punch-drunk heavyweight.

"*Hoahhhhh!*" I shout, sidestepping left and zipping right.

"Motherfuckuh," he grumbles, and doesn't bite. "Yeh dead, Coultuh."

Gabby knows me too well.

That fake didn't work for shit, and he's got me in his sights. Thank God it's only touch. I see Gabby coming in low, like he's actually going to make the tackle and, sure enough, the big bastard does—wrapping up my legs and lifting me. Not a hard tackle, like I saw him do to that poor Danbury scrumhalf at the St. Paddy's Tournament up at Van Cortlandt, guy laying at midfield in the fetal position, vibrating. But a tackle nonetheless.

"Get that shit *outta* here," Gabby says, as we begin our earthbound trajectory. Clutching the ball to my chest, I throw a couple body shots with my free hand into Gabby's concrete midsection. We're both giggling like schoolgirls as we approach the ground, not too hard, but with his weight on top of me.

"*Heeeaaaahhhhfuuuuuhhhhck!!!!*" I scream. Fuckin' A, fuckin' motherfuckin' bitch. Yowww, that motherfuckin' *hurt*. I've been dumped on my ass a million times playing this game, but that frickin' hurt like no one's business. The crack in my neck finally broke all the way through, I know it, I ain't playing rugby again, I ain't *movin'* again, me and Christopher Reeve sitting in our chairs at the home, watching reruns and sipping dinner, Tisa's bastard kid sneaking me a beer. I check to see if my arms can move, but Gabby's body is pinning them to the ground.

"Awright, bro?" he asks.

"Owww, man. Get the fuck off me!"

Gabby starts pushing himself up, blocking out the sun with his big frame. His face grows ashen, his expression sliding off as he continues holding my arms down. He's got on a black jersey with the sleeves cut off, a silver fern and "New Zealand All Blacks" on the chest. His face is sallow. The boys sense something is up and gather around Gabby, their heads in a circle, wearing the same expressionless expressions and bloodless faces as Gabby. Déjà vu all over again. Shit, even Tracy Chapman's pale, and he's black.

"Fuckin' 'ell," says someone with an Aussie accent.

"Sweet mother of Jeezus," says another.

"Motherfucker," says another.

"Owww," I whimper.

These guys have seen all sorts of stomach-churning injuries no man should have to see. It takes a lot to freak them out, but apparently I have succeeded.

My neck is killing me; people always say pain is like a knife stuck in them, and I've never found that to be an accurate description, until now. And Gabby's not even letting me touch the source of my pain, which is driving me nuts.

"Get the fuck off me, man," I say, trying to wiggle my arms, but Gabby continues holding them down. It's like my straitjacket dream with the rats. Will Tisa come to my rescue? Is Gabby fucking with me again? Is this my intervention?

"Where's Demento?" barks Gabby.

"Workin', I think."

"What the fuck?" I say.

"We gotta pull the fucking thing out," someone says.

Fuckin' A, do something, I'm thinking. Pull it out, whatever the fuck *it* is—Glass? Bone?—if it's going to make me feel better.

"Fuck," someone says.

The boys' mugs are *ghastly*. Most of them, I only see them playing rugby and drinking, when they're always happy. I've been in this same huddle as them before, staring in at fractures of the compound and spiral varieties, gashed heads, obliterated noses, Ghetto Ron's newly naked shinbone. But the guys never quite looked like this.

"Hold him down," says Gabby, as Spartacus assumes Gabby's position, his hands on my wrists.

Gabby shifts to put my head in his lap, palming the top of my head with one of his big battle-scarred hands.

"Don't move," he says, as if I could, and I feel another flash of pain.

"*Yeeeowww*, motherfucker!" I cry.

Gabby's pushing a sock against my pain. Spartacus lets go of my arms, and I sit up straight. Gabby's holding a syringe in his hand, its tip shimmering in the sunlight. It's the same one we give out at the center, the Becton-Dickerson 3-millie rig, this one's needle bent at a 45-degree angle, plunger pulled back, chamber filled with murky red.

If this were a sitcom, I would've fainted. My mouth gone dry, I can't speak, and return to my prone position.

"What's the nearest hospital?" yells Gabby.

"St. Vincent's?" someone guesses.

"East side, east side," says Gabby. "C'mon. Gotta be something over here. Bellevue? What's close? Big city, boys. *Think!*"

"NYU Med," someone says. "They're up on like 34th."

"Nah, that one's no good," I say. "Everyone knows that."

That's a lie, but if I go there, it's probably going to get back to Ma at her job over at NYU.

All the guys are silent. I can't believe that, in all our years of practicing rugby here—slamming into each other, baseballs raining on our heads, pit bulls running wild, voracious for white meat, fighting with the Riis project kids—we never had to rush someone to the hospital.

"Beth Israel," I say, annoyed that I have to be the injured party *and* the brains. "1st Ave."

"Bingo," says Gabby. "Who's got wheels?"

"I do," says Tracy. "Got my truck."

He points to where he's parked, on the other side of the field, next to the overpass.

"Beth Izzy—let's go," says Gabby. "You awright, man?"

Michael J. Malone

I nod. I'm scared. Who the fuck left the freakin' needle in the park? Was it the little trannie from Jersey City who swings by the center every Tuesday afternoon? That old Willie Nelson-looking dude from Tennessee? Or the skell with the skin rash from Stuy Town? One of the punk kids that lives in the squats between C and D? Self-centered junkie assholes.

"You be awright," Gabby says, though he's hardly trained to diagnose such injuries.

I'm sure I could've walked, but Gabby scoops me up and carries me—one arm under my back, the other under my legs.

"I'm so sorry, bro," he says weakly.

I nod. I never thought I'd hear those words from Gabby. I almost cry.

"Just fuckin' around, ya know? Just messin'."

I nod again. He's right. We were playing. I'm not mad. Wish I could tell him as much. Instead, I nod.

"You be awright," he says again. The crack in his voice does not reassure me. Ma was right: I got hurt playing *that fookin' poofter game*.

Jogging into East River Park 15 minutes ago, with the river and the Williamsburg Bridge and Brooklyn across the way, was so much more enjoyable than looking back at the city from the park, cars shitting out exhaust on the FDR, and the big, ugly Riis projects looming ahead. Gabby empties me into the front seat of Tracy's pickup. I'm trying to do the "Our Father" in my head, but I keep forgetting the words.

"What the fuck's try-age?" I ask as I fill out the form. At least I'm speaking now.

"*Tree-ahhge*," says Gabby. "It's French for emergency room—something those croissant-eaters know a lot about."

There's a space for my "in case of emergency" contact. I fill in Tisa and her cell number. Man, if this turns out bad, my unborn kid is fucked. A single-parent household, and that parent being Tisa. Or maybe Earl will help raise my kid. Jesus. I cross out Tisa and put down Gabby's name and number, 725-5375. JERK.

"Yeah, man. You grew up in New York City and you never heard of triage before?"

"Never," I say. "I mean, I been to the emergency room tons, just never heard of triage."

"Man, I been in triage a million times," says Gabby, "and never 'cuz I was hurt."

"Whaddya, bring the guys in after you give 'em a beat-down?"

"Nah," he says. "Bein' captain of you knuckleheads, ya gotta make an appearance when one of the guys gets seriously fucked up. Like Giuliani, if one of the

210

NYPD gets shot, or somethin'. I prefer St. Vincent's, 'cuz it's right down the road from MacLennane's."

I've calmed down quite a bit. They gave me ice for my neck, but it's not really that sore, and I'm still holding the bloody sock to my wound, though it's barely bleeding anymore. Just sitting here, waiting to get looked at. I figure, tons of fucked up shit's happened to me, much of it in the last month or so, so if God's going to take me by jamming a dirty spike in my neck, well, that's just tough luck. I ain't gonna fight it. But I don't think he's calling my number. I'm trying to do right by people. Me and Ma have been going to church. That counts for something.

"Emmanuel ...," starts the woman at the desk, "Emmanuel... Brister?"

"Dat is me," croaks a man with dreads. His right arm hangs limply at his side, and his bent bike is propped up against his chair, like a pretzel discarded by quality control. "Dat is me."

Gabby jumps to his feet.

"My man got here befaw he did," he growls, cutting in front of the hobbling, whimpering bike messenger. "Name's Coultuh."

"We all get our turn," says Emmanuel.

"Mr. ...Coulter will get called, I assure you," says the woman.

"Yeah, well, my guy's dyin' over there—,"

The clerk, Gabby and Emmanuel look at me. I shrug my shoulders.

"—and he's tired of waitin'."

"Your friend will be seen as soon as a doctor's available," she says.

"Yeah, well, a doctuh's available to see freakin' Bunny Wailer here," says Gabby.

"Please sit down," she says. "We evaluate each case, and handle them in order of gravity. Please be patient, sir."

Gabby shakes his head and returns to the seat next to me.

"S'awright, man," I say. "I ain't bleeding to death."

"Fucking bullshit," says Gabby. "Been here almost two fuckin' hours."

"Ya know, this never would've happened if you'd just moved to San Fran."

"Ah, fuck you," he says, hiding a smile. "I'm so sorry, Deckie."

"Gab, c'mon," I say. "Shit happens. We were fucking around, we live in a fucked-up city where we gotta share the park with the freakin' junkies, and I got stung. It's gonna be awright."

"Maybe it's a careless diabetic," offers Gabby.

"Nah. Careless diabetics don't make it."

"But careless junkies do," says Gabby. "No justice, man... I wish Demento were there. He coulda helped ya. Where the fuck was he?"

"Working," I say. "Saving other people. You guys did fine. Ya got me here in one piece. I'll get looked at. They'll tell me what's what."

"Well, you're certainly mellow."

"Oh, I'm nervous," I say, though it's more like scared shitless. "We'll just sit tight."

"I'm sure it's nothing," he says. "Just a little pin prick... What's that from?"

We sit quietly and think.

"*Just a little pin prick,*" I sing. I got the tune, but I can't place the song.

"*There'll be no more—*" adds Gabby.

"*Aaaahaaaahhh,*" we howl in ragged harmony. The woman at the desk shoots us a dirty look.

"You get high off that shit at all?" Gabby asks.

"Off the needle?"

"Yeah, man."

"That's hardly an appropriate question."

"I'm just curious," says Gabby, shrugging his shoulders.

"No, I didn't get high off it. Not that I know what heroin feels like."

"Bet it feels *nice.*"

"Yeah, probably. Certainly seems to have a high level of customer satisfaction."

"Some day, when I'm old and near death, I'll give it a try," he says.

"Me too."

"That chick's cute," says Gabby, nodding towards a petite nurse bustling past. "I miss the old-time nurse outfits. The dresses. The hats."

"Yeah," I say. "Scrubs are lame. They hide everything."

A pretty blonde woman enters the waiting room, pushing an elderly lady in a wheelchair. Gabby and I both scramble to our feet to help, but the woman dismisses us with a wave and a polite smile.

"So...what happened with Haley?" asks Gabby. "You okay to talk about it now?"

"Sure, why not. Seeing as I'm in fucking triage. She met another guy. An *ac-torrr.*"

I'm surprised by how much it still hurts to talk about it.

"Really? Like, a guy that gets his headshots done and goes ta auditions and lives off a fuckin' trust fund and tells chicks he's an actor?"

"That's what I thought! But no, this guy's legit," I say. "Been in movies, and shit."

"What's his name?"

I take a deep breath.

"Paul... Rudd," I spit.

"No shit!" says Gabby.

"Heard of him?"

"Sure, yeah," says Gabby. "The big brothuh in *Clueless*...the *Friends* chick's dude in *Object of My Affection*. Yeah, I know who he is."

I would've preferred if Gabby'd never heard of him.

"Didn't know you went for the romantic comedies."

"Who knows," he says. "Various dates over the years. He's a big dork."

That feels better.

"Right, right," I say. "That's Haley's boyfriend."

"Ouch," says Gabby. "Losing her to a tool like him."

I laugh.

"No shit," I say. "Fuckin' A."

"You dug her big-time, didn't ya?" says Gabby, sliding his elbows to his knees and staring at the ground, the cheap plastic chair groaning under his bulk.

"She was a good girl. Yeah, I dug her."

"Sucks," says Gabby.

"Yeah. It does."

"When's the Tisa meeting?"

"Friday."

"This Friday?"

"Yup."

"Dude, you must be shittin' a brick."

"I was, until this happened. Nothing like a potential case of HIV to take your mind off a big meeting."

"Deck-Lin... Colder?" calls the woman at the desk.

"That's my man," says Gabby, hopping to his feet like an expectant father. "He's comin'."

Gabby stands behind me, rubbing my shoulders like a trainer as I walk to the nurse.

"You take off, dude," I say. "Go to MacLennane's. I'll meet you there. Have one ready for me."

"Nah, man," says Gabby. "I'm comin' in."

"Sorry," says the administrator. "Family only."

"This guy's my rugby teammate," says Gabby. "That's family."

"Sorry," she says.

"I'll be here," he says to me. "Maybe I'll try a little rap on that cute nurse."

"You sure?"

"I'm sure, bro. Good luck."

"Alright," I say. "If it's takin' a while, feel free to split. I'll meet ya at the bar. If I find out I'm dyin', guess who's buying the drinks."

Gabby's face turns even more white.

"Kiddin', man, kiddin'. It's gonna be fine."

Gabby smiles uncomfortably and bumps his meaty, scar-strewn fist against mine.

The cute nurse walks me into the patient treatment area, which is a brightly lit, wide-open room. Like St. Vincent's, you get a curtain separating you from the rest of the screaming, moaning, groaning triage guests, but most have their screen open. Maybe I'll pitch a review of ER's and triages for *Time Out*. I look for an old woman in running shoes giving me the thumbs-up, but don't see her. The nurse leads me over to an available bed in the corner.

"Name?"

"Declan Coulter. Yours?"

"Sheila. Birthdate."

"Pour me...another...tequila, Sheila," I sing. A flash of memory comes back. A bar. Country music. Sawdust. Blood.

"Birthdate?"

"Nine-nine-69."

"About to turn...30?" says Sheila.

"I hope so."

"Just have a seat on the bed, and the doctor will be with you shortly," she says. As she walks away, her scrubs rub together and sound like leaves rustling in the wind.

I sit and take in my surroundings. There's an old guy in the bed across from mine, wearing a plaid bathrobe opened to reveal shriveled genitals. He's rocking his head back and forth along the axle of his neck like Stevie Wonder, and he's moaning. I see the bike messenger across the room, Bunny Wailer getting hooked up to an IV, his useless bike propped against the bed. There's a monitor behind me that says DECKLIN COLDER in green type, along with my birthday on a DOS screen. It's making a beeping noise, which I guess means I'm alive. Someone's smuggled a copy of *Family Circle*, circa October 1996, into my little corner of the ward, so I grab it. I flip through and find an article about safe Halloween costumes for kids, one particularly amusing one called the Explorer Eaten By a Boa, that holds my interest until the doctor arrives.

"Deck-Lin Colder?" he says, reading a clipboard. He's got white hair and a bushy white moustache.

"Yes, sir, Declan."

"Hi," he says. "I'm Dr. Goodfriend."

He offers his hand to shake, but keeps it close to his side, so I've got to reach out to meet him.

"Hi," I say. "Cool name."

"Yes," he replies with practiced disinterest. He scans his clipboard. "Stuck by a syringe."

"Yes, sir. In my neck."

"Ouch."

"Indeed."

"And this syringe," he asks skeptically, "belonged to whom?"

"I have no idea. Happened in East River Park. A lot of junkies shoot up there."

"Right, right," he says, still staring at his clipboard. "It's a big problem, the drug abuse."

No shit, I'm thinking. Look at the fucking hole in my neck and you'll see how big.

"So someone...accosted you and...jabbed you."

"No. I fell on the thing."

"Mr. Colder," Dr. Goodfriend begins, looking me in the eye for the first time. "Don't take this the wrong way. I'm not judging anyone here, I'm just doing my job. Are you an intravenous drug user?"

"No, sir," I say. As *if.*

"Okay. This is the time to say so, if you are. We're not the police. We just want to provide the best healthcare we can. I'll ask you a second time."

"I'm not an intravenous drug user," I say. "I'd walk on broken glass before I'd stick a needle in my body. Even if I was an intravenous drug user, I would not shoot up in my neck. I was at rugby practice. See how dirty I am?"

We both look at the dirt stains on my knees.

"Very well," says Dr. Goodfriend.

"So what happens?" I ask impatiently.

"What happens with what?"

"With me! What the hell happens now?"

"Oh, right. Well, don't worry about it *too* much, Mr. Colder. We'll give you a blood test. Have you had a blood test before?"

"Yeah," I say. The pre-nuptial blood test that I optimistically went for a few years back.

"Test for HIV?"

"Yup."

"Negative?"

"Yup."

"OK, good," says the doctor. "That helps."

Minimal sex since then has its benefits, as did Ma's impassioned safe-sex diatribe a decade ago, after she walked in on me and that new wave-y chick from Art & Design. What the hell was her name? Tara? Tamara? I should call her.

"So we'll give you another one. Tell me—was the plunger pushed down while the needle was in you?"

"No."

"You're positive?"

"I tested negative, sir."

"No, I mean, you're sure the plunger was not pushed down?"

"Yeah, I'm sure."

"Good, good," says Dr. Goodfriend, looking a bit cross-eyed as he stares at his clipboard. "That means nothing was injected into you. I can't give you guarantees, but what's on the outside of the needle is mostly harmless. If there was blood, it's dried blood, and has been exposed to air. The virus is not what you might call hardy—it needs a warm, safe environment in which to flourish. There's the risk of tetanus, but in terms of something more serious, I wouldn't lose sleep over it."

"Like HIV."

"Yes, like HIV."

"Geez, that's fucking great," I say, feeling the anxiety slide off my body. Tetanus is child's play. "I'm very psyched to hear that."

I shake Dr. Goodfriend's hand again, and clap him hard on the shoulder, eliciting a displeased look on the doctor's face.

"Freakin' great," I add.

"Good, good," he says. "I'll have the nurse clean up your prick—"

Dr. Goodfriend gives me a wink.

"—and put a bandage on it, and then she'll do your blood test. You *will* have to wait about a month til we're more sure, but again, you'd have to have some mighty bad luck to contract anything serious. You the church-goin' type?"

"Yes, sir," I say, happy to be speaking the truth. "My whole life. Most of it."

"Good man. Sit tight til the nurse comes 'round."

"Thank you, Doctor. Thank you."

"Do you have a best gal?" he asks.

"No," I say, looking at the floor.

"Well, don't be putting anyone at risk until you get the results. Just to be safe."

"Not a problem, sir."

Dr. Goodfriend smiles awkwardly and turns on his heel.

I exhale for what seems to be about 30 seconds, setting forth enough air to fill a beach ball. Of course, I'm not wild about the idea of having blood taken. But after the crap I've been through, it doesn't seem like a big deal. I mean, I'm *not* going to faint, even without my mommy holding my hand. And I'm not going to die; at least, not just yet.

They tell me I can leave, and I hustle out of there before they change their minds, feeling about 150 pounds lighter than when I walked in. As I approach the door to the waiting room, I can see the boys through the window: Gabby, Shady Brady, Tracy Chapman, Ghetto Ron, a few others. They're all in jerseys of varying colors—their old college teams, national team replicas, tournament souvenirs, jerseys they traded with other teams for on our rugby trips, out in Vegas, down in New Orleans. Shady is pouring a Bud tall boy into a Burger King cup nestled between his legs. They've all got Super-size cups, and there's a brown grocery bag of beers at Gabby's feet. A cherubic black security guard in a blue blazer, standing with his hands folded at his crotch, eyes them warily, wondering how to proceed.

I walk through the door to considerable fanfare.

"Deckieeeeeee!" they shout in near unison.

"Boys," I say.

Gabby jumps to his feet.

"What's the good word, bro?"

"I think I'm gonna make it."

"Damn," says Shady. "I had my eye on your apartment. You're rent-stabilized, yeah?"

"Piss off," I say. "I gotta sit tight for a month or so before the results. But the odds of catching something killer is, like, us beating Bainbridge or something."

The boys laugh.

"And you scoring a try," chimes in Ghetto Ron.

"Or you even *playing* in a match," jibes Tracy.

"Seriously," says Gabby. "Y'awright?"

"Yeah, man," I say. "Doc said it's like a million to one, or something. I can live with those odds."

"So can we," says Shady. "Beer?"

"Yeah, man," I say. "I can really, really use a beer."

Shady pours a tall boy into a cup. Gabby claps me hard on the shoulder.

"Watch the neck, buddy boy," I say. "You've done enough damage today."

He laughs and squeezes my shoulder. I sip my beer. It's foamy and warm and delicious.

"Glad you're alright, man," he says. "I mean, I know we ain't gonna know nothin' for a bit, but the doc said it's gonna be OK, huh?"

"Yeah. Million to one."

"Good odds," Gabby says. "You gonna tell yer ma?"

I look at him. We're two kids that just broke a window playing ball.

"Fuck, no," I say. I'll make up some excuse for the Band-Aid on my neck. "I mean, if my ticket comes up, I'll take care of that shit then. But she don't need to know."

"Good," says Gabby. "MacLennane's?"

"Oh, yeah."

The idea of draining a few Guinness at MacLennane's sounds delightful. It's also part of the Guy Code that when you take a hypodermic needle to the neck, you don't have to pay for beers. Shady tops off my cup with more foam. This'll hold me over until I get to the bar.

Lease on Life

Well, after that little brush with death, I suppose I should change the way I live my life: sell all my worldly possessions (meaning my computer, my Skechers boots, a few pairs of jeans, my Ireland rugby jersey), quit my job (well, too late for that) and spend the rest of my life doing nice things for people. That just isn't going to happen. But I *will* stick to the plans I had before. I'm going to buckle down on my novel, I'm going to take care of the two remaining index cards in my life and I'm going to turn 30. And most of that's going to happen in the next week.

So next up is Tisa. Two days. Forty-eight hours. My anxiety will either be cut in half, or multiplied by a hundred.

Tisa's kicking my ass in the unspoken game of tallying up each other's points, and if this were Little League, they'd enact the 10-run Mercy Rule right about now. She and Earl are probably closing on their second home right about now, their little *pied-a-terre* out in Sag Harbor or something, to go with the place in Chelsea. Me? Still living with Ma, but Tisa of course doesn't have to know about that. Realistically, it's not likely that I can get a job in the next week. But I might be able to schedule an interview, maybe with a headhunter or something. Or perhaps one of those resumes I sent out might come through. Then I can tell Tisa, "Well, I'm *interviewing* right now." That's got a good ring to it. And maybe I can crank out the first chapter of my novel and tell Tisa, "Yes, well, my novel is moving along at quite a clip, should be done in no time, blah blah blah." Doesn't have to be good—I mean, she isn't going to read the thing—but it's got to be underway, at least. Maybe I'll even send a few letters to agents. "Yes, been *in communiqué* with a few agents, Tisa," I'll say. "I'm considering my options." Might not be a bad idea.

And the volunteer work, that's always good. I can talk about that for a long time; the well-to-do are always interested to hear what's going on with the less fortunate. I'm a little skeeved to go back after The Needle Incident, but I feel like it's probably a good idea to keep it up a bit longer, keep myself in check, keep filling my days, keep doing stuff for others.

I just hope Tisa doesn't ask about my "little bunny books," as she used to call them. God, I miss my floppy-eared little friend. Hope Sally enjoyed that rabbit stew she made out of him.

I read a copy of the "Our Father" I downloaded off the Internet, though I remembered most of it before looking it up. Please God, don't let Tisa be pregnant. Please God, please God, please God. Please. God.

Ma doesn't have a computer, so she lets me come up to my place to work on my resume, cover letters or whatever else needs doing. So I got Shane MacGowan cranking on the stereo, a cup of tea in hand and I'm ready to write. The white screen beckons like an untouched tub of vanilla ice cream. I switch Shane for Tom Waits, then back to Shane.

Alright, then.

And the phone rings, as I've trained it to do any time I'm threatening to write.

"Hello?"

"Coulter? I can't believe you're freakin' home."

It's a female, one whose voice does not immediately drop my heart into my shoes, or send it flying through my rib cage. I need more women in my life who do neither.

"Who's this?"

"Everyone's favorite former Avatar intern."

"Becky! Jesus, how are you?"

"Alright, alright," she says.

"What's *up*? Never thought I'd talk to you again."

"Thanks, Coulter. Nice to hear from you, too. What we had wasn't enough to keep it going after you got your ass fired?"

"Well, yeah, I guess. I dunno. Wassup?"

"Not much. Well, I guess I'm supposed to say, 'sorry to hear what happened,' and all, but it's probably the best thing that could've happened to you."

"Yeah, I know. I had to get my ass outta there."

"Yes, well, I'm told it's an even more miserable place with you gone. No one talks anymore. They all just work. No more happy hours. Guess you were the glue or something. I should call you Elmer."

"Why aren't you there?" I ask. "What the hell are you up to?"

"Oh, living my little 'Felicity' life—going to classes, hanging out at Dean & DeLuca, having guys traverse the country in an attempt to woo me."

I feel slightly jealous when I think of boyishly handsome WB guys crossing the country for Becky. But more in a brotherly way.

"And?"

"And I switched to part-time at school so I can work full-time."

"At Avatar?"

"Hells no! For my dad," says Becky. "That's why I'm calling."

"It's not to ask me out?"

"Don't tempt me, Coulter. You still single?"

"Painfully so."

"What's new? Are you OK?"

"I'm...fine. Keeping pretty busy, actually," I say, seizing the opportunity to practice for Tisa. "I'm interviewing, doing some volunteer work, working on a novel."

"How Kennedy of you. No pilot lessons?"

"No, not yet. So why you callin'? Just to break my balls?"

"I might have a lead for you."

"Yeah?" I say, sitting up straight. "What's her name?"

"A *job* lead, jackass, assuming the sex mag gig didn't come through. But maybe you just talked your way out of consideration."

"Oh. Right. Sorry. Whaddya got?"

"Ya know my pops? The rich guy?"

"Heard of him," I say.

"He and some of his, ya know, cronies, are launching a little magazine."

"Yeah?"

"You know the Paris Review?"

"No," I say.

Becky rolls her eyes through the phone.

"Is it a show? Some burlesque thing? Need me to write the *Playbill* stuff? I ever tell you, when I was a kid and my mom saw 'Grease' and brought home the *Playbill*, I flipped through it, like, eight times, thinking it was *Playboy*?"

"Will...you...*please*...shut up?" Becky says. "A literary journal, Coulter. We're talking about publishing, remember? Some writer you are."

"Right," I say. "Whaddya gettin' at, Bex?"

"My dad and some of his colleagues are launching a little mag, sort of like Salon, only in print and, hopefully, profitable. Arts, politics, opinion pieces, fiction, etc. Like a *Harper's* for people with social skills. They got the V.C. all lined up and everything."

Viet Cong? Vitae Curriculum?

"We're funded for at least 18 months," she continues. "You got a suit?"

My suit's an ill-fitting mess, but I can borrow one from one of the guys. Mental Ben is my size. Dr. Demento is too.

"Yeah," I say.

"Well, get it dry-cleaned. You're going to interview."

"No shit!"

"Right on, Coulter."

"What kind of job?"

Michael J. Malone

"Associate editor in the book department. Reviews, author profiles, etc."

"Wow... How 'bout senior editor?" I say.

"How 'bout 'don't push it'? How 'bout, 'thank you so much for getting me an interview when everyone else left me for dead'?"

Left for dead. I can still see the fiberglass cow looming over me.

"Yeah, all that," I say. "Seriously, that's way cool, Bex. Thank you so much. What do I do?"

"This dude Jeff Phillips is gonna call you to set it up—he's my dad's partner. No guarantees, but an interview's an interview. Don't screw me—I'm going out on a limb for you here."

"What's your dad gonna do, fire you?"

"Don't fuck me, Coulter."

"I won't, Bex...What's your involvement in this? Publisher?"

"Hardly," she says. "I'll be working in the book department too. Dad figures the real-life experience will be good for me."

"Cool!" I say, picturing me and Becky playing an R-rated version of hangman during editorial meetings, and her covering for me when I call in sick. "What's your title?"

"Senior editor," mumbles Becky. "Department head. Thank you, Daddy."

I start cracking up. What else can I do?

"Fuck off. You're 19."

"I just turned 20."

"Happy birthday," I say. "*You're* a senior editor."

"My dad has lots and lots of dough. And he really loves me."

"You are going to sexually harass the shit out of me."

"You haven't been hired yet, big guy." she says. "Don't flatter yourself. You in, or what?"

"When are you guys launching?"

"Spring 2000, assuming the world still works after New Year's. We got tons to do."

"*Senior editor.*"

"Deal with it, Coulter."

"Guess I'll have to. What's the name of the mag?"

"*Algonquin.*"

"A bit pretentious, don't you think?"

"Well, *Cunning Linguist* was already taken."

"Too bad. That's catchy."

"I thought of *Algonquin,*" Becky continues. "And yes, it's pretentious. But I wanted it, so Daddy bought the domain name off the eponymous hotel."

I seem to recall hearing about this new Eponymous Hotel down on Rivington or something. Total velvet rope hotspot.

"How much they buy it for?"

"He wouldn't tell me. Too much."

"*Algonquin*. Doin' a nice big launch party, I bet?"

"I would assume so, yes," says Becky.

"Lots of booze?"

"Likely, yes. Shall I have Jeff Phillips call you?"

"Yes, definitely. I mean, yes, ma'am."

"Hey, watch it."

"Sorry. Yes, sir."

"Well, I'm glad to hear you're well, Declan, and I'm psyched to see you."

"Yeah, same here," I say. "Thank you, Bex. Honestly, I really appreciate it. I'd be fucking stoked to work f—...*with* you."

"Excellent. We'll talk soon."

"Cool. See ya', kid."

I hang up the phone happily. Tisa's going to be duly impressed to hear I'm part of some hip and artsy-fartsy startup.

And that I'm progressing on my novel, which right now is a blank screen, and will stay so if I keep procrastinating.

And so I commence typing.

ACKNOWLEDGEMENTS
It looks wrong.
ACKNOWLEGEMENTS
Still looks wrong.
ACKNOWLEDGMENTS
Hmmm.

They all look wrong. Thank God for spell-check. But I'm not going to let spelling slow me down now.

For Ma and all the Vipers boys—thanks for everything. We did it!

I print it out, pull it from the printer and smudge the damp ink. Too *Rocky*-esque—*Yo Adrian! We did it!*

For Ma—thanks for all your support. I love you.

Print. Pull. Read.

Too sappy.

Haley—it might've been great. It's not too late.

No.

For Ma and Haley—even though you've never met,
you were both responsible for...

Hell, no. That's never going to work.

For Gabby, Shady Brady and Demento...

What author has friends named Gabby, Shady Brady and Demento?

Bex baby—you rock!

Too unprofessional.

For Mammood. I'm truly sorry. It's all part of the process.

Part of the process? What the hell does that mean? I have to put Mammood behind me, chalk it up to the desperate actions of a desperate man.

For Big Jack. It's my Edwin Drood.

Somewhat intriguing and suitably pretentious, but Ma'll kill me.

For Ma. Thank you.

Yeah.

I read it again.

Yeah, that's the one.

I hit Return and insert a page break.

I'll have this baby done in no time.

Unfinished Business

I throw a few shadow punches at my mug in the mirror: right jab, left jab, right jab, bob and weave, right knockout punch. *BAAAMMM!* Barry fookin' Mc-Guigan is right.

I'm feeling more and more like a fighter these days; maybe I'll drop the rugby thing and take up boxing. At least those guys have the good sense to wear some headgear.

My legs feel like they've got 14 ½ rounds under them. Out of breath, I make my way over to my bed and sit, putting my head between my legs, wishing I had a trainer to rub a cold sponge on my neck and bark advice.

After our phone convo, I spent a lot of time figuring out where to meet Tisa. Scanned the mental Zagat's for every downtown bar I could think of, trying to pick a place that held no sentimental history for us: no fights, no heady feeling of love, no break-ups and, dammit, no marriage proposals. A place where you could have a serious talk without people next to you listening, or seeing you cry, if that should come up. I finally settled on St. Dymphna's. It's a little Irish pub, which I dig, and it's hip and funky enough for Tisa. It's perfect. We have no emotional attachment there. I remember reading a review of the place in that *Time Out* at the laundromat, and it said that St. Dymphna was the patron saint of crazy people.

Perfect.

Of course, when we spoke again, I left it up to her, and she picked the Broome Street Bar in SoHo, wittingly negating my home field advantage.

So we're on in half an hour. And I'm throwing punches at the mirror. Like I did on the tattoo day, all day long I've been trying to keep myself occupied, keep the body doing something so the mind doesn't obsess about what's about to go down, figuring my best plan of attack. Do I try to win her back, help her raise our kid, if that's the hand we're dealt, maybe talk with her about pushing Earl out of the picture? Do I even *want* her back? Do I try to hurt her and even the score (though nothing I could do would get her back for laughing at my proposal, except perhaps jamming a rusty corkscrew under her fingernails and pouring cheap tequila in the wounds).

Well, the answer to all those questions is a big old, resounding "I don't know," seeing as everything depends on whether she's hauling my baby around or not. So I figure my best plan of attack is to not have a plan of attack. Not that my gut's track record is stellar or anything; I just don't have a better idea. So I ran around like a madman all day. Ran to the gym, ran five miles on the treadmill, hit the weights for about 90 minutes and sat in the steam room until I looked like a giant Irish-American prune. Then I took a nice, long, head-clearing walk around the southern tip of Manhattan—over to the west side, through Battery Park, the Seaport and eventually up to East River Park, first time I been back since getting stuck—before coming home to shower and get dressed. And here I am, sweating, out of breath, throwing punches.

I wink at my mug in a false display of confidence that does not fool me, and slide the index card marked TISA into the back pocket of my jeans.

It's about a 20-minute walk to Broome and West Broadway, which means I should have 10 minutes to spare. That's perfect—I want to scope out the bathroom, make sure it's got a knob lock at worst, a dead bolt at best—just in case I have to puke, piss, shit, cry or find some other way of forcing matter out of my body in an emergency situation.

I'm walking like a zombie: slow, methodical, staring straight ahead, oblivious to all around me. Cars whizzing by are streaks of color in the corner of my eye and ephemeral swatches of sound in my ear. People pass engaged in their silly little conversations; I pick up every fifth or so word: visceral, post-modern, Jeter, John Cale, pale ale. It's damn sticky for September; my shirt is stuck to my back, the sweat instantly growing cold.

Walking along 4th towards Broadway I see the posters that line the windows of Tower Records: a new boy band called BBMak, Wyclef Jean's new album, the new Chili Peppers', the soon-to-be-released U2, the boys looking cool while standing in an airport. When I met Tisa, *Pop* was out. A lot can happen in between U2 releases.

I reach for a Shane MacGowan song like a child clutches a security blanket. As I start singing, my fatigued legs fall into a march.

When he stepped up the narrow street, smiling proud and young
Around the hemp, around his neck, the golden ringlets clung
There was never a tear in his blue eyes, but sad and bright were they

I'm singing sort of loud, attempting to replicate Shane's smashed-whiskey-bottle voice. I'm well aware of people halting conversations about letterbox fritters and tofu films as they approach me. I sing louder.

For young Roddy McCorley goes to die on the Bridge of Toome today

Is it a bit of overstatement to sing an Irish freedom song when going to meet your ex-girlfriend? Of course it is; Ma would call me a *fookin' eejit*. Hell, she'd *freak* if she knew I was going to meet Tisa. But singing makes me feel better, so I sing louder and rougher.

It's a dimly lit place. There are three guys at the bar to the left, and a woman about my age, with cropped auburn hair and denim overalls, is seated at a table, looking bored as she leafs through the *Village Voice*. In case of emergency, it appears the odds of the men's room being open are pretty good.

I walk towards the bar and the woman looks up from the table. Her face breaks into a wide grin that makes me think of our first six months together. *Fuck.* Her face is the same, but her belly sticks out, like she ingested a canteloupe. I attempt to raise my right hand to wave, but it's stuck at my side. I try rousing my left hand into freeing the right, but that's stuck too. The only greeting I can offer is an idiotic half-smile, the frozen kind seen in junior high yearbooks, as I approach her.

"Hey, you," Tisa says.

"Hey," I respond in a voice I've never heard before.

"You wanna join me?" she says.

Her hair is unbelievably short, like a boy's. Her belly pushes against the front of her overalls.

"Yeah," I say, hoping she doesn't have to get up and escort me over to the table. Fortunately, I get feeling back in my limbs and begin to walk the final 10 feet. A guy at the bar looks up from his *Post*. He's watching, Tisa's watching, the bartender's watching, and I'm getting real self-conscious. It takes forever to close the gap. When I do, I half expect applause, like it's my first steps since having my legs surgically reattached after an unfortunate subway incident, and the news crews are out en masse.

Tisa's hair looks even shorter close-up; it too is the kind found on boys in junior high yearbooks. We awkwardly kiss on the cheek, keeping enough distance so that we're essentially shaking hands with our right ears. I feel myself hyperventilate as I see visions of the rest of my life spreading out before me: coaching Little League and batting my boy cleanup, attending school plays where he portrays a sycamore. What will we name him? And how do I know he's a he?

"Hello," she says nervously.

"Hello...Tisa," I say. Tisa has Boy Hair. She looks like an entirely different woman. It's the kind of haircut girls get when they're either aiming to flout society's rules about what makes for an attractive woman, or they want to show the world they can place obstacles in front of their attractiveness and still be considered hot, or they're playing a boy, lesbian or cancer victim in a movie. Not sure which Tisa's going for; either way, it's a dubious career move.

Then again, maybe she's not actually playing a cancer victim, but *is* one.

"How's life?" I say.

"Life is good," Tisa responds in an accent that sounds more American than British. "Life is...life. How's your head?"

"Better, thanks," I say, bashfully rubbing my stubbly noggin.

"What were you thinking?"

"I wasn't," I say. "Obviously. I'm so embarrassed. It won't happen again."

"Yes, well, thank God Earl was away."

"Thank God," I agree. As if I couldn't give Leanandhungry a beat-down, even when concussed and horrifically hung over.

"Lookit your hair...," I say.

"I know," she says, fluffing the scruffy back of it. "Short, huh?"

"Yeah. Short, alright."

"Declan, you're supposed to say, 'Yes, it looks positively *fetching.*'"

"It's fetchingly short," I say. "You don't need hair to still look, ya know, good 'n stuff."

"I still *have* hair," she says, tugging on her bangs in an effort to stretch them.

"I know. You look fine."

She whispers "fine," makes a face and looks down.

"You're not...," I start, choosing my words carefully. "I mean, you're OK, right?"

"How do you mean, OK?"

"Like...I mean, the hair. You're not...growing it back...after...ya know... treatment?"

Tisa stares at me with equal parts shock and dismay.

"I'm not getting chemo, if that's what you're stammering towards."

There's an awkward pause, during which Tisa fingers an ice cube in her drink and I put a beer coaster on its side and flick it, making it spin.

The bartender comes by. Tisa waves him off like she's holding in Blackjack.

"Aren't your feet dying in those boots?" she asks, staring at my lightly scuffed Skechers.

"Nah, they're fine," I say. "The boots are, uh, ventilated."

"So what's new?" she asks.

"Oh," I start. What did I rehearse? "Applying to grad school." That's not what I rehearsed. Whoever said anything about grad school?

"Really?" exclaims Tisa, her eyes big as billiard balls. "Declan Coulter in graduate school? *Master* Declan Coulter? I...never... Wow, that's a surprise."

"Yeah, well, I'm not *in* grad school. Not yet. I'm taking the...GSAT's."

"I can't believe it," says Tisa. "I'm quite impressed."

"We'll see where I get in," I say. I'm freestyling now, watch out. "*If* I get in. Should be interesting."

"So you're writing a lot?" she asks. Seems we're both doing everything we can to avoid talking about the baby-to-be between us.

"Yeah, tons," I answer abruptly.

"Will you study writing?"

"Yeah, prolly Creative Writing."

"Still doing the little bunny books?"

"I put Honey Bunny on hold for now," I say. "Wanna concentrate more on the novel."

"And how's it coming?"

"Great, great," I say, eyeing the men's room as my bowels rumble. "I mean, it's a little slow going at times, but I'm building the foundation, ya know?"

"Ooo, exciting," she says without much sincerity.

"Yeah, it is."

The man hiding behind his *New York Post* orders a Jack & coke. I see him watching us, over the paper, in the mirror behind the bar.

"Got a name for it yet?"

"A name?" I say. "Anything but Declan Jr., I guess. Aidan? Evan?"

"Huh? What are you talking about?"

"Names? What are *you* talking about?"

"Your novel, you dolt."

Of course.

If I were to put a name on what I've written so far, it would have to be *Acknowledgements*.

"'The Apathy and the Ecstasy,'" is the first thing I could think of.

"Brilliant. Sounds Gen-X-y. I like it."

"Thanks."

"What's it about?" she asks.

"Friendship. Dudes. A road trip. Maybe a caper or two. There's some Nick Hornby to it. And flashes of Tarantino."

"Good on you," she says.

"Thanks. I'll send a copy along when it's done. Got to read a short story at Troika too."

"That place you used to take me to? The dodgy communist bar with the roaches?"

I don't think I've ever seen any roaches at Troika, though I don't doubt they're there.

"Yeah, I guess so. 4th Street, upstairs. They do readings every Sunday. Real authors, and stuff."

"Congratulations, Declan. What did you read?"

"It was called..."

Shit. I already used its title for my make-believe "novel."

"'L.A. Fadeaway,'" I say, gritting my teeth.

"Ah, the City of Angels," Tisa says as if she grew up there. "What's that one about?"

"Uh, ya know, guys and girls and stuff. Celebrity and obscurity and...the space between them. Speaking of L.A., when'd you move back here?"

"Nearly a year ago," she says.

"Didn't like it?"

"Hated it. Couldn't wait to get back to New York; L.A. made New York actually seem like home. So weird, being twice as far from the family. And everyone's so...well, it's everything you've heard it is. Everyone's so shockingly shallow. And it's such a television town. Television and bad films. And traffic.

"Everyone's in 'the Business,'" Tisa adds, making quotation marks with her fingers. "Declan, I told you all this that night you...visited."

"Right. Sorry. How's the acting?"

"Great, great" she says. "I mean, until this—"

Tisa pats her belly.

"Got it. What kind of stuff had you been working on?"

"A bit of the-*ay*-ter," she says. "A little television."

"Awesome. All because of those headshots I paid for."

"I can pay you back," she says, reaching for her purse.

"Jesus, no," I say. "I'm kidding. I've got money. Glad to hear they helped. So what theater?"

"I played Lady Macbeth in L.A.," Tisa says, pulling on her bangs again. "Unfortunately, L.A. doesn't care a whit about Shakespeare."

"Well, that's still cool, though."

"Yes, well, I was the understudy, actually. But the lead twisted her ankle when Macbeth crashed into her this one night—he was a big lad, big and stupid—and I got the lead for about a week."

"Cool. Betcha kicked ass."

"It went well, thanks. I was chuffed."

"What kinda TV you do?" I ask. "Anything I've seen?"

Tisa swirls the ice around in her drink. I can feel streams of sweat pouring down my back. I envision myself reading *Honey Bunny* to my kid and actually feel comforted.

"Hostess," she mumbles, hanging her head, "on a game show."

"A what?"

She squeezes the lime in her drink and looks me in the eye.

"On a game show."

"Like Vanna White?"

"Sort of."

"Really," I say. "Which game show?"

"Oh, it's this light-hearted show on cable. A funny sort of show, really. Cheeky, like."

"What's it called?"

"It's on at night," she says, hanging her head again. "Kind of late night. 'Bare Market.'"

"What the hell is 'Bear Market'?" I ask, prompting the guys at the bar to turn around.

"Sssshhh," Tisa says, shooting the men a smirk. "Please. They've probably seen it."

"Well, what is it?"

"It's this silly little show, sort of like 'Price is Right,'" she says in a loud whisper. "Where contestants have to guess the price of groceries and the like. It's two lads against two girls. If the lads guess right, the women have to take off a, uh, an article of clothing. And vice versa."

"Bare, like B-A-R-E," I say.

"Right, right."

"And what do you do?"

"Well, I'm not on it anymore, thank God. I wore a short dress and rang up prices on a cash register. It was good fun, really."

"So you didn't have to get naked," I say.

"Gosh, no, Declan. Of course not."

She reaches across the table and slaps my hand.

"Good," I say, relieved but not totally at ease with the thought of cheeseball horndogs tuning in to watch my kid's mom ring up groceries in a sexy dress. "That's so cool!"

"Well, it paid the bills for a bit, and then it got canceled. But I'm back in New York. And it's good to be here."

"'Bare Market,'" I say.

"Yes, well, enough about that."

"You've got a nice place."

"Cheers. We won't have it for long. The rent is preposterous. We're moving to Queens."

Tisa in Queens. I never thought I'd live to see the day she ventured east of the East River.

I clear my throat. "Married yet?" I ask.

There's a brief pause, then Tisa makes a slurping sound as her straw hits air.

"Yes," she says into the straw.

"Congrats," I say. She looks up and smiles. I try to gauge my own reaction, knowing now that she and I will not be marrying. I'm almost sort of kinda happy for her.

"Ta."

"How is ol' whatshisname?" I ask.

"He's grand."

"Guess you got past the Declan flashes," I say.

She takes a deep breath.

"Not entirely."

"Does whatshisname know you're here?"

Tisa slams her drink on the table.

"Declan, stop it! His name is Earl!"

"Earl," I say with a small laugh. Either I'm going to laugh about this guy or cry about him. "Sorry."

"What's so goddamn funny?"

"It's a funny name, is all."

"Earl?"

"Earl," I repeat, laughing again. Hell, she laughed at me.

"OK, we'll stop laughing at Earl's name *now*. And yes—he knows I'm here."

"And Earl's cool with it?" I say, biting my lip.

"No."

"Good. He's still acting?"

"Yes. He does the-*ay*-ter as well."

"So I guess he's carrying the both of you now."

"Well, we've both been sort of...picking our spots...since we've been back. The work he's doing isn't exactly the kind you get paid for."

"It'll pick up," I say, glad to hear Leanandhungry's staying that way.

"It better."

I realize I haven't had a drink yet.

"Whacha drinkin'?" I say.

"Vodka, rocks," answers Tisa.

"Is that OK with, ya know, him?" I say, nodding toward the swell of her belly.

"How do you know he's a he?"

"I don't know," I say, taking a deep breath. "Fifty-fifty odds, I guess."

"Well, you're right."

"When are you due?"

I swear I hear a drum roll off in the distance. Is there a music store nearby? A rehearsal space?

"Christmas!" says Tisa, patting the baby-to-be.

Christmas. December. December is No. 12. Twelve minus nine is...three. Three would be...March. That's when she got knocked up. What month is it? I can hear Demento asking in his Okie drawl. My jersey number is...6. That's June! Recalling my math scores on the SAT's and my difficulty with the month question before, I run through the numbers again. December minus nine is March, and June plus nine is...15! March of next year! Yes. It's true. She's carrying Earl Jr. I lean over and give Tisa a wet, sloppy kiss on the cheek.

"I'm so happy for you," I say. And I am. I wish I had fucking cigars to pass out.

"She's havin' a baby!" I yell to the guys at the bar.

"Woo-hoo!" one shoots back from behind the *Post*.

"Thank you, Declan. But seriously—we went through all this that night. Every damn detail. Do you not remember?"

I shake my head.

"Yes, well, I'm not surprised. I did feel as though I was speaking with a zombie. It was a matter of minutes before you passed out. Couldn't wake you for the life of me. God, what were you drinking?"

"What wasn't I drinking," I say. "Again, I'm so sorry. So, less than... four months to go."

"Yes."

"You look very healthy," I add. "Glowing, even."

"Cheers, Declan. That's very sweet."

"At first, I thought maybe you'd just gotten real fat, like, maybe you'd dealt with our break-up by eating everything in sight. It's happened to other girls I've dated. But you definitely look more, ya know, pregnant, than fat."

"That would've been awkward," she says with a smile. "But if I'd gotten big and fat, I probably wouldn't have wanted to meet you. Not til I lost the weight, anyway. Speaking thereof, you're looking fit."

"Yeah, ya know," I say, my arduous day of exercise and steam room apparently having done its job. "Try to keep in shape...Vodka, rocks?"

"Make it a mineral water," she says. "With a lime. One's the limit these days."

"Me too," I say. "Any more, and I'm a mess."

"Bollocks," Tisa says as I head to the bar.

There's a Sierra Nevada mirror over the bar that's calling my name real loud.

"What'll ya have?" asks the bartender, a guy of about 40 with a big forehead and long gray hair in the back.

"Mineral water, lime. And a club soda, please."

"Wow. Party time," he mocks, then scurries off to make the drinks.

I set the drinks on our table and take my seat again.

"You got a name for the little guy yet?" I ask.

"Either Samuel or Maxwell," says Tisa. "But if the little bugger is born on Christmas, I think we have to go with Noel."

"Cool. I named my computer Kieran."

"Why did you name your computer Kieran?"

"Dunno," I say, feeling stupid. Tisa always made me feel stupid. How could I forget that? "Just figured, ya know, we'd be spending a lot of time together, so he should have a name."

"That's cute," she says. "Besides Kieran, anyone else you spend a lot of time with? Girlfriend? Fiancée?"

"Nah," I say. "Had a girlfriend, kind of a serious one. But we broke up."

I couldn't wait to tell Tisa about Haley, give her all the details about this tall, rich, classy girl with long, blonde hair and a well-connected father, but it doesn't feel that great. Part of me wants to hurt her, but most of me feels like that would just be piling on. I've been at the bottom of a ruck a million times in rugby, studs ripping at your flesh, your bones bending at weird angles, your lungs running out of air, and it sucks. It's dry drowning.

"Oh, I'm sorry."

"Yeah, well, I'm staying single and writing my ass off, and she's dating Paul Rudd."

"The actor?"

"Yup."

"Honest to God?"

"Yup."

"Wow," says Tisa. "He's brilliant. Handsome. Sneakily so. I should give you our headshots."

"I'm not in contact with him," I say.

"So how's the footie?"

"Rugby."

"Right, right. Still playing?"

"Yeah, off and on."

"You lot still losing all the time?"

"Yeah," I say. "We got Forest Hills Irregulars tomorrow. Maybe our luck will change."

"Bon chance," she says.

"Hey, lemme show ya something."

I pull my shirt over my head.

"Declan, I'm a married woman!"

I turn my bare right shoulder to her.

"Lookit," I say proudly.

"Look at tha'," she says, tracing my tat with her finger, like I'd done to her moon tat at the bar years before. "You got it done. Well done, Declan. It's very... Irish."

"It's a harp."

"I can see that. I never thought you'd get it done. Good on you. Cheers."

We clink our G-rated drinks together.

"Yeah, gift from my mom."

"How is your mum?"

"Crazy as ever. She says hi."

"You liar," says Tisa with a laugh. "She doesn't even know you're here."

"You're right."

"We better hope she doesn't walk in."

"She's never in this neighborhood," I say.

Then it grows quiet. We talked about jobs, significant others (Earl!), babies, hobbies and our shrinking pool of common friends. That's really all we have to offer each other.

Tisa smiles at me, and I see tears well up, lacquering her brown eyes. A lone tear breaks free and hits the table, and she wipes it up with a cocktail napkin.

"Why did you want to meet?" I ask.

"I wanted to see you in person, and I wanted to apologize. I'm sorry, Declan."

"Sorry for what?"

"For treating you like shite. You deserved so much better."

"It was a long time ago. I'm over it."

"I'm glad. I mean, I'm so sorry. You were always so kind to me."

I give Tisa a reassuring smile and pat her hand.

"Yeah, you treated me bad," I say.

"I know. I was horrible."

"It was a good lesson. Toughened me up."

"You did not need toughening up, Declan."

"Well, it helped me, ya know, grow up a bit."

"So you're thanking me for treating you horribly," she says, laughing and crying and causing a little snot to bubble out for a split second.

"No. But I forgive you."

"Thank you," says Tisa, reaching across the table to hug me, the Samuel- or Maxwell- or Noel-to-be briefly resting on the table. "That means a lot to me."

"Have a healthy baby," I say, draining my club soda.

"I'll try... You want one?"

"Nah, I'm not quite ready for fatherhood," I say with a smile. "But thanks."

"A drink, you damn fool."

"Ooo, don't let the baby hear you curse."

"Fuckin' 'ell," Tisa says with a laugh, dabbing at her eyes.

"I'm good," I say. "I'm gonna run."

"You're sure?"

"Yeah, I'm fine."

"Positive?"

"Yeah."

"Well, thank you for the drink," says Tisa.

"No problem," I say, as we get to our feet. Outside, the sun is just ducking behind the buildings. It's noticeably cooler.

"How are you getting home?" I ask.

"Gonna walk over to the 1/9," she says.

"OK, I'm heading east."

We hug, and I feel her baby in my gut; I swear I can feel the little guy punch me in the solar plexus.

"Your hair looks great," I say. "Really accentuates your face."

"Thank you, Declan," she says. "You always made me feel good about myself. I like your boots."

"These things?" I say, looking casually at my Skechers. "Thanks."

"Send me your novel when it comes out."

"I will. Send me a picture of your kid. Address is the same."

"I will."

"Thank you."

"Happy birthday," Tisa says over her shoulder, then smiles and heads west, walking with that funny waddle that pregnant women have. I fight off a smile, then let it fly; it's a big one that envelops my face. I take her index card out of my pocket, tear it into four and dump it in the nearest garbage can. Starting up West Broadway, I head towards MacLennane's with a big ol' skip to my step.

If I had the dough, I'd buy everyone there a beer.

"Aye, rise and shine!" sings my mom from the doorway of my childhood bedroom. I lament the hangover pounding in my head. "It's someone's fookin' birthday!"

"Hey, Ma," I mumble, prying my eyes open.

"How are yeh, son?"

"I'm fine, Ma," I say, sitting up and feeling better upon realizing I didn't drink the night before. "How you doin'?"

"Well, to be totally honest, I'm feelin' pretty *daaarn* old now that I've got a fookin' turty-year-old."

"Well, if it's any consolation, I'm feelin' pretty *fookin'* old myself."

She gives me that look.

"Yeh watch yer tongue when yeh talk to yer mudder!"

"Sorry, Ma."

"Ah, no worry, son. Guess yeh can let one slip on yer birthday, eh? Oop fer a little birthday breakfast?"

"Oh, that sounds great. Yes. Yes, please."

"Alrighty, then. Be ready in a few."

"Thanks, Ma."

I massage life into my sore back and pull some jeans on. I won't miss feeling like Gulliver in this ridiculous little bed, but I have gotten used to starting the day with Ma's heart-stopping auld country breakfasts, which are way better than what any of the Uke diners along Avenue A serve up, except maybe Leshko's. Thank God I'm running at the gym.

"Marnin', son," she says, shoveling eggs, greasy bacon, beans and black pudding onto a plate. "Sit yerself down and have at it."

She sets the plate on the table and gives me a kiss on the top of the head. I feel a wave of emotion, a big one. It's her first show of physical affection since she found me. Was she purposely waiting until my birthday?

"You shouldn't have," I say. "It looks wonderful. Thank you."

I take a sip of coffee.

"I'm gonna grab yer gift," she says.

"Aw, Ma, between the tattoo and this," I say, pointing to my plate. "Really."

"Ah, nonsense. This is fer yer last birthday, too, I reckon. Be jest a second."

She hustles out of the room as I butter a piece of toast and dip it in the beans. Not a bad life I got here. I should turn 30 more often.

My mouth is full of fried eggs when Ma's head, a tapestry of reds and grays like a kilt, comes peeking around the entrance to the kitchen.

"Close yer eyes."

"C'mon," I say. "Whaddya doin'?"

"I said close yer fookin' eyes," she says, so I close the fookers.

Michael J. Malone

I feel like I'm 10 and I'm going to open my fookin' eyes to Stretch Armstrong or Electronic Quarterback. I hear the sound of plastic bags crinkling as Ma shuffles into the kitchen.

"Whadja get me?"

"Finish yer meal," she says. "Ye'll get yer wee gift after."

"Aw, c'mon, ya can't do that. I'm gonna eat really fast and get a stomachache."

"Oh yeah? And then what? Yer gonna miss work?"

"Please can I have my gift now?"

"Oh, alright, ya cheeky wee shite," she says, zipping back to her bedroom. Ol' Paula's had a fair bit of coffee today, by the looks of her. I hear the sound of crinkling again, and she walks back in, carrying something behind her back. Stopping in front of me, she brings her arm to the front to reveal a dark gray suit on a hanger.

"Oh, Ma," I say. "It's beautiful."

I'm not so sure it's beautiful, but it's nice. My other suit, which Ma gave me as a college graduation present, is too small, and it's got mud stains on the knees.

I jump to my feet and grab it from her, feeling the front of it, fingering the buttons, checking the label (something called Zvaldi), doing all the things you're supposed to do when someone gives you a suit.

"It's beautiful," I repeat, hugging my mom. "Thank you so much."

"You'll look brilliant for yer interview," she says. "When is that again?"

"Week from yesterday," I say. "Six days."

"Well, try it on and bring it in to get fixed."

"Thanks, Ma. I love it."

"On sale at Today's Man," she says proudly, sitting down with me and lighting up a Kool. "I'll say a prayer the right thing happens with the job."

"How 'bout just asking God to give me the damn job?" I request.

"Och, bite yer fookin' tongue. So we're on for dinner, yah?"

"Yup. Made a reservation yesterday."

"What's the name again?"

"Jezebel Jones," I say. "On B, between 10th and 11th. Just around from Tompkins. *Time Out* said it was great."

"Jayzus, who'da thought we'd ever go to a fancy restaurant on Avenue fookin' B?" she says.

"No kidding. It's not that fancy, though."

The story was about dog-friendly places, so Jezebel Jones can't be too swank.

"So we'll meet next door at Lakeside," I say. "7 o'clock. Have a few drinks, then head over for dinner."

"Yeh can smoke there?" Ma asks.

"Sure."

"They serve Budweiser?"

238

"Dunno," I say. Bud is the only beer Ma will drink. "Prolly."

"Sounds like a plan, then," says Ma. "Yer friends'll meet us at the poob?"

"Yeah. Gabby, Shady Brady, maybe a few of the others."

"A turty-year-old man should not have friends named Gabby and Shady Brady. *Jayzus.*"

"OK, Paul and Malcolm will meet us there. Better?"

"Much," she says, dragging deep on her Kool. "What else yeh have planned for today?"

"The usual," I say. "Gym, writing, the needle place."

"Yeh feel like yer ready to move back to yer place?"

I take a sip of coffee and try to read Ma's face, looking for a trick that's going to condemn me to another few months in 23B.

"Yeah?" I say gingerly, chewing on a fatty piece of bacon, afraid that spitting the fat into a napkin will extend my sentence. I remember us having a very similar conversation in these exact chairs when I moved out nine years ago.

"If aye don't see yez workin' full-time in the near future, even if it's fookin' *Mac*-Donald's, yer arse is back in this flat. Oonderstood?"

"Yes," I say, forcing the hunk of fat down my throat. "Sounds fair."

There's a moment of quiet.

"Today?" I ask.

"Sure, why not on yer birthday? Another fookin' present for yeh, son."

"Thank you," I say, and offer a slight smile. Going to have to start cooking for myself again. There are some aspects of living here I might miss.

"Alright then. Gotta be off to work."

"Thanks for everything, Ma," I say.

"Oh, stop it, yeh," Paula says, slapping the top of my head. *"Fookin' turty.* I'll see yez at the poob, then."

I exit the shower—*my* shower—wrap a towel around my waist and head back to my room. Through the wall I can hear Julio and Marisol entangled in their lambada of passion, her with the *eh eh's*, he with the *mmmm's*. It's good to be home.

I look at the clock: I'm due to meet Ma and the boys in a half-hour. Gabby and Shady Brady will be in a festive mood—the Vipers beat the heck out of the Forest Hills Irregulars Saturday, on that mud bowl out in Queens, so at least we got a win this season. Flyboy and Ghetto Ron both scored twice. Gabby had one, and put this hit on their fullback that had the poor dude on his back, in the mud, for like 10 minutes before they could get him to his feet. We came back to Manhattan like we'd vanquished a Viking army. The boys are probably still celebrating.

Haley's index card is stuck on the mirror above my dresser, next to a Mets ticket stub from the '86 playoffs. Of course, I was supposed to have knocked off all four cards by now. But I look back at the last month or so, and I think I've done just fine. Any more excitement, and I'm afraid my system might short out. Call it a birthday gift to myself—I'm extending my deadline another week.

I pull on my jeans and a thin gray sweater; there's finally a hint of chill to the air, which means the year's best weather is right around the corner. Two weeks until fall…one week to deal with Haley. To make sure I don't forget about her, I decide to carry the HALEY card around until I take care of it. I slide the card into the pocket of my jeans.

Something about having her card in my pocket feels good, or maybe it's just the endorphins from working out. But, as with any thoughts about Haley, the good turns to bad, then progresses to empty. Happy thoughts of her are always trailed like an attentive terrier by thoughts of Paul. Haley and Paul. It still makes me ill to think about them together. But I think about it less than I did a few months ago; like, every six minutes, instead of every five. It's progress, I guess.

I can't help but think, if I'd met her now instead of when I did, well, who knows what would happen. Course, I wouldn't have any dough to take her out. Maybe I'd fuck it up again. Yeah, probably. Maybe I wouldn't. It doesn't matter.

I take her card out again and stare at it: HALEY. I never got a photo of Haley and, at this moment, I can't call up her image in my mind. Paul, I have no problem with. And if I ever come up empty on him, I just have to run out to the video store, or duck into the internet café next to Doc Holliday's. All I've got is this card. Maybe I'll save it after I'm done with it, keep it on my mirror next to my Mets playoff ticket, which I'm saving until the Mets make the Series again. I return it to my back pocket. Keep the feet moving. Think positive thoughts.

Like my novel. I've had a few ideas, and I'm starting to carry a little notepad around. Best friends or brothers, heading west, stopping in Reno, meeting some local girls, one falling in love and one robbing the other girl and wanting to blow out of town. A caper film, set in a buddy book. Not much, nothing to get too excited about, just a few thoughts. But I got about half an hour to kill, so I'm going to sit in Tompkins, dare Giuliani's minions to bust me for having a birthday beer, relax and jot some notes down. And feel like a writer again.

Tompkins is its usual freakshow; the waste-cases sitting at the chess tables near the southwest entrance, oblivious to the gorgeous day, smoking butts, starting hoarse arguments that threaten to escalate to violence but never do. To them, it's always gray and cloudy, with a chance of rain.

I spy another telltale sign of Alphabet City's gentrification; they've put a cow parade statue in Tompkins. Reading the little plaque on its base, I see the bovine is named Cow Punk. It's wearing a sleeveless leopard-print shirt, gold chains around its neck, low-slung black trousers covering its hindquarters and a studded belt around its ample waist. Someone has drawn a syringe and a rubber hose in black marker on the inside of one of Cow Punk's front legs.

The dog-run is its usual swirl of activity; cooped up in tiny studio apartments all day, the dogs are ecstatic to get a whiff of the semi-fresh air and each other, sniffing and humping like men paroled. They run in maniacal circles around a dead tree in the center of the run that serves as their Maypole, its trunk sculpted into a giant bone. The owners stand around in their little cliques, arms folded, newspaper rolled up in their back pockets, some flirting, some discussing the behavior of their dogs.

The Tompkins dog-run has a vibe that's unparalleled by just about any other part of the city; its palpable energy makes it an ideal place to write, to drink, to think. I hop the fence and plop myself down on the bench, opening up my notepad to a fresh page and taking a final gander at the scenery. People yell their dogs' names—I hear Bickle, Buster and Brando, and wonder if it's B-day for the dogs in the run. There's a flier on the gate, announcing a Halloween costume contest for dogs, with Quentin Crisp the celebrity judge.

As happens almost daily, I see another Haley lookalike about 25 feet away. But Haley'd never be in this nook of the city, where the grimy avenues are too east for numbers, sticking out like a leafy salad in one of the Polish butcher shops along Avenue A. I still enjoy watching her lookalike, though, and I'm always up for a reason to put off writing.

She gets closer, and my heart does not leap to my throat, nor does it plummet to my gut. Instead, there's the familiarly pleasant spread of happy chemicals throughout my body, all the way down to my toes and fingers, telling me, yeah, it's her, alright.

I close my eyes and feel a smile creep up.

She's running after a dog, a little Jack Russell with a brown patch around one eye, her running style clumsily graceful, like a dancer dusting off her ballet shoes after years of inactivity. A pit bull the color of my new suit is giving the Jack a menacing eye, sizing up her rear, and Haley, brushing errant strands of blonde hair out of her face, mud splattering her white jeans, looks for the pit bull's owner while gingerly pushing the aggressor's flank—politely suggesting he find another mount.

The pit bull, of course, is undeterred. Grabbing the Jack by the collar, Haley escorts her towards my direction. The terrier puts on the brakes and bends into a squat, as Haley comes screeching to an awkward halt. She scrambles over to the garbage can and finds a clean sheet of newspaper, then picks up the dogshit and disposes of it, before wiping her hands on her jeans.

I would've loved to sit here in anonymity, hiding amidst the frenetic canine activity, and watch her all day. But my right hand rises up involuntarily.

Haley peers across the 20-odd feet of wood chips that separate us, her hand shielding her eyes from the sun that peeks through the tall trees that ring the run.

Michael J. Malone

She lets go of the Jack Russell and takes a step closer, like a kid playing Red Light, Green Light, folding her arms, her face giving nothing away. She tilts her head slightly to the side, like a dog might if he's, I don't know, hungry, bashful, in need of a piss. I never had a dog.

"Hi," I say, realizing that I'm on my feet and walking toward her. I stop about five feet away.

"Hi," she says, taking a half-step back. Red Light. Green Light.

"Well..."

"Hmmm," she adds. "I'd shake your hand, but I'm dirty." "No problem," I say. "Dog-sitting?"

"No, he's mine," says Haley, her eyes boring into my chest.

"Since when do you have a dog? And since when do you hang out here?"

"Just got the dog a few weeks ago."

"He's pretty," I say. "I mean, handsome."

"Yeah, he's a sweetie."

"I see you haven't settled on a dog-run outfit, like everyone else here," I say.

"Yes, well, I s'pose this is turning into it, by default."

The Jack Russell has returned to Haley's side and is staring at me, making sure I don't do harm to the one who feeds him. I smile to let him know everything's cool.

"How are you?" I ask.

"I'm...well. I'm fine," Haley says, her eyes shifting all around. Her dog scampers off to play with the others. She takes a step toward the departing dog, then gives up the chase.

"Let him go," I say. "That's what they do."

"I know. I'm learning."

"What the hell are you doing over here?"

"I'm, uh, giving my dog a run," says Haley. "Like everyone else."

"I mean, why Tompkins? Why not Washington Square? It's much closer to where you live."

It dawns on me that maybe Haley doesn't live over there anymore. Maybe Paul's got some fat pad overlooking Tompkins. The guy whose movies always feature some musical montage that shows him and the leading lady trying on crazy costumes and frolicking in a photo booth while falling in love is keeping it real by getting a place in Alphabet City. I feel my stomach sink.

"I went to Washington Square for the first week or so," she says. "The dogs are too aggressive there."

"Really? More so than here?"

"Yes, definitely."

"Even the dogs in this neighborhood are gentrified," I say. "Well, maybe your dog's just too damn cute."

"That's possible," Haley says with a tense laugh.

The Jack Russell comes cantering back, kicking up wood chips behind him.

I approach the dog and my ex-girlfriend, taking a knee before them like I'd fatefully done to Tisa a few years before. I pet the terrier under his collar, and he happily lifts his chin for me.

"He likes you."

"What's his name?" I ask. As soon as the statement is out, I wish I could reel it back in, fearful of what the answer might be. I recoil when I see Haley's lips poise for a "P."

"Pequod," she says. Of course. Why the hell would she name her dog Paul?

"What's that mean?"

"It's from *Moby-Dick*," Haley says. "You majored in English, didn't you?"

"I think so," I say, rising to my feet. "It was a long time ago."

Haley laughs, but she's still not looking me in the eye. I'm sort of grateful; for some reason, I don't want to see her eyes, knowing, well, where they've been and what they've seen.

"You never struck me as the dog type," I say, as she shoo's a boxer away from Pequod's ass.

"I'm not," she says. "Look at me."

We both look at her mud-splattered jeans.

"You fit right in here."

"Really?"

"No," I say, and we both laugh. "Not at all."

"I'm trying," she says. "I try to talk to the regulars, ask 'em what kind of dogs they have. But they're such snobs."

"How so?"

"Well, I say to someone, 'What kind of dog is that?' and they look at me like, 'Duh! It's a Corgi,' or 'Hello, it's a Pomeranian.' It's kind of embarrassing."

"I can imagine," I say. "So why'd you get the dog, then?"

"Oh," she starts, looking to the sky, "I don't know. Just felt like I, um, I just wanted the companionship."

My heart leaps, just fucking takes off.

"What's up with Paul Fuddrucker?"

"Who?"

The words taste like battery acid.

"Paul Rudd," I spit.

"Oh, him," she says, looking down again. "Yeah."

"He still *The Object of Your Affection*?"

Michael J. Malone

"Stop it, Declan," she says, looking me in the eye. "That's not funny."

"I'm sorry, Hale. It didn't work out?"

"Let's just say, if it did, I wouldn't be here. No offense, Pequod."

She pets the dog and Pequod and I flash grins.

"Me and Pequod keep each other company."

"All I'm gonna say is, Paul is *Clueless*," I say.

Haley smacks me on the arm, causing Pequod to fire off a series of barks.

"Fuck off, Declan."

She sounds like my ma, without the accent.

"I'm sorry," I say, keeping "good Rudd-ance" to myself. "I'm sorry it didn't work out. Honestly. I hate to sound like your dad, but if he doesn't see the good in you, and there's a lot of it, then you're better off without him. I mean it."

"My dad would never say that."

"Well, it's true."

"Thanks."

Haley offers a hint of a bittersweet smile.

"He's a crappy actor, anyway," I add.

"I know."

"*Locusts* was garbage," I continue. "And he looked like a dork in those Buddy Holly glasses."

"He walks his dog over in Washington Square," says Haley quietly.

"Really. What kind of dog?"

"I don't know, some stupid, expensive little thing. Enough about him. How's Honey Bunny?"

"Dead."

"No! What happened?"

"Got his ears caught in the grinding gears of the big publishing machine."

"*Enchanted Meadow* made me cry," says Haley. "I was thinking of reading it to my class, but it was too sad. I was surprised you sent it to me."

"You'd asked me to."

"I'm sorry to hear of Honey Bunny's demise."

"Yeah, me too. My own fault, though. He'll be back. Mark my words. Can't keep a good bunny down."

"I hope so. How've you been?"

I let out an exhale that just keeps coming, and shake my head when I'm finished.

"'nuff said," she says. "Been busy?"

"Busy enough."

"Yes, you look…"

244

Haley is struggling for the right adjective. Haggard? Bedraggled? World-weary?

"...you look the same, actually."

"Thanks. I'm OK. Long story...stories."

"Mmmm."

"Hey," I say, looking at my wrist for the watch I don't wear. "There's a bit more to it. You wanna, maybe, uh, meet some time for coffee? Catch up? I'll tell you everything that's been going on."

Silence.

Haley looks around for Pequod, sees that he's safe and takes a seat on the bench.

"I don't know," she says, her hands flat on the bench, arms rigid, staring at her feet.

"I don't blame you," I say, sitting next to her. "I'm sorry."

"Sorry for what?"

"I dunno. Everything."

"I'm the one who should be sorry, Declan," she says, looking me in the eye.

It's quiet for a minute or so.

"Hey, this is entirely inappropriate," I start. Pequod runs back to us, enjoying the extended stay at the run.

"I wouldn't expect anything less from you."

"It's my birthday."

"Happy birthday," she says, kissing my cheek as Pequod barks. "That's not inappropriate."

"I'm getting there. I'm meeting my ma for dinner. Why don't you join us."

"Your crazy ma from Ireland?"

"That's the one. Ol' Paula."

"I can't," she says. "I've got Pequod."

She pats Pequod's side.

"We're going to this place Jezebel Jones on the corner of the park," I say, nodding in the northeastern direction. "It's actually a dog-friendly place—I saw it in *Time Out*. I'm sure your dog-run colleagues all know about it."

"What kind of restaurant lets dogs in?"

"The kind I'd pick to turn 30 in."

"I don't know, Declan. Look at me. I'm a mess."

I scoop up some wood chips and rub them on my pants.

"Me too. Big whoop."

"I shouldn't. I've got to work out tomorrow's lesson plan."

"How are the kiddies?"

"They're alright. School just started, so they're not driving me mad yet."

"Hey—you wanted to meet my ma. Don't ever ask me again."

"This is all kind of sudden, Declan."

"I know. OK, we're meeting for a drink first. Me, Ma, Gabby, Shady Brady—er, Malcolm."

"How's Gabby?"

"Gabby's Gabby."

"Gabby," she says with a chuckle. "I haven't thought of him since, God—"

"Our Jazz Fest debacle."

"Our Jazz Fest debacle," she laughs. "Yes."

"Come for a drink. You can leave after one. I'll buy."

"You're *not* buying me a drink on your birthday," Haley says.

It's just as well—I've got $10 to my name.

"One drink," I say. "If you're uncomfortable, say you gotta go feed Pequod or something."

Pequod barks at the mention of food and his name in the same sentence, then lies on the ground in front of our bench, cooling his belly on the wood chips.

"You got a million good excuses with the dog," I say.

"One drink," she says, and I smile.

"Cool."

Haley attaches the leash to Pequod's collar and the three of us head toward the exit…

A dog's bark like machine-gun fire snaps me out of my reverie. I open my eyes and shake my head to bring me back to Earth, back to Tompkins, back to this hard bench. The girl across the dog-run looks nothing like Haley. Well, maybe a little bit, in a certain light. She's just another girl who reminds me of her. *Every* girl reminds me of her. This girl's not real. Well, I guess she's real to the people in her life, to her dog. But she's nothing to me.

Slowly getting to my feet, I put a foot on the bench and hop the low fence, heading toward the exit to meet Ma and the boys. I pull Haley's index card out—powder-blue, lined, wrinkled, HALEY spelled out in Sharpie, bent from doing time in my pocket. The card is real. I will call her tomorrow. I promise. I expect nothing of it. But I *will* call. That's real.

Heading out of the park, I flip the card over and return it to my pocket, hoping to bend it back to its original shape.

Acknowledgements

To the Pentameters, especially Joe Lunievicz, Tim Coleman and Aury Wallington, the finest little writers' group in the world.

To my parents—Michelle for the love of books, Richard for the discipline. Sorry about all the curse words.

5232425R00138

Made in the USA
San Bernardino, CA
29 October 2013